D1513683

For my sister, my best friend.

Unstoppable (Pretty Liar Book One).

Written by K.A. Knight
Edited By Jess from Elemental Editing and Proofreading.
Proofreading by Norma's Nook.
Formatted by The Nutty Formatter.
Cover by Opulent Designs.
Art by Dily Iola Designs

PROLOGUE

NOVA

I fist my tanned, scarred hands, ripping the cuts on my exposed, bruised knuckles further. The shock of pain makes my heart race, chasing away the fog and tears.

My body shivers involuntarily, my hair still dripping wet. Today is about torture techniques, and he started early, breaking my weak body over and over. He said it was to test my response to extreme pain and how quickly a child's body could bounce back under immense stress. I didn't please him when I failed to react to the electric shock.

It comes again, and I jerk, my teeth clenched hard so I don't let any noise out. Doing so would either please or annoy him, so I try to distract myself and remain silent.

The sterile white room is thirty steps in each direction—I've counted—the ceiling has fifty-seven tiles, and the door has five locks. Counting calms my brain as the current finally passes through my body, then his distorted voice comes again as he watches me through the two-way mirror.

He's always watching . . . observing.

"Tell me how that feels."

I don't speak.

"Novaleen," he snaps, annoyed now. "You know better. You must answer for my research. How does your body feel?"

I still don't answer. It's a childish rebellion, but one I take pride in, especially when it breaches that cool exterior and brings anything other than cold disinterest to his voice—the voice that haunts my every waking and sleeping moment.

The shock comes again, jolting my body against the table I'm chained upon.

"Answer me!"

I don't, so he shocks me again, barely leaving me time to recover from the last one. He asks the same question again and again, followed by recurring shocks. I still refuse to answer, so he increases the voltage until I scream. The taste of my blood fills my mouth, and my bladder lets go.

"Please, sir, please!" I beg, but it's too late. He's punishing me and reminding me who's in charge. My high-pitched voice cracks and then breaks as my body heaves and twists, trying to escape the current burning through me and setting my brain and body on fire.

"Please, Daddy! Please!"

ONE

NOVA

I jerk awake, coated in a cold sweat, with the sheets twisted around my bare legs. My tank top and thong stick to my body, and my long black hair is stuck to my skin.

Disgusting.

Pathetic.

Count, Nova, count.

I begin to count the specks of light filtering through the curtain, indicating it's sunrise, the bricks on the wall, and then the stains on the ceiling from my neighbour above watering her plants too often. I count until I can breathe again and his face and voice no longer haunt me. I realise then I can still taste blood, and with a sigh, I throw back the covers. I get up to stretch, waking my body before padding to the adjoining bathroom. Flicking on the fan and light, I lean into the counter and stare at myself in the rectangular mirror. My eyes are bloodshot, and my bones stick out from my lack of appetite. I'm getting worse the closer I get to . . . there.

Shaking my head, I push back my wet hair and spit into the sink. I run the tap, watching the pink, bloody water disappear down the drain. Sticking my tongue out, I see tiny puncture wounds from my teeth. I must have bit it in my sleep.

I turn away and crank on the cheap hotel shower. I didn't get in until late last night, and I have another day of driving before the funeral.

Funeral.

Even thinking that seems surreal. He's actually dead. The man who I thought was unstoppable, the man who I thought was invincible, is dead. I should be celebrating, I should be fucking rejoicing, but instead all I feel is lost. For so long, he's been the shadow following me, always one step away, and now . . . what am I running from? What should I do?

And Ana . . . What about Ana?

She's been by his side since I disappeared. What does she think happened to me? I often wonder if she remembers me. Does she even care, or did he brainwash her and turn her into his little clone? She was always so influenced by him, so eager to please. I wonder if he hurt her like he hurt me.

No, he couldn't have. I made sure of that.

But she will be at the funeral, so what do I say? Will she even recognise me? Will she even care?

It's been ten fucking years of running, hiding, and being nothing but a ghost thanks to him. I was just a kid when I left, only seventeen, but she was younger still. She was only fourteen, and that's a long time to spend with a monster like him.

My turbulent thoughts and worries won't help. He taught me not to jump to conclusions and that the only certain thing in life is reality, not the worries in my brain. The only accurate things are what you can taste, see, feel, and explain.

Facts.

Why jump to conclusions? Why worry about what you can't control? Focus on what you can. What can you analyse from the situation? Do better, notice more, and react without emotion.

The command floats into my mind unbidden, like it often does since I heard the news. I had gotten good at pushing the memories away and unlearning everything he taught me, even when it was an impossible task. I settled and even lived a normal-ish life, even if no one ever truly knew

me. But then he died, and it was like opening a floodgate. All that fear and pain came back, drilling into my body until I couldn't even slouch without his annoyed command filling my ears like he was actually here.

I duck my head under the spray and crank the temperature higher, hoping the shock of the burn will wash away everything but the present. Grabbing the cheap soap, I lather it up and methodically wash my body, noting every raised scar—some of which have been dissolved thanks to his miracle serum.

Can't have a perfect being with scars, after all.

Everything had to be perfect and in its place. Everything was carefully controlled based on his whims, and I was designed to appeal to whatever he needed at the time—make me older, younger, more sophisticated, or a street kid.

My first rebellion when I ran away was to dye my once boring blonde, shoulder-length hair midnight black. Now it reaches my hips thanks to him not keeping it trimmed to his desired length. His opinion was that long hair was unkempt, and as I push it back, I see the shimmer of dark blue woven in the curly locks.

Continuing to wash, I run my hand over my defined abs. I could never escape the need for rhythmic exercises, cardio, and weights he trained into me, not to mention survival training and weapons expertise. Jujitsu and every other martial art still live inside my head like a routine I can't escape. At first, I hated the fact that I would wake up at 6 AM and need to run and work out. It was like I'd not escaped him, but now I revel in my strength, in the bliss and nothingness I find when pushing my body to its limits.

Reaching my tattoos, I hesitate. He would hate them and say they make me stand out when I need to blend in. It's the very reason I got my first one at just seventeen, the month after I left. Since then, I've covered my entire left arm in an intricate sleeve of lines, dots, flowers, and mandala, my hand too. Over my right hip, I have a gun, and a skull wraps around the top of my thigh before fading into the black and white piece stretching all the way to my toes. I have a few more here and there, like an under boob one and a piece behind my ear, but they were the most important and beautiful. The black ink stains my

skin forever, reminding me I'm not that perfect creature he tried to create.

I'm real, right down to the chipped, black nail varnish on my toes, my nipple piercings, and the new, unhealed scar running diagonally across my foot from my new bike.

I'm not the same scared Novaleen who huddled before the man who was supposed to protect and love her.

I'm Nova, the badass bitch he created down in those torture chambers, one he could never contain.

I'm his biggest mistake, his loudest enemy, and, if he had lived, his death.

After conditioning my hair, I rinse it away before climbing out and wrapping a cheap, tiny towel around my waist. Swiping my hand through the condensation on the mirror, I stare at myself. I seem more determined and . . . free.

Is that the feeling?

Is that the glint in my emerald-green eyes?

Pursing my thick pink lips, I tilt my head as I analyse myself. I'm tall, like him, at nearly six feet. I used to be lanky as a child, but as I grew, I gained muscle and some curves, with a tight waist, flared hips, and double D boobs. I have long, lean legs, strong arms, and toned abs. Ana was always smaller, and I wonder if she still is.

Stop.

Focus.

Ignoring my invading worries and thoughts, I brush my teeth, comb my hair, and plait it back before putting on a bra and my tight black workout shorts. Moving into the other room, I push the double bed aside to create room, and then, like every morning, I conduct my warm-up routine to fully energise my body and get my adrenaline pumping.

I stretch first before doing cardio with running, jumping, and burpees. Next, I do my sit-ups, Russian twists, and push-ups. Once my workout is done, I stretch out my muscles, feeling the strength running through me as I cool down. I slowly work through some jujitsu, mixing it with Krav Maga and traditional karate. I can never be too prepared,

and the moves are second nature as I work through all of my training, highlighting hold, attack, and defending movements.

Once I'm done, I take a moment to meditate and control my breathing. When my eyes open again, I feel better, and I remember why I am doing this—for her, always for her.

Removing my workout gear, I change into tight black leather trousers and don my steel-toed military boots with knives in each one. I add a somewhat appropriate plain black shirt, which is loose to hide my holsters with small handguns, and as always, I slip my long, handmade necklace over my head then conceal it beneath my shirt—a habit from when I hid it from him so he wouldn't take it, crush it, or use it against me. It is a constant reminder of why I survived.

Of why I still fight.

Grabbing my tight leather jacket, I pack the rest of my duffle, and with one more look to check that I didn't forget anything, I head out of the cheap hotel room. I check out under a false name and a false credit card before heading outside to the one joy in this world I allow myself —my bike.

My Suzuki GSX-R750 is finished in black and fades to red. Riding is the closest I'll ever get to feeling happiness as I race through the world.

There is nothing like it.

Grabbing my helmet, I pull it over my head and crank up the volume of my rock playlist. Everyone else might be sad and mourning . . . but me?

I'm fucking celebrating. I just have to make sure the old bastard is really dead first.

TWO

LOUIS

"Are you sure this is a good idea?" Dimitri asks for the hundredth time.

Nico, who sits in the passenger seat of the big 4X4, just sighs and rolls his eyes. Turning in the driver's seat, I meet Isaac's, Dimitri's, and Jonas's eyes. They are all crammed in the back. Luckily, Nico was too big to fit back there, but those three aren't exactly small. In fact, Jonas is squashed up against the window looking uncomfortable. Nico faces them also, and when he sees them shiver, he turns away, his fists clenching on his thighs. I check him over to ensure he isn't going to flip out at the thought that it could have been him being touched, being near people, but he seems to have it under control at the moment.

"We have to," I remind them.

"What if she doesn't even turn up?" Isaac queries, always the logical one. His slight French accent is still fading after years of living there.

"She will," Nico confirms, and those two strong words are all he has to say on the matter.

"I wouldn't." Jonas snorts. "I'd be sunning myself somewhere with some hot girls and drinking to celebrate."

"She isn't like you." I grin, but it soon fades as I remember everything I read and saw on her. "She needs to be sure. She has to know it's true, that he's really dead."

"Not to mention her sister," Dimitri points out. "She will want to see her."

"Do you think she'll make contact?" I question. I might be the leader of this ragtag band of assholes, but I know when to trust their instincts and intellect. Isaac has a way of seeing people and getting emotional with them, but Dimitri? He can read them, know their thoughts and actions, and put himself into their shoes.

"I'm not sure. It depends on how safe she feels."

"But if you were her?" I press.

"If I were her?" He meets my eyes then, his expression stern. "I'd make contact. Ten years is a long time to be alone and on the run."

Jonas swears, knowing he's right. We all know the effects of extended isolation, anger, and hopelessness associated with being alone for so long. It affects your mental capacity, the way you think, and the actions you take. You become reckless, which he knows better than anyone after spending the most time locked up out of all of us.

"Then it's settled. We go. We keep a low profile and remember our mission."

"Her." Jonas nods, his gaze focusing on the still quiet church we are parked near. It won't be quiet for long. "The bastard who did this to his daughter," he snarls, looking back at us.

"She is like us," Nico states in his low growl.

Jonas nods but grinds his teeth before looking away. Any reminder of the man who changed us sours his mood and makes him unpredictable. His emotions are the very reason he was deemed a failure, after all.

In particular, his hatred towards the man currently awaiting burial in that church.

"She's not the enemy. We need her to finish this once and for all," I remind them, searching their eyes.

THREE

NOVA

The drive to the church located on the outskirts of the small city only takes another hour. It's about thirty minutes from the manor I grew up in, and it's also the church where I was baptised, against my father's beliefs. He didn't believe in God or any deity, only in what he could see, but having unbaptised children made him stand out in such a tight-knit community, and he wanted to blend in. Thus, we were forced to have it done, and now he's forced to have a service and be buried in the very same hallowed grounds he disparaged.

My bike rumbles loudly as I pull into the uneven attached car park, and I make sure to choose a spot near the exit out of habit. Taking off my helmet, I see some older ladies and gentlemen in full military dress staring at me—probably due to the bike's engine—before they turn to greet the vicar waiting at the open double doors. The bells are silent, and huge stained-glass windows allow light to stream into what I know is a vast one-room church with big arched ceilings, old stone pillars with dates and names etched into them, and hard, uncomfortable wooden pews with colourful kneeling cushions tied to them.

Sighing, I turn off the bike before scanning the area and car park, searching for Anabel, my sister. I don't see her, though, and I wonder if she is inside already or if she didn't come.

I think she still likes Father, completely unaware of his monstrous actions, but I can't be sure. She stayed in contact with him and even lived there until about two years ago to save on medical school costs—after all, Father believed in making your own way. He wouldn't have paid a penny for it, no doubt teaching her to fend for herself. More than likely, he was disappointed she never went into research science like him.

She had the brains and the drive. So why didn't she?

I guess I'll find out. I just need to gather my courage, walk my ass into the church, and hope I don't set it on fire. The thought makes me grin before it fades. It's more likely that I'll be recaptured, seen, or stalked—hell, even killed. He could have left orders, and the friends he had could be on the lookout for me.

I don't look like the sweet, willing to obey Novaleen who ran away, however, and that works in my favour.

Hooking my helmet on my bike, I grab my shades and put them on as I swing my leg over, using the excuse to turn and check out the cars behind me. There are a few BMWs, some Audis, a Rolls Royce, a couple of Mercedes . . . and a black 4x4 that sticks out at the end of the row, but I shrug and decide to stop being a pussy and head to the church. If they want me, they'll have to kill me first.

Ducking through the wrought iron gate, which squeaks as I wander down the cobbled path, I join the end of the queue of mourners. When it's my time to enter, I nod at the vicar as he hands me a little booklet and then I flick it open with a snort.

Beloved father and friend. Doctor Davis was an inspiration to everyone he met, a hard worker, and a genuinely good person.

"Bullshit," I mutter.

"Excuse me?" the older vicar asks.

"I said, beautiful." I grin, and he nods but frowns, looking confused.

Heading through the ornate entryway, I scan the packed pews. I don't see the familiar blonde head of hair until she stands at the front, wearing a knee-length black dress, cardigan, tights, and flats. She is completely put together and perfect, right down to the gracious way she accepts condolences and greets people. I can't tear my eyes away from her, but I hear the door shut behind me, so I quickly duck into the end of an empty pew.

A man in the next pew looks over at me and gives me that sad smile everyone wears at funerals. "Did you know him well?"

"Probably better than anyone," I reply.

"I am sorry for your loss," he offers sadly.

"Don't be," I retort, leaning back and kicking my legs up onto the pew. I watch the vicar wander down the aisle to the podium at the front.

The man I was speaking to gawks before leaning in to mutter to his wife who then glances at me. I pull down my sunglasses and wink. She gasps before quickly turning forward, making me chuckle as organ music starts to play.

I almost fall asleep, but then the vicar starts to speak. He drones on about my father, his speech intersected with hymns and loving tributes, and then it comes to her.

Ana.

She stands with her hands clasped at her belly and heads to the microphone, her eyes sad and downcast. Her hands shake slightly, and I know she's nervous. She hates public speaking and being the centre of attention.

Ana clears her throat delicately as I notice her fine features are the same, just grown up. She has the same button nose, slightly round face, naturally thick eyebrows, and light lashes. Freckles dust along her cheeks and nose, and her icy-blonde hair hangs straight over one shoulder. Her makeup is simple, with nude lip gloss, brown eyeliner, and mascara, showing just how naturally beautiful my sister truly is. She possesses the type of beauty everyone envies, even me. Ana was always so graceful and soft spoken, but when she did speak, it was with a level of intelligence surpassing her age.

She is so perfect, unlike me.

"My father was a good man."

Fucking hell, Ana, really? I jerk like she slapped me and close my eyes.

"He gave his life to better this world, first in his service to the country, and then with his innovations in the medical and scientific fields. Given more time, he would have completed such great things. He was a good soul that was lost too soon. My family . . . My family is empty." Her breath catches. "After the tragic death of my sister when she was just seventeen—"

Fucking hell. He told her I died? I didn't expect it to hurt so much, but it does. Did she wonder what happened? Did she miss me like I missed her? At least she had closure and didn't have to wonder if I was out there.

"—my father was never the same."

"I bet he wasn't," I mutter. The people in front glare at me, and I stick my tongue out, but I hear a low chuckle and turn my head, meeting the dark gaze of a huge man on the end pew opposite mine. Four other men sit at his side, each more striking than the last.

They are too beautiful and too smiley to be mourners, so who are they?

Ana's words drag me from their gazes, and I quickly look away, wondering who they are. They are dressed differently than the mourners, more like me.

"And now that I am alone, the last of our legacy, I miss them both so much." A tear, as if she were a paid actor, rolls down her cheek, but I know it's not forged. She's too genuine to lie about something like that. No, she's trying to hold back her emotions, her voice choked. Ana always tried to be the perfect, sophisticated woman he wanted. They don't cry in public, after all, and in his mind, emotions were the mark of a weak or soft person.

"I ask that you remember him for his brilliance, for the love he brought into the world, and the great things he did as we stand together in his memory." She turns to the casket. "Goodbye, Father. May we meet again."

Oh, I fucking hoping we meet again too. I'll kick his ass.

The rest of the funeral is uneventful, and I lean on my bike as I watch them inter him in the ground. Good fucking riddance. My eyes stay on Ana the entire time. She's the perfect daughter—sad but not crying, polite, and quiet. She shakes hands, smiles sorrowfully, and talks with everyone until they finally leave. When she's alone, Ana turns and stares at the grave, then her shoulders finally slump. Her hands twist the material at her hips, showing a little weakness.

I push from the bike and head towards her, only stopping when I am standing silently behind her. My heart skips a beat. Of all the times I thought of seeing her again, of being together, this wasn't how I imagined it. Fear blooms inside me, fear she won't remember me . . . or worse.

"I'm all alone," she whispers, and I flinch.

I wish I could tell her that she's never been alone and explain, but I can't. It's better she never knows and safer that way. But can I do this? Can I step back into her life? And will she just let me?

My decision is taken away when she turns. She startles when she sees me and frowns before her expression clears, then Ana lowers her eyes respectfully. "I'm so sorry. I thought I was alone. Please forgive my outburst," she starts, her lips trembling, though she tries to hide it. She always was too caring.

"Outburst? Come on, Annie, you know I'm the outburst queen."

She gasps and her head jerks up. Her eyes widen as she freezes, probably from the use of her nickname—the one only I use. I see her confusion. Do I really look that different?

Pulling my glasses down, I smile, and she recoils. "Hi, sister."

"Nova?" she whispers before her hand comes up to cover her mouth, and then she steps back. I grab her arm quicker than she can react as her heel catches on the upturned earth and she stumbles. I steady her, and she jerks her arm away like I burned her.

"It's me." I nod solemnly, my fists clenched to keep in the warmth and softness of her skin that's so familiar and different from my scarred flesh. "Been a long time."

"You're dead." She shakes her head and squeezes her eyes shut as she pinches herself.

"I see you're still doing that." I chuckle, unable to help myself. "Annie, I'm not dead. It's really me."

"No, no, I'm finally going crazy. I knew it would happen," she rambles, her cheeks turning pink. She peeks out of one eye and squeaks when she sees me, and I can't help but grin wider.

"Annie, stop. You're not going crazy. I promise it's me. It's Novaleen."

"No, you're dead!" she yells.

"Your favourite colour is pastel blue. You mumble to yourself when you're tired or when you think no one is around. You like to talk your thoughts out loud. You like to wear heels to work so that people have to look up to you instead of down on you." I hesitate. "You're scared of thunder and always used to climb into bed with me—"

"Stop!" she begs, tears brimming in her big eyes before they fall as she stares at me. "It's you; it's really you."

I nod mutely as she continues to stare at me. "He said you died."

"He would." I snort. "I'm not—"

"But that means you left," she mumbles, thinking out loud, and her eyes jerk back to mine and narrow. "You left! I thought you were dead! I mourned you! What the hell is wrong with you?" she rants. "You just left . . . left me alone. Your own little sister. Not a letter, a phone call. Nothing. You let me grieve you and miss you. You left me all alone." Her voice catches, and I flinch. Pain blooms within me, matching what I see in her eyes before anger replaces it, tinged with sadness. "Why? Why did you leave me? Us? And why come back after all this time? Why today?"

"Annie," I start, stepping closer. She stumbles back and holds her hand out as if to physically ward me off.

"No! Don't do that."

"Do what?" I ask, frowning.

"Call me that like nothing has changed. You can't just fucking walk back into my life like you never left!"

"Annie—Anabel," I correct when she twists her lips in anger. "Please, let me explain. I never wanted to leave—"

"Stop!" she snaps, looking at me sadly now. "It's too late, Nova. I don't want your lies and excuses. For ten years, you had a chance to come back or reach out. No matter what happened, you made a choice to leave and start a life without us, without me. No, it's too late. Stay the hell away from me!" She flees, hurrying past me as if she's running from demons from hell, but not before I see the tears in her eyes.

Shit, that went well.

I want to hit something, and my eyes narrow on the overturned dirt. *This is your fault, asshole.* I spit on his grave and turn to follow her, but she's already gone. My shoulders slump as I head back to my bike. I'll have to keep trying. Now that he's dead, there's nothing keeping me from my sister, and despite my nomadic and scary life, I miss her.

Seeing her reminded me of how close we are—were, and how much I love her and want her in my life.

I refuse to let him ruin everything, even in death.

FOUR

NICO

We watch her stride back to her bike with her head held high and lips turned down in anger. We catch a glimpse of her narrowed eyes before she pulls her glasses back on and swings her leg over her ride. She stays settles there and sighs before she looks to the sky as if searching for help. I can't help staring also, but not at the blue horizon, at her.

She's stunning.

She's the most beautiful creature I have ever laid eyes on. I know why we are here, but I can't seem to care as I watch her, analysing each windblown strand of dark hair that I ache to wrap around my fingers. The others talk quietly, discussing how to approach her. She's highly trained, which we already knew, but if we didn't, it's obvious in the way she carries herself, with purposeful fast movements and the weapons she clearly carries. She's just like us, and it's evident.

It's a look we have, something no other beings do.

Like recognises like, and this woman? She's just like me.

Her eyes drop to our car and narrow again as she looks at the darkened glass. I know she can't see us, but the motionless way she stares nearly has me fidgeting. It's unheard of. I can't look away, and the others stay quiet under her watchful gaze, as if feeling the intensity capture me and hold me in place. My breath catches, and my heart hammers until she releases me by looking away. She quickly fires her bike and guns it from the lot as if she knows she is being followed. She probably does since she's good. Really good.

This will be hard.

She will probably try to kill us.

The thought makes me smirk as the car starts, and I turn in my seat to face the front. Let her. It would be the most excitement I've had in a while—hell, the most fun on top of that. What we are doing is important, and we all know the costs of failure. It subdues my mood a little. She might be a beautiful, deadly woman, but she's also the reason we are here.

She's the key to ending all of this.

If only we can get her to listen before she runs or kills us.

FIVE

NOVA

I keep checking my mirrors for that SUV. Something about it didn't sit well with me. It didn't look like a mourner's vehicle, and why was it still there? It had no plates and blacked out windows. No, it was there for a reason. To watch me? Find me?

Is it him?

Fuck. I shouldn't have gone. I knew better. Gunning it, I speed back to the hotel to check in and lie low, but when I turn onto the double carriageway, I spot the SUV weaving in and out of cars to catch up. I pull my visor down and speed up. It's my turn to weave through cars. People honk and swear, but I move as fast as I can. When I look, they are right behind me, so I take a sudden sharp turn, and they do the same.

They are definitely following me.

Fuck.

It's clear I'm not going to outrun them, and as the road widens to an empty path into the outskirts of the city, I know I need to either lose them or hide. They could easily knock me off my bike or ram into me right here.

They keep pace with me the entire time back to the hotel, never losing me despite the crazy manoeuvres I pull. They don't hit me, but I feel the heat and the purr of their engine. Fuck. Sliding into the lot, I park and turn, ready to fight, but the car is nowhere to be seen. I search the road outside and the empty lot.

Nothing.

Shit, am I overthinking things?

Wiping my face, I spare another look at the area around me before turning back and heading up the stairs to my room. I take the steps two at a time, ready to be inside and away from prying eyes.

The spot between my shoulder blades starts tightening and sweating like there are eyes on me, and I make it to the second floor before I hear a slight scuff of a boot on the floor. Everything else is silent. There are no footsteps, but I know they are following me.

I keep walking, trying to discern where they are.

I feel them behind me and risk a small glance without them noticing: five guys, the same five from the funeral. I note several bundles of weapons, the tightening of their muscles, and the intent in their eyes. They are armed and dangerous. Fuck, I was right, and now I'm trapped. I purposely turn a corner and pull my gun, waiting. When they stomp around it, I slip behind them and silently aim.

"Who are you?" I demand. One starts to turn, but he spots the gun and stops before they all begrudgingly raise their hands.

"Who are you?" I repeat, glancing behind me, ready to leap from the two-story balcony and make a run for it. They have to work for my father to attend his funeral. Of course he would be watching. Stupid, Nova.

"Friends."

"I don't have any of those," I snap and start to back away. Obviously hearing me, though I don't know how since I am silent, they turn. The one who was speaking steps forward, and another grins.

"Well, that's lonely," he teases.

I swing the gun to him. "Laugh at me again, and I'll shoot your fucking balls."

He laughs and looks at the others. "I like her; you were right."

I run my eyes over them. I want no part of whatever is happening. Even though I can take on a lot, these men are highly trained, and I can tell when a situation is getting dicey.

Time to bail and regroup.

Keeping the gun on them, I slowly back away as they leisurely step forward. Once I am next to the rail, I put the gun away and smirk at them. "Tell the old bastard if he's alive, he'll have to kill me if he wants me." With that, I grab the rail, haul myself over it, and leap to the ground below. I roll as I land, hearing them swear. Getting to my feet, I glance up to see the others racing down the stairs, bar the biggest who takes a running jump off the balcony to follow me.

Shit.

I start to run, but they chase, and they are good. I don't risk the bike, knowing the seconds it would take to get on it would cost me and their car can clearly out speed me. No, it's better to lose them on foot, and there are more places to hide.

I wind through backstreets, around buildings, and over fences. All the while, they are hot on my heels. I'm usually the fastest person, so fast no one can ever keep up, but they do. Running and hiding isn't working, but I hate that choice anyway, so fighting it is.

I swerve into the street I'm in. Cars honk as I disrupt traffic, picking the alley I want. It's a dead end, so they can't sneak up behind me, and it gives me a better chance of winning.

I turn with my gun in my hand, aim it at the mouth of the alley, and wait. My heart rate slows, and my body relaxes and numbs just as it does whenever I fight, kill, or hunt.

I wait, my eyes open and unblinking. Between one heartbeat and the next, a head pops around the alley. With a slow breath, I fire, and it ducks back with a curse as I wait for the next one to try it. I can do this all day.

"Fuck!" someone yells. "She almost got me."

"I missed? What a shame. I won't with the next one!" I call with a shit-eating grin.

"She's crazy," comes a low mutter, the words carrying on the wind.

"Too right, so just leave, and I promise not to kill you for the insult," I retort.

It goes quiet then, and a hand pops around the alley. I shoot, and it yanks back with a groan. "Wait! Just wait and look!" comes a stern order. The hand comes back, slower this time, to produce a white piece of fabric that looks like . . . yep, underwear. "See? A white flag. We don't want to hurt you—"

"Shame, I want to hurt you," I reply, and I hear a laugh before there's a smack and a groan. My lips twitch involuntarily, and my hands begin to shake from holding my shooting stance. I can't keep this up much longer. I either need to get on with this or drop the gun. I know which option I'll choose.

The only way I'll drop this gun is when they are dead at my feet or if they shoot off my fucking arm.

"Still alive, hotties?" I call with a grin.

"Yep! Just thinking about your ass in that leather—"

I shoot the wall, and there's a chuckle, then a deeper voice asks, "What will make you drop the gun?"

"Nothing you have," I reply conversationally, but I know if I keep shooting, the cops will come, and I don't want that. It seems they don't either because I hear them talking quickly amongst themselves.

"Look!" one yells. "We know you. Your name is Novaleen Davis. You are twenty-seven years old."

I stiffen at that. "Public knowledge!" I shout.

"Your father was not the man everyone says he is. He experimented on kids . . . on you. He hurt you. I'm betting he even locked you up. Am I right? Shocked you? Tested you?"

I gawk silently.

"He did it to us too. He performed so many experiments, they blended together. I hated him so fucking much, hated what he made me into, what he made me do."

"Who are you?" I demand.

There's a moment of silence and then a man steps out. He's confident I won't shoot him, which I don't. "We are like you. Experiments. We are the other children."

My arm drops as I stare at him. "Other children?"

"You didn't think you were the only one, did you?" he asks, arching his eyebrow as the others spread out behind him. Their expressions remain serious as they stand in line, watching me with knowledge only someone my father experimented on could know.

"There were others, Novaleen, so many others. They are all dead now . . . apart from us."

"What do you want from me?" I demand, voice shaking. My mind is overloaded with questions and concerns, but I focus on what I can control and quickly pick the most important question. "Why are you following me?"

"Because we need you to help us finish this and stop what your father started."

"He's dead; it's over," I hedge.

"You know better," the one doing all the talking says. "It will never be over, not until all the research and facilities are destroyed. We can't do this without you, Novaleen—"

"Nova, my name is Nova. Only he called me Novaleen," I snap, and he holds up his hands and smiles.

"I'm Louis. It was what one of the only nice nurses called me way before your father got his hands on me. So, Nova, are you in? Are you finished running and ready to face your past? Or are you not the woman we've been told about?"

Well, fuck.

I drop the gun and stare into his eyes. "Fine, but you're buying me dinner while we talk."

"Deal." He smirks.

SIX

NOVA

They lead me to the closest restaurant, their gazes never straying from me even as I hide my gun behind my coat. We are in public, but that doesn't mean I trust them.

It could be a trap.

Nevertheless, I follow them inside the little eatery.

I ignore the chair he pulls out and sit at another, yanking it in before he can assist me. Pulling my gun from my jacket, I make sure to keep it aimed at them as they choose seats around me. One of them watches me with a smile before another man drops into the chair next to mine.

He's attractive, that's for sure, but he knows it. He has dark, nearly black hair that's cut shorter on the sides and long in the front, so it sweeps across his forehead as he moves. His eyebrows arch over bright, baby-blue eyes that lock me in place, and his pink, puffy lips tilt as he watches me. His strong, square jaw is covered in stubble that's clearly a few days old, stopping at his sharp cheekbones. His nose has a small scar across the bridge, probably from being broken once or twice, and I spot a scar on his left earlobe too. He's a big bastard, not as big as some of the others at the table, but tall and packed with long, toned muscles. It's his eyes, however, that cause me to stare. They are cold but cunning.

"I'm Jonas." He smirks flirtatiously.

I nod in acknowledgement as Louis drops into a different chair. Slowly, all the others do as well, and I run my eyes over them.

The one next to Jonas is taller. He has to be nearly seven feet, with arms thicker than my body and thighs that would make a bodybuilder weep. His face is square and angular, both attractive and strong. He appears stern with his serious, deep-brown eyes, yet his black hair is neatly styled across his head. I spot a lot of scars and tattoos peeking out of his clothes as he meets my eyes.

"This is Nico," Louis informs me, and the big guy nods slightly at me but doesn't speak. He seems uncomfortable sitting in the tiny diner chair. Dressed in all black, he reminds me of an assassin.

"I'm Isaac," the one with the brilliant smile says, reaching over and shaking my hand gently.

He's not testing my grip, just genuinely happy to meet me. Weird. He's only a few inches taller than me, but he still clearly works hard at being strong. His muscles are well defined, but he seems friendly and easy-going. His eyes are almost a grey slate colour, which are filled with warmth where the others' aren't, and are surrounded by long black lashes. His lips are a rosy colour and tipped up into a smile, and they are so thick and pouty, I'm almost jealous. He's ridiculously hand-some, that's for sure, and the longer I stare at his friendly face, the more I'm struck by his features. He has a sharp jaw and cheekbones, a short beard extending up over his lip, and nicely styled hair, which is clearly meant to look like he put no time into it but very obviously did.

Where Nico looks like a killer, this man looks like a model.

"Dimitri," the last man says, his thick accent rolling over his words. He sounds Serbian or Russian.

I analyse him like the others. Fuck, he's attractive too. What are they? A bunch of fucking runway models? His deep-brown and golden-streaked hair is pushed back carelessly and shaved at the sides. His eyes are a warm, honey brown and put me at ease. His lips are in a neutral line, not frowning nor tilted up. As I look at him, his long, scarred fingers tap on the table impatiently, as if playing the rhythm of a song I can't hear. He's the smallest of them, slim too, but there is a shrewd intelligence in his eyes that reminds me not to underestimate him.

I look at Louis again as he sits and scans the room. It's clear he's in charge of this ragtag bunch of men. I would have pegged Nico or Jonas as the leader, but as I continue to stare, I can see why. He's calm, collected, and clearly very smart. He almost emits a friendly vibe, which has me relaxing before I realise it.

He turns back to me like he can feel my gaze, his bright-green irises locking me in place. His hair is pale, almost an icy blond, which is shaved at the sides and then stands up on top in soft waves. He has rough stubble across his cheeks and chin, extending around his thick lips.

"So, what is this, *The Avengers*?" I snort, ignoring my own perusal of them and filling the silence just as a waitress comes up.

"Hi, what can I get you all?" she asks politely. She's a young girl, barely out of her teens. Her cheeks are red, and she doesn't look any of us in the eye for long. I can almost sense her nerves.

"I'll have a black coffee and a burger and fries. They are paying." I grin.

She smiles at me and winks. "I don't blame you, honey, and for you?" she asks the others.

"The same." Dimitri nods.

"I'll have a Caesar salad please," Isaac says, flashing her an award-winning smile that almost has her gasping, but he seems oblivious as she stares.

"I want something meaty, hard, and wet," Jonas purrs, looking me over.

"He'll have the chipolatas," I retort, making Louis laugh.

"I will have the pasta, please," he interjects, "and Nico will have the steak." With that, the woman hurries off to put in the order, and I lean back, crossing my arms.

"Tell me everything," I demand, not giving them any leeway.

"So needy," Jonas teases, leaning over to touch my arm. I grab his hand, twist, and slam his face into the table before letting go and sitting back again like nothing happened.

"Touch me and die," I warn.

Jonas groans but sits back. "Touché."

"Enough," Louis snaps and then looks at me. "I apologise for his behaviour. Like you, we spent a long time locked away. It makes our . . . people skills rusty."

Isaac grins. "Speak for yourself."

"You didn't track me down to reminisce about my dear old daddy and his favourite torture techniques, did you?" I question, ignoring the banter. I'm unsure how to react. I'm not used to having someone look at me and know my past. I feel unbalanced and unsure, like a wild animal backed into a corner, so I lash out with the only thing I can —words.

"No, Nova, we didn't," Louis replies. My coffee arrives, and he waits for her to leave before leaning in and dropping his voice.

Paranoid much? I listen carefully anyway. If what he said is true, and they are all like me, then I have questions. I thought I was the only one.

For some reason, the fact that I'm not helps, even though I know just what that means for their pasts and what happened to them. Besides the flirtatious idiot and the silent, angry-looking Nico, they seem pretty well adjusted. So, what happened to them, and why have they suddenly tracked me down if they knew about me before?

"You must have a million questions."

No shit.

"First, what I said is true, and if you agree to help, we will answer any questions you have about our pasts, what happened, and who we are. For now, I will give you a quick rundown. Your father is dead—"

"Stop fucking calling him that."

He looks confused, but Nico leans in. "She means Father." His voice is dark, low, and raspy, and I jerk my eyes to his. He stares back before I incline my head.

"I do. That monster was nothing but a jailor to me, but you know that."

"Very well. Dr. Davis is dead, but his research is still out there, and as we have discovered, it is still being used."

"Impossible," I snap.

"I'm afraid not. It seems he had a partner," Jonas mutters angrily, the flirtatious idiot nowhere to be seen, and in his eyes, I see such anger, such hate, that even I look away.

"And that partner is continuing with the work. We were locked up all around the world in different countries, always alone, but it appears there are more. These are not focused on children, but on grown men. In particular, soldiers. You see, Nova, he took the . . . research he did on us and proposed that if reduced to a serum and training, not only could it make the perfect soldier, but a super soldier. The child experiments were deemed a failure—too risky and too challenging on a young mind—but on a highly trained individual? It works. It makes them everything he wanted them to be, and he was doing just that. We need to find these facilities and stop what is happening before it's too late."

Blowing out a breath, I think over his words as the food arrives. "Why me?"

"You knew him better than anyone. You were his favourite, Nova, and the only successful experiment on children. We were all deemed failures and supposed to be terminated. He might have been a monster, but it seems he couldn't bring himself to kill children, so he kept us instead and raised us under lock and key. I escaped and hunted down other children. These are the only ones who are still alive. His partner does not have the same qualms about killing innocents. So, Nova, you ask why you? We can't do this without you. We need your insight, your training, and your mind to end this. We must go to the beginning, to the very first lab and experiment—your old house. We cannot get in, but you can."

"Fuck," I snarl as I grip my mug. "I vowed not to go back there," I admit as images of the horrors I endured there flash in my mind. I raise my gaze, allowing them to see the haunted shadows in my eyes. "If I do this, it will truly end?"

He nods. "We have to, you know that. No one should suffer like we did. He's dead, and it's time his research was too."

"So, it's this ragtag bunch of lost, abused kids to the rescue?" I scoff.

"We have some help," Isaac says with a grin and nods at my food.

"You should eat." I sense his worry, so I grab the burger, take a huge mouthful, and start to chew with my mouth open to make a point. For some reason, it makes Nico's lips twitch, and I am entranced by the movement, but when I meet his eyes, they are empty again.

"Help?" I ask once I've swallowed.

"You'll see," Jonas answers, back to his smiling happy self. How weird.

"Eat, and if you still agree to help us, we will take you there," Louis offers as he takes a dainty mouthful of food.

"Fine." I sigh. "Looks like we really are The Avengers . . . just hopefully without the tragic deaths and terrible costumes."

"I don't know, you do look good in leather," Dimitri teases, making me snort as I grab a fry and throw it at him.

If Dad could see me now, he'd have a fucking heart attack, but it would be worth it.

My mind is still whirling over the fact that I am not alone, that there are others like me, and as they talk and laugh between each other, I analyse them. I wonder just what my dad did to them and why they were to be terminated.

I guess I'm going back down the rabbit hole.

SEVEN

JONAS

I watch as she finishes the whole plate, appreciating a woman who knows how to eat, and when she burps, I almost swoon. There's something about Nova.

She cools the anger inside me, especially when she gives as good as she gets. The others refuse to play my games, to tease or joke, but it seems her twisted, dark sense of humour is the same as mine.

It's probably a result of our fucked-up pasts. Her dad made me into a psycho, then he determined I was too fucked up in the head to continue on. He said I was consumed by too much anger and hatred, and that I couldn't be trusted.

Basically, I was a wild card.

A threat.

Therefore, I was not useful, as if spending fourteen years being locked in a bare, white room and being experimented on wouldn't do that to a kid. Seriously, what did they expect? A normal, functioning child? And they say they are the smart ones.

Isaac speaks, and I look at him. He has his own issues, for sure, but he seems more normal than the rest of us. He can even blend in with civilians, speak, laugh, and act normal. Underneath that soft, caring façade, however, I know deep, lingering pain and anger festers insides him just like with all of us.

Nico feels it even more than me, Dimitri harnesses his, and Louis tries to control his turbulent hatred. Me? I give in to it and let it help me, but it does make my moods unpredictable. Maybe that's why her eyes keep flicking to me when I clench the silverware. With a smirk, I bring it to my mouth and lick it as she watches. She rolls her eyes and looks away, but I notice a flush on her cheeks—she liked what she saw.

I like having her eyes on me.

That's bad, but it's too late to care now.

She's one of us, and we are stuck together.

"We should get going if we want to get back before they wonder where we are," Louis says, wiping his mouth as he pulls out money to pay.

"You mean before they wonder if we have finally lost it and gone AWOL?" I snort and lean into Nova, careful not to touch her. I saw her eyes when I did it the last time, and I know she wasn't here with me. She was somewhere else, probably with the monster who fucked us all up. "They need us, you see, but they are also fucking terrified of us. It makes them uncomfortable that we can be so clinical and cold when on a mission. Oh yes, Nova, they need us, and they hate it."

"Enough," Nico snaps and stands.

Louis drops money on the table and nods at Nova, letting her go first. She ignores it and waits, so I stroll out first. "If you wanted to look at my ass, you should have just asked," I tease.

Something whizzes by my head, embedding in the restaurant door, and a laugh booms out of me when I see the knife and feel the slight cut on my cheek. She storms past me, plucks it out, and twirls it as she glares at me.

"I'll admit you've got a nice ass, but it's a shame about the mouth," she remarks and then pushes outside, leaving me gaping after her.

Isaac chuckles and follows her. He escorts to her bike while the rest of us pile into the car. Louis leans out of the window and calls, "Follow us."

"Believe I won't try to escape?" she taunts, straddling the machine, and my mouth dries as I imagine her straddling me like that.

"You are free to go. We are not like him, Nova, but I think you'll follow."

"Why is that?" she grumbles.

"Because you're interested now, and you hate what he did as much as we do." With that, Louis rolls up the window and pulls away.

I turn to watch out of the window, and a few seconds later, Nova turns on her engine and follows us out into traffic, making me smile. This may be business, and we may have his twisted experiments to end, but it doesn't mean I'm not enjoying our latest group member.

She's an improvement on these grumpy bastards, that's for sure.

I'll work *very* closely with her.

The drive takes over an hour and a half, the base set up as close to the old mansion as we dared without tipping them off—not that we had much choice. It was a military decision, the government's secret operation location. It's hidden, so if you don't know where to look, you would think nothing of it.

I can almost sense Nova's hesitation as we lead her through winding country lanes, with rolling hills on either side of us. There is no one for miles. I wonder if she thinks it's a trap. Probably, but the girl is fearless. She doesn't turn back, and when we pull into an old, abandoned barn to park, she follows us in before turning the bike off and walking over to meet us.

Her first question makes me laugh. She isn't concerned for herself but her bike. "Will it be okay here?"

"Yes, there are cameras and a fence, though you wouldn't see it, not to mention the sensors. This barn might look rundown, but it's maintained and made to look this way," Louis explains calmly before jerking his head at her. "Come, you can meet the people we work for. They are funding this operation."

"Yeah, real cheerful bastards." I laugh, walking backward to keep her in my line of sight. Nico rolls his eyes and trips me. I leap to my feet and swing, but Isaac gets between us, as always. Dimitri mutters something and rushes to catch up with Louis, probably antsy to get back to his computers and whatever shit he was doing on them.

Nico circles until he's behind her—a habit. I see her shoulders tense, but she doesn't protest, even as her eyes scan everything. She's probably spotting all the hidden cameras in the trees as we move through the scrapyard. It's a trap, of course. The cars and bits of metal are rigged with bombs, sensors, and even landmines. I did it myself.

You can never be too careful, and their security was almost laughable. Dimitri said even a child could hack it. They didn't like that, but they grudgingly took our help.

Nova stops abruptly, her eyes narrowing. "Let me guess—C4 hidden in the cars, cameras in the trees, and sensors all over the place."

That's so hot, I almost groan. "You forgot the mines."

"Of course." She nods and moves over to me, meeting my eyes confidently as my cock jerks. "I would have added a few hidden weapon caches and bail out bags." She strides past me, and I reach down to rearrange myself.

"I love her already," I mumble, and Nico glares at me, so I turn and follow her, my eyes locked on her ass.

Across the next hill is a sharp incline, which is easy for us. We cover the ground in under a minute, as does Nova, who effortlessly keeps up, but for some soldiers this is a struggle—pussies.

When we reach the top, she looks around. "There's nothing here," she snaps. "If this is a trap . . ." She draws her gun and points it at Louis.

He holds his hands up and nods at Dimitri. "Do it."

Concerned and looking for a way to disarm her, Dimitri moves over to the sensor. I move to her left, just in case she attacks, and Nico steps to her right. Isaac just sighs.

There's a buzz, and Nova's eyes narrow, but she doesn't move until the grass-covered panel in the ground parts in the middle and rolls back. She turns, dropping her gun to her side, and watches as it reveals a yawning abyss. I move closer, and she spins, aiming her gun at my head.

"Stop getting so fucking close, chuckles," she warns. "What is this place?"

"A hidden bunker. Our new employers are almost as paranoid as Dr Davis," Dimitri replies. "It's safe."

"Nothing's safe," she mutters, but she puts her gun away and moves towards the other guys. When the platform arrives, she steps onto it and turns to us. "Well, come on then. What are we waiting for?"

Even Nico grins as we all hurry on, surrounding her, and then Dimitri presses the button, causing the platform to descend slowly. The lower we go, the darker it gets, with only emergency lowlights embedded in the dark-grey metal walls. The circular chamber stretches deep into the earth, with the bunker built below, although *bunker* may not be the best word. The level numbers whizz by as Nova parts her legs, steadying herself. We finally slow and come to a soft stop before a ramp leading to the closed, bombproof bunker doors.

Stepping off the platform, I gesture at them as I wink at her. "Well, come on then, Nova, time to save the world."

EIGHT

ISAAC

The doors open, and a few soldiers nod at us. They don't like us, but they appreciate that we are here to help. They almost blend in with the walls in their black fatigues, and Nova pays them no mind as we lead her deeper into the labyrinth. The first room is a quarantine, questioning, and security room. After passing more doors and taking another elevator, we stop at the command room, which fills the whole second floor.

Louis nods at me, silently telling me what to do, then he looks at Nova, needing to speak to her since she hasn't been with us long. "Isaac will escort you. You will be given a chip to get in and out of the area and any rooms. Everything is open to us, but without it, you will be locked out. I'm going to debrief while you do that. When you are done, they will escort you back here to meet the people behind everything." Without waiting for her to respond, he merges into the hustle and bustle of the command floor.

There are about twenty computers all facing the wall of screens in the back, showing video feeds of active missions and other stuff. More soldiers are positioned at each, along with scientists. The generals are gathered in a glass conference room overlooking the entire floor, and that's where Louis heads with Nico following behind, ready to protect him. Dimitri and Jonas come with me, but they will undoubtedly split off to go train. Jonas is always on the move. When he's not fighting or training, he is cleaning and assembling his weapons.

I analysed his mental state when he was first brought in. I was more suitable than any of their medical staff to assess him after living as he did. Unlike myself, who compartmentalises everything that happened and looks at it logically, Jonas lets his anger control him, very much like Nico. Where Nico is scarred from his past, however, Jonas is fuelled by it. It means he's always moving, fighting, flirting, or fucking. He needs to move or he will think on it.

I have tried to offer them all advice and counsel at some point. Sometimes they speak to me—mainly Louis and Dimitri, though it is only when they have no choice—but we all prefer to fight our own demons. We were beaten, tortured, and made to believe that any weakness meant pain, and that's a hard cycle to break.

We return to the elevator, and Dimitri and Jonas get off on the accommodation and training levels. Jonas winks at Nova, who stands by my side. "See you soon, Nova. We can play then."

"I will shoot you," she threatens.

"Oh fuck, please do," he begs with his hand over his heart as the door closes.

"Please ignore him," I tell her with a friendly smile, trying to put her at ease.

"Trying," she mutters. "Plus, I'm used to much worse."

I tilt my head in consideration, using her words to ease into a conversation as the elevator lowers. "Is that so?"

She sees my obvious approach to get her to talk and sighs. "Let me guess—shrink?"

"Doctor." I shrug. "Habit, sorry."

She shivers at the word *doctor*, and I frown. "I'm not like him," I state, but there's a coldness between us, as if she has a basic distrust of the profession. I don't blame her, especially when all she has ever known from them is pain. I will earn her trust.

This makes it hard to complete my next tasks though. I need to check her out and implant the chip in the lab, where all my supplies are. If I give her any pain in the lab, it might only encourage her fear of doctors, as well as reinforce her anger and distrust of me and the other guys. Knowing I have no other choice, I lead her out once the elevator stops.

This corridor is lined with rooms, and our footsteps are loud on the metal as we turn a corner, the cameras watching her.

"This place gives me the creeps," she mutters. "Feels too much like my dad—Dr. Davis's fucking torture labyrinth."

"The others feel that way too," I share, giving her a bit of their weakness to gain her trust.

"But not you?"

"I guess I got so used to a clinical setting and living underground that it almost feels like home to me. Up there"—I point above ground —"is where I feel out of control and cornered."

I see her pondering my words, and I'm glad I could tell her that as we arrive at my lab door. The window to the left shows the interior, and her footsteps falter.

"What is this?" she demands, and I turn to see she has her gun out again. A siren goes off, but I hold my hand up to the cameras, indicating that I have this. The siren stops, but I know they are watching us, and it served as a reminder that she is surrounded and alone with us. I see fear and anger in her eyes, and I know she's thinking of trying to escape.

"You can leave at any time," I assure her softly, imploring her to trust us. "You are not trapped, not like before. This is for our safety so they can't find us."

"The lab," she snaps.

"It's where I work, where the chips are," I explain quickly. "Without it, you will be unable to walk around freely, and I don't think you would like that."

She stares me down, and I wait. It's her choice. I won't make it for her. She's been through enough, we all have, so her distrust isn't misplaced. It's built from years of pain and abuse, just like every single one of us. We might be what others consider superhuman—I hate that word, knowing it's a mix of nature, nurture, and genealogy—but we are still human. We still carry grudges, feel pain, and experience fear, but unlike others, our fear makes us dangerous and deadly.

Nova is no exception. She is a weapon, and right now, that weapon feels cornered.

I step back to give her more room, and the door opens. She stills and looks behind me. I know what she sees. I've tried to make it as calm and homey as possible by painting some of the walls, hanging posters and paintings, and dotting the space with sofas, chairs, and plants. Yes, there are computers and equipment, but it's more like a fancy office than a cold, sterile lab. I see her noting the difference, but it wars with her terror of the places she was hurt in.

"No," she snaps, stepping back, refusing to enter the lab.

I reach my hand towards her. "We all have to face our fears eventually, Nova," I murmur. "I used to hate labs too."

"Then why?" she croaks, true terror in her eyes mixing with the ghosts of her memories—the same ones we all carry.

"Because I refuse to hide from them." She flinches. "This is just a space. It can't hurt us. He did, not the equipment. This equipment saves lives. Think of it like a gun," I reason softly. "The gun isn't inherently evil. It's the user that chooses the path it takes." Stepping back, I wait. "Come in, and I will tell you more."

When she doesn't move, I leave her to think it over. I walk through the room, humming, trusting her not to shoot. I'm showing her I'm not afraid. I light some candles and prepare the chip as well as some needles and vials, since we need to do a blood test to ensure she is healthy and that *he* did nothing to her. One of the other children was purposely infected with a disease to see if it would change the way her body adapted to training.

I almost shiver in horror at the thought. He was a monster, a true monster. Doctors are meant to heal and protect, not hurt. It goes against everything I believe in.

I hear a noise but don't turn, focusing on my task as I hum until there's a deep sigh. "I don't know how you could become a doctor."

"It was easy," I reply as I turn and gesture to the seat near me, but she remains standing, so I shrug. If that's what makes her feel more in control, then okay. "I'm good at science. It made sense to me when human nature did not," I explain. "I like to help people and figure out problems. I hated labs for what he did in them, but I can understand the beauty and science behind it. It doesn't mean I agree with what he did, but I can understand the sophistication and work it took." I hurry on when her eyes narrow. "The things he did with research, however, were monstrous, and I'm sorry that ever happened to you," I offer softly.

She nods but doesn't look away, and I pick up the chip gun. "This will hurt, but only for a moment. It's an RFID chip that will be implanted into your hand; that is all. It's simply a key."

She nods and relaxes a little as I talk her through each step. When I get to the blood work, she snarls but stoically stands as I take the vials. I stroke her hand and squeeze it, talking about everything and anything until it's over. She's very much like Nico, who struggles with touch and medical equipment. It will make my job harder, but I find I like to comfort her, especially when her eyes soften a tad when she looks at me as if I am protecting her. Unlike the others, where it's my duty and what I'm good at, this feels different.

If I were Jonas, my chest would puff out, but instead, I have a dopey smile on my face.

The others hate my chatter, but she doesn't seem to mind, so I don't stop. "Other children?" she finally asks, interrupting my story of a time when Jonas shot up my lab.

"Hmm?" I ask as I analyse her blood.

"The other children. You said . . . Where are they? Are there any here?"

I round my shoulders and turn, playing with my coat. We had mentioned some had died, maybe it's hope that she's asking if any survived. "No." Pursing my lips, I think of the best way to explain it. "Louis is better at answering your questions—"

"Please, Isaac, I need to know," she implores, her eyes widening.

Whether it's her round, trusting eyes or the hand she places on my arm, I find myself answering. I am unable to say no to her. A dangerous thing, I know, but she has her father's magnetism, if not his streak for cruelty.

"They are dead."

She flinches but nods, probably already guessing that.

"According to his notes, some were . . . terminated. They failed some of the experiments, so he, um . . . Those that survived were pushed further. He would infect some with diseases or genetic impurities, as he liked to call them. Cancer, MS, or congestive heart failure were introduced into their bodies to see what effects could be created. Some died when they could have been saved. One I read about, a girl, killed herself at only thirteen."

"Fuck!" she cries, smashing her fist into the table. I surge to my feet and rub her back.

"I know, it's horrendous, but that's why we must do this. We need to stop anyone else from being hurt like us."

"Why me? Why us?" She tilts her head, and I see tears in her eyes. "When I thought it was just me, I could survive. I asked why all the time, but I survived . . . and the others . . . I didn't know. I left and ran like a coward while they suffered because I thought I was the only one. Fucking foolish. I could have helped them!" she yells, but then her voice breaks as she tries to hold back her tears.

Her pain calls to the caring part of me, the doctor part, though I know it's a lie—it's deeper than that. Her pain feels like a knife in my heart.

I wrap my arms around her. She's stiff at first, but then she relaxes, turning to bury her head in my chest as I stroke her back and hair.

"There is nothing you could have done, nothing any of us could have done," I murmur. "You were a child yourself, and you did the best you could to survive the unimaginable. We all did. We have a chance now to make it right, so do not let guilt change you, Nova. It was Dr. Davis who did this, not us. We are innocent, but we have a chance to avenge them and save others. Do not let the past fill you with hatred until you blindly fall into the madness like he did. Let it guide you instead. Learn from it, and let's do better."

She nods and pulls back slightly. Her eyes are rimmed red, and tears stain her cheeks, yet she's utterly beautiful. Then it hits me. I was looking at her like another patient, as if I knew when I looked too hard, I would see it, but now I can't not. I can't look away from her as my hands tunnel into her hair and touch her as if I can't get enough. My gaze drops to her lips then up to her eyes.

She's stunning.

She's so strong, beautiful, and intelligent.

It's a powerful combination that leaves me breathless, and for the first time in my life, I want to lean into another person instead of being the person they lean on. It makes me want to break all my carefully built rules and kiss her.

I can tell she feels the same because her eyes widen and her breath picks up, causing her chest to rise and fall against my own. Her hands clench the material of my coat, and a blush flushes her cheeks as we stare. We are both fighting the electricity between us, one that's so potent, I'm surprised we haven't set the room alight.

Something grows between us the longer we stare, and then I start to tilt my head down, unable to resist her.

Nova is one of us. I would never hurt her, not like other women, and it's that knowledge that has a slight groan leaving my lips as I finally give in. I lower my head, and she doesn't move away, making me believe she feels this too. Whether it's the desire to feel loved since we spent our childhood alone or she simply wants me as a man, I can't tell, and I don't care.

The spell is broken when we hear footsteps.

She jerks back, wiping her mouth like I kissed her, and looks at the door. I turn, my lips dipping into a frown as disappointment fills me. What was I thinking? She won't trust me if I force myself on her like that. I don't know what came over me. It's clear Nova is deadlier than we expected, considering I almost gave into the dark urges inside of me when I am usually perfectly in control and calm.

The beauty standing next to me nervously buzzes with embarrassment as Dimitri steps into the room. As usual, he enters farther than the others who would simply wait outside, as if by doing so he is telling his past to go fuck itself. He appreciates knowledge and computers as much as I do, though he hates how he obtained his interest for them.

I quickly turn back to the computer as I breathe deeply and pretend to analyse my notes.

"Louis is ready. Are we good to go?" he calls.

"Go?" I jerk my head up like I was consumed by work and not the woman next to me. I am no better than Dr. Davis at this moment, almost using her weakness to take what isn't mine. I close my eyes as hatred for myself builds. "Yes, of course. I need to stay and look at these results."

"Okay . . ." He frowns, sounding confused. "I'll escort Nova then."

"Yes, do that." I turn away quickly so he doesn't see the strong emotions in my eyes. I feel her looking back at me before she follows him out without a word. Unable to resist, I lift my head and watch her go.

With each step she takes, my heart slams, begging me to chase her and finish that kiss.

What is happening to me?

Was he right about the reason I was supposed to be terminated? Lowering my head, I press it against the screen to cool my overheated skin and try to ignore my body's urges. I will not become the creature he told me I would be, not even because of her.

And I have to work with her.

Fuck.

NINE

NOVA

I follow Dimitri quietly, and he doesn't break the silence either. He seems nervous about my presence, flicking his fingers against his leg as we rise in the elevator. All the while, my mind goes back to what almost happened, what I almost did.

I almost kissed the doctor.

What a fucking idiot. He was obviously embarrassed after. He was only trying to be polite and professional, and I cried, raged, tried to shoot him, and then almost kissed him.

I'm a mess.

Poor man, no wonder he didn't want to come with us.

Feeling the need to fill the silence and escape my self-destructive thoughts, I glance at Dimitri. "Where's Jonas?"

"Stabbing stuff," he mutters, eyeing me before looking away. "I'm sorry. Next time, I will let them know you would prefer for him to escort you."

With that, he steps out of the doors when they open, and I tip my head back and groan. I'm so rusty at conversation and being around other people, I'm fucking this up. Great. Just great. Even though I know they don't have to like me, for some reason, it feels important, especially if what they say is true, because it means they are the only other ones in this world who knows what it's like to grow up the way I did.

I'm pushing them away by almost kissing and attacking them.

I'm surprised I wasn't terminated like the other kids, since it's clear I'm not as capable as these men here who have adapted to this world. Not only that, but they are actively using the training and strength my father gave us to make the world a better place while I just ran and hid.

Sighing, I follow Dimitri as he leads me through what they called the command floor. I analyse the huge screens that cover the back wall, showing this base as well as my old house. Scientists and soldiers are working everywhere, but Dimitri heads right to a set of metal stairs on the left that lead up to a glass room overlooking it all.

He opens the door without knocking and steps inside, holding it for me without looking at me. Great.

Inside, there is a giant rectangular table, a fridge, and a kettle on the counter at the back. The dark-wood table is surrounded by chairs, only two of which are in use. Louis sits in one, and in the other is a man in full military dress, with grey hair and sharp, cold blue eyes. It's clear he's a commander of some sort.

Just who are these people?

"Please sit, Nova," Louis offers, sounding friendly enough. I step inside, and Dimitri shuts the door harder than necessary, leaving me with them.

Before Louis is some water, and the other man has a mug. "A drink?" Louis asks as he stands.

"I don't suppose you have whiskey," I joke before sitting, automatically propping my heels on the table, but the commander glares at me, so I slowly put them down and cross my arms. "Water will be fine, thank you." I remember my manners, even though they irritate me, and Louis moves around as I glare at the military man. I refuse to be intimidated. He eventually looks away, and I want to whoop in pleasure, but I refrain and smirk instead.

Louis places a glass of water before me and sits. "Nova, this is General Smith."

"Of course it is," I mutter, making his eyes narrow further until he's basically just squinting. "I've been poked and prodded, and I followed you into a hole in the ground, so tell me everything now," I demand.

"Do not make demands, girl. You are only here because they believe you can help. We voted against this—"

"Well, whoopty fucking doo. I'm here because you obviously need me, so shut your trap and let the person actually in charge talk." I look at Louis then to see him trying to hide his smile behind his hand. He coughs as the general stands.

"You deal with this. Get her in line or it's all your asses," he barks and storms past me.

Louis sighs. "He really is in charge. This is his operation, and his team was the one that found out about the other experiments. We were brought in as . . . consultants because we know Dr. Davis's ways, his type, and, well, we are stronger and more capable than his soldiers."

"Then I'm here for you, not him." I shrug and put my feet back on the table. "And I'm running out of patience."

"Of course, well, you know the basics. Your father had an unidentified partner, and we know he's still running experiments—not on kids, but soldiers. We have to stop him. The government didn't know about his involvement or that he was conducting these studies, but they do now, and they want to put a stop to it—"

"I'm betting it's to save their own asses," I scoff, and he smiles sadly. "Oh, come on! If it gets out that one of their scientists knew he was experimenting on kids? Bad press."

"You're not wrong. They are doing this for their own reasons, the same as we are. We believe the best place to start is at the house where his main research was. Maybe there are hints regarding other locations or who his partner was. We have only found three additional old research facilities other than where we were kept, but they were all abandoned years ago. We are at a dead end, and that's why we need you."

"Why? Go to the old house and look," I mutter, feeling both annoyed and scared at the thought of going back there.

"Nova, he left the house to you. It's yours."

I flinch at that, thinking of Ana. Why me? But more than that, it means he did it as one last kick in the teeth. Here, have the place where I abused and experimented on you for years.

The dick.

"Not only is it illegal for us to go in, which, yes, we would do to stop this, but we couldn't find his lab. We tried."

I still at his words, going cold. "What?"

"It's there; we know that. You were a kid when you left, but I'm betting you remember the way in and out of it. It's clearly hidden, like this place, and we could spend years searching and never find it. We need you to get us in, Nova. Help us stop this and stop others from enduring what we did."

I get up and start to pace. Fury and terror fill me at just the thought of going back to that place. I vowed I'd never go back, ever, yet he's asking me to voluntarily go there. It doesn't matter that my father is dead. It matters that ghosts and memories still haunt that place.

"Fuck!" I snarl, smashing my fists to the table. "Even from beyond the grave, he's fucking me over."

"I'm so sorry, Nova. I wish we didn't have to involve you, but we do. We would leave you in peace—"

"I have never known peace," I mutter and close my eyes. "I can't remember," I croak.

"Try harder," he implores. "Calm down and focus. You don't even need to go there if you can show us on maps—"

"I can't. I'm sorry. I blocked so much of that place out. I would either be drugged through vents in my room and wake up down there or be blindfolded."

"Oh," he mutters, obviously disappointed, and for some reason, I hate letting him down, which is why the next bit spills out.

"I only saw it once. I can remember pieces, but not enough to direct you. I'm sorry."

He stands. "Don't be, we can work with that."

"We can?" I ask, eyebrow arched.

"Yes, come." He offers me his arm, but I ignore it, and he still smiles as he opens the door. "But first, you should rest. We will work on this tomorrow. It's been a long day, and I imagine you are eager to sleep."

Not really, I want to get this over with, but it doesn't seem to be up for discussion.

Louis spots Dimitri at the bottom of the stairs, working on a computer. "Dimitri," he calls, and Dimitri lifts his head, meeting my eyes before he looks at Louis. "Can you escort Nova to the spare room near ours?"

Louis looks at me then, not waiting for an answer, and I see Dimitri sigh. "Rest, and we will begin tomorrow. You're safe here, Nova." With that, Louis disappears down the stairs where Dimitri is now waiting for me.

"Come," is all he says.

Great.

TEN

DMITRI

I feel Nova's eyes on me as I guide her back to the elevator, but I don't look at her. The first time I saw her, I was struck like an electric charge from a machine, and she restarted my cold heart. I don't know why. It's not because she's beautiful, she is, but it was something in her eyes, in her determination to survive.

She is broken, just like me, but she is also able to function.

It makes my fingers twitch to figure her out, to peel back her exterior like I would a machine and fiddle. Even now, I tap my fingers to resist touching her.

Once the elevator stops, I rush out, trying to escape her presence and her sweet scent, but then her voice splits the air, making me stumble. The soft, purring tone heads directly to my cock in a way it shouldn't, hardening it uncomfortably so.

"Look, I didn't mean it to come out the way it did earlier, okay?" she says, and I turn back to see her looking at me. "I don't prefer Jonas or any of you. I barely know you. I was just curious about this place and a little nervous. I want to talk and fill the silence. I'm sorry if that upset you."

Fuck, of course she didn't mean it that way. I don't even know why it's been bothering me that she asked for him, as if I weren't good enough. Like she said, she doesn't know us, so why did it hurt? Why do I wish she said my name? She's looking at me kindly now, not him. It doesn't make sense. Computers, cameras, and equipment make sense, but people? Not so much.

I don't even understand my own turbulent feelings regarding the beautiful woman waiting for a response, so I put those thoughts away to answer her.

"I understand."

She nods but seems to be waiting for more. "You're not a talker, are you?" she teases, grinning.

"I'm better at fixing things," I admit as she comes to my side, and we start walking again.

"Fair enough. So where did my dear old daddy keep you?" I flinch, and she winks at me.

"Prague," I mutter. "It was a nice city from what I saw of it."

"Exotic. I simply got a basement."

I can't help but smile. "I had no windows."

"Windows?" She gasps. "What a luxury! I had no bed, just a floor to sleep on."

"At least you had somewhere to lie down. I had to stand." I find myself teasing her, and we are both smiling. It's only then when I realise she put me at ease. How strange. No one, not even the others, can do that, and I've been with them for years.

"Come on, this way to the rooms. They aren't big or even comfy, but they are private, and there's a bed and pillows."

"God damn, you run a five-star hotel," she teases, walking next to me with strong strides.

"Wait until you see the food," I joke as we reach the room between Louis's and Isaac's. I open the metal door and let her enter first. There's a metal single bed to the left with the bedding folded at the end and a towel. A door to the left leads to a small en suite, with the wall caging in the bed. Each wall is made of metal, and there are no windows, just a bright white light above, a small desk to the right, and a wardrobe.

"Wow, there's so much room," she teases, sitting on the hard bed. "You guys really know how to spoil a girl."

"We do." I grin. "Your RFID chip will let you in and out. Try to get some sleep. I'll get some water and supplies delivered." I turn to leave, and she calls out.

"Dimitri?"

"Yeah?" I ask, looking back.

"Thank you," she offers softly, appearing happy.

"You're welcome, Nova." I shut the door after me, a smile on my lips as I turn to leave.

Maybe people aren't as bad as they seem.

ELEVEN

JONAS

Where is my little Nova?

I'm annoyed at myself for getting distracted and not following Dimitri when he left. He came back to our training room, and after quizzing him, I learned she is staying in a room near ours, though he seemed annoyed at me asking.

Rolling my eyes at that, I slick back my hair as I make my way there. I haven't planned what I'll do when I get there, but it's pretty obvious Nova is as attracted to me as I am to her. Honestly, it's been too long since I've had my dick sucked, and never by a beauty like her. My cock hardens in my trousers as I remember the way she tried to kill us. I've never been with someone as dangerous as us, so I usually have to hold back, worried about hurting them. Our lives don't leave a lot of time for fun, never mind relationships even if I did want one, which I don't. Women are hard work, so I'd rather just fuck their brains out and leave them in ecstasy than deal with one all the time. If there isn't one about? Well, I always have my fist.

Speaking of, I stop at the next corner and slip my hands in my jeans. I palm my hard cock and give it a squeeze before stroking, recalling the fire in Nova's eyes and the expert way she held her gun. A groan escapes as I speed up my strokes.

When a soldier rounds the corner, stumbles to a stop, and gawks at me, I almost sigh. There's never any privacy around here.

"S-Sir?" he sputters, his eyes dropping to my cock before they slam shut. His face is bright red. Why is he embarrassed? Is it because my cock is a lot bigger than his? That must be it. It's very nice looking, after all. Or maybe he liked what he saw.

I pull my hand free and go to walk by him, slapping his cheek softly with the hand that just grasped my dick. "Sorry, I'm not into dudes, though never say never, but I feel like I would like mine prettier, you know?" I whistle as I walk away, happy to have set the record straight.

Maybe I should try sex with a guy, that way I wouldn't need to find a wet and willing pussy. I would miss it, but then I remember Nova has joined our team and perk up. She'll eventually come to me. How could she not? I'm the best-looking one, I can make her scream in ecstasy, and everyone loves a good quick, dirty fuck. I'll just make sure I'm available when she asks, like now, in case she needs to . . . let out any stress after the day she's had.

The only empty room in the dead-end corridor they placed us in sits between Louis's and Isaac's rooms. I slip into mine, which is opposite, leaving the door open. My room hasn't been touched, thank fuck, not since the first day when they sent someone in to clean while I was working out and I threatened to blow up the whole bunker. I mean, really, the person placed all my C4, guns, and knives in a box. A box! How dare they! They are perfectly placed, scattered around my room in what Louis calls chaos but I call order. I know exactly where everything is—

Shit.

I left a mine switched on.

Rushing to it, I turn it off with a laugh. That was close. If I had lain down with that under the pillow, it would have been bye-bye Jonas. I do a few burpees before taking a shower and changing into some shorts, nothing else. After all, I worked hard to have an impressive chest and abs, though Dr. Dickhead always told me vanity was illogical. I can't help but flex in front of the mirror before flipping off his ghost.

Suck my pecs, you dead bastard. I look good, more muscle for your daughter to hold onto as she rides me.

A few hours later, just when I'm about to get bored and knock on her door, I see it open. Perking up, I slide from my bed in the dark, not bothering to turn the lights on as she steps out, wearing skintight shorts and a bra. The sight of her is enough to have me coming in my shorts, and when she turns, I have to bite my fist so I don't call out. Her ass is peachy and round, and the shorts hug it perfectly.

Stepping out after her, I tilt my head when I realise she hasn't heard me as she treads softly down the corridor. She should be sleeping. The others will be working, but I promised to keep watch in case she needed help. It was an excuse to get close to her.

She reaches the steps that no doubt brought her to the room.

Clever girl.

Is she going to try and escape? I almost hope so. Tracking her, hunting her, and then fucking her into submission would be fucking amazing.

But no, she uses the chip to enter corridors and wanders aimlessly. I track her the entire time until she turns into a hallway. Speeding up, I turn the corner just as a leg darts out, slamming into my side. I tumble into the wall, the breath knocked out of me, and before I can move, an arm bands across my throat.

"Why are you following me?" she hisses.

Smirking, I let her touch as much of me as she wants. "I was curious. I was waiting to see where you would go. If you're bored, Nova, I could occupy you."

"I'm sure you would," she scoffs but doesn't let go. She seems unimpressed, so I need to show her how strong I am. I quickly grab her, spin, and slam her back against the wall, placing my arm across her like she did to me. Her breasts heave, and I lean in to try and look down her bra.

"Pig," she snaps and brings her knee up to hit my jewels.

I block it and step back. "If you wanted to spar, all you had to do was ask." I shrug.

"You have a training room, I presume?" she responds, straightening.

"Yes," I purr.

"Show me," she demands.

"Why? You'll be too scared to fight me and worried I'll kick that tight little ass." Her eyes narrow in anger, which is just what I want. It's clear she's unbalanced down here. I don't blame her; I hated it too. I loathed being confined underground just like that bastard did to me. Even the thought has my hands fisting at my sides. I know what helps me, and it should help her too. She's like us, after all, so I antagonise her.

"You couldn't beat me with two hands tied behind my back, though I don't think yours would fit around your muscular back," she growls.

I smirk. "So you noticed my muscles?"

Her hands go into the air. "Are you dumb or something?"

"Want to find out?"

"Fucking hell," she mutters, turning away.

"Come on, Nova, I'll show you, and you can take all that aggression out on me. Don't worry, I'll try to go easy on you."

That does the trick. She storms after me as I lead her to our training room. I don't tell her that having her under me is exactly what I want. I'm a greedy bastard, and I want to touch her. Plus, fighting always leads to other things, especially this time. I'll make sure of it. She needs to feel less alone, less scared, and more in control. I'll offer her that and whatever else she needs.

I can take it. I've had worse.

TWELVE

NOVA

That cocky, egotistical, sexy—*wait, what?*

No. Not sexy.

He's an asshole.

It doesn't matter that his ass is tighter than a goddamn peach or that his arrogant, dangerous smirk has my heart clenching. It also doesn't matter that when he was pressed against me, it made me wet as hell. I left my room for a distraction after not being able to sleep, and I guess I found one in the guise of Jonas.

He leads me to a set of double doors and winks. "Ladies first."

Rolling my eyes, I shimmy past him, and he spanks me as I go, making me realise that was the only reason he wanted me to go first. That, and when I look at him, his eyes are locked on my ass hungrily. I can't help it. I smile. He's so forward with what he wants, and yes, definitely a little crazy as well, but aren't I also?

I guess we all are.

Thanks, Dad.

"Are you going to stand there fantasising about my ass or actually spar?" I joke, crossing my arms. His eyes quickly jerk to my breasts, and his tongue runs along the front of his teeth. I don't know why the sight is so sexy. Maybe it's the way his eyes sparkle or just that this bastard is hot as hell, but it has my pussy clenching. I appreciate a good fuck as much as anyone, but this one has strings, and I don't do strings or attachments. I only do strangers.

Jonas wouldn't be that.

He strikes me as the type who would want to fuck all night and then brag about it.

What is it about the cocksure assholes, though, that makes a clever woman weak?

He's clearly deranged and fucked up from his past, but damn if I'm not curious if he fucks as good as he looks.

"I'd rather have the real thing, but fantasies will do for now, unless you want to fuck instead of fight . . . or both?" He grins as he advances on me. I slowly step backwards, already having scanned the room when I walked in, so I know there are huge mats in the middle of the room which I lead him to now like a dog.

I ignore all the weapons on the wall, the athletic equipment to the right, and the assault course to the left—I'll explore those another day. For now, my entire focus is on Jonas. He could strike at any moment.

Once I feel my bare feet sink into the mat, I hop backwards, only stopping once I'm in the middle of a sparring ring. Tilting my head, I run my eyes down him, searching for weaknesses. I've fought a lot of people before, usually during training supervised by my father or on missions, but never one as skilled as Jonas. It's in every line of his body. He works hard to be the best, to be strong, just like me. It's probably another trait from our fucked-up childhood. It will make him unpredictable, wild, dangerous, and an actual challenge for once. The thought has me bouncing on my toes in excitement. Life has almost been too easy up until this point.

"Come on then, crazy, show me what you've got. Show me what I'm missing out on," I purr, widening my stance to prepare.

His eyes narrow, and his grin kicks up a notch as he steps closer. He begins to circle me, shirtless and shoeless, as his eyes roam over every inch of my body. I feel his gaze like a physical touch, but I focus on the shifting I hear, preparing for his first move. The anticipation has my heart slowing and going into business mode despite the electricity in the air. I'm not fighting to avoid punishment from my father or even for money—no, this time, I'm fighting because I want to know exactly how dangerous the men I'm going to be working with are and to see if they can keep up.

I hear the whistle of air just before I see his arm darting past my head. I throw myself to the side, rolling away and to my feet, having to leap back to avoid his oncoming attack.

I move across the mat, on the defensive, as he kicks and punches. Weaving around me, he lands a few hits, winding me, and I bend over. With my eyes narrowed in anger, I meet his gaze. "You're dead," I hiss.

I lunge forward with all my strength, throwing him to the floor. I manage to get a few kicks in before he grabs my leg and pulls. Bringing my knee against his face, I hear his grunt of pain as I wiggle from his grip and get back to my feet. He climbs to his own, ignoring a trickle of blood running from his nose as I circle him.

"You're good, Nova, but not quite good enough." He flies at me again, mixing moves from different martial arts to try and throw me off. He should know better, though, because I'm Dad's first experiment. He taught me all the same and more.

We fight hard and fast, equal in each way.

He's harder, but I'm faster.

He staggers, and I take a shot, leaping into the air and circling my legs around his neck. I slam him down and quickly spin, my knees going to either side of his hips. I press my arm across his throat as I grin.

"Got you," I declare.

Panting, he stares up at me, and I watch as his shock melts to vibrant lust that I can almost taste. "Nova . . ." He groans. "If you keep me pinned much longer, I won't be responsible for my actions."

I know exactly what he's talking about. My wet pussy is sitting right on a steel rod.

He has a massive hard cock, and he's looking at me like he wants to do something with it. For a moment, I almost let my intentions sway and give into the desire between us before I lean down.

"Maybe next time. I've got a busy day tomorrow, and baby?" I purr, giving myself a moment of weakness to lick his lips, making him jerk beneath me. "You'd need hours to fuck and recover from me."

Rolling free of his body, I stand and give him one last grin. "Good-night, Jonas. Try not to break your hand while you're thinking of me."

His groan follows me back into the corridor, as does the sound of his breathing picking up, and when I look back through the closing door, he has his shorts down. His heels are planted against the mat as he lifts his hips and thrusts into his hand, which is wrapped around a hairless, huge, hard cock with piercings glistening in the lights.

Swallowing, I force myself to leave before I go back in there and finish what we started.

THIRTEEN

NOVA

I woke up early. My body is sore from sparring with Jonas last night, but that aching pain tells me I worked hard. It's addictive, and I stretch out my muscles before showering. Once I get back to the bedroom in a towel, I root through my bag for something to wear. The tiny towel almost slips, but half my ass and legs are already exposed thanks to the ridiculously tiny thing.

Just then, the door slams open without warning.

Instead of panicking, I grab the weapon I hid in my bag and turn. I drop the towel, uncaring about modesty as I hold the knife out, my body reacting before my mind could even play catch up.

Jonas stands there, his eyes wide before they narrow in desire and slide down every inch of my body. I spot Louis coming up behind him along with Nico. Great. Dropping the knife with a sigh, I glare at him. "Ever heard of knocking, asshole?"

"If I had, I wouldn't have gotten to see all this." He gestures at my body. "And god fucking damn, Nova, if it isn't a sight."

"Jonas," Louis snaps and politely brings his eyes to mine. "I'm sorry, Nova. We will give you a moment to dress."

Rolling my eyes, I place the knife in the bag, ignoring the obvious groan. I look back over my shoulder as I pull out some stretchy black shorts and a crop top. "No point, you've all seen me now. What's up?"

My eyes flick to Nico for a moment, expecting the silent man's judgement, but in those dark eyes I see . . . heat. It makes me shiver, and I quickly look away, busying myself with getting dressed.

Unlike the others, Louis doesn't seem fazed. "Okay, well, Jonas was supposed to *knock*"—Louis says it loudly as if to chastise the man— "and invite you to breakfast where we can discuss what will happen today."

"Okay, one sec." I pull on my shirt and straighten it on my chest. My nipples pebble through the material, but every person has them, so I ignore it. I don't get those weirdos who are so offended by nipples. It is a bit chilly down here, though, so I grab an oversized hoodie and pull it across my shoulders, but I leave it unzipped for now. I add some trainers, and then I'm ready to go, pulling my wet hair over my shoulder to dry. When I look back, they are all staring at me.

Louis quickly clears his throat and brings his gaze back to mine. I guess he's not as unaffected as he seems. "Shall we?"

"Lead the way." I wave him on, and as I pass through the door, Jonas leans into me.

"I'm going to wear out my hand tonight thinking about you, unless you'd rather just provide me with the real thing?" he flirts.

"In your dreams." I elbow him, and he laughs.

"Always," he calls as I fall into step with Louis.

Nico is behind us, and when I glance back, drawn by the feeling of his gaze, I see his eyes locked on my ass. When he realises I've spotted him, he doesn't have the decency to act ashamed—no, a small grin teases his lips before disappearing, as if it were never there.

Men.

A part of me is weirdly happy he was looking at my ass though. Being surrounded by so many attractive, strong men has my hormones going wild. I don't know if it's because they are like me and know my secret or if I'm just plain fucking horny, but I want them all.

Even cool and sure Louis.

I'd like to take them for a ride just once to see if they really are as strong as they look. After all, Dad was all about expanding the human mind and trying to make the perfect weapon. Did he succeed? Could one of these men actually kill me?

Why is that thought so thrilling?

No one else has ever gotten close, but I guess only time will tell. I don't trust them wholly, I don't trust anyone that much, but there's definitely a bond between us all since we share trauma and went through the same things. Maybe that's why I feel like I know them already and fit in so easily.

I remind myself to build my guard up though. Just because we have a common enemy and similar pasts doesn't mean they won't fuck me over when they get what they want. For all I know, they could want Dad's research to continue it, but I don't believe that. They seem too angry and fucked up by their pasts to want to inflict that on anyone else, but I don't trust the government, that's for sure, and they are pulling their strings.

I'll keep my distance for now, and I'll do what they want me to do so I can end this, even if it means killing them if they get in my way.

Before this, I was lost, but now I have a purpose, and I know it's right. I have to finish this. It started with me, and now it ends with me.

Louis leads us through the corridors and down a level to a cafeteria. "Go grab a seat over there with Dimitri and Isaac. I'll get your food."

I hesitate, hating that show of weakness, but then I nod and stride over, sitting on the metal chair opposite them at the long table. "Morning."

Dimitri smiles. In one hand, he has a book which looks like gibberish, and in the other, he has a spoon in some porridge. Isaac has a tablet in front of him showing charts, along with a full plate of fruit with toast to the side.

"Morning, Nova. How are you feeling?" he asks cheerfully, closing the tablet's cover.

"Oh fuck, you're a morning person!" I playfully groan, making him grin wider. Dimitri chuckles as he shuts his book.

"Holy shit, you got D to shut his book. It's the boobs, right, D?" Jonas asks as he plonks his tray down next to me, grabs his chair, and sits backwards.

Dimitri just rolls his eyes as he stirs his porridge.

"Maybe it's my winning personality," I deadpan, making Isaac laugh.

Louis places a tray before me. It has fruit, toast, cheeses, and a croissant, as well as some water and cranberry juice. Offering him a, "Thanks," I pick at the fruit as he sits next to me with an omelette. Nico sits next to Dimitri with a full English breakfast spread out on a massive plate. When he sees me watching, he sighs and offers me the plate, so I quickly pass him mine and take his, digging into the food.

"Did he just share food?" Jonas whispers.

A spoon flies through the air and hits Jonas right in the face, and I almost choke on my beans when I see Nico staring innocently at him, even though we all know he threw it.

"Children," Louis mutters. "Behave."

Smirking, I devour my food.

"Fucking hell, hungry?" Jonas nudges me.

I freeze as memories flash through my head, and then I drop my fork and turn my glare on him. "My father used to starve me to see how my body and mind would react under stress. I almost died more than once, and then when he would let me eat, he would make me so sick I hated it. When I got free, I was fucking poor and couldn't afford food either, so excuse me for enjoying it when I can," I snap.

His eyes widen and then narrow, filling with anger. "If he wasn't dead, I'd kill him."

"Join the fucking club," I mutter but settle down. When I glance back at the table, the others are staring, but luckily, there's no pity in their eyes, just understanding. I still hate all the attention. "So today?" I prompt.

Louis takes the hint, sipping his coffee and settling back. "We will hook you to a machine to help enhance your memory until we can figure out the entrance to the research area."

"Machine?" I arch my eyebrow. I didn't have a clue how they were going to do this, but Louis seemed so sure.

"Machine." Louis nods. "Dimitri."

"Anything in your past is stored in your brain. You only need the right stimuli to access it. Correct, Isaac?"

"Correct. The right triggers, words, or even sights or smells could help. The machine will assist with this," Isaac explains.

That's not what I was expecting at all, to be honest.

"This machine can help you access your memories. It was originally one of your father—Dr. Davis's creations, but Dimitri has since worked on it to make it safer, cleaner, and stronger. All you need to do is relax and trust us. We will be with you the entire time to guide you through it. If you want to stop at all, just let us know. I'll monitor your vitals too," Isaac says, looking worried even as he comforts me.

"Stop coddling her." Jonas snorts. "She's not a baby. She can handle this. She survived Dr. Dick and his experiments, so this is nothing, right, Nova?" He winks at me.

For some reason, that puts me at ease as well, and I grin. "Sure."

Dimitri squeezes my hand across the table, and Louis notices, his eyes narrowing in calculation and contemplation.

"Nico, take Dimitri to check the machine one last time," he orders, and Dimitri stands, blushing.

"I was just about to do that," Dimitri mumbles, throwing me one last look before hurrying away. Nico lumbers to his feet and follows him wordlessly.

I wonder what that was about, but I don't ask, too focused on what's to come.

What exactly will they see when we dive deep into my fucked-up memories?

My screams? My pain? My tears?

My hopes?

Or worse . . . my weaknesses?

FOURTEEN

NOVA

U nable to eat after their explanation of what's going to happen, I wait for them to finish. Bile rises in my throat, and my memories crowd my mind. I'm unsure if they will be able to see them, but regardless, I'm betting that they will be able to guess what I'll see from my expressions, and that terrifies me.

Isn't it bad enough that I survived it and did what I had to do? For them to know what I did, though, and who I was . . .

The mere thought has me on edge.

I barely listen to their chatter as I am led to a room near the labs but off a different corridor. Once the door is opened, I freeze as fear rolls through me in waves. There's a metal chair in the middle of the room with a spotlight above it and a footrest swung to one side, with two padded armrests waiting for me to be tied to them. I can almost hear my father's voice. I have no doubt that this was his creation, but I can also see Dimitri's changes. There's a cushion on the back for comfort, there are no restraints, and the room is warm and comforting. There's also a computer to one side, but other than that, there is not much else.

"It's okay," Louis promises as he steps into the room. "We can stop at any time."

Dimitri heads to the computer and starts it up, and I flinch when it whirrs.

"We are not him," Nico states behind me.

I know it's true when they let me choose and don't drag me in. Instead, they wait. It's my choice, my body, and my mind. Taking a deep breath, I allow myself to be brave one more time and step into the room.

"Take a seat when you're ready," Louis instructs as he moves to the side. Just then, a screen I didn't notice comes down from the ceiling. "Through a lot of science that I won't explain to you because it will bore you to death, we are able to project some fragments onto this screen," he tells me as I slowly walk over and perch on the seat.

I am ready to leave at any minute, stiff and scared, but I'm also unwilling to let fear beat me.

"To do so, I have to implant this at the base of your neck," Dimitri murmurs. "It can be disconnected at any time, and I will numb the area—"

"Don't," I mutter and look up at him to see he's shocked. "I don't want to be numb. I'd rather feel it." Old fears, I guess.

He nods like he understands but looks at Louis who stares at me in contemplation. "It will hurt," Louis warns.

"I've survived worse," I remind him as I sit back.

"Do it," Louis orders, keeping his eyes on me. "If she says she can handle it, she can handle it."

Smart man.

The others spread out, watching and waiting. I almost feel comforted by their presence. Before, this would have felt like an experiment, but they have all survived shit like this, and I know no matter what the reason, they wouldn't let me get hurt. They are like me.

They are me—the experimental children of a mad doctor.

"Okay, I'm going to implant it. Take a deep breath for me," Dimitri instructs.

Isaac hurries over, takes my hand, and kneels. "Eyes on me," he orders, his voice soft and reassuring. Before, I had to grit my teeth through the pain and focus on the cracks in the wall, but now I focus on his caring eyes, on the way his lashes fall across his cheek, and the tilt of his lips—

Fuck!

I jerk, but the pain is over just as fast as it began. My head swims a little, and I feel sick as the chip wires into my brain like an octopus stretching inside and curving around the stems. My fingers tighten, gripping Isaac's hand with all my force, yet he doesn't complain. He kneels patiently, stroking my hand as I breathe through it. When I jerk my head in a nod, he stands and squeezes my hand once more.

"You've got this, Nova. We will be right here the entire time."

I nod again, feeling nervous now, before I turn my head to meet Dimitri's eyes. "Do we guide the memories? I have a, erm, lot of—"

"Nova," Nico says as I stumble over my words. I look back at him, and he smiles softly. "We all have a lot of bad memories we don't even want to remember, never mind want anyone to see."

Fuck, he knows. He knows that I feel exposed, vulnerable, and weak.

"We won't look. I promise you that. Your pain is your own, and your memories are too. We will only look when it's time," he promises, and I believe him.

"Okay, let's just bloody do this," I mutter, leaning back in the chair.

"I can strap your arms down if you want," Dimitri offers, and I snarl without thinking. "Okay, never mind, it was just to stop you from moving, but that's fine. Okay, we are going to inject you with a hallucinogenic to help. It's short-lived, so we have to be quick. Our metabolism burns them off too quickly."

"Too fucking right," Jonas mumbles, and when I spare him a glance, he frowns. "Doctor Dick created the serum using me as a lab rat."

Well, shit, that explains a lot.

"If you just roll with it, it'll be easier. If you try to fight it, it will hurt and make you sick for days," he cautions.

"Okay." I feel the prick, then an icy cold liquid moves through my arm and up my chest.

"Okay, Nova," Louis begins, his voice reassuring yet firm. "Take us to your home, to the estate. See it, smell it, and remember it."

I close my eyes, finding it easier than staring into their hopeful gazes, and then I do just that. I recall the way the rain would wash the huge gardens clean, and how it would fall through the big oak tree Ana and I used to play under, the leaves bowing under the weight. I remember how the fog would roll in through the moors, surrounding the old, red-brick building sitting in the middle of nowhere, giving it an eerie look.

There's a gasp, and when I open my eyes, the image, the memory I'm seeing in my head, is projected onto the screen. It's fuzzy, like a dream, and when I focus too hard on that, it falls away.

"Focus, Nova. Close your eyes. Go back to the estate," Louis instructs.

Taking a deep breath, I settle back.

Ana runs across the cobbled back patio, her dress flowing behind her as I chase her through the open back doors and into the cold, quiet kitchen, our bare feet loud on the cold tile.

She turns around to whisper, "Shh, we don't want to wake Dad."

Nodding, we sneak over to the fridge.

"Focus, Nova. Lead us to the entrance," Louis murmurs, his insistent yet soft tone piercing through the memory until Ana's face disappears.

Turning, I leave the kitchen. Like always, there's only minimal light out, and never enough to fill all of the unused, dust-collecting rooms. When I was younger, the dark scared me, until I grew to realise that it was what was waiting in the dark that scared me more.

"Good, where now?" Louis prompts.

I hesitate at the base of the grand wooden staircase. For a moment, I can't remember.

"You've got this," Isaac encourages, so I slow down and let my body lead.

I turn without thought, instinctively knowing the way. Slowly moving across the tile of the entryway, I see the huge double front doors are shut against the storm. I turn and peek at the stairs like I did when I was a kid. At the top, I see the flickering light from my father's study, and fear pumps through me, so I turn away and hurry on before he spots me.

Ana would be reprimanded for being out of bed late, but me?

I would be punished.

I come to the hallway, stilling before the cold darkness of it. The doors running the length of it mock me before I suddenly hear footsteps on the stairs. I turn slowly, and fear fills me until I'm choking on it.

"Focus, Nova. He's not there. You're alone, and it's daytime. You're okay."

The light he tries to bring to my memories is swallowed as I hear *him* heading towards me, and I know what is coming.

"Nova, have you been a bad girl?" The disembodied voice causes me to run.

Their voices become lost—no, that's me. I'm lost in my memory, consumed by snapshots of pain, screams, and torture. I see myself being drowned. I see the fire on my skin. I see the pain. I see the one I don't talk about before I skid to a stop.

I'm in the lab.

Oh God!

"Nova!" Nico snaps. "Pay attention, you're not there. Go back—"

It's too late.

Looming above me like a nightmare is my father with a gun in hand. I know what he's going to say before I hear it. "Kill him or I'll kill her."

I scream and fight. I hear the others trying to calm me down, and I try to change the trajectory of the memory, but then he's there. The man is tied to the chair, afraid and wide-eyed.

The gun is in my hand—

"No!" I roar as I lift it and shoot. The shot is deafening.

My eyes snap open, and I fall from the chair before scrambling across the floor. I press my head to the tile and try to breathe.

A hand touches my shoulder.

"Nova."

All I see and hear is him as my memory and the present fight each other. The feel of the warm, smoking gun and seeing the excitement and pride in my father's eyes is too much.

I jerk to my feet, knowing I look wild as I swing around before locking eyes on the door and sprinting through it.

"Fuck! Nova, wait!" someone shouts.

The corridors blur as I run through them, trying to outrun my demons.

My past.

My sins.

I run as far and fast as I can, trying to outrun my nightmares, my memories, but they are still there.

I skid to a stop, blinded by my memories, as I slap my hand out. It finds something cold—a wall, I think—and I press against it. My breathing is ragged, and my nails dig into my palms, drawing blood. I try to force the memories back into the box where they belong, but I opened it, and now they refuse to be forgotten.

"Nova." His mocking voice echoes around my head. I feel him behind me, waiting, so I spin and lash out, but someone catches my fist.

Their hand is hard, scarred, and warm.

It's not my father. He never had scars or calluses.

I blink, and light pierces my vision before the nightmares swallow me again.

"Nova, Nova, look at me!" I hear someone's voice, but it morphs into my father's. "Fuck, I knew we shouldn't have done this. Look at me, come back, you're not there. He's not there."

All I hear is him.

Father.

My torturer is coming for me again.

My hands are pinned to the wall as I try to fight them.

A dark, brooding voice barks, "Nova, stop, it's me!" but it's lost in the haze. "Fuck this," the voice mutters, and then suddenly something warm starts building inside me.

Hands drag along my sides, pulling me closer, and then lips are on mine. The shock of it causes me to freeze, and the softness invades my thoughts. The person deepens the kiss as they nip my lip, making me gasp before they sweep their tongue into my mouth. Each touch, each breathy moan and rub of their lips yank me back from my nightmares until I feel the cool tile of the bunker under my feet and the heat of a large body before me.

Thick hands caress my body until my clit throbs in time with my wild heartbeat. My head is tilted back, and something unmovable and hard is pressed to every inch of my front. The kiss pulls me from the abyss, and then it's over.

The person pulls away, so I slowly blink my eyes open.

"Nico," I whisper, and he pulls me closer, cradling my head to his chest.

"Thank fuck," he rasps, holding me.

I'm still dazed as my hand drifts to my lips.

He kissed me.

Nico kissed me.

Pulling back, he frames my face with his large hands and peers into my eyes. "Are you okay?" he asks worriedly.

I nod, and he frowns.

"I'm okay," I say, my voice hoarse. "You kissed me. Why?"

He swallows, his eyes drop to my lips for a moment, and when he speaks, his voice is silky and low. "It was the only thing I could think of to bring you back."

"That's the only reason?" I flirt, my lips tipping up into a smirk.

His own part in a grin as he holds me against him, letting me feel the evidence of his desire. "Maybe, maybe not."

"Nico! There you are! Is she okay?" Louis barks, and I hear the others running towards us, but I'm still trapped in Nico's dark gaze. His eyes tell me a whole story full of his worry and desire, and then he blinks, and just like that, a shutter comes down and he steps back.

I instantly miss his heat, so I wrap my arms around myself and turn to the others as they stop before us. They look me over before turning to Nico.

"I'm okay." I sigh. "I got lost in the memories is all."

"I know. We saw," Isaac hedges, wincing when I shoot him a look.

We become quiet then, none of us knowing what to say. After all, they just saw some of my deepest darkest secrets.

"Your dad was a real prick," Jonas finally says, breaking the silence.

I can't help it. I burst into laughter.

"Yes, yes he was," I agree.

FIFTEEN

NICO

She stands at my side, and her laughter fills the air, putting us all at ease. I thought we had broken her. I thought we had finally done what her own father couldn't. She was trapped there, and she didn't even see me—she saw him.

I know that feeling.

My own PTSD and nightmares are similar, and I learned how to bring myself back from them the hard way. I couldn't do that to her, and kissing her was the only idea I had, though a part of me can admit I've wanted to do it since I met her. I should feel guilty that I took advantage of the situation, but I don't. How could I with her sweetness still on my lips?

I look down at her. Her eyes sparkle with amusement, and her body shakes with it. She's just as beautiful as when I first saw her.

I knew back then she was like us. Some of the others wondered if Dr. Davis took it easier on her since she was his own blood, but he didn't. If anything, he was harder on her.

This woman at my side is a warrior. She has survived the unthinkable, and she is still able to laugh.

It astounds me.

She looks up like she feels my gaze, her laughter fading into a knowing smile that has my cock hardening. "Thank you for coming after me," she murmurs softly just for me.

"Okay, well, let's go take a break. We can try another day if you want to," Isaac starts.

Her head whips around, and before she speaks, I know what she's going to say. It's what I would do. Nova doesn't give up, especially with others depending on her. "No, we go back and try again. I think I can get there. It was just a shock is all."

He groans. "Nova."

"Nova," Louis calls. "We almost lost you. We can find another way—"

"No, this is the way. Everything I went through . . ." Her voice breaks, so she swallows. "It has to mean something. I have to do this. You understand that, right?"

We do. After all, isn't that why we are all here?

"It's her choice," I state, interrupting their bickering, and they all turn to me in shock. They are probably wondering why I agreed with her, since I'm the one always trying to outrun my demons. Here I am, however, standing with her as she faces her own. They all know parts of what I went through, especially Louis since he was the one who found me, and he looks at me now knowingly.

Swallowing, I allow some weakness to enter my words. "If I could help save people, even if it meant experiencing everything again, I would. I survived it once. I can survive it again." Looking at her, I nod then add, "They are just memories. They can't hurt you anymore."

"Thank you." She reaches out and squeezes my arm before rolling back her shoulders and stepping closer to them. "Then let's get back to it," she says, walking past them.

They all turn, eyeing her, but I see their pride and wonder.

I feel it too. Her strength astounds me.

We follow after her. Her father might have been our torturer, our enemy, but his daughter is our salvation.

She reminds me of what it means to be unstoppable.

SIXTEEN

LOUIS

O nce we're back at the lab, she sits in the chair and waits with her chin tilted high in defiance, daring us to stop her. We won't. This is her choice. She knows her limits better than we do. After seeing hints of her past, though, I don't think there is anything she couldn't survive. Her father was an evil, cruel man. He did terrible things to me for most of my childhood, things that have left me scarred, but to do that to your own daughter . . .

It must be soul destroying to wonder why your father hates you so much. At least he was just a stranger to us, but to her, he was supposed to protect her, love her, and teach her right from wrong. Instead, he broke her over and over.

He tried to ruin her.

He did not succeed, though, because there is one thing his data could never tell Dr. Davis, and that's a soul's strength. Children like us are unbreakable. Unstoppable.

Just like his daughter.

She could choose to hide and spend the rest of her life in peace, healing from what happened, but instead, she's here, choosing to help us end this once and for all. And that is something he never could have explained with tests or genetics.

It's something you are born with.

"Are you ready?" I ask, knowing she won't back down, not when she has set her mind to it. It's an attractive quality, and my opinion of her triples tenfold.

"No, but let's do it." She grins, making Jonas laugh.

He blows her a kiss. "That's my girl."

She flips him the finger before closing her eyes and focusing on her past. The transformation instantly comes over her. Her eyes tighten in pain, her lips tilt down, and her cheeks pale. She looks like she's seen a ghost, which I guess she has.

Her father.

The man she was running from for so long, whom she's facing now for us.

Her first memories are the most painful, the ones she clearly doesn't want us to see, but our minds have a funny way of doing what we don't want them to. No one says anything. We just watch stoically as a little girl screams and begs her father to stop. As her memories progress, she becomes more silent in them. Her tears and screams fade into nothing, until all that is left is a broken little girl who realised asking for help did nothing.

My heart breaks at seeing her that way.

She is alone and so scared.

Memories of my own childhood filter through my mind—the very same memories we all try to push away so we don't have to live with their scars.

Seeing hers, however, brings all of mine to the surface.

I would scream until my throat bled and scratch at the walls until my fingernails broke and bled. Those were only the days when he locked me inside alone, wanting to see how starvation and darkness would affect my mind.

It didn't break me.

I refused to let it.

It was one of the nicer experiments he put me through, and better than the electrocutions, water, and gasses. Those haunt me even to this day.

Nova's gasp draws me back to her memories, pulling me from

mine.

The torture and experiments she suffered fade, and then it's dark, but I hear Dr. Davis's voice clearly. "Remember, Nova, we focus on nothing but the darkness. This is a secret, isn't it?"

"Yes, Father," she whispers.

The lab.

He's leading her to the lab. She told us he blindfolded her.

When my eyes go to her, I realise she's counting something. Steps? Turns? It's all fuzzy to us, but she looks determined. "Nova, are you trembling?" I ask.

She nods, still mouthing numbers and words to herself before the blindfold is abruptly ripped away. Bright white light pierces her eyes, making her rear back in both reality and memory. She's in a white room, the one from before, and on the table are restraints and a machine I know very well—the shock machine.

The memory suddenly changes, and she's already in the chair, her body shaking with fear.

"Crank it higher. I want to see if she can withstand the same amount as before or more now that she is used to it," Dr. Davis calls.

"Nova, come back!" I demand.

"Can't," she whispers as the machine is turned up. The shock goes through her, and she jerks and screams in the chair.

"Turn it off!" I yell, rushing to her side. Isaac hits the kill switch, and she slumps.

I lift it gently, noting her closed eyes and parted lips.

"Nova?" I ask worriedly. Fear fills me at her silence, at how little she feels in my arms . . . breakable almost.

Isaac moves to my side, checking her pulse. "She's alive, just passed out. The sudden pain of the memories must have been too much. Let's get her to the lab where I can monitor her."

"Will she be okay?" I ask, even though I should be more concerned about the entrance to the lab since we have been looking for it for years. "Isaac," I snarl when he doesn't answer.

"I don't know," he admits nervously. "We could have fractured her brain. Only time will tell."

"Gentlemen, who cares? Did she get the information?" the general barks. All of us were so focused on Nova, we didn't see him come in.

Turning, I block his view of her. Jonas and Dimitri quickly move to my other side, doing the same, while Nico steps up next to Isaac and lifts her, hiding her from him. All of us are protecting her, and he sees it, his eyes twitching.

"Do not forget who is in charge here. She is nothing but a tool," he snaps. "I want that location in two hours or you are all let go."

Fuck.

"Understood." I step forward, feeling angry now. "But you will not interrupt again. You need us, and do not forget that, general."

His face reddens as he turns and storms away.

I slump slightly as I scrub my face. "We don't have long. Let's get her to recovery and make sure she is okay, and pray she remembered or we are all in trouble."

All our hopes are pinned on Nova now.

SEVENTEEN

ISAAC

I watch the slow, even rise of her chest worriedly.

The things we saw in Nova's memories . . .

No wonder she ran and didn't want to help us. No wonder he kept her close. She wasn't just the first experiment; she was the worst. I can't even imagine everything she went through, but seeing those snippets was enough to know that this woman lying in the hospital bed before me is a fighter.

A survivor.

She deserves to be free of this life and her past, not dragged back to it, but that's her choice, and I won't make it for her. It might help her let go if she is able to destroy what he did, or maybe it won't help at all. Only time will tell, and I will keep a close eye on her to make sure her mental health isn't affected by this mission.

I have my own personal mission now—to save Nova and ensure she has the life she deserves.

It is clear her father, her family, or the world has never given her anything, but I will. I'll help her find her place and her happiness, even if it takes years. The doctor in me feels the need to give something back to this sweet suffering soul and prove the world isn't all bad. Nova craves love and a home. That much is obvious.

I'll help her get that.

I stand softly and check her blood pressure again. I gave her some fluids to counteract all the drugs she was given, and I've also checked her heart and head to make sure everything is okay. It is physically, but the mental pain?

I can't do much yet.

Now, we just need her to wake up. I kicked the others out, not wanting her to be overwhelmed when she wakes up. She will probably be embarrassed, and maybe even lash out because of that, feeling vulnerable and off kilter. I've also lowered the lights to change the room from something clinical to cosy. I spotted the layout of her father's lab from her memories, which is similar to this one. No wonder she didn't want to come in here.

It's probably a trigger for her, like chains are for me.

Her blood pressure is normal, so I sit back and double-check all the medical details I have on her while I wait for her to rouse. A lot is missing from her childhood, since only the public files are available. Hopefully, when I find her father's notes, there will be more. It leaves me blind, however, and wondering if she has any undiagnosed illnesses or broken bones. I wouldn't put it past him.

There was another one of us that we found as a child, who was left with chronic pain from purposely broken and unfixed hands, ribs, legs —not to mention all the internal scarring from procedures. Eventually, it got to be too much for him. I tried to help, and we got him morphine —well, actually, we stole it, and that's when we came up on the military's radar—but even then, it wasn't enough. He was in so much pain all the time. Not that he would admit it, but we saw it. It drained what was left of him, and he was unable to fight. He couldn't take it anymore.

He killed himself by stepping in front of a bus.

I close my eyes in pain at the memory. I was only a teenager, but I should have done more. There had to have been something, anything, other than just ending it.

I carry that guilt and blame, and I know the others do as well, especially Dimitri.

He made his choice, but we have to live with the consequences.

A slight change in Nova's even breaths jerks me from my memories, and I blink my eyes open, sit up, and push away all those thoughts so they aren't as obvious on my face. She needs me to help. They all do.

I need to be their rock, but they have no idea that I'm crumbling myself.

Her eyes slowly open, hazy and disoriented. Dragging her tongue across her lips, she tries to sit up and groans when she falls. I catch her then gently prop her up with some pillows.

"Slowly, Nova," I murmur, and her head turns as she meets my eyes.

The pain, embarrassment, and fear in her eyes undoes me.

I stare, unable to look away, until her lashes cover her gaze, and when she looks at me once more, her eyes are empty. Her guard is up again. "What—" Her voice cracks.

Turning, I grab water and press the cup to her lips, tipping it. She drinks as she watches me.

"Only sip a little. We don't want you to be sick," I caution.

Nodding, she pulls away and sighs. "What happened?" she asks, her voice clear now.

"The overload was too much for your brain, and it caused you to pass out. I'm so sorry about that. I have flushed the drugs from your system and helped rehydrate you. You may feel weak for a little while, so you need to rest." I sigh when she slides to the edge of the bed and arches an eyebrow as if to challenge me on that.

"You're not going to rest, are you?" I murmur even as a smile curves my lips.

"Nope, not my style, doc." She winks then stretches, groaning when her bones pop. It's obvious she doesn't like to feel weak, and resting in bed isn't Nova's style despite how much she clearly needs it. I wonder if she has ever let her soul rest or heal a single day in her life.

"Well, that was fun," she deadpans.

"Your sarcasm is intact, so you'll be okay."

She laughs. "That's your opinion, doc."

"It certainly is. Now—"

I'm interrupted when the door opens. I glance over and harden my expression, the teasing words dying on my lips. Sitting up straighter, Nova follows my gaze and stiffens. Every inch of weakness and embarrassment disappears, until only Nova the fighter exists.

The rest of my team stands there, their expressions a mixture of relief and worry as they stare at her—apart from Jonas who grins at her suggestively.

"Nice. Glad you didn't die before I got to fuck you."

I shake my head, and Nico smacks him. It makes her laugh, though, before the last person's voice interrupts—the general.

The asshole didn't care if she was okay. To him, she's disposable and only as useful as what she can provide. We all are, and he's made that very obvious, hence why everyone is on guard around him.

Louis's eyes tighten as he steps forward, ignoring the general's disgusted snort and obvious impatience. "Are you okay?" Louis asks.

"I'm fine."

Even if she wasn't, I doubt she would admit it in front of the general, whom she clearly doesn't trust or like.

"Great, now do you have the location?" the man in question demands, uncaring about her health. She ignores him and looks at Louis, which makes him smile.

"Do you remember the location, Nova?" Louis repeats kindly.

She shrugs. "I do."

"We have to know. Tell us," the general demands greedily.

Louis's eyes cut to him in a gesture only we would understand. Nova inclines her head slowly and looks right at the military man.

"I know it, but I won't tell you." He starts to sputter as she grins. "I'll show you."

Clever girl. She just ensured she has to come with us so we can guarantee everything is done properly.

It infuriates him, and he starts to storm away. "We leave in two hours. Make sure she is ready," he snarls just before the door shuts behind him.

Nova slumps. "Guess we are going on a road trip," she comments in the tension-filled room.

"Isaac, double-check her. If she isn't ready, we can wait. I will deal with him," Louis promises.

"I'm fine," she snaps, but he ignores her, knowing she won't admit if she's not. "I will get us all ready. Once we're on the road, we all stay together."

He doesn't say why, but it's obvious.

He doesn't trust them either.

"You are completely healthy," I declare as I pull the blood pressure cuff off.

I knew she was, but I was hoping to find an excuse to give her some time to recover from what happened mentally before being pushed back into the very place where all her nightmares began.

"I could have told you that, doc," she teases, getting to her feet. She stumbles a little but holds up her hand to ward me off when I go to help her. "Dead legs," she explains, stretching. "Okay, where are my clothes so I can change?" She peers down at the ones she passed out in.

"Jonas selected some for you."

She groans as I point to the chair. "It's probably a thong and nothing else."

"I had Dimitri help him to make sure it wasn't." I grin, having thought that myself.

Nova nods in thanks as she grabs the clothes and starts to strip. I turn away to give her privacy, not that she requested it, but just because she is getting naked doesn't mean she's giving me the consent to stare at her body.

No matter how much I want to.

Instead, needing to distract myself from the thought of her naked, mere inches away, I repeat drug names in my head until I've calmed down enough to talk.

"You know what we saw doesn't change anything, right?" I don't know why it's what enters my head, but as soon as it comes out, I know I need her to understand this.

I hear her freeze, and I feel her eyes lock on me without even looking.

"I just mean . . . your past, Nova. It changes nothing. In fact, we think you are incredibly strong to have survived it—"

"So, you've been gossiping about my torture? Nice," she spits.

"No, not at all," I reply hurriedly before sighing. "There isn't much privacy down here or between us at all. We've all seen each other at our worst and best, and shared pain and nightmares. Yours are no different, Nova. What I'm trying to say is that we understand."

"Sure." She snorts, annoyed at the way this conversation is going.

Knowing I'm losing all my progress with her, I try a different angle and expose myself so she doesn't feel as embarrassed and, therefore, defensive. "Your father had specific experiments he did with me—"

"Isaac, you don't have to—"

"I do. You need to understand you are not alone." I turn to look at her then, keeping my eyes locked on hers and nowhere else. "He had specific experiments," I repeat. This isn't easy to discuss, even though I know it's safe with her and she needs to hear this. "It would usually involve playing with my genetics and digging in my head to see what made me tick. He knew I liked medicine and wanted to be a healer, so he would devise scenarios to test my morality and abilities. He would pit self-preservation against my need to save others."

"Isaac," she whispers.

"Some of the choices I made . . ." I shake my head. "I will have to live with them forever. They will haunt me, and I promised myself if I made it out of there alive, I would earn back my soul and help as many as I could."

"Isaac, we all did what we had to in order to survive. We were kids," she reasons. "We should have been protected and learning right from wrong, not holding people's lives in the balance."

"Still, I knew some of the choices were wrong. I should have died instead of saving myself." I let her see my pain, the one I hide. "I should have died before I let him hurt someone else. I never should have chosen my own survival over that of another. Child or not, I made those choices. Yes, he put me in those situations, and I will never forgive him for that, but I am the one who is haunted." Swallowing, I look away. "So, I understand more than you might think. We blame ourselves, Nova. We hold the pain and guilt while he gets to forget and move on. My body is riddled with his scars."

I pull back the sleeves of my shirt to show her the thick, mottled marks around my wrists.

"These are from his chains. He liked to take everything away but my brain. I hated it. I fought and got nothing for it but more pain. He wanted to expand the human mind, Nova, but all he did was destroy it."

"I know," she whispers.

"I survived, but at what cost? We all have these questions, these regrets, worries, and nightmares. I cannot begin to understand what you went through, but you are not alone. We all have our own horrors, things we wish we could forget but can't. Look closely, and you will see we all may be different, but we all carry the same scars."

"Thank you for telling me, Isaac," she murmurs, laying her hand on my shoulder. "I know you won't listen to what I'm going to say, because I wouldn't either, but you need to forgive yourself. You need to accept what happened and find a way to live with it. It's clearly still hurting you. Don't let him. He's dead, so the only way we can ever truly move on and let his pain die with him is to forget the ghosts he left inside of us."

"It's easier said than done, Nova. You know this yourself." I cover her hand and smile at her. She smiles back sadly, and for a moment, nothing else exists except this emotionally scarred, intelligent, beautiful, brave woman staring at me as if I'm the reason she's here—and then it's over when she steps back, realising she is still half naked.

Clearing my throat, I look away. I caught a glimpse of her body despite knowing it was wrong, and what I saw will stay in my mind longer than any bad dream or nightmare her father imprinted there.

"Well, at least he brought me a bra," she teases, and when I look over, she's slipping into a leather jacket. She looks unbelievably sexy and badass in skintight black jeans, a high lace bra under a white tank top, and boots.

I thought Dimitri was supposed to help Jonas.

The pervs.

"Good, then if you're ready, we should go." I stand and approach her. "If you can't do this, we will understand and fight against the general on your behalf."

"No, I can do this. I want to do this. Just . . . don't leave me, okay? I have a feeling this is going to be hard."

"Never," I promise, knowing how hard it was for her to ask. "We will never leave you alone again, Nova." I take her hand and kiss it.

"Then it's time to go home."

EIGHTEEN

NOVA

W hen we find the others, they are waiting at the exit elevator, all geared up in black. Jonas wears a matching leather jacket—he winks at me when I notice—with some black leather trousers and no shirt. I see a lot of weapons on his body; he doesn't even try to disguise them. Dimitri is at his side in a long-sleeved black shirt, slacks, and trainers. Isaac nipped on the way to change, and now he sports a black denim jacket, trousers, and shirt. Louis looks every bit the commander in utility pants, which are tucked into black boots, and a black T-shirt that showcases his very hard muscles.

"We look like the Care Bear version of an assassin squad," I tease.

"Maybe we need matching uniforms with nicknames." Jonas smirks. "I would be BD, short for Big Dick."

"Enough," Louis snaps.

Turning, I see four soldiers heading our way in formation. At least they are dressed in plain clothes, but Christ, the way they move gives them away. They are all stiff, hard, and uncomfortable. It's clear they don't like working with us as much as the general.

Great.

"We have been ordered to accompany you," the one at the front says. He has greying hair, crow's feet around his eyes, and a mole above his lip. He's also clearly older than the rest and in charge, if the sharpness of his order was anything to go by. "The general said there are to be no arguments. We are to report straight to the address here and then back to this bunker. No stops, no interruptions. Nothing but the mission." He narrows his eyes like he expects us to fight him on it.

"Sir, yes, sir!" Jonas calls, saluting him mockingly. "Would you also like to search my anal cavity for tracking devices?"

The man narrows his eyes and looks at Louis. "Control your people or I will report that they are not needed."

A tense staring match begins, so I step between them. "They are needed. If they don't go, I won't, and without me, you cannot access the estate or the lab. The general might have ordered you, but we are in charge here, so watch your tone, stay silent, and follow us if you must, but don't get in my fucking way, toy soldiers."

"Watch who you talk to like that, street rat, or we'll put you back where we found you," the soldier sneers.

That, of course, doesn't sit well with us.

I hear them all move, snarling as they form a line behind me. They stand at my back and side, defending me.

It's something I've never had before.

It's nice, even though my neck does prickle from their proximity. "Are we going to have a problem here?" Nico snaps. "Because we could easily . . . resolve that." The words hang in the air.

It's a clear threat.

Lines have been drawn.

The soldiers shuffle and actually reach for their weapons, but it's evident that fear passes through their eyes and bodies.

Just then, an announcement comes over the speaker. "No fighting, just get the job done, now," the general snarls.

"Guess we are working together for now," Louis mutters. "Men, weapons down." He includes me in his order, so I shrug and look away before Louis moves to my side, his voice lowered. "We will keep an eye on them. You don't have to worry, just lead the way, Nova."

It's time to go back to where it all started.

NINETEEN

JONAS

O nce up top, we split up. Our cars are hidden in the old barn.
I don't know where the soldiers go, but when we emerge
onto the empty country road, they are waiting in two black
SUVs. It alerts me to the fact they have a hidden cache somewhere they
haven't told us about. I narrow my eyes at that, making a mental
reminder to find it when we get back.

Even if it's just to play with their toys.

I knew the general lied when he said he had no nukes.

"Why do you look like you just hatched an evil plan?" Nova grumbles, scooting away from me. She's pressed between Nico and me, so I
move over again, ignoring the empty space between me and the door,
much preferring to have her plastered against me.

Nico sighs and presses against the door uncomfortably. I see his old
ghosts rearing up, but when Nova looks at him and smiles, his eyes
warm. His entire focus is on her now, and not the cramped situation.

In all honesty, we were all surprised that he volunteered to sit back
here. He never does, always preferring to sit up front, and we never
questioned it because we understand triggers better than anyone. He
hopped right in today, however, and when he met our eyes, he said not
to question it.

I see Louis in the driver's seat, throwing him worried glances and me harrowing ones, so I move back slightly, very slightly, to give them more room.

"Nico, Jonas is going to do bad things. If he gets his cock out, do I have permission to cut it off?"

"Why? You liked looking at it last time." I grin, reaching out to play with her hair. She smacks my hand away and rolls her eyes while the others gawk at my statement.

I let them think what they want, sitting back with a smug smile.

"If he gets it out, I'll cut it off for you." Nico grins at her, and they share a secret look that has my eyebrow rising. I meet Dimitri's eyes in the front passenger seat before he turns away, but I saw his envy. Interesting.

Isaac sighs in the back. "Please don't. That would be a lot of blood, and I'm wearing my nice jacket."

"Did doc just make a joke? Holy shit," I tease, looking back at him. His eyes are locked on a screen, and he flips me off without looking, making me chuckle as I lean into Nova.

"It seems you have them all on their best behaviour, trying to show off for you, Nova," I purr.

She shivers, but when she turns to me, her eyes narrow in fake anger. Under it, however, I see lust. She can't hide it from me for long. Oh no, Nova wants me just as much as I want her. "Or maybe they just aren't assholes like you, Jo."

"Oh, Jo! Are you giving me nicknames now? That's fine with me, baby, though I would prefer Big Coc—"

"Enough," Louis snaps from the driver's seat. "Don't make me come back there."

"Nice going, Nova. Way to get me in trouble," I tease with a wink, waiting for the hit to come from Isaac when Louis gives him *the look*, but instead, Nova reaches out and smacks the back of my head.

"Behave, and I'll let you show me your collection of toys."

I almost choke, and then she closes her eyes slowly. "I meant like weapons—"

"Can't take it back!" I shout, leaning in and wiggling my eyebrows. "I have this really long vibrating—"

This time, it's Isaac who hits me, but I see Nova chuckling softly, so it's worth the momentary pain.

"We know the location of the estate. We will be there in just over two hours," Louis informs us, the mood in the car sobering at the reminder of why we are here. I feel Nova stiffen, and before I can make a joke to help, Nico reaches out and covers her fisted hand on her thigh, offering her support.

It helps, and she leans into him, placing her head on his shoulder. I feel his shock ripple through the car, and ours also—both at him reaching out for her and for him touching another person voluntarily.

Nova is changing things, but is it for the best?

I end up napping out of boredom, and when I wake up, I'm curled around a grumpy Nova who pushes me away with a knife to my throat. Her and Nico are playing some weird game in Latin, Isaac is working, and Dimitri is playing with a machine while Louis drives.

"How much longer?" I whine.

"Ten minutes," Louis barks, cranking up the radio to ignore me.

Looking out the window, I realise we are winding through country lanes up a small hill in the middle of nowhere. When I look back at Nova, she's gone quiet and pale as she stares outside.

"Nova?" I murmur.

"It's been ten years since I ran down this road. It took me hours, and I tore up my feet. It was freezing, and when I finally managed to find someone willing to give me a lift . . ." She shakes her head. "Ten fucking years, and it still hasn't been long enough. I can already feel the evil he poisoned this place with leaking into the car."

"You're not alone though, Nova," Dimitri reminds her. "We face this together."

"D is right," Nico says, placing his hand on her shoulder. "Ten years is a long time, Nova. It's time to face your fears. That is all that exists there now: your own fear and memories. He cannot hurt you here anymore."

"I'm betting he will find a way," she mutters. "One last barb, one last ounce of pain wrung out of me . . . That was his style, and you know it." She turns away and looks out of the front window. "I swore I would never come back to this place."

Unsure what else to say, I reach for her hand, Nico takes the other, and Isaac's palm lands on her shoulder, offering support. Dimitri turns, setting his hand on her thigh, and even Louis reaches back with one hand, squeezing her knee for a second.

In that moment, we are like children huddling together in the dark, looking to each other for comfort from the big bad monster.

But we aren't children anymore, and at least now we have each other.

Louis stops the car then turns his head to meet her eyes. "Tell me to turn back now, and we will."

"What?" she asks.

"Tell me you can't do this, and fuck orders, we will leave. We will find another way. You're more important than what is in your head." There's an impatient beep behind us from the SUVs. They're probably wondering what we are doing, but Louis pays them no mind.

She jerks at that, her mouth opening and closing before she swallows. "I can do this," she finally answers. "I can. Just don't leave me, okay? We do this together."

"Of course, and any time you want to leave, we will." He nods. "Are you sure?"

"I'm sure," she responds, and without waiting, Louis turns forward and drives down the narrowing road to the driveway leading to the estate we can now see.

Within five minutes, we are before the huge wrought iron gates. The black paint is chipped and peeling in places, and the golden crest of Dr. Davis's family sits proudly in the middle of the designs. They stand close, with a guard station to the right which is empty.

"He never had guards because he never wanted them to know what we were doing here, not until the end, but I always knew there was no escape. He kept me here out of fear, not out of lack of freedom . . . fear for my sister." Her whisper reaches us all, and we jolt.

He kept her here by threatening her innocent, untouched sister.

Nova endured all that pain and torture for her sister, Ana, and now she wants nothing to do with her for saving herself? For finally running?

Selfish bitch.

If she knows, then she's worse than her father.

The gate doesn't open, so Dimitri gets out, noticing a control panel. "Do you know the code?"

"It's the first four digits of pi," Nova snaps. "The pretentious bastard."

Dimitri nods and puts in the numbers, and with an audible beep, the gates start to swing open. The groan of the worn metal is loud as he gets back in the car. We wait for them to fully open before Louis drives through them, followed by the SUVs, which have been tracking us this entire time.

The drive winds through the estate's grounds. Upkept grass lines the driveway on either side with flower borders, and to the left, we see what must have been the servants' quarters in a separate building. When we turn into a circular gravel driveway, a large water feature with two small girls in the middle is switched off, the grey brick green from time.

Nova and Ana maybe?

Either way, it's nothing but a reminder for Nova as we park before the huge estate. Her hands clench ours, but we don't complain, as she stares at the old, towering brick manor where she was abused by her father.

She gazes at the large, ornate bay windows downstairs then the small balcony up top. Gargoyles are poised on the pointed roof of the three-story manor. The entire structure screams old British architecture, and the dark, ominous feeling about the place is only confirmed by Nova's fear of it.

It could have been beautiful once, but it seems like Dr. Davis didn't care about the upkeep, so he let it begin to rot away, like his mind.

"We don't have to go in," I start, but Nova climbs over me, kicks the door open, and slides out as if she doesn't do it now, she won't at all.

Nova is facing her fears head-on.

TWENTY

∞∞∞ NOVA ∞∞∞

I don't wait for them as the other car pulls up. I can't, because even seeing this place is enough to send me running for the hills. I hate it here. The memories are already winding around me like fog on the moors that surround this hellish house. I can feel them looking for an entry, for my weakness. I can see my father's silhouette in the window the night I ran and hear my sister crying for me.

Can a place really be haunted by what transpired?

If so, this one is.

It should be burned to the ground and left to rot, but here I am, standing before the antique, ornate wooden doors with my heart in my throat like I'm a child again. Lifting my hand, I swing the gold door knocker and wait. A shiver goes through me as I remember that night.

The lightning crackled across the sky, followed by a clap of thunder as the harsh wind whipped around me as I ran and ran. My feet were muddy and slippery, and my dress stuck to my tiny body as a deep chill set in. It took weeks to stop shivering.

No one answers, so I try the door, and it swings open with a creak, admitting me to the entryway. The wooden spiral staircases rise before me, and the same rug lies over the cold tiled floor. To the left is a painting of my father, Ana, and me, which was painted when we were children. Stepping closer, I see the hopeless, sad look in my eyes as my father stands with his hand on my shoulder, like a threat. I was silently screaming for someone to save me, while Ana smiled happily up at him.

I fucking hate this painting. If I could, I would tear it down and burn it.

"Hello, M-Miss Nova?"

I hear a gasp and spin. The guys are hesitating at the door with the soldiers, but coming from the kitchen, wiping his hands on a tea towel, is Bert. He's older now, his hair thin and greying, and there are more wrinkles around his thin lips and kind brown eyes. He's hunched as well, when he used to stand tall and proud, but the ever-present suit is still in place.

"Bert," I whisper.

I thought he would be gone. Other than Ana, he was my only friend, my only confidant. Father hired him as a butler, but he was more than that, much more. He looked after the staff and house, and he helped Ana and me grow up. Bert was kind and caring. He even taught me to play the piano and read me stories when I couldn't sleep.

He was the father I always wished I had.

And I left him too.

However, he knew why—at least partially. At first, he didn't, but as I grew older and more withdrawn, he started to realise something was happening. He hated my father for how he spoke to us, and I know he saw the way Father watched me. He was also aware of the nights I wouldn't spend in my bed, and when I could make it to breakfast, I was usually in pain and tired.

He never spoke it out loud, but he knew. He tried to protect me as much as he could in those final months, talking to me so I didn't retreat inside myself, and the night I left, he was the one who helped me.

He brought me clothes, money, and supplies to set me free. The only thing he ever asked of me was to run and never look back.

"Nova." He shakes his head. "What are you doing here? You promised you would never come back."

"I had to." I move closer and take his hands in mine. "He's gone. He can't hurt me anymore."

He flinches and closes his eyes. "I'm so sorry, Miss Nova. I stayed to protect Ana. I often think about what happened. I should have done more."

I silence him by pulling him into a hug. "You did everything. You saved my life, Bert. I've been eternally grateful for it all these years. Thank you. I never said that."

He cups my cheeks and looks me over. "You grew up so much. Look at you. You are more beautiful than ever, but to me, you'll always be my little Nova chasing butterflies."

I can't help but smile. Someone clears their throat, and he drops his hands before straightening. "Oh, forgive me, I got carried away." He flushes slightly. "Are these your friends?"

"In a way." I smile. "Bert, I need my father's research."

"Why . . . ?I . . . It would be in his office," he begins, turning to the stairs.

"No, the kind of research he hid," I correct.

He frowns, not quite understanding, but he nods anyway. "Of course, this is your house." I don't correct him. After all, it's never been mine. "I will put some tea on. You know the way." He begins to turn before looking back at me. "I'm so glad you are okay. I have wondered about you every single day since that night, hoping you had a better life. Did you?"

I nod. "I did."

"Good, good, that's all that matters." With that, he hurries to the kitchen, uneasy with showing his emotions past his duty.

"Who is he?" Isaac asks as he comes to my side.

"An old friend," I reply, watching him go. "He saved my life."

"Then we all owe him a debt. Are you okay?" he whispers low enough for only me to hear.

"I-I don't know," I admit. "But I have to be." I turn to the soldiers and others, trying to fight off the emotions whipping through me like a gale force wind.

"I think the entrance is right down—"

"Who the—please move," comes a stern, feminine voice from behind the soldiers at the door.

Ana.

She slides through the busy doorway and stops, her mouth dropping open as she looks around at everyone before her gaze lands on me.

"Hi, Annie Bannie," I say softly.

"What the hell are you doing here, Nova?"

"I finally came home," I answer lamely.

She crosses her arms, her usually friendly eyes sparking with anger. "Get out. Get out now. You don't belong here. You're not welcome."

I flinch at the venom in her tone. "Ana," I murmur as Bert comes down the hallway.

"Miss Ana, how lovely to see you."

"Bert," she greets, softening briefly before looking back at me. Her face clouds with rage and betrayal again. "I don't want you here, and neither would Dad. Get out, this isn't your house."

"Actually, it is."

TWENTY-ONE

NOVA

Both of us turn to Bert, confused and shocked.

"What?" we ask in unison as she steps closer, dropping her crossed arms as he smiles at us both. I didn't believe that I truly did own it after all. I thought it was another trick.

"It's so good to see you together again."

"Bert, please, what did you mean?" Ana demands. It's the harshest she's probably ever spoken to him, but he takes it in stride.

"I simply mean it is her home. It's in her name, Miss Ana. I know you haven't seen the will yet, but I was the one to witness it for him. Your father, well, he left everything to Nova."

The silence could be cut by a knife.

Shock fills me, then anger. It's just another way to get back at me, another fucking punch in the gut and a way to haunt me even as he's dead.

"You can't be serious." I laugh.

"Deadly, I'm afraid." Bert nods. "He expected you would be angry, upset even, but he told me to tell you one thing. Please excuse me if it's not verbatim, it's been many years. 'Novaleen, the house, the money, and the labs are all yours to do with as you wish. I hope they help you understand. I hope they set you on the path.'"

"What the fuck does that mean?" I snarl, throwing my hands up.

"I do not know."

"Dad knew you were alive? And he left everything to you? The kid who ran away?" Ana almost screeches.

"If you need money, you can have it—" I start as she snorts bitterly.

"I don't need money! I just didn't want my childhood home being destroyed or sold! It was all I had left of you, of us, and now him." Her face scrunches like it used to when she was sad. I reach for her, but she jerks away.

"I don't want it, any of it," I tell her. "I have my own life, my own things. It's all yours, I promise, I just need to get something—"

"I don't want it. Congratulations, Nova. As usual, you get all the attention and everything you ever wanted." With that spiteful comment, she flees, leaving me staring after her. Everything I ever wanted? All I ever wanted was to be happy, to be safe, and to be with her again.

TWENTY-TWO

DMITRI

My eyes lock on the retreating form of Nova's sister, my fists clenched at my sides. I wanted to chase after her and demand that she listen to Nova, but how can I make her see when she is so blind to the truth? So lost in the love of her father that she doesn't see the ghost of the woman he broke before her. When I glance back, it's to see Nova's stricken face before she shuts it down, turning that emotion inwards. I never had a family or siblings to care for.

To love and miss.

Nova did—does, and to see them turn their back on you? It must be indescribable. I want to scream at her sister and tell her what Nova went through to keep her safe, but as I go to chase her down, Nova's voice cuts through the air like a command.

"Don't."

I look back, and she shakes her head at me sadly, as if knowing what I was going to do. "Let her go. She has every right to feel the way she feels. She owes me nothing. It's probably better if she hates me anyway."

"She doesn't know," I snarl, getting angry on her behalf. For a moment, I see sadness in her eyes before they turn cold again, but she can't fool me. I saw the hope, pain, and heartbreak written there.

"And she never will. It would break her heart more than I ever could," she replies before sighing. "Let's just find the fucking lab and leave this bloody place so I can burn it down once and for all."

"We must insist you find the lab also," a soldier sneers, uncaring about the fact that Nova is clearly upset and already feeling triggered by being in this fucking awful horror house.

Louis throws them a withering look as Isaac moves over to Nova, whispering in her ear. She smiles slightly, and jealousy pounds through me for a moment before I toss it aside. There is no room for jealousy here, and I'm glad he got her to smile. When he leans back, she nods, squeezing his shoulder.

"It's down here, if I remember correctly." She turns and freezes for a moment, blinking at the dark, empty corridor. We all move closer, knowing the signs—after all, we struggle with them too.

"Nova?" I murmur.

"Yeah, sorry," she whispers, but her voice is shaky. "Fuck, I hate this place."

"We do not have time for memory fucking lane," one of the soldiers snaps.

I turn to knock him out, but Nico beats me, fisting his hands in the man's shirt. "You do not get to fucking speak to her. You know nothing of what we survived. If I hear one more word come from your mouth, I'll rip out your tongue and give it to her as a gift," he snarls, and then with an effortless move, he launches the man across the reception area and right out of the front door, where we hear him hit the car. The alarm sounds as he groans. Turning back to us, he winks at Nova.

"Just taking out the rubbish."

I can't help but laugh, and she does too, even as the other soldiers start barking orders and surroundings us.

It's going to be a long day.

TWENTY-THREE

NOVA

I stare at Nico, extremely turned on by that display. I shouldn't be, since it was angry and chaotic, but I hear the man scream, and shit, it has my pussy clenching as I look at his bulging muscles. It's only when another soldier clears his throat as the others leave to fetch their comrade when I turn back around. I shake my head, remembering that there is no time for flirting or even figuring out if Nico would throw me like that.

My steps are slow as I make my way down the corridor. I feel their eyes on my hunched back and sense their worry, and it only fills me with shame. They think I'm weak and stupid—

No!

It's my father's voice and insecurities rearing their heads, so I push them back, knowing they are only concerned about me. There is something about shared trauma that bonds people. I trust them more than I ever knew was possible because we are the same—same wounds, scars, fears, and hopes. They would never judge me, only support me, and that level of trust and support has me standing up taller, knowing I can do this. I have to so I can find peace, not just for me, but for them. We also need to finish this and stop what my father did, so it can end with us.

My steps become steadier, my hand dragging down the wall as I walk. The shakiness disappears once I realise their strength is my strength and that I'm not alone anymore. My father's ghost can't hurt me here. They won't let it.

The hallway turns darker the deeper we go, and memories assault me from every corner, but I grit my teeth and force myself through them. They cling to me like the cobwebs in this house. Those silky strands wrap tighter around me until each step is heavy and dragging.

His grip tightens on my too young hand, tugging me down the corridor. I dig my feet in, not wanting to, a wordless whine on my lips. My eyes dart around behind the blindfold desperately, seeking help.

Seeking something that won't come.

Someone to save me.

He throws my hand down like a petulant child, and I feel his fingers on my face as he moves closer. The heat of his body makes me shiver, and the faint smell of whisky on his breath as he spits his words makes me recoil as far as I can. Pain already racks my body, but it is nothing that will compare to what is to come now that I have tried to defy him.

A useless rebellion.

In the long run, it will only hurt me longer if I fight.

"Now behave, Novaleen. You know why I do this. It's to help you and to better mankind. It will expand the human mind . . ."

Panting, I lean into the wall, pushing through the memory. It fades away with a mocking laugh. For a moment, I'm still that young, scared, pained girl who's lost in the dark, reaching out desperately for someone to save me, only for my hand to be taken by the monster.

Betterment of mankind? It's such bullshit.

All of his research was utter bullshit. All he did was scar children and force them to become wounded adults. Yes, we are stronger and faster, and we have higher IQs and survival skills. That part of his research might have succeeded, but everything else?

It failed.

We aren't supersoldiers. We are too broken for that.

"Nova?" Louis's soft voice pierces the haze of anger and resentment, reaching for me in the dark.

They aren't coming to save me from my father, but instead, they are right here in the darkness along with me, and their hands are in mine as we face our demons together.

"I'm fine," I mutter gruffly, pushing away from the wall, shaking yet again.

It's just a place, Nova, just a fucking place. Get over it and man the fuck up.

With that thought repeating in my head, I lift my foot and take one step, and then another. The world around me is a blur, my racing heartbeat roaring in my ears as I focus on my feet and nothing else, like that will stop the memories from reaching for me again.

Flashes of them move past my eyes, but I ignore them as best as I can as I lead them to the lab.

"No, Daddy, please, I'll be good. I swear!" My young self struggles to walk as he pulls me down the corridor, sighing in disgust before slinging me into his arms and carrying me into the lab. It's the only time he ever carries me.

Next, I silently walk down it. I'm older and not even reaching out anymore. I'm just silently and numbly walking after him.

The years pass through those memories, from a sobbing, begging child to a stern, dead-inside teenager. My understanding of the world evolved alongside my understanding of the father who only saw me as an experiment, and never a child. Once upon a time, I loved him. I used to stay awake at night, begging for signs to tell me what I did wrong to make him hate me so, before I realised he didn't. He never loved me either. He didn't have children for that purpose. We were just another scientific research opportunity for him, nothing else. It made it easier when I realised he didn't hate me but, instead, felt nothing, so I made myself the same, hoping it would be easier.

It wasn't.

In that numbness, cracks formed in the dark as my silent hopes for a family, for love, tried to break through and pierce the shadows.

I finally stop, and when I do, I realise I am just above the steps and the hidden door to the lab. My hand reaches for the knob, but I snatch it back like it burned. The wood warms, screams fill the air, and hands reach under the door for me—familiar hands.

Mine.

I stumble back, turning to look at the others, seeking them out amongst the madness.

"I can't . . . I can't go down there," I mutter, my voice shaking. I hate to admit that one weakness.

"It's okay. We've got it from here," Louis promises, stepping up to my side. He places his hand on my shoulder, grounding me. When my eyes meet his and I nod, he passes. The others squeeze through, putting their bodies between the door and me. I move farther and farther away, and with each step I take, my breathing gets easier, freer, and lighter, until I'm leaning into the wall, almost sagging in relief.

"It's locked!" Louis calls, and a part of me relaxes at not having to face whatever demons are lying in wait in that torture lab.

"Open it!" a soldier commands me.

"I don't know how," I mutter, not looking at them. "It was always open."

"Figure it out now!" the head one orders, his hand reaching for his weapon again. I'm feeling too vulnerable for this, and not like my usual, argumentative self. Luckily, Jonas slides before me, his arms crossed.

"It's a fucking high-tech security lock. She wouldn't know how anyway, so back the fuck off before I decide to play Nico's game and see how far the soldiers can fly."

The soldier stands down but doesn't look happy, and we spend the next twenty minutes in uncomfortable silence as they work on the lock. I stay as far away from the door as I can. Jonas is before me, grinning suggestively at me as he blocks my view of everyone and anything but him.

"I bet I could make you shake harder." He winks.

It's so out of the blue that a laugh escapes me and a true smile crawls over my lips as I face him. That rat bastard, he's never going to let me live it down.

He grins, wiggling his eyebrows. "Knew I could make you laugh. How about next I make you choke—"

"Jonas!" Dimitri snaps, making me grin wider.

"How's it going?" I call out, and he grunts.

"Bad," he mutters, so I quiet down and leave them to it.

The time passes slowly. Bert silently comes out with drinks, and I smile in thanks but can't bring myself to drink anything. A phone rings, breaking the silence, and we all turn to the soldier who pulls it from his pocket.

"All phones must remain on silent for the performance," Jonas jokes.

He ignores us and answers the phone, barking answers. His face twists in displeasure at the conversation before he hangs up. "Move out, men."

"You're leaving?" I ask, my eyebrow arched.

He grinds his teeth and looks at Louis. "There's an emergency back at base, so orders have changed. We are to leave, while you are to remain here and get into that lab. We will be back to help with the collection of the research, understood?"

"Aye, aye, captain," Jonas jokes.

"Understood," Louis snaps, unhappy with the order, but when the soldiers leave without another word, we all relax without their presence.

"Thank God, finally." Dimitri sighs.

We all turn to him as he straightens from the lock, blinking as we gawk.

"What did you do?" Louis sighs.

"I just set off a few alarms and sprinklers at the base with a tiny fake fire to get them to leave." He grins, and all of us laugh. "Hey, I hated them as much as you. Plus, I don't like the way they spoke to Nova."

My heart warms, and I smile at him. "Thank you, Dimitri," I tell him sweetly.

"No problem. Now let me crack this baby," he mutters, focusing on the lock as if no one else in the world exists, and to him right now, no one else does. His single-minded focus is sexy as hell. I wonder if he focuses on other things . . .

No, don't go there.

Not wanting to just stare at him and knowing it might take a while, I push from the wall. "I'm just going for a walk. Don't worry, I'll be okay," I call before they can ask. Instead of going outside, though, I decide to walk upstairs. I feel their gazes on me as I reach the top and turn right. Once out of sight, I allow myself to show a little weakness. My hands drag along the walls as I walk like I did as a child when we were playing.

Flashes of my and Ana's laughter have me smiling as I stop before a closed door.

My room.

I shouldn't, but I can't resist as I reach for it and push the door open. The wood creaks from years of disuse, and my nose crinkles as stale air hits me. I guess they didn't want to keep this room open. When I step inside, nostalgia fills me.

It's smaller than I remember.

The single bed with the princess curtains sits to one side, all made and clean. Teddy bears are perched on the seat under the window with the books I read when I got older. The mix of my childish room and collection of stuff as I grew makes me wrap my arms around myself.

There are still boy band posters hung haphazardly on the wall, CDs piled up on one side, and my old iPod too. There is no TV, since Dad said it was bad for the brain before bed. Clothes are also folded in the drawers and hung in the wardrobe. Everything is how I left it.

It's like I never disappeared.

I wonder if Ana ever came in here and if she missed me as much as I missed her.

All I ever wanted was to love and grow up with my sister to keep her safe, and now we are strangers.

It's so odd how you can go from knowing everything about a person to knowing nothing, from best friends to strangers. The love you have for them is still there, but there is a chasm between you, filled with everything that has happened, and both sides fight not to fall in.

Sighing, I throw myself down on the bed like I had done countless times in my childhood. My hands automatically go up and under the pillow, but I freeze when the fingers of my left hand touch something. Flipping, I lift the pillow and slowly extract the slip of paper.

It's a torn out, lined page that's haphazardly folded. Sitting up cross-legged, I slowly open it. The edges are jagged where it was ripped out of a notebook, but the sloppy handwriting is more familiar than my own.

Ana.

I miss you, Nova.

That's all it says. I reread the sloppy, black inked words over and over. The paper is yellow from age, yet it still has the power to break me.

My heart cracks, and the yawning abyss finally takes over as tears fill my eyes and slowly slide down my cheeks.

Gripping the page, I hold it to my heart and close my eyes.

"I missed you too, Ana bug," I whisper brokenly. "More than you could ever know."

TWENTY-FOUR

LOUIS

Not wanting to leave Nova alone here, especially after we forced her to come back to a place that hurts her, I venture upstairs. The place is dull, over the top and filled with stuff, but dull. There's no life here, and I can almost feel the pain and heartache. At the top of the stairs, I hear a little noise and turn right, following it. I stop at the doorway to her bedroom where she sits on the bed, holding a crumpled piece of paper with tears in her eyes, and I swear internally.

Feeling like shit for interrupting, I begin to turn away when she wipes her tears and her head jerks up to find me. I lean harder into the door, crossing my arms. I won't let her see my worry or my pain—pain caused by hers, the very same one we all carry.

Her agony is so much more, though, because she lost her sister in the process. We had no one to lose, but she did.

"Are you okay?" I ask softly.

Swallowing, she folds the note in her hand and looks down at it before her shoulders slump. That usual, cocky force of nature persona is gone, and in its place is the scared, broken little girl her father created here. "No, not really."

"Can I do anything?" I inquire honestly, and in this moment, I would do anything to see her smile again and help her rebuild her walls. If I could tear this place down for her, I would, but we know how to endure pain for the greater good, and that's what she's doing right now: enduring her nightmares to stop this and save others, even as her shoulders sag from the weight of it.

Shaking her head, she wipes at her face before standing, pocketing the piece of paper, and looking around the room. "It used to be my sanctuary. He wouldn't come in here. It was the only few hours of peace I ever had. Ana and I played here, and I read her bedtime stories. I used to do these elaborate voices and act it out for her. Sometimes, it was the only thing I would say all day. This was the only room in this house where I was happy. Now it's just cold and empty like the rest of this fucking torture mansion." Looking at me, she smiles sadly. "I shouldn't complain. At least I got a house and a sister, while you guys—"

I shake my head and move closer. "Do not compare pain. Ours doesn't detract from yours or vice versa. We were hurt by the same sick man, and we are allowed to hate him and what he did, to suffer from it in whatever way we need to survive." I place my hands on her shoulders, and she leans into me. "But you do not have to do it alone anymore."

Looking up at me through her lashes, she searches my face, and the expression painted across her features kick-starts my heart until it's racing as I stare back.

"What if we can't stop this?" she finally whispers.

"We have to," I murmur equally as soft, our whispers creating a barrier around us. "We are the only ones strong enough to. We didn't get to pick our lives, but we can still take a stand to stop this and save others. Afterwards, we can be whoever we want."

"But that's not true, is it?" She sighs and looks away for a moment, and I instantly miss her eyes, almost slumping from the force of her gaze being removed from me, searching my very soul. "We will still be the same fucked-up, overtrained people. There's no place in society for us, so where do we go then? Where do we belong in a world we protected from an evil they didn't even know about?"

"Together," I reply instantly, not even knowing where it came from.

Her eyes jerk back to mine, searching them in shock. I meant all of us, but deep down, I also meant that she belonged at my side. I don't know if it's our trauma that is pulling us together or the strength she exudes that makes me unable to leave her, but since the moment we met, I haven't been able to stop thinking about Nova. This mission is the most important thing to me, as well as keeping my men alive, but she snuck her way in there, winding through my body and heart so quietly, I didn't even notice until I couldn't stop thinking about her.

I have shouldered the burden of leading our people, of protecting them in any way I could, since I was young, but with her, I feel like a man, just a man, standing before a woman he likes.

A lot.

With her, I am not Louis the leader, the freak the military fears, or the experiment her father saw. I am just a man, and she sees him like no other ever has. For a moment, I allow myself to be weak, and my eyes drop to her lips, which part on an inhale. I wonder not for the first time what it would be like to kiss this wildcat, this living tornado, and taste the pain and beauty on her lips.

"Boss man!" The echo of Jonas's voice has me stepping back and dropping my hands to my side.

The desire pushes back and is replaced with a business-like demeanour. Her lashes close for a moment, and when her eyes open again, the same determination I feel is reflected there.

"I thought you would want to know we got in, but if you need thirty seconds to finish like normal, then we can—" There's a grunt, no doubt someone hitting him.

"We better get down there before they start killing each other," I murmur as I offer her my hand. "Shall we?"

Nodding, she takes it, and I squeeze hers, letting her know that whatever she'll face down there, she won't do it alone.

TWENTY-FIVE

NOVA

I grip Louis's hand like a lifeline as he leads me downstairs, lending me his strength. The others wait at the bottom, watching me carefully, so I give them nothing. I don't want them to think I'm weak. It's just a place, just a fucking place, and my father can't hurt me anymore.

I repeat it silently as Louis turns us to see the open door that leads to the one place in this world I never wanted to go again. Darkness mockingly creeps out of it, its tendrils reaching for me. Releasing Louis's hand, I step forward, my chin notched back.

Breathing slowly, I force one foot in front of the other, my hand curled around the lingering heat of Louis's palm to remind me that I'm not alone. It's easier than before, and once I'm in the doorway, halfway between worlds, I close my eyes against the darkness before me.

The feel of my father's orders washes over me, as does the way my heart would always stop when I stepped over this threshold because of the pain I knew was waiting. Lifting my foot, I step willingly inside for the first time ever.

I still then, my nose twitching at the slightly old smell of the place, as if it hasn't been touched in a while, but under that is the antiseptic cleaner my father used meticulously, the one that would always follow our sessions. Swallowing past the ghosts that want to take over my body, I walk farther inside, knowing the way in the dark better than in the light.

I feel the others hesitate, but I don't stop, my feet automatically taking me through the space. It's as if my father is right there at my side, his commanding presence filling me with fear more than safety. I can almost see him out of the corner of my eye, but I shake my head and stop, knowing it's inches away.

Lifting my hand, I stroke the glass that separates me from the room where some of the most horror-filled days and nights of my life were spent.

"Light, anyone?" someone mutters.

"To your left, there's a bank of switches, two steps," I murmur, remembering every inch of the layout. After all, I used to count the bricks and study the tiles, anything to forget the pain rolling through my body every time I was here.

There's a moment of searching, and then I hear the click. The lights bloom to life with a buzz, long ones attached to the ceiling and walls, washing the area in a bright white light that's also too painful to look at. I blink past the sting and then look at the room beyond, one that hasn't changed. The metal chair is still neatly tucked under the table as if it's waiting for me. No doubt the scratches in the cushioned leather handles from my nails are still there too. The table is spotless and clean, and the chains are neatly coiled in the middle. The floor and ceiling are still immaculately tiled—a hundred exactly on each.

The cot in the corner is made up and waiting for the other types of experiments, and the cameras in each corner no doubt turned on with the lights. I don't need to look behind me to feel their shock and horror, nor do I want to.

"Holy fuck," someone whispers.

I couldn't agree more. It's so clean and perfect, yet I remember the walls being covered in my blood, the echo of my screams filling the space, and the smell of burnt skin and melted plastic. I recall the sight of the burns on the table and floor and the shattered glass on his work-tables, a consequence of his anger. I remember it all.

Thousands of memories converge on me as I close my eyes and

press my hand to the glass. I can see her, the younger me, doing the same,, her eyes filled with tears and exhaustion, and her forehead resting against the glass as I do the same now.

"Please, help me," I would beg.

It's as if I can touch her, can reassure her that we will get out, but I can't. She turns away, dropping her hand, leaving a slight smear in her hopelessness. With her back to me, her head drops back as she screams and screams, letting out every inch of her pain and agony.

It will never echo around the house, though, only down here, haunting me even now.

"I'm sorry," I whisper. "I'm so sorry it took me so long to get us out," I murmur, needing to get it out. "I'm sorry it still hurts, and sorry we are still just as angry and lost."

"Nova?" someone calls behind me.

With one last look at my past, I open my eyes and pull away from the glass, leaving an identical smear across it as I turn to them. They are standing at the door and watching me with sad, knowing eyes. I see no pity there, only horror and anger on my behalf.

Turning, I scan this side of the office. It's still the same, and everything is exactly in its place. The rows of books on the small shelf in the corner are all perfectly lined up with the edge—his notebooks. The filing cabinets are locked and spotless, and the corner desk holds three computers, ready and waiting. To the right is his whiteboard with mathematical and scientific equations I could never follow, no matter how much I tried. His equipment sits before it, like the centrifuge. I look at it all idly, numbly.

Nothing has changed.

In all the time I've been gone, I changed nothing.

"It's so . . . normal," I mutter. "It shouldn't be this empty, as if this place didn't destroy me."

"Once we've searched it, you can rip it to pieces," Nico tells me, coming closer and stopping before me, blocking my view of the room. "You can destroy it all for all we care."

Nodding, I turn back to the room and hit the switch on the wall. The door to the left of the glass slides inwards, and I step to it. Nico follows me, not asking me if I'm sure but silently supporting me.

Moving deeper into the room, I stop next to the table, sliding my fingers across the metal I used to trace over and over.

A shiver rolls through me. I feel so weak just being here. My breathing starts to pick up, and a scream lodges in my throat. I can barely see, can barely hear. I'm losing it. Fuck! But Nico notices. He turns me and cups my cheeks hard, the slight pain bringing me back from the edge.

"Focus on me, on my voice. Count with me, okay? That's it, slow breath in, slow breath out. Focus on breathing, nothing else." With him instructing me, I work on getting myself back under control until I'm blinking before him. I feel tears in my eyes as I meet his stricken gaze. I know he struggles too, but only someone who has flashbacks would know how to bring you back so quickly and recognise them so easily.

What haunts Nico?

What does he see when he closes his eyes?

"You are safe. He's not here. He's dead. You are safe, you are alive, and we are here. Nothing in here can hurt you unless you let it, baby," he murmurs, pulling me against his chest, the steady thump of his heart grounding me. "That's it, breathe for me and remember who you are, not who you used to be."

His low, calming voice grounds me like nothing else, and I stand in his arms with my face pressed into his chest, gripping his shirt as I finally let out all the hurt, pain, anger, and hopelessness. I scream into his chest, the sound ragged and filled with horror, as tears flow down my cheeks.

He holds me steady, whispering to me and stroking my back as I sob and scream. Other hands join his, stroking me, and they add their voices until they drown out my own thoughts and turbulent emotions.

I don't know how long I stand there before I lift my head and look around at the men standing with me in my solitary pain, the men who are quickly becoming family and something so much more. Their hearts echo my pain, and yet they are ready to defend me, their eyes filled with their own tears.

Their own pasts.

Suddenly, I'm better, feeling emptier than I ever have before, like I've cried it all out. I have no doubt it will happen again, but I do feel better getting it out. Dimitri reaches out and strokes my face, wiping away my tears as I swallow.

"Thank you," I whisper.

"That is what family is for," Isaac murmurs, squeezing my hand I didn't realise he held. "We all break sometimes, but we are here to hold each other up when the darkness becomes too strong."

Smiling at him sadly, I step away, needing a moment to rebuild myself. There's a noise that has us all whirling around with our weapons raised before we realise who it is. It doesn't escape my notice that they move closer to me as well, far enough away to fight if need be but close enough to protect me, but it's only Bert.

His eyes run over the room in horror, his hand pressed to his mouth. The sound was a tray of tea shattering on the floor. When his eyes meet mine, his entire body shakes. "I never knew it was—"

"I know," I murmur, putting away my gun and stepping over the threshold. I kneel before him and start to pick up the broken pieces of china. Standing with those pieces in my hand, I stare down at the beauty of their jagged, shattered edges. "It will never be the same, but you can fix it with a little love and patience," I murmur, knowing he understands I mean more than the china as I carefully place it on the tray he now holds. "It might even be stronger than before, and different, but still as beautiful as the others."

"The broken ones always are because they are different and they stand out. Their healed wounds are a mark of their inner strength," he whispers, his hand covering mine. "I should have killed the bastard."

It's so out of character for him, a laugh barks out of me as I pat his hand. "Well, he's dead now, so let's focus on better things, like that amazing chocolate cake you used to make."

Smiling, he leans in and kisses my forehead. "Anything for you." He begins to turn before hesitating. "I am glad you found a family, Miss Nova. A real one, I mean. You always did have the biggest heart I had ever seen. Whatever your father—the doctor did to you here, it doesn't define you. He was a monster, but you are better than him in every way. Remember that." With that, he hurries away, leaving me staring after him.

"Nova, we need to start looking. You don't have to help," Jonas says, sounding serious for once.

Shaking my head, I turn to face them. "I want to help. Let's get this over with." I head over to the cabinets as they share a look.

One of pride.

I start with the folders as Jonas works on the cabinet locks. Dimitri works with Louis on the computers, while Isaac goes through folders near the medical station. Nico paces, watching everything and everyone with gritted teeth—mainly me, as if he's worried for me, but I keep my head down.

When I find anything that could be relevant, I mark it and add it to the pile in the corner. I'm working my way up to my father's journals, knowing they will hurt and trigger me, but once I shut the final folder, I can't put it off any longer. I feel them watching me carefully as I select one at random and flip it open.

His messy scrawl covers every page with diagrams, equations, and even pictures. It falls open on a page, and I inhale, closing my eyes for a moment. Nico is there instantly, placing his hand on my shoulder, so I show it to him, and he growls. Ripping it from my hands, he stares at the picture as if he wishes he could destroy this whole place for hurting me.

But they can't protect me from my past.

"It has already happened," I remind him.

"What is it?" Isaac asks worriedly.

"Just a picture." I pull it out of the journal, holding it in my hands. I stare down at my own sad, tear-filled eyes. I was young, and it was one of the first months I spent down here. The white gown I have on falls from my too slim frame, my face is pale and scared, and my hair is shaved off—a mental test.

My hand reaches up now to touch my head before I drop it and trace the photo instead. When I see the machine behind me, I sigh. "I remember this. It was one of the first times I realised my father truly didn't care if I lived or died. I was broken-hearted."

"What did he do?" Louis asks slowly. He knows if I'm talking, he should probably ask, but he doesn't want to make it worse.

"EST," I murmur. "Electroshock therapy, though it wasn't therapy. He wanted to see how I would react to extreme pain and how it would affect my brain waves at such an early age. More than anything, it was a test to see if I could endure it. It was this night he told me he was proud of me for the first time, and that I would be his best yet. It only got worse from there." I go to tuck the picture away, but Nico takes it from me and places it in his pocket.

"To remind me," he murmurs.

I don't know what to say, so I flip through the notes. "It's just his thought processes and findings on some of his early experiments." I clear my throat before I read his notes out loud. "If we are to expand the human mind and reach all it is capable of, then sacrifices must be made. We have already established a baseline that pain can help trigger these changes. Extreme stress, exposed at an early age, is helpful in unlocking the brain's secrets." Shaking my head in anger, I carry on. "I am hoping constant exposure to both fear and pain will develop the brain in further ways, mouldable at such a young age. Coupled with training usually given to soldiers, and learning equivalent to those given with high IQs, we can reach the results we need to prove my theory correct—that the human brain can be changed and expanded. That we can be better, stronger, faster, smarter, and more capable. A new race of beings, unmatched by any. By manipulating the brains of our children and selective breeding, coming generations will be nearly superhuman." Shutting the journal with a sneer, I toss it to the floor.

"Bullshit. That might have been his aim at first," I scoff before turning away. "But he began to like the pain he caused and the experiments he conducted. It wasn't just to make us better, as he called it, but to satisfy his sick urges and theories. It was never as simple as proving that theory. It was to test our humanity and how much we could endure."

"Nova?" Dimitri whispers.

I shake my head again. "Sorry, I'm okay. I'll keep looking."

"Never apologise," Louis orders. "You are right. Your father might have started as a scientist, but he broke his oath. It was about so much more than creating the perfect human, and we will prove that."

I hope so.

TWENTY-SIX

DMITRI

I keep my eye on Nova as I hack the doctor's terminal. I have to leave some programs running to try and crack some of the encrypted notes and locked folders, which could take weeks, but I also search the computers and hard drives for anything I can get to.

Minutes turn into hours, and all of us are still working.

We hoped it would be easy, but we should have known better. That doesn't make us give up, though, because we are destined to stop this once and for all. If not for us, then for Nova and all the children who didn't make it. None of us deserved what he put us through, but we can make it right. We can't change the past and what we endured, but we can stop it from happening to another. We just need to find the right pieces of the mad scientist's puzzle.

Louis forces everyone to take breaks except me, knowing he wouldn't get me to no matter what. Nova sits with me every now and again, talking and joking, distracting me from the screen even just for a few minutes. She doesn't get it though. I'm determined to find the information for her.

I need to do this.

It's all on my shoulders. Even Louis is trying to help, but none of them are as good with computers as I am. I feel that heavy weight until my eyes sting, my hands cramp, and my back aches, but I still keep going late into the night. The others stay with me, and food is brought but it remains uneaten. We all continue to push forward, refusing to stop when we are this close.

Then there's a ping. We cracked a folder. I quickly navigate to it, saving it in case there's any kind of virus or trap. It's labelled with a date, and there are video files inside. I stiffen when I examine them, wondering what they are and if I should play them.

"Louis," I murmur, and he turns from the screen next to me. "Should I play them?"

It must catch the others' attention because they crowd us, and I feel Nova's hand on my arm. "Play them," she orders.

Louis nods, so I pick one at random. It loads quickly, and we all swear. Nova freezes, and I wish I could protect her. I try to close it, but she knocks my hand away.

On the screen is a screaming Nova. She's young, an early teen, and her hair has grown back, but it's stuck to her skin with her sweat. I can't see what is being done to her, but she's screaming, and her father is watching her from the corner while making notes. I close it and open another, only to see her at another phase in her life.

She's curled into a ball, sobbing on the cot.

Another one has my eyes closing. There's a gun between her and a man on the table.

All of them are of her torture, her experiments, and all the while he's there, watching and making notes. Closing them, I lean back and scrub at my face. Those images will haunt me now as well.

What she endured . . . *Fuck.*

I'm more determined than ever to make them pay, but when I look up to her, I find her eyes still locked on the screen. "I-I need a break," she murmurs and hurries from the room, wrapping her arms around herself. We all track her worriedly.

"Don't," I murmur when I feel Nico begin to move after her. "She needs a moment. She will feel raw and weak with us all seeing her pain. Give her a moment alone." I hate it as well, and he hesitates before sinking heavily into a chair, holding his face.

"How could he do that to his own daughter?" Isaac murmurs sadly. "How—" He shakes his head, looking away.

"Because he believed it was a necessity." I hate that I think like him. "Love is a useless sentiment, a useless feeling, remember? He never loved her or cared beyond her purpose in his experiments. She was just like us—a thing to use."

"Save them all and any others you find. We will all watch them so we know what she was forced to survive and to remind ourselves why we are doing this, but she will never see, do you understand me? Not ever again. We cannot protect her from her past, but we can protect her from this," Louis orders, and we all agree.

She shouldn't have to watch them again, not when they still fill her every waking and sleeping moment, but I will watch every single one, even when it fills me with hatred and helplessness. I will keep them with my own memories and pain, so whatever happens next, I'll remember why we are doing this now.

Not just for us and the other nameless faces, but for her.

Nova.

TWENTY-SEVEN

NOVA

L ouis forces us to rest, but I can't sleep upstairs, and the others seem reluctant, so Bert brings in sleeping bags and sets them up in the unused living room I have no memories of. They take turns sleeping. Louis checks in with command. They aren't happy, but they understand that we need time to go through all the findings and research for what we are looking for.

Everyone sleeps but me and Dimitri.

He never stops or moves from the computer.

Slipping from my sleeping bag, I tiptoe past a snoring Jonas and over Nico, who's near the door. I spot Louis at the front door, staring out, and Isaac in the kitchen, so I move back to the computers and Dimitri. From the doorway, I see his hunched over form. His eyes are red and raw, and the light from the screen gives his face a hollow look.

"You should rest," I murmur, and he jumps like he didn't hear me creep up. Blinking, he rubs at his eyes as I move closer, pulling a chair over to sit at his side. He looks back at the computer with a grunt, so I cover his hand on the mouse. "Dimitri, you need to sleep, you know that. Your brain needs rest."

"I'm fine." He shrugs off my hand, and I debate walking away, but something is bothering him. "I can't stop, okay?" he finally says as I stare at his profile.

"Why?" I murmur, needing to know.

He turns to look at me, his gaze pained and dark. "Because I need to do this for you!" he rages, tugging at his hair. "I can't stop what happened, but I can do this. I can find the information that will help them, you, and us stop this. That might give you peace and a better future. I'm doing this for them as much as you. How can I sleep when I know that with each minute I wait, another child could be hurt, and that you are stuck in this place that haunts you?"

He's doing it for me.

I sit back, blinking as I stare at him, and suddenly I can't stop myself. Leaning forward, I cup his face and the stubble there, and I kiss his warm, soft lips. He freezes as I pull back, pressing my forehead to his. "Thank you," I murmur. "I do hate it here, but I would hate it even more if you were to get sick because of me. I can endure this. It's . . . better with you all here. I know how important this is, I do, but so are you. Do not kill yourself for answers. They will come when we need them. Louis and the others need you for the long run, not just for your mad computer skills." That makes his lips curve, and mine follow as I search his eyes. "I need you, okay? So please, sleep and eat."

The smile drops, and our breaths mingle. "You need me?" he echoes.

"I do," I admit, my voice hoarse, "in more than one way, but right now? I need you to sleep, please." I lean in and kiss him softly again before standing, then I offer him my hand.

He swallows, glancing at the computer before taking my hand. "Just a few hours," he concedes, making me smile wider.

"Fine by me." Squeezing his hand, I lead him from the room. Louis is at the door, and I almost stumble, but there is no judgement or jealousy in his eyes. I only see gratitude. I nod and lead Dimitri to my sleeping bag, where I tuck him in like a child as I brush his hair back. "Sleep, the computer will be there when you wake up."

His eyes start to close, but then his hand moves to squeeze mine. "I need you too," he whispers, and just like that, he's asleep.

I sit back on my heels and watch him before forcing myself to stand

and move to the kitchen, unsure what to do with the feelings inside of me. Isaac is staring out of the kitchen window with his hands wrapped around a mug, and he appears to be miles away. I slip inside, and he jumps, turning to look at me before getting to his feet.

"Let me get you one." He quickly pours me a mug, and I sit opposite him, drawing my knees to my chest as I balance the mug that's filled with some kind of herbal tea. I raise my brows, and he grins sheepishly.

"It's good for the soul," is all he says.

"Okay, Dimitri is resting," I tell him, taking a sip and almost groaning as the warm, comforting taste sinks into me. Isaac's eyes are wide.

"And how the hell did you manage that?" He gapes, making me laugh. "Seriously, we've been trying to learn how to for years. Tell me your secrets."

I lean in and look around like we are being watched. He does the same with a grin, and I crook my finger until he comes closer, then I press my mouth to his ear, ignoring the pulse of desire it sends through me as his scent wraps around me. "Feminine wiles."

Sitting back, he chuckles. "Well, we never stood a chance then."

"Nope, sorry." I wink while taking another sip.

"How are you doing, really?" he asks over his tea.

"Probably about as good as anyone would be," I admit, not wanting to lie. "But I've survived worse."

"Yes, but you're not alone anymore," he murmurs, eyeing me.

"I know, I know." I wave it away. "There are just some things you have to deal with alone."

"I can understand that." He nods.

"What about you?" I ask, tilting my head. His eyebrow arches, and I laugh. "Oh, come on, this can't only be affecting me, so how are you, Isaac?"

"I, um, I don't think anyone has ever asked that," he says quickly.

"Then I'll ask every day. Come on, you have all seen my deep, dark secrets," I joke.

"Truly, it's not easy," he admits as if he's ashamed to share it. "It reminds me of my own . . . imprisonment," he hedges.

"In France, correct?" I ask. He still has a slight accent.

He nods. "Not that I saw the place. Maybe I will go back and visit one day just to see the beauty I knew lived above my prison." He sips his tea, his eyes going far away. "My cell wasn't quite as grandiose as yours. It was in the basement of a house on the outskirts of the city. It was surrounded by land, though I never saw the sun much. I was kept in a room bigger than that one, with a bed, a toilet, and a shower. That was it." I reach for his hand, and he takes mine with a sad smile. "I spent so many years there, I thought I would go mad, but I didn't. Instead, I filled the time by learning everything about medicine I could. I thought maybe it would impress him, but I would also be able to look after myself."

"And did you?"

He nods, squeezing my hand before he stands and pulls his shirt up. I inhale when I see the healed marks on his chest, and then he peels back the sleeves, where there are scars raised around both wrists. "For years, he was obsessed with capture, with chains restricting my movement to see if it would help my brain grow if I couldn't focus on my body." Sitting, he takes my hand again. "To this day, I hate them . . . when I see them on the table." He looks away in shame, so I force his face back to me. "The only reason I didn't sink into my own memories was because I needed to be there for you."

"Isaac." I swallow. "I'm sorry. These words feel inadequate, but they are true. I'm sorry for what he put you through, but I'm not sorry it brought you to me."

"No?" he asks. "You might be soon."

"Nah." I squeeze his hand with a wink. "All families are dysfunctional. No matter what, though, he cannot take away your achievements, your good heart, and how you take care of everyone else. When do you look after yourself?"

He swallows, and I smile sadly. "Exactly what I thought." Standing, I round the table, take his tea, and put it down as I sit on the table before him. "You need to look after yourself and give yourself that chance to heal. You do not have to bear the brunt of all the weight alone. That's why we are together. Right now, I'm betting you are in here worrying about them all out there"—I jerk my head towards the other room—"and how they are handling it, while coming up with plans to reduce their stress without even considering your own."

He's silent, but he knows I'm right.

Leaning forward, I capture his chin and force his eyes to mine so he can't look away from me this time. "You can't save anyone if you don't save yourself first," I tell him before I stand. "I mean it. I will ask how you are every day, and I want the truth. Now get some rest. As a doctor, you should know how sleep deprivation works on the brain."

"Is that an order?" He laughs as I put the mugs in the sink.

"You bet." I grin at him and smack his ass as he walks past. "Go sleep, doc. I'll keep watch."

Once I've cleaned up, I move through the house, seeing them all resting except for Louis. I find him at the computer, and I sit at his side. He meets my gaze with a grateful smile.

"Thank you for getting them to rest."

"Any way I can help." I shrug it off, but he turns my face back to his.

"It's a big deal, Nova, thank you." I hate the kindness in his tone, so I clear my throat and look at the screen, blinking. "What is that?"

"That," he begins, and he seems pained. "Is something that would destroy Dimitri."

I flinch, and he nods.

"That is Bassel, Bass for short. He was one of us."

"The one Isaac spoke of," I mutter. "He . . . He killed himself, didn't he?"

"Yes, when the pain became too much." The young boy on the screen looks so lost and sad, my heart aches for him. "Your—the doctor didn't just do mental experiments, but physical. He wanted to see how life-long chronic pain could affect you. He carved up his insides so badly, there wasn't a day when he wasn't in agony. We supplied him with morphine as much as we could, and he was constantly high on it just to be able to sleep or breathe. It's why we got caught in the end, but before we could help him too much, he walked in front of a bus. He left us a note that said he couldn't do it anymore, couldn't fight the pain, and that he was sorry."

"Fucking hell," I murmur softly. "Dimitri—"

"And he were lovers." Louis smiles. "They were so close, they were inseparable. It hit Dimitri hard when he died. He buried himself further into his love of machines, losing himself in them and pulling away from all of us. He had no drive for anything but revenge, and then you came, and you reminded him of friendship, love, and a future. I cannot thank you enough for that. We were going to lose him like we lost Bass, but you are saving him."

"I'm not doing anything," I reply worriedly.

"You are. You just don't know it."

"Will you tell me about him? Bass?" I ask, changing the subject. I want to know more about the man who could have been a friend, who went through what we did.

"Dimitri knew him best, but he had this laugh that would light up the room, and he was so creative. He would tell us stories and act them out. He liked to paint . . ." For the next hour, Louis lets me fall in love with a friend. It's easy to see how much he cared for the man, and how deeply they are all connected. The stories make me laugh as much as they make me cry, and when he trails off, I'm almost desperate to know more about someone I will only know through them.

Someone I couldn't save.

Someone my father killed.

TWENTY-EIGHT

NOVA

I get a few hours of rest once Jonas comes and takes over, and I wake to the sound of grunting. When I open my eyes, I realise Nico and Jonas are sparring right there in the hallway. A nervous Bert flits around them, making sure they don't break anything. Sitting upright, I feel my mouth dry at the sight of their huge, glistening muscles as they move with precision and speed that rivals mine.

That's when I realise I haven't trained or sparred in a few days, and it's evident from my turbulent emotions and nightmares from being back here that I could use it. Rolling out of the sleeping bag, I rip my long shirt over my head, leaving me in a sports bra I fell asleep in and biker shorts. I tie my hair back, grinning when Jonas spots me. His eyes widen before they simmer as Nico lands a hit that sends him flying back into the wall.

"No fair! Her tits distracted me!" Jonas groans.

Nico whirls, his eyes widening as I move towards him with purpose. "I think they would distract anyone," he murmurs. "You want in?"

I nod, rolling my shoulders back. "Both of you against me. I could do with a challenge." I smirk.

"Oh, she has a death wish." Isaac sighs, leaning against the wall as he comes from the kitchen.

"Or maybe I'm just that good." I wink at him, ducking below a hit from Jonas, who wasn't really trying. They circle me as I stand there.

"Are you sure about this?" Nico asks, giving me a way out.

"I've fought bigger and faster opponents." I grin. "Killed them too. Bring it, baby."

"When I win, I'm going to fuck her." Jonas laughs.

"Master Jonas!" Bert snaps.

"Sorry, Berty." Jonas winks as I give him a grin.

"If you can beat me, I might just let you," I murmur. He didn't expect that, and I use it. I launch myself at him, tackling him to the floor before rolling to my feet as I smirk down at him. "But fight properly."

"I won't hold back," Nico warns, his voice a whisper behind me as I duck a punch and spin to face him, sliding back.

"Good, then neither will I." I smirk at him, seeing the flare of desire in his eyes.

Glancing over, I see Jonas push with his hands and flip back to his feet. "Oh, this will be fun." It's the only warning I get before he comes at me. He's fast and feral, with no rhyme or reason to his movements. I duck and weave around him, managing to land a few hits before I'm kicked back into the table with a grunt. The vase there tips to the side in slow motion, and we all watch it drop to the floor and crack. All eyes go to Bert, whose eyes narrow before he looks at me.

"Kick their asses."

I can't help but laugh as I nod and throw myself back into the fray, ignoring Isaac's, "Now you've done it."

Nico manages to grab me from behind, but I use his body and height and throw myself back, flipping over him and taking him down. He rolls back to his feet, though, and then they work together. One is always behind me, and one is always in front. But what I said is true—my father and his mentors used to blindfold me and throw me into the ring with their guards.

I am used to being outweighed and outnumbered.

It's fucking thrilling for me, in fact.

Adrenaline courses through me until I can't help but laugh as I spin away from a sweeping leg. Despite their words, they are still going easy on me, so I decide to up the ante and force them to take this seriously. They wouldn't go easy on each other, so I won't let them go easy on me.

As Jonas chases me, I race towards the wall, kicking off it with three steps before I flip over him, then I wrap my arms around his head and bring him down in a headlock as he snarls, elbowing me. I grunt from the pain and hold tight with my hand on my wrist, tightening my hold.

There's a cheer, and when I glance over, I spot Dimitri and Louis watching from the hallway leading to lab room. I grin as I release him and roll, avoiding Nico's silent sneak attack I sense coming up behind me.

"About time." I grin, and then there's no room for talking as they turn and come at me faster than I thought possible. They aren't normal guards, and this isn't typical fighting. I should have remembered that. They are like me—stronger, faster, and harder—but fuck if that isn't a turn-on. It's an actual challenge for once. I don't have to hold back the strength of my punches. I split Jonas's lip, where that blow would have knocked someone else out. Nico's punch to the gut only winds me, where it would have taken anyone else down.

Jonas kicks out the backs of my knees, and the pain is sharp. I fall forward, hitting the floor with my bare hands and rolling as they follow me. I roll back and forth to avoid their kicks before stopping in front of Nico. I grab his foot as he brings it down, grinning up at him. I twist, and he growls, having no choice but to turn with it or break his foot. He spins away, and I sweep Jonas's legs out, watching him tumble as I climb to my feet.

I'm panting slightly, and my body is lit up with excitement. For some reason, a thought flickers through my head

If this is how they fight, imagine how they fuck . . .

That idea distracts me enough that Jonas manages to grab me and lift me into the air with a hand on my throat, squeezing so hard I gasp. I slam my hands down in a V, but it doesn't affect him as his eyes smoulder up at me. "I think I'll let them all watch as I take my prize," he says before he throws me.

Instead of hitting a wall, I hit a solid chest as arms catch me midair. Nico.

His mouth meets my ear, and somewhere along the way, this fight has charged with sexual tension strong enough that I could cut it with a knife. I feel his very hard, very big cock pressed against my ass as he holds me, letting me feel just how much he is enjoying this.

"Maybe I'll join in," he murmurs into my ear before bringing me down in what I can only describe as a WWE move to the floor. Groaning, I stumble to my feet and wipe my mouth as my heart skips a beat.

"Fine, you want to play like this?"

"Oh shit," someone whispers. "It's about to get good."

"I think I should leave," Bert mutters.

"Good call," someone else replies, but I focus on Nico, who's coming at me again. They want to win just as much as I do. It's not in our nature to submit or give in, so I fight back, even though I'm starting to realise the odds are stacked against me.

They are fucking superhuman.

They don't stop.

I try to tease them like they teased me, but it doesn't work because they are so focused on winning.

I dodge one attack, only to fall into another. I do manage to bust Nico's ribs and take them down to the floor, but they just get back up. I can tell they feel the same as we dance around the foyer. They are both panting, covered in cuts and blood, as I get back to my feet again despite the pain and exhaustion flowing through me.

"Fuck, you can take some punches," Jonas remarks breathlessly, his hands on his knees and head bent down so his hair falls into his face. He straightens with a groan and cracks his back. "Come on, let's finish this."

"My thoughts exactly," I retort.

Nico nods, blood running from his nose. They share a look again, and then we are back at it, clashing in the middle. I duck their punches and jump over their kicks, giving as good as I get. One movement slides seamlessly into the next, mixing martial arts together. I bust open Jonas's nose, and Nico splits my lip. I kick Nico back to a wall and take Jonas down, grabbing a piece of broken vase and pressing it against his neck with a grin. "Submit."

"You," comes a growl, and I feel a sharp edge of a glass vase pressed to my own neck.

Laughing, I toss the glass away and get to my feet as Nico does the same. "Well, shit, it's a draw." Louis sounds shocked.

"Good fight, boys." I hold out a hand to Jonas, who is grinning madly at me. He accepts it but pulls me down so I sprawl across him with a groan. Gripping my head, he gives me a hard, swift kiss that leaves me breathless and clears all thoughts from my head.

"Since I didn't win, I at least get that." He smirks and then rolls us to our feet, putting me on mine as I gawk at him. "Well, look at that, I finally shut her up."

Rolling my eyes, I swallow my shock. I'm about to walk away when Nico grabs me, spins me back to him, and tilts his head down. I freeze, thinking he's about to kiss me as well, but his tongue darts out and traces the cut on my lip, tasting my blood. The stinging sensation makes me gasp as he pulls back slightly.

"I'll collect my kiss when I'm ready," he whispers and then spanks me. "Go get washed up, it's time to eat."

Unsure what the hell just happened, I blink and accept the clothes Dimitri holds out to me. "I've never seen anyone lose against either of them separately, never mind together," he tells me, stroking my ego, which is bruised.

"He's right." Louis nods. "Now back to work." He claps.

I nod at them with a small smile, happy they aren't watching me strangely after Jonas's kiss and Nico's near miss, before I hurry to the stairs where Isaac is standing.

With my clothes tossed over my shoulder, I stop beside Isaac as he hands me a warm mug. I meet his eyes over it. "Are you okay?"

His eyes widen before a soft smile curls his lips. "Yes."

Nodding, I turn and head upstairs, feeling all eyes on me and not minding one bit.

TWENTY-NINE

NOVA

"**B**ert, I said I'm sorry!" Jonas whines as I step into the kitchen. My hair is still wet and hanging over my back, and I'm dressed in skintight black yoga pants and a crop top. I lean into the door and watch as Jonas follows an angry Bert around like a kicked puppy. With his lips pursed, Bert sniffs, ignoring Jonas as he cooks.

"Please, my man, I just want those epic pancakes you made," Jonas begs. "I'll go and clean up the vase. I'll even get you a new one!"

Shaking my head, I stride to the table and take a seat next to Dimitri, who smiles at me. I grin back and knock my shoulder against his as we turn to watch the show, but then Nico comes in and steals all of my focus. My mouth becomes dry, and my thighs clench together as desire pounds through me.

He's shirtless, wearing low-rise grey joggers that do nothing to hide his thick thighs and slightly hard length. I scan his impressive abs and Adonis belt, leading down to the joggers and then back up to his huge pecs. I get lost in his muscles before there's a whisper in my ear.

"You're drooling," Dimitri teases.

"And you wouldn't?" I mutter.

"Oh, I do," he purrs.

I throw him a mock glare and wipe my mouth, even as my eyes jerk back to see Nico grinning at me, flashing straight white teeth, as he purposely heads over, leaning over the table to kiss my forehead. "Good fight. Next time, don't hold back so much. You can't hurt us."

I swallow and nod, not trusting my voice when his man boobs are so close and I have the irrational urge to flick his nipple. Fuck it. I tweak his nipple, laughing when he jerks back. "Same goes for you." I ignore the looks thrown my way, especially the dark, hungry one Nico gives me as I grab a plate and start to load it with fruit and pastries, whistling happily.

"Fucking hell," Nico finally mutters as he sits opposite me, bringing his pecs back to my line of sight as I munch on fruit. There is a crash, and I jerk my gaze up to see Jonas on his knees before a shocked Bert, who dropped a pan.

"Please, Bert, I'm not into guys, but I'll blow you if that's what you want."

I frown at the panic winding through Jonas's tone. Looking at Louis, I see him sigh, scrub at his face, and nod at Dimitri.

"Dr. Davis used to starve him as an experiment and withhold his favourite foods as punishment and to taunt him," he whispers sadly. "When we found him, he was half dead and crazed. He panics about food."

"Fuck." I climb to my feet and head over, my hand going to Jonas's shoulder. He looks up at me sadly with haunted eyes, completely broken. Getting to my knees, I lean into him as I stroke his face, comforting him as tears fill his eyes. He's terrified that someone will let him starve again and tease him with what he wants but can't have. "Go sit down, baby, okay?"

He still seems concerned, but he stands, and with sagging shoulders, he heads to the table, not meeting anyone's eyes. I look at Bert who tracks him with a shocked, saddened gaze.

"We all have our issues from my father. Do not ever withhold food from them again, do you understand me? I know it wasn't meant as a punishment, but we've been treated as lesser humans since we were kids. Everything you can imagine was used as punishments. Don't do that to us, please," I beg when he looks like he's about to cry.

"I swear, Miss Nova, I didn't—"

I grab his hand and squeeze. "I know, my friend. I'm just explaining. Now, how about some pancakes?" I say happily. I meet Jonas's eyes. He looks hopeful, like a child perking up.

"I will fill the entire house with them whenever you want, sir," Bert tells Jonas, his back straightening and eyes determined, as if he would cater to his every whim to not see that look again. Turning, I sit next to Jonas, placing my hand on his thigh under the table. He jumps but settles into my side as I fill his plate.

"Eat for me," I murmur, and he quickly dives into it as I meet Louis's grateful gaze.

Not ten minutes later, a plate stacked so high with pancakes I can't see Bert over it is placed before Jonas, who looks lost for words. Tears actually well in his eyes. "The doctor was a cruel man. I am not him. I'm sorry, Master Jonas. I meant no disrespect. You are always welcome in this house and in my kitchen, so never hesitate to ask for what you need. A friend of Miss Nova's is a friend of mine." With that, he bows to Jonas and goes back to making more pancakes, as if he truly will fill the house with them.

Jonas just stares at them, so I lean in and break the moment, knowing he will hate that we all saw his weakness. I would. "Are you just going to stare at them, or are you going to eat them before I decide I want them?" I tease.

He blinks when he turns to me with a bright, unguarded smile on his lips. He looks so innocent for once that it stops my heart. "Thank you," he tells me, squeezing my hand before taking a pancake. I stare as he eats, and something shifts inside me. A barrier falls before this equally damaged, crazed man, and a sense of protectiveness roars through me, the force of it scaring me. I return to eating but make sure to watch him as he carefully eats and treasures the pancakes as if they are a gift.

And in a way, they are from Bert, to show Jonas not everyone in this world is the same.

When Jonas sits back with a groan, I see the usual mischievous sparkle in his eye and relax a little. He's back, and he's not lost in the past anymore. "Next time, I'm going to cover your entire body in them and eat them from you," he warns, closing his eyes before he cracks one open when I laugh. "Hell, maybe I'll even fill your cunt with syrup and drink it from you."

"Jesus," Louis mutters, making us all laugh, but mine is tense and filled with desire.

Jonas hears it, his grin knowing as he strokes my thigh under the table, heading higher and higher until I scoot my chair back suddenly. I am not ready to go there, not with him. I fuck for fun and never remember them. I know it wouldn't be like that between us, and I don't want to lose them.

I like them. They are starting to feel like family, and I don't want to do anything that will ruin that, even if I know it would be amazing—okay, better than amazing. Fucking spectacular.

"I suppose we better get back to work."

A flash of hurt echoes in his eyes as he turns away. Licking my lips, I look away and meet Louis's concerned gaze before he stands.

"You're right, back to work. Let's find these bastards."

After five hours of helping everyone that I can, I go for a dinner break that Louis orders with Dimitri at my side. He's teamed us up since he told us Dimitri listens to me. Jonas says I have some kind of weird pussy power over them.

That got him a smack, even if it was the first time in hours I cracked a smile.

I don't know how they manage it, but they bring me back from the brink when I'm in there, and I'm grateful for it. They keep the atmosphere light and teasing, and if it wasn't, I think we would all sink into the depths of what we are looking through and handling.

Bert makes us a basket for dinner and shoos us outside, saying he needs to clean and we need sun and fresh air. Grinning, Dimitri takes it from him, and we head out back. I lead him to my favourite spot. I used to read and hide out here all day if I could to avoid my father. Bert reminded me of it with a knowing look, and although I've never taken anyone there before, even my sister, I take Dimitri, knowing he will understand why I needed it.

I don't anymore, but it's nice to share those places with someone who will understand and not judge you.

Crossing the huge back garden and walking past the pool that haunts me, I smile back at him as we reach the tree line and I duck under a low branch. The leaves crunch under my boots as I lead him deeper into the woods.

"If you are taking me out here to kill me, can I eat first?" he jokes from behind me.

Laughing, I hold a branch for him. "If I were going to kill you, I would have brought a shovel." I shrug. "Plus, I'm too hungry to kill."

"Good to know," he mutters. "Always keep her hungry."

Shaking my head with laughter, I duck under the two huge stones that lead into the dark crevice between. "Oh, this isn't sketchy. She's definitely going to murder me," I hear him say, but he follows me anyway, and when we come through the other side, he gasps.

"This is my favourite place in the world," I tell him, looking out at the land that has remained unchanged. "It's where I used to come to get away from it all." Stepping over the soft grass, I kick off my boots and wiggle my sock-covered feet into it with a sigh. The sun filters through the trees, warming us against the slight chill. "I would spend hours up here, reading and imagining I was the characters in a book. I would pretend like I was in a different land, envisioning a prince coming to rescue me," I admit as I look back at him to see he's listening carefully.

"Here, I was in a different world, and for a few hours, I was just a child, and I could be anything." I turn to face him as I spin. "A pirate rescuing his love from a stolen ship, a wizard going to school for the first time, a high priestess winning the war for her people. I could be anything, and I was. When my world came crashing back down, I took their strength and lessons with me to survive."

"Thank you for showing me this place," he murmurs, crossing to me and cupping my chin, forcing me to meet his eyes so I can see the truth in his gaze as he speaks. "I know that wasn't easy. I am so happy to be here with you, in the place that saved you, so I could meet you. Let's eat, and we can read for a while for old time's sake."

"I'd like that," I murmur softly with a smile just for him. I hope my place can become his and help him when he needs it. It can be his escape from the reality of the harsh, uncaring world we live in.

For a moment, we just stare at each other from inches away, and his eyes drop to my lips before he clears his throat and steps back. I turn to hide my disappointment, knowing it's for the best, and look out at the place I've brought him.

The cliff overlooks a raging river below where you can spot deer sometimes. The sun shines brightly through it, almost making it ethereal, and on foggy days, it transports you to a different world. The trees make natural arches above us, creating a barrier from the summer sun and keeping it warm in the winter. The grass is soft and dotted with flowers that have me grinning. There are also some rocks worn from age that I used to lounge on under a tree for shelter, soaking in the sun glistening across the worn grey space.

There's just something so beautiful here, and since it remained untouched by the horrors of my life, I found solace in its unreserved neutrality and softness. It reminded me that there was good in the world if one looked hard enough. Probably an idiotic thought as a child, but I did whatever I could to get through. Crossing the distance, I sit with my back to the natural seat of the rock, and he does the same opposite me, opening a basket similar to the ones Bert used to sneak to me when he knew I was coming out here.

Dimitri laughs, and I see why. Inside are little sandwiches cut into squares with the crust off. "I hate crusts," I admit. "He remembered."

"He loves you." He shrugs as he takes some for himself. There's a spread of different flavours—ham and cheese with honey mustard, garlic cream cheese and red pepper, egg mayonnaise, and BBQ pulled chicken. He's made a feast. Dimitri also pulls out scones with homemade jam and clotted cream, little cakes, and crisps.

"Wow," he mutters.

"He doesn't like people to go hungry." I shrug as I unwrap the sandwiches and dig in, gratefully taking a napkin and paper plate from him, and then he divides it out and begins to eat himself. As we do, our eyes wander to the land around us.

"Did you have a place like this?" I ask, curious.

"Not really. I escaped into the never-ending line of computer code," he replies. "If I focused enough, it swept me away from my body and the pain in it, as well as human emotions such as loneliness, hunger, and sadness."

It makes more sense why he loves anything that has to do with technology. It's like my meadow. That's where he feels safe and happy.

"Then I found it in a person as well, and he became my safe place, my hope." He swallows and looks away as I slump, saddened by his pain.

"Bassel," I murmur. He jerks in shock, and I smile sadly. "I saw a picture, and Louis told me a little. I'm so sorry, Dimitri."

He swallows, his face pale as he looks away.

"Did you love him?" I ask. I shouldn't pry, but he needs to talk. I can see that he's keeping it bottled up, and that won't help. I know.

"With every fibre of my being. He was my best friend, the only one who understood . . ." He looks back nervously. "I love the others, and they are my brothers, but they are stronger than me. They understood the violence or the beauty in the science. Me? The world didn't make sense to me, and Bassel was the same. He didn't get people or the world. He floated in pain, wanting to escape. We found it together. I tried drugs with him once, but I didn't like how they felt, too out of control. With him, though, I was in control, and I was strong. Someone needed me, and I wasn't alone. I still wake up expecting to see him there."

Tears roll from my eyes, and he reaches out and captures one, bringing it to his lips to kiss.

"He would have liked you," he murmurs as I smile.

"Really?"

He laughs. "He would always say, 'Trust the crazy ones, they know something we don't.'" I laugh with him, and he grins. "He had this unique way of looking at the world. He said the broken were beautiful and that we understood something no one else ever could. He told me one day I would understand that love could be as healing as it could hurt. It did hurt with him because I loved him, Nova, but he loved the pain meds more. He couldn't exist without them, and I saw him withering away before me. I would wake up to a ghost, a stranger, towards the end. We were so young, so lost, and clinging to each other. He told me once it wasn't a partnership, but a necessity for us to survive. It was a love created out of desperation and pain, not friendship and need, but it was what we had. In the end, I lost him, and the pain was too great."

"He killed himself?" I ask, knowing sugar-coating it won't help.

He nods. "I found him," he admits.

"Jesus, Dimitri, I'm sorry." I reach for his hand, and he looks down at our intertwined fingers as he speaks, as if he's gathering strength for his words.

"At first, I was so angry at him for leaving me in this fucked-up world. He left me alone. Nova, I was furious with him and hurt. I even hated him a little for it and thought it was selfish." He peers up at me as if he's expecting recrimination, and guilt fills his eyes.

"I think that's normal," I hedge. "You are allowed to feel however you want. You lost someone you love, so you have to just feel it."

"That's what Isaac said, but more . . . technical." We both laugh then. He's bitter and sad, so I slide closer, and he rests his head on my shoulder as I stroke his back.

"Then I just missed him so much it broke the last parts of me your father wasn't able to."

I swallow my own pain and tears. This is about him, not me.

"Now I can hardly remember him or the sound of his laugh. It's like he's fading all over again, and that scares me."

I cup his face and force him to look at me. "No one is ever truly gone. They live on in our memories and our love for them. You may forget some things with time, but you won't forget the way he made you feel and the love you shared. You won't forget the important things—that you loved each other—and in the end, that's enough."

"You think?" he asks, searching my gaze hopefully.

"Yes, and you'll see him now and then in other people, in places and things you shared, and be reminded of that love. Like now. You remember him as you tell me about him, right?" I smile, wiping away the tears that fall. "So, tell me everything you remember about him, and I will remember him with you. That way he will never be forgotten, and if you start to forget, I will remind you."

"Promise?" he whispers.

"I promise," I say solemnly with strength infused in my voice. "He was so loved, Dimitri, and sometimes that isn't enough, but you have to know you did everything you could. Now you need to live for both of you. Let him live through you. Sometimes . . . Sometimes people aren't meant to be here. I believe it happens for a reason, despite everything I have survived. It's not about being strong or weak; it's about nature. It takes the best of us, and Bassel? He sounds beautifully brilliant. He had to be for you to love him. Forgive him, Dimitri, for leaving. It's time. He was human and imperfect. He felt like he had no other way out, and I have no doubt that, in the end, you were with him, and he wasn't scared because of that. He was happy to go into the light knowing one day, you will join him."

"Do you think it hurt?" he asks, sounding like a child seeking comfort.

"No," I answer seriously. "I think for the first time in his life, it was probably the only moment he wasn't in pain or afraid."

It seems to settle him, and he leans into me. I hold him as he cries and lets it all out. When his tears dry up, the birds chirp above us as if signalling a fresh start. He leans back, and I clean his face, and then we start to eat again.

Here, in my meadow, in my safe space, he tells me about the man he loved, and I keep him in my soul with the man next to me, remembering and loving him for both of us.

THIRTY

NOVA

fter leaving the meadow, Dimitri kisses my cheek and
hurries back to the computers. For a moment, I let my hand
linger on my cheek, wishing it had been on the lips. I've
been so starved for contact that these men, these ridiculously attractive
men, have driven me wild with their teasing touches and looks.

I have lady blue balls, in all honesty. Remembering the way their
sweaty bodies pressed to mine as we fought and the promise in their
eyes . . . Yeah, it has me hurrying upstairs to my bathroom. I need to
blow off some steam so I can focus on why we are here.

Kicking the old wooden door shut, I stand before the mirror above
the sink, one of my hands holding the porcelain edge. Usually I would
turn away, but the spark in my eyes has my breath whistling from my
lips. It's something that wasn't there before . . . .They were always
dead.

Cold.

Now they are burning up.

My black hair is mussed from the wind, and my face is bright with
happiness. Is this what this feeling is? Closing my eyes, I let my hand
slide into my jeans, tracing over my knickers before slipping under.

Widening my legs, I spin so my back is against the sink as I stroke my pussy.

I'm wet from thinking of them.

From chaste kisses and teasing looks.

Fucking hell, I'm like a teenager, but it doesn't stop me from flicking my clit with a muffled moan. With my other hand, I nudge my top up and cup my breast through my bra, rolling and tweaking my nipple. Pleasure explodes through me as I pant, my finger rubbing my clit quickly, but for a moment, I imagine it's not me.

I imagine it's them.

Their hands cupping my breasts and playing with my nipples. Their mouths sliding across my skin and marking it up. Their hands inside my jeans, touching me, sliding down my wetness to push inside before moving back to my clit. Their mouths pressing to my ear. No doubt Jonas would whisper dirty promises, Isaac would keep a watchful eye, Dimitri would hold me up, and Nico would destroy me and make me his all the while Louis watched on. All working together to make me come.

I don't have time to think about how fucked up it is. I'm imagining all of them fucking me, and my imagination gets the better of me. I visualise Nico on his knees before me, gripping me meanly as he jerks me closer, his mouth sealing over my pussy and dominating it. I see Jonas at my side, stroking my breasts as he whispers in my ear. I imagine Dimitri on the other side, doing the same, while Louis watches it all with his hand on his cock and Isaac stands next to him.

Shit, shit, shit.

My clit throbs in time with my racing heart as I speed up my fingers, needing to come so badly but not wanting this fantasy to shatter.

"Good girl, I told you I would claim my kiss."

Nico's voice echoes in my head, and a gasp leaves my lips as I slide my hand down my dripping pussy and thrust two fingers inside myself, pretending they are his. I widen my legs farther as I thrust in and out of my pussy, hitting my clit with the palm of my hand each time until I'm almost coming, my back arching and mouth falling open.

A noise has my eyes opening, and at the sight of the peeling wallpaper, reality comes crashing down and embarrassment chases away the desire.

I pull my fingers from my pussy, about to berate myself, when there's a husky groan. My head turns, and my eyes clash with Jonas's bright, lustful gaze. He's poised at the door, his fists clenching the wood as he watches me, his nostrils flaring.

"Don't you dare fucking stop," he growls, stepping into the room and kicking the door shut behind him. "Watching you touch yourself is the most beautiful thing I've ever fucking seen. The best fucking torture I could have ever endured."

"Jonas . . ." I lick my lips, unsure what to say, but when his eyes drop to my glistening fingers and his body shudders, I slide my hand back inside my jeans. "Like this?" I murmur, playing along. He's igniting my lust again, only this time I can't control it. It storms through me like a wildfire as I hold his gaze while I stroke my clit.

"Fuck," he groans, reaching down to rearrange himself. My eyes lock on the huge bulge in his joggers, and I remember the sight of him fucking his hand. I moan and my pussy clenches. I'm dying to know what that magnificent cock would feel like inside me.

"I did watch you." I rub faster, my other hand gripping my breast harder as I rock my hips, fucking myself. "I watched you touch yourself. I was so fucking wet I could barely sleep."

His eyes narrow, neck straining. "I came harder than I ever have in my life, and I had to stop myself from hunting you down and forcing you to your knees to taste it. I wanted you to see what you do to me, baby."

Groaning, I speed up, and his eyes drag over my body possessively, hungrily, but I'm about to come, and I don't want to yet, so I pull my fingers free and suck them clean, moaning at the taste of my desire.

He snaps, lunging for me, grabbing me, and turning me.

He presses me to the edge of the sink as his hands slide down my body to grip my hand again. "Don't stop. Watch yourself as you come, watch as you touch yourself for me." He quickly unzips my jeans and pushes them down so he can watch, his hard cock pressed to my ass.

His fingers nudge my knickers aside to expose my glistening pussy to his hungry gaze. He grunts, his hips jerking forward as he pants. "Fucking hell, look how wet you are. You better touch yourself before I decide to eat that pussy until they have to rip me from you."

"That's not a threat," I purr, even as I touch my clit.

"Like that?" he murmurs in my ear, licking and biting it. "Is that what gets you off?"

I nod jerkily, rolling my hips as I rub my clit furiously before sliding my fingers inside myself. His eyes darken, almost turning black, as if they are sucking all the light from the room so he can watch me. One of his hands grips my breast for me, pinching my nipple hard.

I cry out as I speed up my fingers, so close to coming again. "You're close. I can almost see it." He groans, rolling his hips into my ass, humping me. "Fucking hell, I've never been so turned on. I haven't even got my hands or mouth on you yet, and I'm about to come in my joggers."

The idea of him coming from watching me has me picking up speed and closing my eyes, but he twists my nipple so hard, they shoot open.

"Eyes on us," he snarls, biting my neck. "You will always keep your eyes open when we fuck, baby, so you can see what you do to me. So I can watch you come apart and see all those walls come down as you explode."

"Holy fuck," I whisper, desperately rubbing and flicking my clit now, and with a knowing smirk, he bites down on my neck at the same time he pinches my nipple.

I shatter, and explosions rock through me. My legs shake from the force, and a moan is trapped in my throat as I fight to keep my eyes open through the crashing waves of pleasure.

As he rocks none too gently into my ass as he watches me come apart, I can't pull my eyes away from the man behind me—the man framing me like I'm a fucking masterpiece painting and he's simply been made to hold me up.

"Good girl." He pets my oversensitive pussy, making me jerk before he steps back and laps at the palm of his hand, tasting me. Snarling, he pushes at his joggers as if needing to touch himself just from the taste of me. I turn and almost fall, having to hold myself up as I watch him. I redress as my tongue darts out to wet my dry lips. My pleasure ebbs, even as my pussy clenches at the sight of the man before me. He's wild, panting as he tries to find his own pleasure after helping me find mine.

It's that thought that has me stepping forward. Reaching up, I drag his head down and slam my lips onto his. He freezes for a moment, not even breathing, before he groans into my lips. Gripping my hips, he jerks me closer, trapping his hard length against my belly and rocking into me like he can't help it. I slide my tongue across the seam of his lips, and when he opens for me, I sweep inside, tangling with him. Both of us become lost in the other.

His kiss turns feral and hard, just like I expected. Our teeth clash, almost drawing blood from my lips, and I still can't get enough. I have to rip myself away to breathe, and when I do, I shove my hand into his joggers, curling it around his cock. His hips jerk forward, and his eyes close for a moment.

"I want to watch you this time. I want to watch you make yourself come for me," I order him, gripping him hard as I stroke him. "I want to see how you like it."

A noise invades for a moment before I ignore it, focusing on him as I stroke his length. His head falls back, his eyes closed in bliss and agony. His neck strains, his veins throbbing with his pleasure. He loses himself to my hand, but another noise distracts us, and I jerk my head around, listening.

It's shouting.

"Jonas . . ." I stop, looking at the door. The need to rush down there and confront the situation wars with the fact that I *need* to see him come.

"Let them fucking kill each other," he growls, thrusting into my hand. I laugh, I can't help it, and then I press my head to his chest, hearing his racing, thundering heart. "Hell, let the whole world burn around us right now, and I wouldn't give a fuck."

Smiling, I reluctantly remove my hand from his joggers and press a kiss to his chest before stepping back. "Later, baby. Then you can feel how frustrated I've been since you chased me down." I wink and move to the door. He grabs me, spinning me and slamming me to the wood. His lips come down on mine, hard and fast.

He gives me a brutal kiss before he presses his forehead to mine, both of us panting and fighting the need to tear each other's clothes off. "Now, we are even," he murmurs, his voice like gravel, echoing around me. He grabs the handle and rips open the door. "Let's go save the idiots so I can kick their asses."

Taking his hand, I let him tug me downstairs, trying and failing to ignore the desire storming through me again.

Unleashed by him.

THIRTY-ONE

NOVA

I have to try and focus on the shouted words as I hurry downstairs, hand in hand with Jonas. I still feel the heat of his cock warming my palm, and my knickers are drenched with my own cream from our encounter, but as soon as I reach the bottom step, all that pleasure and afterglow fades, and my throat clenches in panic and something else . . .

Hope.

At the front door, unsure and hesitant but standing her ground, is my sister. Ana wears an expression that echoes one I usually wear, although it's slightly more nervous, and she has her arms crossed as she stares them down.

My men.

Standing together, side by side, Nico, Dimitri, Isaac, and Louis create a barrier as if to protect me from her. After all, they all saw how much her anger and hatred of me killed me last time, but she's my sister. Squeezing Jonas's hand for strength, I carry on until I stop next to them, sparing her a look. "What's going on? I heard shouting."

For a moment, all eyes are on me. Louis's eyebrow arches at my flushed cheeks and rumpled clothes, but it doesn't faze any of them as they return to glaring at Ana. What did she do? She jerks her gaze to me and looks me over as her lip curls.

"Oh yes, she's clearly so fucking traumatised," she spits haughtily.

"Huh?" I frown, confused. "Someone fill me in."

"We were trying to educate your sister"—Nico spits the word like a curse—"about exactly who you are and what you went through."

"You what?" I snap.

They know they have fucked up because they won't meet my eyes, but Nico does. "I couldn't stand her insulting you like she did. I didn't tell her everything, just some bits."

"Oh yeah, because she was clearly fucking abused," Ana snarls.

The urge to run consumes me, but when I meet their eyes, I see their confidence in me and the strength they are offering. They want me to tell the truth and stop protecting her. After all, that's what I'm doing. I am protecting her from the truth, but she's not a child anymore, and she deserves to know, even if she won't believe it.

That actually terrifies me, but with her note burning a hole in my pocket, I stop before her, blowing out a breath. We are night and day. Two very different sisters.

"Of course you wouldn't think I was. I protected you from it, Ana," I tell her softly. She jerks and meets my eyes with derision. I rush forward, knowing she's the only person in this world who could flay me alive anymore. The anger in her gaze makes me raw.

I want her to believe me, but I made my decision, and now she needs to make hers. I will give her all the facts, knowing she will need them. Her scientific brain is unable to accept anything but evidence.

"Father hurt me, Ana." Her mouth opens on a rebuttal, but I surge ahead. "For years. He was not the man you knew, sis. He wanted me to feel like this. He wanted me to feel isolated, ashamed, helpless, and alone. I was scared to tell anyone, scared to tell you because I needed to protect you, even if it meant hurting myself in the process. He knew that by separating us, it would turn us on each other. Ana, you know deep down what I'm saying is true. You know he was capable of being cruel and cold if it got him what he wanted. You must have noticed the changes in me. I tried so very hard to hide the evidence, but I know you saw it, even if you didn't understand it."

"Stop," she demands, shaking her head. "I can't believe you are trying this."

"What?" I ask, frowning. I feel the guys step closer behind me to protect me.

"To disparage his name and make me think he was evil. He was a good father. It's not his fault you are a selfish bitch who skipped out on her family. You can't come back and spin these lies now because you aren't the favourite anymore. Did you know that? You were always his favourite. Whatever I did was never good enough and could never hold his attention while you were around. When you left, it was like you died. Those were the best years of my life because he finally paid attention to me."

Fear pounds through me at the fact that I might have missed him hurting her like he did us, but when she carries on, I realise he didn't.

"He finally loved me," she confesses. "Just because you messed up, that doesn't mean you can concoct these stories. You are probably doing it for money."

"I don't want money, Ana," I reply sadly, rubbing at my aching heart. "I just wanted you to finally know the truth because I hate this. I hate you thinking the worst of me. He knew you would. He encouraged it, knowing that even if I was protecting you from afar, he was driving a wedge between us. It was a final blow to me, the only way he could hurt me anymore. I never should have left you with him, Ana, and I'm sorry. I ran because I was scared. You're right. I was scared he was going to go too far and kill me, but I protected you. I promise."

"I don't need your protection!" she screams.

"You did! He was a monster!" I yell, ripping up my shirt to show her the scars he left behind.

"Those could be self-inflicted. You are so delusional." She looks away.

I realise she will never believe me, too blinded to what truly happened, or maybe her mind is rejecting it to protect herself. Nothing will change her mind, unless . . .

My shoulders sag at what I'm going to have to do. I was a fool to protect her from this for so long, but I refuse to lose her again. I refuse to let him win on this. "If you don't believe me, then let me show you."

"Nova," Louis snaps and turns to me, searching my eyes. "You don't have to prove anything to her. If she doesn't believe you, then that's on her. She knows deep down what her father was; she just doesn't want to see it. She doesn't want to confront the fact that she let you be hurt over and over and did nothing about it."

I cup his hands, leaning into him for a moment. "I have to do this. She has to see. She deserves the truth as much as we all do." I look back at her. She's watching us with a confused expression. "Give me five minutes. If you still don't believe me, you can leave and continue to hate me. I will leave you alone."

"Five minutes," she agrees. "Lead the way."

I turn and find Bert there. He steps forward and takes my hand. "For what it's worth, Miss Nova, I never doubted you, but Master Louis was right. I was scared to tell the truth, for it meant that I was involved in something so terribly vile. My excuses and apologies don't matter. I let him hurt you, and I never did anything. For that, I will spend the rest of my life apologising."

I shake my head and kiss his cheek. "It only would have gotten you hurt, my friend," I admit honestly. "I often begged for someone to notice, but I was selfish because it would have ended their life. You do not take responsibility for the vicious, cruel nature of that man, do you hear me? We are all victims here." When he nods, I look back at Ana, who looks unsure.

Bert straightens. "I can help you now." He looks at Ana then. "Miss Ana, everything Miss Nova is saying is true. Please do not make her relive this for your own peace of mind. She has already suffered so much. If I could protect you both from this, I would."

"I need to see," she responds, and he sags. I pat his hand as I pass, heading to the lab.

She follows me, as do the others, and at the door, she hesitates. "I didn't know this was here."

"No, he never wanted you to. This is why you never saw or heard it. This is the place of my nightmares," I tell her coolly as I step inside. I don't look around as I sit at the computer and pull up what I need, but when I look up, I see her staring at my cell in dawning horror. When she looks around and then back at me, there is fear on her face—a child's fear that the man she loved, the man she looked up to as a hero, was actually a villain.

I have to burst her bubble, but I nod at the screen. Slowly, she steps behind me. I meet my guys' eyes in the doorway. They crowd the entrance, offering me their friendship and love.

"I don't want your pity or sympathy, sis, only for you to believe me. You are the only person in this world I care about believing me. After, I will answer everything you want to know." I hesitate before pressing the button. It's a random video file of me. My dad is there, talking and introducing it before it pans to the cell.

Ana gasps, the pure horror in the sound making me curl into myself. There is a surly, angry teenager strapped down to the bed. My head is turned as I glare at him, and he stops before me, device in hand. My eyes spit fire at him, even as he touches it to my chest and my body jerks with the shock, a scream leaving my lips.

I pause it, but she pushes me aside, her hands shaking as she clicks another. I don't watch what's playing, and instead, I watch her. Her face is pale, and horror and agony are written across her features as she watches video after video of me being tortured by our father. I was experimented on under her nose. I watch the moment her life crashes down around her and all the lies are unveiled. Her eyes dart to mine, filled with tears, as her lips quiver. Her gaze silently begs me to protect her from this.

For a moment, she's the little girl I used to hold as she slept. She's asking me to protect her from the monsters in the dark again, but I can't, not anymore, because the monsters are real, and they got me.

"Ana, it's okay—"

"How can you say that?" she screams, but it has an edge of hysteria to it. "I can't breathe. Oh my god. I need to get out of here." She rushes to the door where my men are. They look at me as she beats at them blindly, trying to get them to move. When I nod, they step aside, and she rushes out. I hurry after her in time to see her burst out of the front door. I step out after her as she falls to her knees, gripping the gravel like a lifeline. An anguished scream rips from her throat.

The sound burrows into my heart, another scar to add to my collection.

I stop before her, kneeling as her tear-stained face and hopeless eyes lift to see me. "I-I didn't know," she whispers, her voice ragged. "I swear, Nova, I didn't know."

"I know you didn't." I take her hands in mine, brushing off the gravel and rubbing them to stop them from hurting—an automatic response to her pain. "I never wanted you to. I thought by not knowing, I could protect you from it. From him."

Her eyes close for a moment. "Everything was a lie."

Leaning in, I press a kiss to her head like when we were kids. "Not everything, sis. Not us. Never us."

I simply hold her as she cries into my chest, her hands pulling me closer as another piece clicks into place in my heart. I look at my men who are gathered at the door, protecting me from afar.

And since I arrived, I smile for the first time.

THIRTY-TWO

LOUIS

Ana's hands shake as she grips the mug and takes a sip. Her face is still pale, and she's in shock. Her eyes go to Nova, as if she's worried she will disappear. I know the feeling. She sits in silence on the sofa. I'm opposite her on the other one, and Jonas is stretched out next to me, still glaring at her.

I know that feeling too. He's still angry at the woman who hurt our Nova, but she was a child, and she didn't know better. Then I remember how adamantly she fought her, and how she didn't even believe her for a moment, and that anger does not fully dissipate. Nova might love her, but that leaves her open to getting hurt, so we will protect her from everyone, even her sister.

Nico blocks the door, as if worried she will run again. Isaac watches her worriedly before looking at Nova with open admiration. Dimitri is tapping his fingers in the corner, clearly wanting to be at the computer but staying for Nova, who hurries back in and wraps a blanket around Ana, protecting her yet again.

But did she ever protect Nova?

No.

After five more minutes of silence, Ana lets out a breath, places the cup down, and turns to her sister. "I need to know everything."

"There is a lot. Ask whatever you want. I have no secrets." Nova sits opposite her sister on the sofa, one leg bent up with her arm thrown over the back. She appears casual, but I see the tremble of nerves and the tightness of her body. I wish I could lessen what she's feeling.

"Do not harm her more than you already have." I lean forward, and Ana jerks her gaze to me. "Remember, Nova still has to live with this, so do not make it worse just to settle your curiosity."

"Louis." Nova sighs, but I shake my head.

"No, I don't care if she is your sister. She doesn't have our loyalty; you do. We will protect you, even from her." I want her to realise how serious I am, and the smile that curls up her lips steals my breath.

"Then let's start with who they are," Ana says, nodding in understanding at me, so I settle back. If she takes this too far, she's gone.

Nova hesitates and looks at us, so I incline my head, telling her to let her in on the secret. "The other children." She blows out a breath. "I wasn't the only child Father experimented on. He had children all around the world, from different walks of life, but they had one thing in common—no one cared if we were hurt or missing."

"But why?" Ana asks.

"He wanted to expand the human mind," Nova repeats before she shakes her head. "But the truth is, he used us, experimented on us, for his own gain. For research. He liked playing God. There were more, but they didn't make it. For the last few years, I've been on the run to avoid him and his clutches, just trying to survive and keep you safe, but with his death, a chain of events was set into motion. They found me"—she grins at us—"and chased me down to prove who they were. Together, we are going to stop his research once and for all."

"But he's dead. It's stopped," Ana protests.

"No, it hasn't. It's still happening. Children are still being hurt, and we are going to put an end to that. We are going to destroy it all, and his name will go down in the history books for what he truly was. That's why we are here, in his lab, looking for our next location, our next research facility."

Ana looks shocked and seems to be absorbing it before she looks around. "He hurt you all too?"

I incline my head. Nico grunts, and Isaac offers a gentle, "Yes." Dimitri just looks away, and Jonas snorts. "Quick on the uptake." He looks at Nova, his eyes softening. Later on, I need to address where they were and why they came out looking rumpled. Jealousy roars through me before I seal it up. "Are you sure she's your sister, baby?"

Ana blinks. "Baby?" she repeats.

Nova flips Jonas off, but he just laughs. "Questions, Ana," she reminds her.

"Right." Ana sits up, flicking off nonexistent lint, and I see the calculation in her gaze. She's now the scientist, not the scared child.

For the next hour, Nova answers question after question about the science, their father's co-workers, the experiments, and everything and anything in between. I butt in when it gets too hard for her, and Ana deftly avoids those conversations. That's when I realise something else. She recognises the signs of PTSD and abuse now, and she seems to know how to deal with them. *Strange.* Why didn't she notice them before? Or was she purposely blinding herself to them with her hatred?

Ana finally sits back, drained of questions and looking exhausted. "I just can't believe"—she shakes her head—"that he did this, that he got away with it. That I never noticed."

"He was good at playing the perfect, doting father," Nova comforts her, easing her guilt when she shouldn't. Ana was a kid, that's true, but so was Nova.

"So what now?" Ana asks.

"Now?" Nova repeats in confusion. "Now nothing, you go back to your life—"

"I can't do that." She sits up, forcing Nova to blink. "I can't. I need to help. I need to make this right. Our father—he was a monster; you're right. We need to stop what they are doing."

"We?" I repeat, looking her over. "You have no skills that are of use to us, and everything you know is from us. You don't know the locations or anything of use. You aren't as fast, strong, or capable as us. Go back to your life."

"No." She meets my eyes, and I see a spark of Nova there. "I will make this right. I will protect my sister."

"Ana," Nova starts, but I lean forward, a tiny spark of respect starting to form for the younger woman. She might not have known then, but she does now, and she's choosing to help us.

"I can read my father's research. I worked with him for years—not on this, but I can read it. I can help," Ana reasons. "Please, let me make this right."

I can see Nova doesn't want her involved in this and wants to protect her, but she deserves the same rights as us. "Fine, you can help with the research, but that is all, understand?"

She nods quickly, determination on her face. "I can help." She seems to be telling herself that.

"You won't get in the way, do you understand?" I demand, and she nods again. I see fear in her eyes as she looks at us. Good, she should fear us because her sister is quickly becoming our whole world, and we won't lose her, and anyone who stands in the way of that or jeopardises that won't have our mercy. "What kind of scientist are you?"

"I work with the brain." She blushes. "Mainly the effects of war and PTSD. I work with veterans . . . ," she trails off. "Ironic, I know."

Tell me about it.

Nova looks at her sister with nothing but pride as I sit back. "Dimitri, show her to the lab."

He turns to face me, not looking at her. "I won't work with her there," he snaps.

"D, please." Nova stands, going over to him.

"No, Nova," he retorts. "She hurt you. She didn't believe you. I won't."

Ana looks like she's about to cry, but we all watch as Nova stops before D and their heads bend together. They whisper before she sighs and looks back at me, defeat in her expression.

"Fine. Ana, you will take the research to your room here."

Ana nods, looking at Dimitri in shock before bowing her head, shame in her expression. I stand, and Dimitri slips from the room. I follow him before nodding at the others. I need to talk to him. He's hurting, and he's protective of Nova, but I can't let him get lost in his grief again. Not like with Bass.

"Nova." I look back at her, silently communicating for a moment before speaking. "Look after them for a moment." I narrow my eyes on Nico and Jonas. "Do not kill her sister; it would hurt her."

It's the only thing that would appeal to them. I know that. If I'd said it was wrong, they would have laughed. If I'd argued she didn't know, they wouldn't care.

They will do nothing to hurt Nova, however, and I see my order hits its mark, even as Ana pales, realising she's surrounded by killers.

"Now, back to our mission. We have information to find, so let's not waste time." I slip from the room, intent on protecting my family.

Including Nova.

THIRTY-THREE

NOVA

I watch Louis go, my heart racing from the look he gave me. It told me he would protect me no matter what. I look around and realise they all would, even from her. Dimitri was so adamant about hating her for what she did to me, he refused to listen to reason, and even gentle Isaac doesn't seem happy with her.

"Would . . . Would they really kill me?" Ana asks, fear in her voice.

"Yes." I won't lie to her. "So don't give them a reason to." I move to Nico and meet his angry gaze. He eventually looks at me. "He's right. If you kill her, you will ruin me in a way my father never could." He flinches, and I kiss his cheek.

Jonas watches me stride towards him, his eyes hazy with madness and lust. I straddle his lap, uncaring who's watching, as I grip his chin and force his head back to meet my eyes. I need to penetrate that fog and make him understand. After all, he's the wild card.

"You touch one hair on her head, and I will chop off your dick."

"I knew you liked it." He grins, gripping my hips and tugging me over his hard length. I try to swallow my gasp as I narrow my eyes. "Though chopping it off to keep for your pleasure is sexy as hell, I'll admit to liking it where it is."

"Jonas."

"Nova." He grins, and I have to fight my own as I grip his chin harder, making his eyes smoulder from the pinch of pain.

"Please," I beg, and that makes him jerk, his eyes turning serious. "Please don't hurt her."

"I would do anything for you," he replies, and I don't know what's scarier: his madness or the fact that when he says that, his gaze is clear and serious for the first time since we met. Sighing, he looks over at Ana. "Fine, you're safe from me. Thank your sister for that." He leans up and kisses me quickly. "Now, if you're not going to ride my dick, let me go so I can deal with this hard-on."

For a moment, I debate it before sliding off his lap. He stands and stretches, and Ana quickly averts her eyes as Jonas winks at me and then wanders off, leaving me shaking my head.

"He scares me," she murmurs.

"He should." I look back at her. "I'll go get the research for you." I look at Isaac then, and he nods, letting me know he'll watch her as I stand. Although I am thankful for him, I still hurry. They watch me, but I force myself to head back to my sister and hand her his books to start with.

Holding them tight, she nods at me, taking this seriously, and hurries off as well. I watch her go before looking at Nico and Isaac. "Well, we are all on break, right? So what shall we do?"

Nico groans as Isaac laughs. "I have an idea."

I wiggle my eyebrows, even though I know that's not what he means, but it's nice to see them both grin. To be honest, I'm exhausted from this conversation and from seeing my sister hurt, and as usual, Isaac notices, so when he leads me outside into the sun, I turn, wondering what he's doing.

"Let's play hide and seek." He grins, jumping on the spot. "I could do with some exercise, and I never got to play it as a kid."

"Me either." Nico frowns. "What do we do?"

"You never played hide and seek?" I stare, open-mouthed. I know they are doing this for my benefit, and it makes my heart melt as I grin. "Oh, this will be fun."

"What are the rules?" Nico demands seriously.

"I count to thirty, and you hide while I do. We will limit it to the trees and property here. No going too far or out front. If I find you, you're it."

"I'm so going to win." Isaac grins. "Cover your eyes, sweetheart." Laughing, I do as I'm told and spin around, starting to count. I hear them racing away, and I can't help but laugh, just like they knew I would.

When I've finished counting, I drop my hand and look up for some reason, spotting Ana at the window of her room, watching us. She looks so alone and so lost that I hesitate, but with a determined grit of my teeth, I turn back to my men, knowing they did this for me. They are right. I need some laughter and fun. She's made her bed, so now she must lie in it. I can't protect her from everything, and it's time I started living for myself.

I run into the forest, leaving her behind to find her own way, and a weight I didn't even know I was carrying lifts with each step I take away from her and that house.

THIRTY-FOUR

ISAAC

Grinning, I press my back to a tree. I don't really want to hide, since I want her to catch me, but I want to listen to her giggle as she searches. Her steps are loud despite the fact she knows better. She's enjoying this. This is exactly what she needs, and honestly, so do we. We've been working so hard that we haven't just had fun or enjoyed life in far too long. Nico needed a distraction from his anger at the world and her sister, and I did as well, so this seemed like the perfect thing to do.

The sun shimmers through the trees. It truly is a beautiful estate, despite everything that happened here. I can't hear or see Nico, but I know he will take this very seriously. I have different plans, and I don't even realise it until I hear her draw closer.

Seeing her coming down the stairs with bruised lips, mussed hair, and a glowing expression was enough to cause feelings, such as jealousy and possession, that were so strong, it scared me. I told myself I wouldn't make a move on Nova, not after the kiss, but I can't resist.

I really can't.

She makes me want things I have no right wanting, and I'm tired of hiding my desires and trying to be her friend when she clearly doesn't want that. She crossed the line with Jonas, but that doesn't mean she's willing to with the rest of us, and yet I can't hold myself back from chasing her now.

I'm hunting her even though she's the one searching.

I'm leading my prey into my trap, and I'm not bothered by that in the slightest. She giggles, and I tilt my head, realising she's close. Suddenly, she jumps out from behind the tree, her grin wide and carefree. "I got you!"

"No, I got you." I smirk as I tackle her, lifting her over my shoulder. She laughs, and when I throw us down on the leaf-covered ground, her eyes alight with happiness.

She's so fucking beautiful.

I must say it out loud because her laughter tapers off, and her eyes turn dark with desire, dropping to my lips. She wants me to kiss her as much as I want to. Her legs frame my hips, and our bodies are completely pressed together, so I can't hide my rapidly hardening cock from her. When she feels it, her mouth forms a perfect O, and she doesn't pull away.

"This isn't in the rules," she teases as her hands stroke up my arms and loop around my neck.

"We make our own rules," I murmur as I lean down, unable to resist feathering my lips across hers.

She groans. "I like our rules better."

Laughing, I swipe them across her chin and cheeks. "Me too. So what do I get for letting you catch me?" I purr as I lift my head up. Her pink little tongue darts out and traces a path across her lips.

"What do you want?" she flirts, playing the game, but I'm done with games.

"You," I snarl and drop my lips to hers.

Tangling my tongue with hers, I swallow her moan as I tilt her head back and dominate her mouth, taking over every corner and tasting every inch until she's panting beneath me and rolling her hips, dragging her warmth across my hard cock. I nip at her lips as I pull back, grinning at her.

"Hold on," I order as I kiss down her chin and neck, nudging her shirt down to place a gentle kiss on her rapidly beating heart. Moaning, she tightens her hold on my hips, lifting her own to roll her cunt against me. I move slowly, taking my time. I want to remember this, the taste of her skin, the feel of her silky warmth, and the sounds of her moans, so when the darkness takes over again, I can push it back with this.

She watches my every move as I push her thighs apart, pull off her trousers, and settle between her legs. Her knickers are wet with desire, and I press my nose against them before inhaling deeply, filling my lungs with her sweet scent. Groaning, I dart my tongue out to taste her before looking up. Her head is back, her neck arched, so I bite down on the soft, silky material and tug them aside to expose her pink, glistening pussy.

"So pretty," I murmur as I stare at her, reaching out with shaking hands. I part her lips and lick my own, staring at her swollen clit and pretty hole that's begging for me to fill her.

"Isaac." Hearing her moan my name has my throat thickening with desire and something much deeper.

Swallowing the words I want to say, I drag my tongue along her pretty pink cunt.

The gasp she makes has me doing it again and again. I love her reactions and need them all. I watch her carefully as I stroke, lick, and explore her pussy, noting what makes her sigh and what makes her cry out, and then I use it against her.

I need to feel her come for me and be as crazed for this as I am. I'm not as wild as Jonas, but I have the insane need to taste her pleasure and to make her mine. Panting, she drags her hands up her shirt, tugging at her nipples as I watch.

"Fuck, you are so beautiful, Nova," I tell her, kissing her clit in that maddening way she both loves and hates. "So bloody beautiful, and you taste so good. I could eat you all day."

"Jesus, Isaac," she calls out, looking down at me.

"Don't believe me?" I dip my fingers into her tight, wet heat, stroking them inside her as she rolls her hips to fuck them, and just when she has a rhythm, I pull them out. Ignoring her cry of anger, I lift my fingers to her. "Taste yourself, taste your desire for me."

With her eyes locked on mine, she leans up and wraps her lips around my fingers and sucks, tasting her own desire for me. When she moans and drops back, I smirk.

"Told you, darling, you taste like fucking heaven, so be a good girl and lie back and let me enjoy my new favourite meal."

"Don't let me interrupt you," she mumbles, but then she moans when I suck her clit into my mouth in punishment.

I tease the swollen nub as she lifts her hips and grinds into my face. Releasing it, I nip and lick at it until she's panting heavily and widening her legs. Grinning, I switch between licking and sucking her pussy, teasing her, then I drive her higher by dipping my tongue inside of her before flicking her clit as I thrust two fingers into her tight channel.

I grind my hard cock into the ground, and the pain and pleasure mixes together until I'm nearly spilling in my pants just from tasting her.

"Isaac!" she yells, gripping my hair and tugging me as she rolls her hips. "Shit, I'm so close."

"Let go," I murmur against her sensitive skin, turning my head to nip her thigh. "Let go for me. Let me watch you come, Nova. Let me feel it against my tongue."

My words send her off the edge. Flattening my tongue, I lap up her release before plunging my tongue into her clenching pussy as she cries out and writhes beneath me. I lick and lap at her, desperate for more of her addictive taste, and I don't stop until she tugs my hair until it hurts.

Letting her pull me up her body, I meet her blazing eyes.

"Fuck me right now," she orders, lifting her legs to wrap them around my waist.

"Anything for you." I chuckle as I lean down and kiss her, letting her taste her release. Swallowing her moan, I reach down and pull my hard cock free, stroking my length before settling between her thighs and dragging it up and down her cunt. I let her feel the blunt end of my cock as I nudge her clit over and over.

"Isaac," she warns as she pulls back, biting my lip until it hurts.

Grunting, I line up with her pussy, lifting one of her legs higher as I kiss down her cheek to her ear. "I can't wait to feel you wrapped around me. Fuck, I've thought of nothing else since I first saw you, and how pretty you would look beneath me, taking every hard inch."

"Fuck," she groans, closing her eyes as she lifts her hips, trying to take me inside.

Grinning, I nip her ear. "Hold on, beautiful." Then, without warning, I slam inside of her, unable to go soft or slow. I still once I'm balls deep, closing my eyes at the tight, hot feel of her gripping my cock. She feels like a fucking vice, making me tremble with the need to move. Her hands claw at my back as she rolls her hips, trying to get me to move, but I wait, savouring the first thrust, the first moment of her.

I know there will never be another that feels this good, whom I want this much.

"Isaac." My name on her lips is my undoing, so I pull out and slam back in, filling her before speeding up my thrusts. Both of us need to come, even as much as we want this to last.

I lose myself in her body, kissing her while I do, and she fucks me right back, meeting me halfway, encouraging me to go harder and faster in the dirt.

"God, you feel so fucking good," I rasp when I have to break away to breathe, my head pressing to hers. "So fucking good, Nova. How can you feel so fucking good? Like heaven, Christ, I could spend the rest of my life inside you and die a happy man."

Her eyes round as she stares at me. "Don't say shit like that to me. We don't get forever; you know that."

"Then I'll take what I can get, which is right now, with you dripping beneath me, begging for me," I promise as her hands slide down my back and tug my pants lower.

Her hands grip my flexing ass, and her nails dig in until I groan from the flash of pain. One of her hands flops to the ground next to us, gripping at the dirt and leaves as she cries out for me, her eyes wild as she meets my gaze.

Glancing up, I spot Nico half hidden behind a tree. His dark eyes are lit with hunger as he watches us. Smirking, I slam into her harder, making her scream, and then I look back down at her, watching her take my cock and give as good as she gets.

Her hands drag up my back to my neck, and without warning, we flip. Grinning down at me, she lays her hands on my chest and starts to bounce on my cock.

"Fuck," I murmur, watching her amazing tits sway with her movements. "Goddamn, Nova, you are too fucking sexy. You're going to make me come before I even get you off again, and I consider myself a fucking gentleman, darling, but with that hot body riding me? All that goes out the window."

Her head falls back as she winds and rolls her hips, chasing her own release.

"Use me to come, fucking ride me until you do," I growl, gritting my teeth against the pleasure storming through me. My balls are heavy, and my abs are tightening, but I hold back, feeling her tight, wet cunt engulfing my cock over and over until she grinds herself deeper and screams her release.

Then and only then do I flip us. I pull out of her as I press her front into the dirt and wrap her hair around my fist. I pull her head back, arching her for me as I slam back inside of her dripping, milking cunt. I hammer into her, chasing my own release. She claws at the ground, pushing back to meet my thrusts as I take her brutally, knowing she can handle it.

I need to fill her with my cum, and I can feel my release approaching. Pleasure bows my spine until I can't hold back anymore. Yelling, I explode, filling her with my release as she cries out, coming again and gripping my dick, milking it of every drop of my release. Moaning, I fall forward, resting my head on her sweaty back as I bury my cock deeper, wanting to keep my cum inside of her so she'll think of me later.

Breathing heavily, she falls forward against the ground, and we just lie here before I gently pull out of her and roll to my back next to her. A smile I can't stop curls my lips. I'm almost giddy, and I am so happy, my heart feels like it's going to burst. When she reaches over and takes my hand, I almost declare my feelings for her there and then, but I don't, knowing it will freak her out.

Nova is like a wild animal. She craves freedom, not chains, and I will never contain her like her father did.

I turn to stare at her, and she watches me with knowing, smug eyes.

THIRTY-FIVE

DMITRI

"**D**imitri," Louis calls after me, but I ignore him, not wanting to talk.

My emotions are too messy, too volatile, to speak to him, and he'll want me to talk it out. That never works. Instead, I'm going to lose myself in the one thing that still makes sense—computers —but I should have known he wouldn't let me. He follows me into the lab as I sit.

"D," he begs, "talk to me. What's going on?"

I shouldn't respond, shouldn't unleash the tornado of fury inside of me. I should focus it and never let it out, as her father would say. Emotions make you weak. I try, clenching my hands on the desk and closing my eyes to count like I was taught.

"Is it her sister?" he questions, hoping to understand.

One mention of her, and I'm turning with a curled lip, my nostrils flaring with the fury I can't contain. Not when it comes to Nova. For so long, I lived in nothing but code and flashing screens. There were no emotions and no connections, I was just adrift online, but then she came and she yanked me into real life, sending me tumbling around with things I haven't felt in years. Memories, pain, happiness and hope are all tangled up inside of me because of her, yet she also settles it.

Her soft smiles, stolen touches, and comfort anchor me to this world and give me a chance to breathe.

Is she right? Is Louis? Do I retreat into computers because it's easier not to feel anything? If so, it's the coward's way out, yet aren't I doing that again? Afraid of the true depths of my feelings for this woman we only just met?

Bass would call it fate. His smile would crinkle up in that adorable way, and he would chuckle at my uncomfortable thoughts and my bumbling attempt to express what is happening in the vortex in my head. He would tell me to go for it, to take the leap, because even if you hit the bottom and crash, the fall would be worth it.

Is Nova worth it?

Yes. I know that one hundred percent, which is why I'm so angry on her behalf.

For so long, my life was carefully filed inside of my brain, locked away in folders with passcodes, but now, she's the virus infecting them, and I can't even be mad about it.

"D," Louis demands, sitting next to me and turning to me as I sort through my muddled feelings.

"I hate her," I finally admit.

"Who?" he asks, his brow furrowed. He's dragging the words from me and leading me to a confession. That's how Louis operates. He sees what we don't inside of ourselves and finds the best way to coax it out, whether it be potential, trauma, or hopes. He protects us by knowing everything he possibly can, taking the blows for us, and keeping us together by pure grit.

"Her sister," I snap, trying to control my anger. It's not directed at him, after all.

He watches me carefully, the only one who knows what I'm truly capable of. "D, breathe."

Nodding, I count, and only when I feel like I am on stable ground do I carry on. I'm still angry, but I'm not about to go out there and wring her fucking neck. "Okay, why do you hate her sister?" he asks slowly when he sees I'm calmer.

I give him an exasperated look, and he grins. "I know why I hate her, but D, why do you hate her?"

"For hurting Nova and not believing her. Fuck, you've seen Nova, Louis. She's loyal to a fucking fault, and even after all these years, she protected her sister. I saw her face when Ana"—I sneer the name—"said she didn't believe her. It broke her, Louis, in a way even her father wasn't able to. It fucking killed her. She's been betrayed, used, and hurt by her own family for so long, yet she still protected her. How fucked up is that?" Swallowing, I look back at the computer and close my eyes. "I would have done anything to have someone willing to protect me like Nova protects her sister, and yet she doesn't even care. She threw it all away."

"I know. I'm angry too. All we can do is be there for Nova and protect her because fuck knows she doesn't protect herself, even from her sister."

I nod, drumming my fingers on the desk.

There's a scuffle outside, and Louis jerks up. After peering out, he shrugs at me and sits down heavily. His eyes are still locked on my profile, and after my outburst, I just want to go back to what makes sense, like finding answers on this hard drive, but I know he won't let me. He has something else to say. I can feel it. He was like this when Bass . . . well, yeah, then.

He was worried I was going to explode and watched my every move.

He once told me people fear Nico and Jonas because they look like they are willing to kill because of the darkness in their gazes, but they should fear me because I would destroy the world and stand in the flames before they even realised I was a threat.

I guess that's not wrong.

We are all a little fucked up, even Isaac who plays the perfect, doting doctor, and our fearless leader has a dark side, not that he lets it out often. That iron control was built to contain what lies within.

"You're letting her get close," Louis finally comments, and I almost laugh at the absurdity of it. If I wasn't, I wouldn't give a shit about her weak sister.

"And you're not?" I retort, lashing out in my own anger, but he doesn't react to the barb. He simply sighs and sits back. His response only deflates me and makes me feel like rubbish for taking my issues out on him when he's only trying to help.

"I am, and that's what worries me," he finally admits, sharing a shy grin with me. "She is magnificent, isn't she? When we suggested finding his daughter, I never thought we would find *her*." He shakes his head with a laugh. "Who knew such an incredible woman could be born from such cold hatred."

"Diamonds are crushed, not made," I reply simply, and he laughs, nudging me.

"Maybe tell her that." He winks, and I can't help but smile. The phone rings, and we both look at it, understanding washing through us. It's a reminder of our duty and what we are doing here, and all traces of amusement disappear as he extracts it from his pocket and answers it with clipped greetings.

He barely speaks, and I can only hear the vague hum of words on the other end, but we all know who it is. When he hangs up, his expression is closed down and serious.

I raise my brow, but he just scrubs at his face, and it's then I realise he looks tired. Not just now, but always, as if this life is slowly draining him. Was I so self-centred and locked in my own world that I didn't notice my friend, my brother, was suffering too? I want to ask, but I know he will just close down further, so instead, I file it away for now.

"Same shit, different day. We need to find something soon. They already don't trust us as it is, and I don't trust them not to lock us up and throw away the key. Humans are good at that, hurting those they are scared of."

Just then, there's a beep on the computer. If I were a man who believed in fate, I would have said it was exactly that, but instead, I know it's just a coincidence. Turning back, I raise my brows at what I've got.

"Well, we might have something. I'm finally into the encrypted files, so let's take a look at what the good doctor felt he had to try and hide."

THIRTY-SIX

NOVA

Grinning, I let Isaac chase me to the main house. Nico catches me halfway, slinging me over his shoulder as he strides into the kitchen. Laughing harder, I smack his ass, and he does the same to me.

"Oh, hi, Bert," I hear him say.

Mortification fills me as I lift myself to peer over at Bert who is just smiling like this is a normal occurrence. "Is anyone hungry?" he asks us.

"Starving," Isaac replies, smirking over at me. The desire I see in his eyes makes me shiver where I'm perched on Nico, who spanks me again.

"I could always eat, especially something sweet," Nico teases, but Bert is oblivious.

"I could make a fruit cocktail for you." He looks around seriously. "Five minutes."

"Add peach if you have it," Isaac replies, licking his lips as he moves closer to me.

Okay. I slide from Nico's back before they can cause me to self-destruct, and with withering glances at them both, I hurry away, but I can't help but smile when I hear them bantering and laughing with each other. I soon sober up, though, as I move upstairs, heading to the shower, knowing I have leaves and dirt in my hair and clothes. At the top of the staircase, I hesitate and move to Ana's bedroom door, peeking inside.

I need to check that she's still here and that she's okay.

She's hunched over on her bed, with folders and documents spread out in an order only she'll be able to understand. Her hair is pulled back in a clip, and her face is bare and locked in concentration. For a moment, I don't see her now, but as she was when she was a kid. She would focus so hard on her homework to be the best and to understand as much as she could, always hungry for knowledge. Briefly, she's not Ana, the grown woman, but Annie, the little girl I ached to protect from ever seeing the evil in this world.

Slowly, I shut the door and move away. After calling down to make sure Bert will send her some food and drink, I force myself into the bathroom. She's not a little girl anymore, and she doesn't need me there making sure she sleeps and eats. She needs me to trust her, and after I demanded that she trust me, I can offer her that much . . . right?

Once in the bathroom, I quickly strip and put my clothes in the basket. Turning on the shower, I wait for it to warm up as I look at myself in the mirror. There are leaves and twigs in my hair, my cheeks are flushed, and my eyes are bright. I look happy.

I look healthy.

If my dear old dad could see me now . . . With a self-deprecating snort, I hop into the shower, cranking the heat up to the point where it almost burns off my skin, and only then do I sigh, my eyes sliding closed as I just relax under the punishing spray.

My head is tilted back, and water sluices over my tired and aching muscles, and that's when I feel it. I jump and try to spin, but hands grab mine before I can attack the intruder, and they are slammed to the wet tile of the bathroom wall.

I kick out, but a warm, hard naked leg wraps around mine, trapping me, and I freeze. Warm breath blows across my neck as the water continues to pound down on me, almost obscuring my vision as I blink away the water droplets.

It's one of the guys, I know that, so I relax a little more. The force of his groan shakes my body as he presses against my back, letting me feel every hard inch of his body, including a massive hard cock prodding my ass.

I almost smirk, having my suspicions on who it is, but I play along, letting him lead this time.

Curling his hands in mine, he drops his head, his tongue darting out to lap at the water on my neck before he licks up to my ear. "Now, where were we, baby?"

I shiver at the hungry words.

Jonas.

"Well, by the feel of your cock, you were hoping to bend me over and fuck me, I'm guessing," I tease, pushing my ass back to rub against him. I shouldn't. I just fucked Isaac while Nico watched, but there's a madness in Jonas that I crave. While Isaac softens me, and Nico encourages me, but Jonas? He frees me, meets me head-on, and I find myself licking my lips in anticipation. A savage hunger races through me so suddenly, it steals my words.

"Or maybe I was imagining just slamming you up against this wall and fucking that tight little cunt until you scream for me again." He grunts, bucking his hips against my ass. "But I'll take you how I can get you, baby. So tell me, Nova, are you wet for me?"

"Why don't you find out?" I taunt, but my words are breathless. Anticipation floods through me, making me tremble with the need I feel for this man and a hunger they all seemed to have awakened.

Don't get me wrong, I love sex, but it's never felt like this before. Maybe it's because I know I can fully let go with them because I can trust them.

The chuckle he lets out is edged by madness. He slaps my hands harder against the wall. "Do not fucking move or I'll just slam into your cunt and fuck you until I come and leave you wet and wanting." The threat hangs in the air, and it turns me on more than it should as his hand slides up my arm and down my body, making me suck in a breath when he purposely catches my tightening nipple and then covers my mound. He grips it as he bites my leaping pulse.

"Oh yeah, baby, you're wet for me. I should be nice, taste that little cunt, and make you break apart, but if you want nice, you should have fucked the others. Me? I'm fucking mean, and I don't give a fuck if you aren't wet enough for my huge cock. I'm going to fuck you so hard it will hurt, and you'll love it, won't you?"

"So much talk," I snap. I want to turn on him, but I don't because I want what he is offering more. "Tell me, Jonas, are you all mouth?"

His hand slides back up my body to grab my neck roughly, and his teeth meet my ear. "You know I'm not, but how about I remind you, baby, since you seem to have forgotten? You think being a bitch will make me fuck you faster? Just for that, baby, I'm going to be mean. Keep your hands there the entire time or I'll walk away." With that, he reaches up and grabs the showerhead. I blink, wondering what the hell he is doing, but he kicks my legs open and, with a mean laugh, aims the spray right at my cunt.

Fuck.

The pressure hits my clit, and he moves it closer until it's just beating at it. "Let's see how long you can last, shall we, baby?" he taunts. "Let's see how quickly you'll come for me, so desperate to ride my cock."

"You're a prick," I snap, even though I roll my hips, that relentless spray making me cry out despite my words.

Laughing, he slides his hand down and circles my trembling hole. "You can lie to me all you want, but your body tells me the truth. It tells me how much you want this, how much you want me, Nova."

Narrowing my eyes, I kick back, but he just laughs. My eyes close, and my hips rock into that spray, but they fly wide open when I feel something hard, round, and cold at my entrance.

"Jonas!" I snap, but then I scream when he pushes it inside of me, forcing me to accept it. I stiffen, but he presses the showerhead right against my clit until I moan loudly, my pussy relaxing against the invasion and taking it deeper. It's wide, impossibly wide, but fuck if it doesn't feel good. My hips kick without me meaning to, sinking me deeper onto it, and when he finally stills, I look down. My head hangs between my trembling arms, which are still pressed to the shower wall, to see his hand wrapped around a bottle of what looks like shampoo.

He's fucking me with a shampoo bottle.

Oh fuck.

"Get that out of me now," I snarl, feeling embarrassed. When he starts to pull it out, the pinch of pain is eclipsed by the pleasure, and I whimper.

Laughing, he slams it back inside of me, setting a steady, brutal pace as he fucks me with it.

"Nah, I don't think I will. I've got to get you nice and stretched for my cock. Now watch me make you come, baby. You think you can resist this?" he growls into my ear, grinding against my ass. "Yet here you are, letting me fuck you with an inanimate object because you are so greedy for my cock."

"Fuck you!" I snarl, but he just laughs and speeds up, slamming it inside of me, and despite my protests, my abject horror at what is happening, I find myself pushing down to take it, letting the beating of my clit push me over the edge, and without even wanting to, I come hard, right as he slams the bottle inside of me and presses the shower-head to my clit.

My hips jerk, and he groans into my ear, grinding his cock into my ass. Sagging, I press my head to the wall, and he takes pity on me and pulls the showerhead away, the bottle too, leaving me whimpering at the almost painful pressure of it. A moment later, his hand is there, cupping my pussy. "Next time, be a good girl, and you'll get my cock instead of this."

He pulls away, but fuck that. If I have to submit, then so does he. I didn't let him do that to me, no matter how good it felt or how much I liked it, just so he could walk away. I pull my hands from the wall and spin to him, kicking him back. He looks shocked but laughs. I fling myself at him, and he catches me with a groan, his hands going to my ass and hoisting me up as our lips meet.

The kiss is hungry and desperate, and then I'm suddenly slammed back into a wall again, only this time it's my back that meets it hard enough to force the air from my lungs and pull me from his greedy mouth to suck in lungfuls of air. I wrap my legs around his waist and reach between us, gripping his hard cock and slamming myself down on it.

His eyes widen as he moans, his hand slapping against the wall as he holds me there. "Fuck, Nova," he yells. "Are you trying to kill me?"

"No, baby," I taunt. "If I was, you'd already be dead. Now be a good boy and fuck me."

"God fucking damn it, we are going to make some incredible babies." He groans, lifts me, and drops me onto his cock.

"They would be psychopaths," I retort as I reach out and grab a fistful of his hair and yank his head back. "Now stop fucking talking, you crazy bastard, and fuck me."

For once, he listens to me, his lips curling in a snarl as he slams me back into the wall with the force of his thrusts. There is no room for talking as he hammers into me. His huge, pierced cock hits that spot inside of me that has me raking my nails down his back to grip his flexing ass, urging him on as I slide down his dick to take him faster and harder, until there's nothing but jagged breathing and moans between us. I hit the tiles with each hard thrust, and I feel them crack, break, and cut my back, yet I don't care.

I want more.

Like walking a tightrope, I'm ready to fall at any moment, only this time he'll be coming with me. "Jonas," I moan, and it only urges him on. He grunts as he fights my fluttering cunt, gripping me roughly. There's nothing but madness in his eyes, and I love how focused he is on me, how he doesn't care if he could hurt me.

He just fucks me, hammering into me like it's his life's mission.

With his next thrust, he grinds into my clit, and I tumble from that tightrope, falling with a scream. My nails cut into his ass to keep him inside of me as I writhe on his cock. Fighting my tight hold, he flexes his hips twice more before stilling with his own shout. His cum splashes inside of me, almost too hot to handle as I fight his hold, nearly causing us both to fall.

Finally, the pleasure ebbs, leaving me exhausted, satisfied, and boneless in his arms. I feel his legs shaking as he holds us up, leaning into me to pin me to the wall so we don't fall.

"Holy fucking shit," he whispers. "I would say I went to heaven, but we both know I would end up in hell. I guess that makes you my punishment, baby, and I am so fucking okay with that."

I can't help but laugh, and it isn't long before he joins in.

Fucking hell, if we are supposed to stop and save the world, then we are all fucked.

THIRTY-SEVEN

NICO

The screaming finally stops, and with a forkful of fruit held midair, I trade a smirking, knowing glance with Isaac. Bert is blushing hard, and the radio is cranked up to drown it out as he moves around the kitchen.

Poor man.

But I'm glad to know she's a screamer.

Finishing my meal, I sit back and look at Isaac, who ducks his head slightly. "Got to be honest, doc, I didn't think you'd be the first to crack."

He rolls his eyes, delicately eating his fruit just like he ate her cunt in the woods while I watched. "I couldn't help myself," he finally admits.

"Yeah, I think we are all feeling that way when it comes to her," I respond as my gaze goes to the ceiling again, wondering if we will survive her.

"We have something. Grab the others," Louis calls to us before hurrying back to the lab.

I share another look with Isaac. "Rock paper scissors for who goes and gets them?"

"Fuck no, he will murder me. You go," he replies instantly.

Rolling my eyes, I get to my feet. "Pussy."

"Nah, that's what I got earlier." He toasts me with his bowl as he stands, and I can't help but laugh.

Shaking my head, I thunder upstairs, letting my footsteps be heard to give them warning. I see Ana peek out of her room, but when she sees me, she ducks back inside quickly with a pale face and fear in her eyes. I almost snort. Smart girl, that one.

Rapping my knuckles on the bathroom door, I swing it open, ducking the knife I know will be coming as I do. It sails over my head as I grin at them, noticing Nova's flushed cheeks and half-dressed state. Jonas is naked and proud, but I blink.

"Where did you pull the knife from? Wait, I don't want to know." I groan, rubbing my head. "Louis needs us in the lab. He found something." That sobers them, and Nova gulps, but her back straightens.

That's my girl.

Turning, I pluck the knife from the wall and toss it to Jonas without looking as I head back downstairs, giving them time to get dressed. At the lab, Louis is pacing, Dimitri is rubbing his head, and Isaac is leaning back against the wall, his face closed down. I arch a brow but lean behind the computer and wait.

A moment later, Jonas saunters in naked with a pancake in his hand. When he sees us all watching, he grins. "What? I worked up an appetite."

Nova comes in then and smacks him as she goes past. "Idiot," she mutters, but she's nervous as she moves around to stand near me. "What did you find?"

Louis looks at me, and I lean back, wrapping my arms around Nova and bringing her into the shelter of my chest. She's stiff for a moment before she melts, propping her chin on my arms as she looks between them.

"Just tell me," she finally snaps, and a grin flits across Louis's face before it locks down.

"We don't know. It's a video file addressed to you. We haven't watched it yet," he answers.

She becomes rigid against me, and she's barely breathing, so I lean down and kiss her ear, unable to help myself. I hate the anxiety spiralling through her. "Breathe, baby," I remind her.

She lets out a low breath and sucks in another, shivering against me before straightening. She's strong and brave, such a fucking fighter. "Then play it."

I hold her up as much as she holds me up, especially when the bastard's face comes into view on the screen. The room is silent, memories no doubt crowding all our minds of when we last saw him. She pats my hand, comforting me, even as she fights her own demons.

He's older than the last time I saw him, wrinkled, and appears weak, but he still has those sharp, cold, evil eyes. As I see him now as an adult, and not from a child's body and mind, I can't believe I was ever scared of him. He's just a man.

That's all.

He's just a man, despite how we built him up in our minds. His brain made him seem immortal and invincible, but he's not. He's just a man, well, now a dead man, but that doesn't mean he isn't fucking with us from beyond the grave, and I hate that she has to face him again.

"Hello, Novaleen." She startles, so I tighten my hold, even as the others move closer as if they can protect her from his ghost. A slight smile curls his lips, and she shivers. I don't blame her. It's a cruel, mocking smile. I don't think he is even capable of a real one. "If you are watching this, then I am dead."

"No shit," Jonas mutters as he blows out a breath.

A chair creaks on the video from where he is filming in this particular room, exactly where Dimitri is sitting. He must realise it because he stands in disgust and backs away, as if not wanting to be tainted by being near where he was. "I know you hate me, I understand the emotion, but I want to explain myself. I did what I thought was best for mankind. I thought I was bettering humanity and I could play God. I truly believed it was for the best of our people, and a few sacrifices and suffering, including yours, daughter, were worth the end result, but I see now that I was wrong, very wrong. In the name of advancement, I hurt you, and I stole yours and many others' innocence, and only now, at the end, are my sins catching up with me." He lets out a cold, bitter laugh. "Strange how you think about the beginning at the end. I did love you. I need you to know that, Novaleen. You were brilliant, the very best of me and the world. The capacity for greatness you have was revealed in every experiment I have ever conducted. None ever compared."

"Bastard," she mutters.

"But you threw it away. If you are watching this, it means you're back, though, and despite what you think of me and my research, there are some things you need to know and do, if not for me, then for those like you—those still out there enduring the same treatment as you. There are other children, lots more. Some are grown, and I hope you find them, but some are still young. It's bigger than the children now. I needed help, Nova, and that was my first mistake. I needed funding, and I sold my soul for that. The man who no doubt killed me and will be searching for you now is the very same man still conducting my experiments, and despite what you think about me, he is evil. He doesn't want this for advancement, nor to help people. He wants to hurt them, use them, and profit from them. I did this for knowledge, but he does not. There are no lines he won't cross. I'm afraid I have once again put you in danger, but I know you are smart and strong enough to stop him."

He moves closer, his face filling the frame.

"And you must stop him, daughter, otherwise not only will my research be corrupted, but it will be sold to the highest bidder. It would destroy the world as we know it. I can never ask for your forgiveness for what I did to you and the others, but in my last act, I am trying to make things right as much as I can. All of the lessons I taught you will come in useful now, Novaleen." His eyes narrow as he drags that out, like it's important. "You will need them all. Find the others like you, tell them, and let them help you stop this. At the end, I hope you find peace." He sighs, scrubbing at his face in an unfamiliar sign of stress and exhaustion. "She doesn't know, Nova. She doesn't know what I did, and she doesn't know what you are, that you're alive somewhere out there. She doesn't know the deals we made to keep her out of it, but she must be included now. You will need her."

"Ana?" she murmurs, confused.

He glances behind him, then, before looking back at the screen. "I don't have long, but I will not run and hide. He will kill me, Nova, which I'm betting you will be glad about, but heed my warning—he will stop at nothing to protect his secrets. You think I am the devil, daughter, but you are wrong. You are going to meet him, and I wish I could see you all in action, but it is not meant to be. Stop him. That's my last order to you." Then he's gone.

A picture of a notebook flashes on the screen for a split second, and then the video cuts off.

"If he wasn't already dead, I would kill him." We all jerk our heads up, not realising Ana had joined us. Her expression shows she is heart-broken, and anger flashes in her eyes.

"That's the first smart thing you've ever said," I mutter, and she throws me a glare before blowing out a breath.

"He knew you would need my help. That picture at the end of the message . . . play it back. Yeah, there, stop," she instructs Dimitri, glancing over the gibberish. "I can decipher his notes. These are locations."

"Locations?" Louis demands.

"Yes, it seems so. Locations and numbers . . . No, wait, ages, I think. Fuck, you think these are other labs he . . . experimented at, don't you?" she whispers, looking at us.

"Only one way to find out," Nova grinds out. "We hit them all and destroy everything he has. Ana, you stay here and keep working. None of this leaves this house. If anyone tries to take it, you kill them." She steps from the circle of my arms, moving towards her sister. "I'm trusting you to do this."

"I won't let you down," Ana promises, her back straightening. The two sisters, night and day, face each other.

Nova looks us all over. "Pack your bags, boys. We are going on a road trip." With that, she storms from the room, and Louis watches her go before nodding.

"You heard her, pack up. I want wheels up in an hour." He follows after her, pulling his phone out.

"I guess that means I need pants," Jonas grumbles, making us all laugh despite what we just saw.

THIRTY-EIGHT

NOVA

There is no time to waste, so I pack as quickly as I can. As I stare down at my bag, his face flashes before my eyes, and my hands curl into fists. Anger, resentment, hope, and fear fill me.

I hated him, but seeing him brought back all those childhood feelings of wanting to be loved, and I hate that more. I hate that even at the end, he's still playing me, using me, and ordering me around, even going so far as to involve Ana, knowing I would have no choice then.

Whoever this mystery man is, he killed my father, and for that I'm grateful, but if he is doing worse, I'll kill him myself and bury his body right next to my father's grave.

Determined, I zip the bag closed and toss it over my shoulder, finding Louis in the doorway, watching me.

"Just wanting to check your state of mind."

"Pissed, hateful, and wanting to kill someone," I reply, and he grins.

"Good." He pushes away from the doorframe.

Shaking my head, I drop my bag in the foyer as Bert comes in, holding a bag in his hands.

"I packed as much food as I could." He hands it over to Nico, who stops next to me, his own bag slung over his shoulder. "I've also included pancakes for Master Jonas."

"You da best, Berty boy," Jonas calls as he leaps from the balcony and lands next to us with a smug grin and kisses Bert's face.

He blushes and grins at Jonas before looking at me. "Please be safe, Nova."

"Always," I promise, kissing his other cheek. "Take care of Ana for me."

"I will." He nods solemnly. "We will be here when you get back, all of you." He looks around at them as the others come in with their belongings packed up. "None of you are to get hurt or killed, do you understand me?" he orders, and we all nod like naughty children. "Good, and if you get arrested, call me." He steps back, his eyes glassy with tears just as Ana hurries down the stairs. She throws the guys a nervous glance before she hands me a journal.

"Here's as much as I've found so far, as well as the locations. I have Louis's secure number. If I find anything more, I will send it to him."

"Be smart and safe." I hate it when I almost repeat my father's words. "I will be in contact when I can. Stay here with Bert." She nods, and we share a look, unsure what else to say, the years still arching between us. I sigh and grab my bag as I head towards the door where the others are already loading the cars.

"Nova," she calls. I turn back, and Ana races towards me, wrapping her arms tightly around me. I freeze for a moment before melting and wrapping my arms around her as well, kissing the top of her head.

"I'm so sorry I hurt you as much as he did, but I'm here now, and I will make this right. I will help, even if none of you believe me. I'm . . . I'm just so sorry. I love you, Nova, I always did, always will. Come back home soon." She steps back, dashing her tears away.

I nod at her, unsure what to say, so instead, I pull out the note that was folded under my pillow. "I know. I love you too," I tell her, and Bert steps up, placing a hand on her shoulder as I throw my bag in the car and get in.

"So where to? I'm betting the secret military peeps won't be happy about this." I smirk.

"What they don't know won't hurt them." Louis grins over his shoulder. "I just told them we have a few leads and are going off grid."

"And how did they take that?" Isaac asks curiously.

"Started shouting, so I hung up, but we should get going before they track us. Your sister will be safe, but us? We might get locked up."

"Then let's go." I nod, sitting back next to Nico. Jonas and Dimitri are in the other car behind us.

I flip through the journal and pick a location at random. "The first coordinates are somewhere in Berlin. Wait, how are we getting there?"

They share a look before laughing as I frown.

"Wait, what's so funny?"

That just makes them laugh harder as we pull away.

THIRTY-NINE

NOVA

N ow I know why they were laughing. Two hours later, we pull into a private airstrip, and sitting on the tarmac is a private jet. The stairs are down, and the lights are on inside. The cars stop before it, and I lean forward.

"Erm, okay?" I say to no one in particular, but they laugh and get out. Hoisting my bag up, I follow them onto the plane. They are all comfortable and instantly settle in. Louis talks to the pilot and assistant while I just stand there looking around.

Behind me is a small galley and the cockpit, and before me is something out of a movie. It sure beats the shit hole hotels I stay at, that's for sure. To the right is a full-on sitting area, with a sofa along the plane's wall covered in cushions and blankets, perfectly decorated. Two huge reclining leather chairs sit opposite on either side to create a square, with a table in the middle with a fruit bowl on it. The carpet is soft and fluffy under my dirty boots, and I cringe, feeling out of place.

Behind the sofa is another one where Jonas sprawls out, his arm behind his head and feet kicked up. To my left are two reclining chairs that are facing each other with a table between them, and at the back are three more chairs. All are done in luxury prints and leather. I feel like a dirty thief. The curved ceiling is filled with warm LED lights that are dimmed to create a soft atmosphere, and it smells expensive in here. Hell, there is even a full-length window in the ceiling, which I stare at incredulously.

There are two closed mahogany doors at the back. I'm guessing they are for the toilet, but I don't dare explore. I hesitantly sit on one of the chairs. Dimitri sits down heavily on the sofa and pulls his laptop out as Nico takes another chair at the back and instantly kicks back, going to sleep. Isaac grins at me as he passes and takes the spot next to Nico, reclining it and taking out a book.

They seem comfortable here and used to it, which has me frowning as Louis comes back to us and sits in the chair opposite me with his legs crossed. A very beautiful stewardess in a suit closes the door and smiles at us before moving back to the galley.

"Take off in ten. Refreshments will be served in an hour or so," Louis tells me.

I've bitten my tongue enough. I have to know.

Leaning across to Louis, I narrow my eyes. "Who the hell does this plane belong to?" I hiss.

FORTY

He grins, and there's a shuffling sound at my side. I turn my head to see Dimitri ducking his head in embarrassment. "What?" I ask, confused.

"It's Dimitri's," Louis explains, sparing a clearly worried Dimitri. "He made some money online, and he is very good at it, but he always felt like he didn't need wealth, so he shared it between us to help keep us afloat and not dependent on doing things with our skills—things like this plane so we can get around uncontrolled."

I blink, looking at Dimitri and then around again. He bought them a plane?

Dimitri feels my gaze and sighs, looking up at me. I lean across and take his hand, squeezing it. It doesn't change how I feel about him. He freezes, searching my gaze. With or without money, I care for them all, but in all honesty, I would feel more comfortable sleeping on the floor together again, and he must sense that because he smiles softly at me.

"Money is just another necessity, like food or shelter. You need it to survive, and anyone who says differently has never had to be without it. I simply made us some so we didn't have to exploit ourselves and could fly under the radar, same as the military, to protect my family," he explains logically, and I swear my heart actually melts for this man. He simply found a way to make money to protect his family, to provide for them, and to offer safety the only way he could.

Money changes people, but not these people.

"The plane's nice," I comment with a shy grin, "but I prefer the shitty hotel you found me in."

He cracks a smile but still seems worried and embarrassed. Sitting back, I keep my eye on him as we take off, and once we're in the air, he still won't look at me.

Blowing out a breath, I meet Louis's gaze, silently asking him how to fix this and assure D that I don't care. Louis nods, and I follow his gaze to the back of the plane and the doors there. Frowning but trusting him, I stand and hold out my hand to Dimitri.

He doesn't notice at first, and then he seems confused, but he trusts me and takes it. I haul him up and tug him behind me. Ignoring Jonas's knowing look, I take the first door, but it's a huge bathroom with a shower. The second door leads into a bedroom, and my eyebrows rise. I almost whistle but know it will only upset him, so I don't say anything about the emperor-sized bed made with silk sheets, the mirror along the wall, and the dimmed light fixtures and glass ceiling. Turning, I drag him in and shut the door.

A plan comes to mind, and I know how to show him how much I see him, how much I appreciate him.

It's something that has been brewing since the meadow, if I'm honest.

"Nova?" he asks, sounding confused, his eyebrows furrowed. Smirking, I plant my hand in the middle of his chest and push. He stumbles back to the bed, his legs spread.

Kicking them farther apart, I drop to my knees between them. His eyes widen, his mouth drops open, and lust blows his pupils as he stares at me.

"Dimitri, baby, if you didn't have a private plane, I couldn't do this," I purr as I slide my hands up his solid thighs to his waist and unbuckle his belt.

"Nova," he whispers raggedly. "You don't have to—"

"I want to," I promise. "I want to taste you and see you come apart for me. I need to be in control as much as you need to let go." Leaning up, I press my lips to his and nip at his lower one. "So let go, baby."

Moving back down, I slide his belt out, the slick of it loud, and he groans. Smirking smugly at the uncontrolled desire smouldering in his eyes, I flick open his trousers and slide my hand inside.

He moans when I grip his huge, hard shaft. He's massive and so hard it has to hurt. "Poor little Dimitri, so needy," I purr as I pull him out. He helps me push his trousers down, his eyes wild as he watches me. His chest heaves with his ragged breaths, and I've barely touched him.

This will be fun.

Grinning, I drop my eyes to his cock and lick my lips at the sight of him.

"Fuck, Nova," he growls, watching me, but damn, he's got a pretty cock. That's not a word I use lightly, but Jesus. He's long and thick, veiny and hairless, but when I spot the ink on his cock, I raise my eyebrows.

He grins shyly. "A dare with Jonas," he mutters.

I lean down so I can see what it says, then I laugh when I realise it says, "Ride me."

"Oh, don't worry, I will," I promise with a wink before dragging my tongue down his veiny length, tasting the musk that is all man and Dimitri. "Lie back, baby, and let me have some fun."

Tugging at his hair, he falls back, his spine arching as I suck him deep. "Holy fuck!" he yells as I take all of him to the back of my throat and hold him there before pulling my mouth away and licking down his length.

"I can't wait to have this inside of me," I purr against his skin, rubbing the tip of his leaking cock across my lips. I taste his precum as he watches me with dark eyes. Locking my own on his, I swallow him down again before lifting my mouth and bobbing on his cock, sucking hard and fast. I wrap one hand around his base to hold him still for my exploring mouth, twisting harshly.

Moaning loudly, he grips his shirt and lifts it to expose his tanned, cut abs, making me suck him harder, and his hips jerk up.

I dig my nails into his abs and scrape down, making him cry out as

I suck him down hard and fast. My head bobs faster now as his hips jerk, forcing my mouth lower on his cock. He fucks my mouth, his hand darting down to grasp my hair and drag me down his length, but I don't let him take over.

I slow until he releases his tight grip slightly and lets me do what I want. "Please, Nova," he begs. "Your mouth is too fucking good. I'm going to spill."

Pulling my lips free, I slide my hand up his abs and down again as he watches me. "Then spill, but it will be down my throat because I want to taste everything you have."

"Fuck," he groans, falling back onto the bed. I can almost taste his desperation to come, but he holds back. His other hand fists the bedding as I play with him, licking and tasting before sucking him down again.

I bob faster and harder until he's slamming down my throat, his loud moans echoing around me.

Cradling his balls, I suck him all the way down to the back of my throat before I squeeze. His cock jerks in my mouth, and his release spills down my throat as he writhes. I suck him dry, only pulling my mouth away when he sags back, breathing raggedly. I clean every inch of him with my tongue as I wait for him to open his eyes.

"See? Private planes are good."

Watching such a brilliant, strong man come undone just from my mouth empowers me like nothing else ever has.

He watches me, his chest heaving and cock dripping in my saliva, like I'm a dream, and I start to wiggle, trying to ignore my wet pussy. Desire coats my cunt from the taste of him and the way he gave in for me.

He sits up, and I almost fall back, but he grabs me, throws me onto the bed, and is on me in seconds. He flips me so my face presses against the comforter and drags my pants down, then his hand presses to the back of my head, keeping me there as he jerks my hips back.

"D," I pant, but it turns into a scream when two fingers spear inside me. "Holy fuck!" I shout, pushing back as he starts to fuck me with them.

"It's only fair," he tells me, his voice dark and rough. "You got to taste me, and now I get to taste you and see you come apart for me. Damn, look how wet you are from sucking my cock. You love it, don't you? You loved tasting me, loved swallowing my cum like a dirty girl."

"Yes," I say without hesitation, pushing back to take his fingers deeper. My pussy pulses around them as he grinds his hand into my aching, throbbing clit.

"I can tell." He groans. "It's so fucking sexy. Look at you. Your pretty wet pussy spread for me. Fuck, Nova, I've never seen a prettier pussy," he praises as he adds a third finger. It's my turn to grip the silk bedding as I moan, pushing back to fuck myself on his fingers. A release is already building inside me, the slick sound of him pumping into me turning me on more.

"I wonder if you taste as good as you look," he purrs.

"I know I do, so why don't you find out?" I taunt. He doesn't reply, but a moment later, he pulls his fingers free of my clinging channel, and there's a wet sucking sound and then a groan.

"Fuck, you're right. You taste delicious. I need more. Be a good girl and let me lick this cunt."

I'm about to reply, "Be my guest," when he grips me tighter.

He yanks me up higher, and one hand slides under my body to press down on my stomach, while the other holds me still for him, and then he seals his mouth onto my cunt.

All forms of niceties are gone, and in the place of a shy, unsure Dimitri is an animal. His tongue thrusts inside of me until I cry out. "Fuck!" I yell, and knowing the others can hear me only has me crying out louder and grinding against his face.

Pulling his tongue from my pussy, he laps at my clit until my hips jerk. "Scream, let them hear, let them all sit out there with stiff cocks, imagining what I'm doing to you in here," he growls against my pussy, the vibrations making me cry out.

"Then make me," I retort, spreading my thighs wider.

"Oh, I plan to, pretty pussy Nova." Without waiting for a reply, his talented mouth returns to my pussy, licking from clit to ass like he can't get enough of my taste. He circles my clit before dipping inside of me.

He does that over and over before I push back impatiently. Chuck-ling, he grips my hips, keeping me still for his mouth, and sucks my clit, making me scream for him just like he wanted. I almost come, but just as I'm about to, he stops, leaving me panting, dripping, and unsat-isfied. His fingers stroke over my pussy like a caress.

"I didn't say you could come yet, Nova," he warns.

"Fuck you," I snap, frustrated.

"Not this time. Next time, I'll have you under me with those claws in my back. This time I plan on licking this cunt dry," he says, and when I slump, he licks my cunt again. Desire explodes through me as he twists his tongue around my clit, giving me the right amount of pressure. I push back, and this time, he thrusts his fingers inside of me, letting me fuck myself on them as he licks and sucks my clit.

It's too much.

"Now, Nova. You will come now," he demands, and without waiting for a retort, he sucks my clit again.

I come with a scream, my thighs clenching and pussy clamping. I come so hard I see stars, and he laps up my release. His tongue dips inside of me alongside his fingers to taste every drop until I'm spent, and I fall to the bed with his fingers still inside of me.

Slowly, he pulls them out, and when I blink my eyes open, they are next to my face. His thick digits glisten with my cum. "Suck them clean, Nova, and taste how hard you came for me."

I open my mouth, and he thrusts them inside, watching me as I suck and lick them clean just like I did with his cock. When he pulls them free, I groan and roll onto my back, watching him. His cock is hard again, and his other hand is wrapped around it, stroking leisurely as he takes in my spread thighs covered in my cream, my breasts that are almost falling from my shirt, and my eyes heavy with pleasure.

"Fuck, I've never seen such a beautiful sight," he growls, his teeth sinking into his lower lip as he speeds up his hand on his cock. I can't help but watch, my gaze darting from it to his eyes until, a moment later, his cum spurts across my spread pussy and thighs, making me whimper.

He pumps his cock, squeezing every last drop of cum out before slumping next to me. His hand goes to my pussy and rubs his release across my oversensitive flesh before dipping his fingers inside me.

"Next time I come, it will be inside you," he murmurs.

"Fucking hell, I've unleashed a monster." I laugh as I turn my head. He grins, looking relaxed and happy now, as he pulls me against his side. I go willingly and burrow closer, watching the sky above us in the ceiling window.

"I like this plane now," he declares, and I can't help but laugh.

FORTY-ONE

NOVA

B y the time we have cleaned up and changed, we are landing.

"I've never been to Berlin," I comment as I lean forward to peer out of the window. "What's it like?"

"Beautiful," Louis murmurs. "I've been once for work, but the snippets I saw were stunning." Standing, he offers me his hand. "Let's do this, Nova."

Nodding, I take his hand, and with our bags slung over our shoulders, we disembark the private plane. There are two taxis waiting outside, and Louis pays them a heavy sum to keep quiet about what they saw. It's not foolproof, but we leave as little of a paper trail as we can as we speed through Berlin.

I don't know where we are heading, but I soak up the views. Tourists flood the streets, and the shops and cafes are full and bright with light. Seeing the modern amenities mixed with the old, historical elements almost entrances me.

"We would usually stay at a shitty hotel with a don't tell policy, but since it's your first time in Berlin, why not go big?" Louis winks down at me. "If they are going to find us, they will anyway, so it doesn't matter where. Plus, they will be expecting us to fly under the radar. Instead, we will blend in by remaining in plain sight."

"What do you mean?" I ask, drawing my gaze away from the window to him.

"Luxury, baby. We are spending our time here in luxury, just like you deserve." He winks, and I swallow as I look back out the window. Not long after, we have to get out and walk down a huge shopping district called Ku'damm. There are restaurants, cafes, and shops lining every corner and side of the street. He's right; we easily blend into the crowd. We stop before a massive, six-story building placed between two equally large buildings, the hotel name boldly displayed at the top.

"Zoo?" I ask, and Louis grins as he heads inside.

I follow after him, gawking when we plunge into a different world. A sumptuous, darkly lit interior greets me with epic decorations, and a dramatic tiger rug leads to a reception area. I find myself gawking at everything as Louis heads right up to the desk. I barely hear what he says, but I notice it's in German, which makes my eyebrows rise. When he comes back, he slings his arm around me and leans in as if to kiss me. "We got the penthouse, baby," he purrs then looks to the guys. "You are in rooms next to us."

"Bastard." Jonas grins but winks at me. I let them lead me to a bank of elevators, and from there, we head up. The guys are, in fact, in rooms next to us. When I walk into the penthouse, I freeze. I'm used to shitty hotels with questionable bedding and dirty old bathrooms.

Not here.

Light almost blinds me from the floor-to-ceiling windows with views of a courtyard below. Sofas and chairs sit to my right with a table between them. A partial wall with a fireplace is to my left, and when I peer through, I can see into the bath. There's a dressing room, a huge king-sized bed, and a bathroom that almost makes me weep with an epic tub and huge shower big enough to fit four people. There's also a minibar and so many amenities, I don't know where to look. I just wander around in awe.

Louis lounges on a chair with his chin on his chest, watching me. "Like it?" he murmurs, and I swallow as I turn to him, my back to the windows.

"I love it, but are we—"

"Don't worry about it." He stands smoothly and pads towards me, taking my chin and lifting my head. "Just enjoy it. Yes, we are here under horrible circumstances, but it's time you saw that the world has more than death and darkness. A little bit of luxury won't hurt you. It might even do you good." He winks before sobering. "We are as safe here as anywhere. There are plenty of entrances and exits onto a busy area of Berlin that we can get lost in. I did my research and set up backup meet points, but for now, we set up shop. Everything here is soundproofed, so we use this as base." Just then, the door opens. He doesn't break apart from me, just watches me. "And we prepare."

I nod, and only then does he step away. The others make themselves comfortable, with Jonas peering through the fire and then back at me. "I know where I'll be spying," he teases, making me roll my eyes.

"Nico, order room service and check the floor. Jonas, help him," Louis orders. "Dimitri, get set up. Isaac, check the room."

"For?" I ask curiously, crossing my arms.

"Bugs and cameras, wiretaps, anything." Louis grins at me. "You can help him."

Isaac takes my hand, and we start in the bedroom, working our way through the entire suite. By the time we are done, food has been delivered on a silver trolly they rolled in themselves, not wanting staff to enter the room. "We are good." Isaac nods as he sits and picks up a lid, munching on some fruit while Jonas grabs a handful of chips and starts eating.

"Good, then let's begin."

Stretching out my back, I walk to the windows and look out at the darkening city before me, the lights stealing my breath with their beauty. Sometimes it's easy to forget how big the world is, and how beautiful and crazy it can be with so many unexplored places. Especially when you are so focused on the present and the little places around you.

But seeing it now steals my breath.

Nico snores, making me turn with a grin. He's cramped up on a tiny chair, snoring happily away, with his head back and one leg bent up uncomfortably. His other leg is thrown over the edge, and one arm hangs down. The other is under his head. Jonas shakes his head and goes back to cleaning the weapons. Dimitri and Louis are on the computers, checking our trail and locating the next stop as well as hacking security cameras and planning in case anything goes wrong. I was helping out, but my eyes are almost crossing. I'm not made for computers. Shaking my head, I grab the blanket that's neatly folded on the sofa and drape it across Nico, tucking him in before wandering to the bedroom to find Isaac curled up there, fast asleep.

We are supposed to take turns sleeping, and it's not mine, but I need a break from the screens and from . . . everything. It's all so much. I feel like I've not had a moment alone since they invaded my life, and although it's been for the better, and we have important things to do, I know I need some quiet time and space to regroup. I need to build up the barriers around myself again that protect me from being hurt, the very ones they have been smashing down since day one with soft smiles, teasing words, and protective hands.

They make it very hard for a girl not to fall for them, but I can't. I know that. We can have our fun and enjoy every moment until our pasts catch up with us, but people like us aren't made for love, and we don't get a happily ever after. We just get now.

Reminding myself of that, I slip into the bathroom and decide to run a bath to ease my aching muscles.

There are fancy ass toiletries on the side, so I fill the bath with them before stripping and stepping into the hot running water. I groan as I sink into it, my head falling back as I drape my arms on either side, letting the warm water wash away today and my worries.

Once we destroy everything my father built, we will go our own separate ways, right? If I am not careful, I will miss them something fierce. I'm not used to being alone anymore. I look for them in the silence, letting their laughter wash over me and their smiles ease my concerns.

I lean on them and trust them, and when they are gone, I will be alone again, which means before then, I need to protect myself so when they leave, it won't break me. I can admit to myself that they could destroy me in a way Father never did. With their kind eyes and friendship, they filled a hole in me I didn't know I had, and although they wouldn't mean to, they would break that last part of my soul and take it with them. But they deserve to live and find happiness when this is over, and this cannot last.

We were brought together by my father, by our trauma, but it won't be enough to stay together.

I will only have me at the end, and I remind myself of that over and over, even when I hear Jonas laughing with them and Nico's snores.

Slowly, my thoughts settle as I turn off the tub, just soaking and allowing myself to rebuild as the night passes.

My eyes open, and my heart freezes when I see Louis turned in his chair, his eyes locked on me. The whole world falls away as I stare into his eyes that are so hungry, I actually shiver in the tub. Dimitri is oblivious, and so is Jonas, so it's just Louis and I locked in a stare before his eyes very purposely drop to my exposed breasts and then crawl back up to mine.

When he turns away, I gasp and slump, free of his gaze. Shaking off my lust-filled thoughts, I submerge myself under the bubbly water, trying to remind myself to protect my heart from them.

Even if they are set on stealing it.

FORTY-TWO

NOVA

"Get some sleep," Louis orders the others. "We begin in the morning."

Groaning, Jonas drags Dimitri out, Nico following with a yawn. Isaac smiles at me and kisses my cheek.

Louis turns to me. "We will take the first watch. I'll keep an eye on the hallway cameras, and you can keep watch on the target location. Let me know if anyone comes or goes."

I nod and sit next to him, curling up in the long shirt I stole from one of them. My wet hair is plastered to my back as I focus on the screen before me. Nothing much happens, just the same old building we have been reconning all day, and an hour or so later, Louis brings me coffee, and we keep watch, protecting our family.

Staring at the screen eventually gets boring, so I look at Louis, watching the play of light on his handsome, sharp features. His hair looks darker in this light, and his eyes appear tired.

He feels my gaze, and his lips quirk up, but he doesn't look at me. "Problem, Nova?"

"Just looking." I grin, unable to help it. "Seems only fair since you got a good look at me."

His head swings to me slowly, his eyes gleaming with amusement and lust that he doesn't even try to hide. His gaze drops to my body again. "You wanted me to watch."

As soon as he says it, I realise he's right. "Maybe, and you want me to stare, talk to you, and tease you, or you would have had any of the others in here with me."

"Maybe I was just keeping an eye on trouble." He grins, flashing white teeth as he leans in. "And you are trouble, baby, down to the core."

"Yet you can't stay away," I murmur knowingly. He leans back, glancing at the screen before turning slightly to take both me and it in.

"Maybe not, or maybe I just want to keep you away from them." I flinch, but he doesn't hold back. "I see them with you, and, well, you are a part of this family, and I will always protect you, and them, from this."

"This?" I swallow, confused at the turn this took.

"You." He takes my hand and won't let me drop it when I try, yanking me closer. I fight him, and he lifts me and pins me between his body and the table.

Stilling, I glare at him. "I don't want to hurt them. I'm not my father," I snarl, darkness clawing at me.

As if he can see it, he pinches my chin until I focus on him and his words. "I never said you were. I know you are nothing like that monster, but you don't see it, Nova. We were just heartless men searching for purpose, and you have given them hope. You bind us tighter than ever before, and yes, that terrifies me. Not for me, but for them. It is my job to protect them. I pulled them from their cells and promised them revenge and protection, and I will always protect them, even over my own wants. You have the ability to hurt them, Nova, and you know it."

I nod but lick my lips, the truth spilling free. "But you have the ability to hurt me too," I admit, and he flinches, searching my gaze. "I was just thinking that you all strip me bare. I'm used to fighting alone, living alone, and then you all come and fill me with life. You remind me how to laugh, and you show me joy and friendship. It scares me because what happens when you leave and I'm alone again? You say

I'm a threat to them, but the truth is, Louis, it's all of you who are the threat to me."

"Nova," he murmurs, his grip on my chin turning soft as he pulls me close and wraps his arms around me. I press my head to this throat, just breathing in his scent. I should pull away and focus on the cameras, but I can't. He strips me bare, revealing all my fears, hopes, dreams . . . everything. It's like he can see them clearly, even clearer than I can.

"How about we promise never to hurt each other?" he finally responds.

Pulling back to see his face, I search his gaze. "Just like that?"

"Just like that. We have had enough hurt to last a lifetime. Who knows where this mission will take us? Instead of wondering and fighting what's all between us, let's just give in and promise not to hurt each other."

A naïve promise? Maybe, but it's a desperate edge we are both clinging to.

The electricity returns between us as his eyes darken. "Promise?" he murmurs, his voice rough.

"I promise," I whisper.

"And I promise not to break your heart, Nova, but I never said anything about your body." He slams his lips onto mine, pushing me back to the table. He grabs my hips and drags me farther down his lap until I'm perched over his very hard length. Groaning, I run my hands up his shoulders to his hair where I grab on and kiss him back, giving as good as I get. Pulling back slightly, I can't help but smile. "Is that another promise?"

"Baby," he warns, his eyes narrowed, "it's a threat." He yanks me back to him, kissing me so hard I can't remember the hurt or anything but the taste of him on my lips and the feel of his hands roving possessively over my body.

Snarling, he lifts me and walks us across the room, slamming me into the wall there.

I watch him through simmering eyes as he kisses down my neck and then back up, nipping my lips as he nudges his thigh between my legs, rocking the hard length against my pussy. I moan his name, watching his eyes blow as I do, and his grip tightens until it hurts, so I do it again.

"You'll be screaming my name in a moment, Nova," he promises against my skin as he slides his lips across it. "You'll see just how mean I can be, and you'll love every hard inch I give you. Fuck, baby, I've never forsaken my position, but right now, I will, so keep your eyes on those cameras for me while I taste what's mine."

Dropping to his knees before me, he holds me effortlessly in the air, keeping his eyes locked on mine. "Cameras," he barks, reminding me. "Or I'll stop and let you sit with wet underwear all night, imagining my cock and tongue inside you."

Huffing, I drag my gaze to the monitors, groaning when he rips off my underwear with his teeth before he attacks me with his mouth. He tears down my defences as he drags his tongue from my clit to my ass and back again, tasting every inch of me. I grab his head, trusting him to keep me up, and narrow my eyes on the screen. I try to concentrate as he attempts to rip me apart with pleasure.

His wicked tongue circles my oversensitive clit before lashing it, making me buck and cry out. My eyes slide shut for a moment, and he stills with his tongue against my clit. He only carries on when I open my eyes again.

"Good girl," he coos, the vibration of his voice making me cry out and tilt my hips. Chuckling, he drags his tongue down my pussy and circles my hole before thrusting into it. I rock and ride his tongue as one hand holds me up, and the other circles my clit in a maddening pace.

The screen is fuzzy as pleasure arcs through me, my panting loud. Louis does what he does best and takes control, giving me the freedom to let go as his tongue circles back to my clit and his fingers slide down my wetness and thrust inside me. He stretches me around his digits as he starts to fuck me with them. "You taste so good, Nova." He groans, licking his lips as he watches me, fucking me with his fingers until I'm reaching for release just from his touch. "No wonder they all need this pretty pussy. You're enough to make a sane man wild, Nova, and drive any man to distraction. Are you still watching those cameras, baby?"

"Yes, fuck, yes," I call out, my eyes locked on them like a lifeline, fighting the urge to look down. His lips wrap around my clit, and he sucks.

The pressure is too much, but I'll be damned if I don't grind against his face as I come. Pleasure explodes through me, and I basically drown him in my cunt, but I somehow manage to keep my eyes open while doing it. He continues to lick my pussy before sliding back up my body. His face is coated in my release, and as I watch, he wipes his face with his hand and drags his tongue down his palm, tasting every drop of me.

"Fucking delicious," he growls, the wild look in his eyes so unhinged.

This is so unlike Louis, and it makes me desperate. Grabbing his shoulders, I wrap my legs around his waist and snap, "Fuck me so we can work."

"Such a pretty, dirty mouth, baby." When he leans down to kiss me, I taste my own pleasure, and then his hand is on my throat, pinning me to the wall as he squeezes. "You move those eyes from that camera one more time, and I'll bend you over that computer and take that pretty perky ass until I fill it with my cum and then leave you hurting and wet. Understood, baby?"

"Bastard," I hiss, hiking myself higher. I glance back to the cameras as I reach between us to stroke his cock. "You can have my ass later, now shut the fuck up and get inside me."

"Such a sweet talker," he purrs, smacking my hand away and freeing himself. He's still fully clothed, and both of us know that this is a quick fuck to get it out of our systems. We need the release or we will be useless, yet the freedom I find in his touch is like nothing else I can explain.

I've been in control my entire life, meticulously aware of every action. I never even drink just to be safe, and now with Louis, I can fall because I know he will catch me.

And I do.

I keep my eyes on the cameras and trust him to give me the pleasure I need. Praising me, he lines that huge cock up to my pussy, and with a squeeze of my throat, he slams me down on him. He takes me rough and hard, forcing me to stretch around him. I cry out, almost shutting my eyes before I remember.

Snarling, I lean into him, biting his shoulder through his shirt to keep him inside of me and my eyes on that screen. With a yell, he pistons into my cunt, taking me rough and hard, slamming me back into the wall with each thrust.

His cock is huge, and it borders on painful, but it's absolutely perfect, and those little cameras become my everything as he steals my body one thrust at a time.

"Fuck, you feel so good, baby, too tight, too fucking wet." He pants into my ear, the sound so sexy I clamp around him. "Fuck!" he roars, hammering into me. Gone is the cold, unemotional leader, and in his place is a wild, lust-driven man. "Don't fucking do that, Nova," he growls. "Not unless you want me to come in two pumps like a teenager," he threatens, and even though he tries to slow down, he continues to pound into me.

"Louis," I snap, "please." It's a plea, a demand.

"Hold on, baby. I've got you," he promises, and the hand that was on my throat slides down and circles my clit. "Come for me, let me feel it on my cock. Scream so they all hear and they all know that you're mine right now. I bet they are in the other rooms, listening and stroking themselves, wishing they were me, but they aren't, and you're all mine. It's my cock you are riding so good, my cock you are drenching, and mine you will come on until you pass out," he purrs, and fuck it that isn't the trigger I need.

I come on command like a cum slut, clenching around his cock, and my eyes close with the force. He either doesn't care or doesn't notice, fucking me through it.

The other guys, the cameras, the mission, everything is forgotten in the pleasure Louis is dragging out of me, draining every last drop. The orgasm turns into two and then three, flowing through me, and he still doesn't stop.

"I can't," I whisper, but both of us are too deep to stop. "I can't, another—"

"You can and you will," he demands, slamming his lips to mine. He swallows my sobs as he fucks me, and I feel the wall dent behind me.

His hands hurt where he holds me, and my cunt drips so much I bet it's on the floor. My clit throbs painfully, and yet when he snarls, chasing his own release, I come alongside him.

I scream my release into his lips as his hips stutter, and his cum splashes inside of me as he groans my name.

We stay locked like that, both breathing raggedly as we shake from the aftershocks. He kisses me softly. "Shh, baby, I've got you," he promises. "You did so good, so fucking good, Nova. Jesus, you feel amazing. It's never been that good. No one has ever made me want to forget everything before," he murmurs, pressing his forehead to mine.

A noise has us both looking behind him.

Panting, I look around to see Jonas watching the cameras and us, holding popcorn in his hand. "Don't let me stop you," he drawls, making me groan and drop my head to Louis's shoulder, which shifts with his chuckle.

I'm just about to shout at Jonas for being a perv when something on the camera catches my eye.

"Movement, there's movement!"

FORTY-THREE

NOVA

We watch the cameras until morning. All we saw was a hooded man leaving the front door and slipping into an idling car before it pulled away. No one came back, and no one else went in.

It's been hours, and nothing.

"It's time," Louis finally says. "Get ready, we are going in. We need to find the research there and destroy it."

"And if there's a kid there?" Isaac reminds him softly.

"Then we save them and get them somewhere safe, somewhere far from their reach," Louis commands, giving us all a pointed look, so without any more conversation, we all jump up and get ready.

We are going in as soon as the sun sets and need to be ready to find out just what my father was hiding around the world. Is it another kid? More torture in the name of research? If so, who was the man who came out of the house, and why has he not been back?

I guess wondering won't change anything. Instead, I dress in my usual black jeans, tank, and zip-up bomber. I plait my hair back and grab the cap on the table and tug it down, then I add some knives, avoiding guns. I could use them; I'd just rather not.

I lean back and watch the guys get ready. They are all wearing black, and seeing them like this makes my mouth dry. Tight black T-shirts cling to their muscles, black cargo pants are tucked into boots, and their holsters are hidden under their jackets. Seriously, they look sexy as hell. Louis is perfectly dressed, while Jonas is mussed and his shirt gapes slightly to show his pecs. Isaac's outfit has more pockets for first-aid supplies, Nic has more weapons strapped to his body, and Dimitri is carrying a laptop. When they all check themselves over, I can't help but smile.

It's an important mission, but jeez, they look cute, like toy soldiers but oh so damn sexy.

Shaking my head, I clear my throat. "Let's go."

We wait until the sun sets to make our move, watching from bushes both in the front and rear of the house. No one comes or goes, and there's no movement at all. A bad feeling starts building in my stomach, but I keep it to myself as the instructions come through my earpiece from Louis, who's in the front with Isaac and Dimitri. I'm with Jonas and Nico in the back.

"Five minutes, and then we move. Set watches." I hear Nico doing it and trust him to alert us. Jonas is busy drawing dirty stick figures in the mud, and when I glance over, he wiggles his eyebrow, pointing at an elaborate sexual position.

"This is for us to try later," he teases.

"Jonas, you perv—wait, is that even possible?" I tilt my head, looking over the diagram as I feel Nico's eyes on me.

"Yes," he grunts, and we both swing our heads to him, wearing twin expressions of shock. His face is cool and collected as he watches us back.

"Well shit, you dirty dog, Nico. I didn't know you had it in you." Jonas almost whoops as Nico rolls his eyes, but when I wink at him, a grin tugs at his lips as his watch counts down.

"Remember your position and check the corners. Dimitri has disarmed all alarms and cameras. The main focus in the house is the mainframe and command centre. Get any research or data before it's wiped. Ours is to check every other room in case there is a . . . subject being held here. Understood?"

"Yes, boss." I salute, making Jonas grin.

"As long as I get to be behind Nova, I'll behave." I realise that is exactly why they put Jonas with me. Jesus, I'm like a psycho's babysitter, if the baby was an almost seven-foot, built, weapons expert with enhanced senses and intelligence.

"Louis, am I with Jonas to make him behave?" I mutter as I look back at the darkened house.

"Yes," he answers without shame, making my eyes narrow.

"And Nico?" I hedge.

"To make you behave." He chuckles. "Sorry, baby, but we all know if anything goes down, you and Jonas are firing first."

"Touché," I mutter, even though I'm annoyed and, yes, slightly turned on that he thinks that much about me. Grinning over at Nico, I wiggle my eyebrows. "I guess that means you get to punish me if I misbehave."

"Oh fuck, me, me, let me!" Jonas shoots his hand up, and without looking, Nico knocks it down.

"No, that's my job as this unit's commander for the mission." The heated look he gives me makes me want to misbehave just to see what he would do. As if reading it on my face, he moves closer in his crouched position and wraps his hand around my neck, twisting my head back until it hurts, and I meet his gaze.

"But if you're a good girl, you'll get a reward too, and trust me, baby girl, the reward is better," he promises, his lips almost touching mine.

"Fuck, you two would make beautiful babies," Jonas randomly remarks, his eyes wide and confused. We both turn, so our cheeks touch, and stare at Jonas, who is just grinning at us, and then we glance back at each other and laugh.

Just then, his watch beeps, and he transforms back into commander mode. "Thirty seconds until we move. Stay low, silent, and keep your faces hidden just in case. Watch for traps, and be aware of what is within." With that, he moves to the edge of the bush, gun in hand, as he counts down silently. I slide behind him, palming a blade while Jonas pats my ass from behind me, sighing dreamily.

"If I'm good, do I get to eat your ass later?" he whispers in my ear.

"We both know you'll prefer the punishment," I murmur, and then Nico starts to move, and Jonas quiets down as we hurry in a crouched run to the back door. It's a seemingly normal house in a rural area, but we all know it's a lie. The windows are dark on both the second and first floor. I peeked in the one next to the back door earlier that leads to a kitchen and a hallway. Dimitri found some blueprints, but we all know it has probably been modified by now. However, it did show a basement.

Which is where we are assuming everything is.

I move past Nico to take my position at the door, quickly picking the lock and grabbing the handle as he counts down with his fingers. On three, I rip it open, and he rolls in, sweeping the room before a whispered, "Clear," comes. I hear Louis and the others coming in the front in my earpiece, but I focus on keeping them safe. It never mattered before, when it was only me.

If I messed up, it was only my life, but now it's theirs too, and I refuse to let them down.

I follow Dimitri as he sweeps the room, and Jonas brings up the rear. We move through the silent, empty house. There is a layer of dust everywhere and old furniture covered in sheets, but the dirty floor has booted footprints leading to the hallway. We follow them and see Louis shadowed by Isaac and Dimitri. Isaac breaks off with Dimitri, and Jonas and I break off. They sweep upstairs, and we sweep the rest as Louis and Nico watch the door. Every corner must be checked before we go down there. We don't want to be crept up on.

When it's clear, I call it out and move back to the door to see them hurrying downstairs. Once there, Nico points at Jonas and at the ground. I feel him grumbling, but he agrees to stay and watch our backs while we head downstairs.

Nico opens the door for Louis, who strides in. Nico and I are next, followed by Dimitri and Isaac. The stairs creak as we walk down them, and we flick on our torches, lighting the way. It's deeper than I thought possible, but I'm betting they built the house to conceal this. At the bottom, the corridor runs left and right. Louis points right and heads that way with his team, while Nico and I go left. There's a corner up ahead, and I peek around it before rolling and coming up with the knife just in case, but there's no one there, so I wave and move on. Nico moves past me, his eyes sharp as his torch lights up the white walls that make me shiver in memory.

This place is definitely one of my father's locations. It has the same clinical feel to it. Recycled air and pain almost circulate in the air. The corridor ends at another set of stairs. These are metal and only have a few steps, and once we are down them, we freeze side by side in a huge laboratory and observation room. There are computers and workspaces everywhere. Notes are scattered all over the floor, half-trodden and destroyed, and each computer seems like they were broken in a hurry.

"Fuck, boss, they knew we were coming. Everything has been ransacked," Nico informs the others as he walks through the room, which extends both left and right, but I move straight ahead to the glass window running along the whole front wall.

When I look out, I see nothing but white. I follow it down, and what I see makes my heart skip as a scream claws at my throat.

Spinning on my heel, I find the entrance to the left and hammer on the red button. The door opens with a hiss.

"Nova!" Nico growls, but I ignore him as I race to the other door and smack the button, turning to see it close the outer one before the inner one opens. Putting my knife away, I rush down the metal steps, my booted feet loud as I land on the tiled floor, sliding in the blood there.

I don't breathe until I'm next to it. My fingers hesitate before I press them to the body's neck, knowing he's already dead. When I don't feel a pulse, I let my head fall back and scream.

And scream.

There are panicked questions coming through the comms, but I rip it out as I swallow my pain and glance down at the boy. Just a boy. Just a fucking kid. No older than fourteen, he wears a hospital gown like I used to wear. His head is shaved, and his bright blue eyes are locked on the ceiling. His hands and feet are chained to the operating chair.

The whole room is a fucking sterile operating theatre and prison, but I can't look away from him, noting his slightly parted, bruised and cut up lips. A scar runs across his forehead and down to the slit neck.

The blood is dried there, pooling onto the floor. His body is cold and going into rigor. He's been dead a while, I know that, but it doesn't stop the agony from forming a ball in my chest and mixing with my fury. He was just a kid, just a fucking kid, and they slit his neck like he was an animal.

I hear them then as they come into the room, and I turn to face them. I don't know what they see on my face, but they still, worry in their eyes as well as pain. "He's dead. He was just a kid. He's dead."

Isaac moves closer, taking my face and searching my eyes before examining me. "She's in shock, but she's okay," he tells the others before moving to the kid.

I don't watch as he examines him.

"From the wound and rigor, I'd say he's been dead about seven hours," he murmurs.

"They killed him today. They knew we were coming, and to hide it, they killed him rather than let us save him." My voice sounds weird and faraway.

Dimitri steps into the room, staring at his phone. "Everything has been wiped, cleaned out entirely—" He jerks his head up and stops, his face paling when he sees the kid.

"They knew," I snap at Louis and storm past them. I need to move, to do something. In the other room, I ball my hands into fists, and then with an anger-filled scream, I yank on one of the desks and throw it. Once I start, there is no stopping.

I throw chairs at walls, smash beakers, and crumble equipment in my wrath. Computers are destroyed and paperwork is ripped up until I just rage and take it out on the room. When I stumble back, my chest heaving, I don't feel any better, but the room looks like how I feel inside—a destroyed mess of pain.

Arms wrap around my waist and turn me. I sink into that warm embrace, pressing my head to a solid chest. I feel their heartbeat as they try to soothe me, stroking along my back. "Collect what you can," Louis orders, and the chest in front of me sighs.

"Shh, I have you," Nico murmurs, and I realise he's holding me.

Once again, he came after me and brought me back, and when I lift my head, I meet his knowing eyes. He glances down at me, flicking glass off my shoulder. "We need to move quickly. Are you okay?"

I nod and step back and look at the glass before glancing away. "We bury him," I tell them, leaving no room for argument.

"Nova, we can't," Louis starts, and I whirl to him. "We can't. I want to, but we can't. If his body is found, there will be questions we can't answer. Plus, it will expose us all. We have to burn this place to the ground, so no one ever finds it."

"He deserves better than being burnt to fucking ashes and forgotten," I yell, knowing I'm being irrational and taking it out on him when it's not his fault.

"He's dead," he snaps meaningfully, making me flinch.

"Boss," Nico snarls, but Louis narrows his eyes on him, silencing him as he steps before me.

"He's dead, Nova. He doesn't know or care anymore. I will not risk my family or you to bury the boy, no matter how much I want to. I vowed to protect you, and I will. He burns with all this, and I fucking pray that wherever he is now, he's free of this hell."

"He was just a kid," I whisper, my lip quivering.

"So were we. We will get the bastard who did this, and when we do, he's yours. Until then, we need you to keep it together. Can we count on you?" He searches my gaze as I breathe through the pain and anger until I feel more whole.

"Yes," I mutter and meet everyone's gazes, but they look away, working quickly to take anything that might be useful. Embarrassment heats my cheeks as I clear my throat and look back at Louis. "Yeah, I'm here."

"Good." He squeezes my hand as he passes. "Then let's do this and get out of here."

FORTY-FOUR

NOVA

After clearing the house of anything useful, we find some gasoline in the shed outside and fill the house with it. Standing in the back garden, I toss the lighter inside, watching as flames engulf the house of horrors. We stand side by side and watch it burn away all evidence of the evil done here and the boy's body within.

Closing my eyes, I say a prayer for him, something I've never done. I pray to a god I don't believe in to protect him and give him the happiness he deserves in life. When we hear the sirens, we disappear back into the darkness.

We don't know where to go, and we're unsure of our next move.

Luckily for us, we have Louis who barks out orders. We grab our stuff from the hotel and check out. If they know we are in the city, they might come for us, so we need to move fast. When we load into the plane and take off with no direction in mind, we are all feeling angry, hurt, and lost.

Dimitri spreads out the papers and computer parts he saved, giving us a purpose. It keeps my mind off what happened and the boy, even though I know I will see his body every time I close my eyes. Instead, I sort through the papers while Dimitri and Louis pick at computer parts.

An hour later, Dimitri's head jerks up.

"I have it!" He hurries off to the cockpit, and when he comes back, he grins at us. "They tried to wipe all of the hard drives, but in their rush, they didn't corrupt them enough. I managed to save some documents on another location, another experiment, which they were comparing this one to."

"That's great." Louis sighs, clearly relieved, the only sign that he was as worried as us. "So where to?"

"We are going to Scotland," Dimitri tells us as he shuts his laptop and stretches. "We might as well get some rest and then we'll hit the ground running when we get there. The notes on this one are odd."

"Odd how?" I ask, and he looks at me, not with pity, but understanding.

"The age . . . It isn't a child."

Unsure what we will find when we land in Scotland, I spread out across the bed in the back of the plane. Right now, I'm grateful Dimitri's money was able to provide this. We are all drained after this mission. We knew it would be bad, but we never expected that. We should have.

My father is dead, though, so then who killed the boy?

And why?

How did they know we were coming?

I have so many questions and not enough answers, and my turbulent thoughts only quieten when Isaac slips into bed next to me, taking my hand. "Are you okay?" we say at the same time and share a grin.

"No," I admit, and he nods.

"Me either," he murmurs.

Closing my eyes, I turn and lay my head on his chest, sliding my leg over his.

He sighs contentedly and wraps me in his arms. "We have to do this, Nova. I just wish I could make this easier for you, for all of you."

"We do this together," I mutter, listening to the steady thump of his heart. "I should have expected . . . but yeah, I guess I didn't. It made it so much more real again, that's all. That poor boy, what he went through . . ."

"We all did. Part of me is happy that he at least escaped the future we had, but either way, we cannot change what happened. We can only prevent it from happening again, and we will. No doubt there will be more horrors the deeper we investigate, but you are right. We will do it together, and when there is nothing left but the ashes of your father's research, we will mourn them."

Lifting my head, I meet his eyes. "You are amazing, you know that?" I tell him, and he blushes even as his eyes drop to my lips. Leaning in, I allow myself a little weakness and kiss him softly. "So amazing," I whisper huskily against his lips as the bed bounces, rolling me into Isaac.

Grinning, I pull back and turn to see Louis stretching out next to me, closing his eyes. "Don't mind me," he murmurs, even as his hand snakes out and tangles in my hair. He sighs and settles down as if he just needed to feel me, so I snuggle between them, not even cracking an eye when I feel the others climb on, and we lie in a tangle of legs and arms.

There is a grunt and a smack.

"That better be your gun," Nico snarls, and when I laugh, Jonas does too.

"Nah, I'm just happy to see you."

There is a yelp, and when we look, Jonas is on the floor. He glares at Nico before pouting at me as he climbs up and lies on the full length of my body, burying his head in my chest. "He's being mean, baby," he whines.

"Nico, be nice." I grin as he huffs, wrapping his hand around my ankle. Dimitri's head is on my leg, and something settles deep inside me as I look over them.

"Sleep," Isaac commands. "Dream of good things," he whispers in my ear.

Closing my eyes, I can't help but smile and feel protected and loved. I'm not alone, I know that, but there are people out there who are, and they need our help. I cannot afford to break, not now, but I know with the guys by my side, I never will.

FORTY-FIVE

NOVA

By the time we catch a taxi into Scotland, we are all ready to stretch our legs and walk around. The air is cool and fresh, and the castle casts a beautiful shadow across everything we pass. The mixture of old and new buildings is incredible. I've never been to Scotland before, and my eyes are wide as I try to drink everything in. I know we are here for work, but it doesn't stop me from bouncing in my seat, wanting to explore the little shops and climb to the castle and do the ghost tours. The taxi takes us just off the main road to a side street of houses. Once there, I pay and slip out, stretching my arms up into the air. I giggle when someone tickles my side and smack their hands away, then I turn and glare at Jonas who just winks.

"Guess this is home for a few days," I comment as we stare at the three-story house.

Isaac hoists his bag into the air and takes off towards the front door. "Yep, I made sure we could just let ourselves in so we didn't have to meet anyone. It's private and gives us the cover of tourists we need. So get settled, but keep your bags packed. Dimitri is going to work on the next location information."

"Does that mean we can explore?" I almost bounce up and down.

Louis looks back at me, his eyebrow raised, and when I glance over, Nico and Jonas are at my side. Jonas is pretending to pray, but Nico just rolls his eyes. "Actually, I set up an automatic system to work on the encoded information. It could take hours, so there's no point in watching it," D calls and smiles at me. "How about we all explore, and get some good food and some drinks? I'll get a notification on my phone if anything comes up."

"D—" Louis starts, but when he looks all of us over, his resistance crumbles. "Fine, a few hours, no more!"

Grinning, I jog over to him and kiss him. "Thanks, boss man," I purr, smacking his ass as he turns and unlocks the door for me.

"Bloody woman is going to get us all arrested. I can feel it," he mutters, but I ignore him as I head down the long hallway. There is a living room to the right, and beyond that is a dining room, kitchen combo with huge glass doors that open to a beautiful Zen garden with swinging chairs, bean bags, artificial grass, a pizza oven, a grill, and even a hot tub. Jesus. Heading back the way I came, I leap up the wooden stairs two at a time. On the first floor are three bedrooms and a bathroom.

"You're on the top floor!" Louis calls up. Listening to him, I hurry up the second set of stairs, hearing the boys fighting over the rooms on the floor below me. There's only one bedroom up here. It has an en suite, and it takes up the entire top floor, with a bed big enough to fit us all and skylights that let in the beautiful soft daylight. The carpet is white and fluffy, and there is a sofa to the left under one of the skylights, a flat screen TV, and a glass partition into the bathroom with a huge waterfall shower, golden clawfoot tub, and matching his and her sinks.

There's abstract art above the bed, but the decor is all very simple and pretty. Throwing my bag down, I strip off my jacket and stretch, needing to loosen my muscles.

I hear footsteps but don't turn. "This room is pretty big for just me," I call out to whoever is there.

"And me," Louis replies, surprising me. I glance over as he tosses his stuff next to mine and winks at me as he lies back on the bed. "Perks of being in charge, I get to pick the rooms." His tongue darts out then, licking his lips as his eyes run down my body. "Are you sure you don't want to stay and explore here?"

"As tempting as that is," I purr as I crawl onto the bed and up his body, "I need food."

"I could feed you, though I am starving too," he admits, making it clear by the stark hunger in his eyes it's not for the same thing I am.

Laughing, I smack his chest and go to roll off him, but his arms wrap around me and flip us, pinning me facedown on the bed. "I think I'll eat my fill first," he purrs into my ear as he captures my hands and holds them against the middle of my back. He kicks open my legs and covers my jean-clad pussy with his hand, making me groan.

I could get out of this position, but why would I want to?

Especially now that Louis is finally playing and giving in to this heat between us.

"Louis," I mumble into the bedding, faking a struggle to at least pretend like I'm fighting it. Arching my back, I try to buck him off, but he simply grips my pussy harder, making me still.

"Good girl," he praises and starts to stroke me through my jeans, digging the seam into my clit and making me gasp as I push my ass back into his hands. I give up. Who am I to complain if he wants to make me come? Especially since my knickers are already wet.

"Whoa, we didn't get invited to this. I want in!" Jonas calls, his footsteps silent so I didn't even hear him come upstairs. "Guys, come look at this!"

"Make sure to leave no traces of ID, check every window and door, and put up the cameras and alarms," Louis orders, all the while stroking my pussy through my jeans. It shouldn't be so hot, but it is, and I wiggle below him. I'm needy as hell now.

"Seems like we have time for me to eat that sweet little cunt like I've wanted to every moment of every single day since I met you. I'm tired of fighting it, Nova. I'm tired of holding back, so be a good girl and scream for me."

"Louis," I murmur, "I need to help them—"

"Shh." He smacks my pussy and keeps me pinned with one hand. With the other, he starts to wiggle my jeans down my ass, leaving me in a lacy thong with my ass in the air. His hand strokes up my leg and over my cheeks, ignoring exactly where I need him to touch me. "Fuck, you are way too beautiful. Look at that." His voice is soft as his fingers feather across my pussy and the thong there, feeling how wet I am for him. "So strong and certain until I touch this little pussy, aren't you? You are probably going to destroy us all, but I will enjoy every second of it. Life is too fucking short not to have what I want, and Nova? I want you so badly. Fuck the rules. Fuck everything but this need."

"Shit," I mumble. "If you don't—"

His hand lands on my ass in a rough slap. "Shh, Nova. You're not in control here, I am, and I'll taste this cunt when I damn well want to. First, I want to look at you." His mouth moves closer, and I hear him inhale deeply. "Fuck, you're a masterpiece."

"Louis," I beg as he hoists my ass into the air, the heat of him behind me making me shiver.

I never beg for anyone, but for him?

Fuck, I might just learn to.

"So demanding," he teases as his thick fingers stroke along my dripping folds, avoiding where I need him most. "Such a beautiful disaster, Nova."

"Fuck you!" I go to flip over, but he slaps my ass hard, making me groan as his fingers thrust into me, giving me what I want.

"Behave, and you'll get exactly what you need," he promises. His fingers curl and stroke inside me, making me moan as I push back and fuck myself on them. He lets me, his thumb rubbing my clit. Pleasure slams through me as he shows me what a reward would be like.

And then his fingers still.

"Are you going to behave?" he murmurs slowly, like he has all the time in the world.

I squirm on his fingers, and pleasure arcs through me so much, I want to say fuck it, turn over, and make myself come, but I don't want that.

I want him.

Clenching my eyes shut, I breathe slowly before nodding.

"Words, Nova," he demands, his mouth almost touching me now.

"Yes! Fuck, I'll behave," I snarl.

Uncaring about my angry tone, he darts his tongue out and flicks my clit, making me gasp. "Good girl."

I fall forward when his mouth seals on me, giving me the pleasure he promised. He takes no prisoners as he methodically decimates my cunt with his tongue, his fingers stroking inside me as he licks and sucks every inch of my pussy.

He leaves no inch untasted in his conquest to destroy me.

I moan and writhe below him, pushing into his mouth and fingers as he sucks my clit before moving away and down. He doesn't give me enough to get me off, only winding me up more.

"Louis!" I practically scream, rolling my hips to try and move him higher.

He ignores me, taking his time and learning what makes me moan, but he never lets me come.

"You taste so good, baby," he purrs as he laps at my entrance while he thrusts his fingers in and out of me. "How can someone who has experienced such pain, bitterness, and sin taste so fucking sweet? I could eat you all day. In fact, I just might."

Shit, shit, shit.

I'm so close, I can feel it, like when you are standing on a mountain and about to drop down the other side. My whole body shakes with anticipation, and my pussy clenches on his fingers.

"Boss, you want the cameras on the back too? There's no entrance point that I can see, but I want to be sure," Dimitri calls, his voice closer, and I feel his eyes on me. The fact that they are talking business while I'm almost coming on their leader's face is ridiculously attractive.

Louis lifts his mouth from my cunt to speak. "Yes. Better to be safe than sorry."

I want to scream. I was so fucking close! Louis chuckles like he knows my thoughts.

"Got it, enjoy your snack." D laughs as he walks away.

"Oh, I will. Now where were we?" he purrs, sealing his mouth back to my cunt.

"If you don't make me come, I'm going to fuck myself," I snarl, knowing I'm being a brat.

"Is that right? I don't take well to threats, Nova." His words vibrate my pussy, making me gasp. "But luckily for you, I want to see you shatter more than I want to punish you." His fingers slam into me, fucking me hard and fast as he lashes my clit and sends me spiralling over the edge with a cry.

"Again," he demands.

I shake my head, falling forward, but he hoists me back up. "I can't —" I'm too sensitive. I try to push him away as the aftershocks of the orgasm tear through me, but he licks me through it and out the other side, forcing me to reach for another one.

"You can and you will," he orders. "Now be a good girl and come all over my tongue for me."

"Louis!" His name is practically a scream. His other hand holds my cunt open for him as he sucks my clit, scraping his teeth against it until it almost hurts, and despite my protests, I come again, all over his fingers and tongue, and he laps up my release.

"Good girl."

Collapsing to the side, I turn to see him, his mouth and chin dripping with my cream as he licks his fingers clean, watching me. I roll to my knees and grab his head, kissing him deeply, tasting my release on his lips. I slide my hand down his body to his hard cock and grip it through his jeans, but his other hand circles my wrist as he pulls from my lips.

"No, darling, this was about you, not me. I don't need you to think you have to touch me to make us equal. Making you come was more pleasurable than even your talented hand." He kisses me again. "Go get ready so we can go explore like you want to, but remember, Nova . . ." His other hand slides around my throat, gripping it tightly and tilting my head back until my eyes open and lock on his determined, hungry gaze. "When you come back to this bed tonight, you're mine, all fucking mine, and I plan on spending every minute between those pretty thighs as you scream for me. It's your choice. I'm done fighting this tension between us, and I plan to give in to you completely, so this is your last warning, baby. If you step into this room after nightfall, you won't be leaving until I've fucked every single inch of you."

Fuck me.

I almost come just from the threat. He tightens his hand on my throat, using all of his strength. Dominance pours from him in waves, and usually I would fight it, needing to be in control, but something about Louis gives me the strength to let that go and just be in the moment, trusting him to keep me safe and happy.

That terrifies me, and he watches the emotions play across my face before leaning in and kissing me softly—a promise of what is to come. He won't let me back away or hide.

Not this time.

As much as whatever is happening between us all scares me, the thought of living without them now terrifies me even further.

Louis leaves me after that, no doubt checking on the others.

He leaves me to my muddled emotions and clenching sex.

After changing out of my plane clothes and taking a whore's bath in the sink, I slip on some ripped black jeans with a white top tucked in loosely, and then I add a belt and some black boots. I even brush my hair and apply lip gloss and grab some shades, just in case. As I'm about to head downstairs, my phone vibrates, so I sit on the bed and accept the call from Ana.

"Hey," she says then hesitates. "I just wanted to check in and see how you are." I pull the phone away with raised eyebrows before putting it back to my ear.

"Yeah, we are all okay," I admit slowly. I am unsure what to say, not wanting to make her mad again.

"Okay, where are you now?" she asks, clearly nervous and trying to start a conversation.

"Scotland. We got another hit. The last one, well, they were dead, and it was all ruined. Let's leave it at that. How are you getting on?" I find myself lying back, feeling awkward at first, but as the conversation goes on, I smile, missing this connection between my sister and me. Although we have a lot to work on to trust each other again, this is a start. She reached out, and that makes me beyond happy.

"Hard," she grumbles. "His writing is worse than a doctor's—oh, wait." She laughs, and I laugh with her. "But I'll get there, I've been sending anything I've managed to translate to Louis, which isn't much yet."

"You'll get there; you always do. Let's be honest, you're smarter than me or Dad, so there is nothing you can't do if you just put your mind to it." I find myself needing to comfort her. I love my sister, and everything I've done is for her. Although I'm starting to put myself first and I'm still upset about what happened, I can't just stop loving her.

She will always be my Annie.

"Why are you always so nice to me? Nova, for so long, I pushed away memories of you because it hurt too much. I was angry, but under it was pain. I forgot how you used to tuck me in every night and make up these elaborate stories. I forgot you would hold me when I cried or clean my cuts or create these incredible worlds for us to play in so I didn't feel lost and alone when Dad ignored us, which was always."

"Annie," I murmur, the old nickname just slipping out, but she interrupts me.

"No, you need to hear this. The point is . . . I forgot. I forgot everything you did for me out of my own selfishness, but I'm remembering now, and I'm so sorry. I am so sorry I ever doubted the girl who promised to protect me, who fought off bullies and protected me from falling from that stupid old tree." I smile, remembering that day. "I'm sorry I didn't believe you. I will be for the rest of my life, and I'll make it up to you because I missed you, Nova, so much. If you are willing to, I'd like us to be sisters again. I'd like to have a family again, with you."

I remain quiet, and she swallows. "I—sorry, I shouldn't have—" She sounds dejected.

Life is very much like the weather. You get some good days and some bad. When it's sunny, you forget about the rain, and when it rains, you long for the sun. No matter how much she has hurt me, she will always be my sister, and she's offering me something I've wanted for so long—to be together again.

Everything else is just rain. It's beautiful and sometimes painful, but in the end, the sun always comes out.

"I would like that," I admit softly. "It's all I've ever wanted."

"Me too," she replies.

I hear Jonas yell, and I grin. "I have to go, there's work to be done, but I'll talk to you later, okay?"

"Okay," she replies softly.

"Make sure you eat and sleep, Annie," I order as I stand.

"Yes, Mum," she mocks like she used to when we were kids, the nostalgia quickening my heart rate as I rub the aching organ through my skin. "Love you, Nova."

"Love you too, kid," I reply before hanging up. There's an extra bounce in my step as I head downstairs. Now I just need to destroy all of Father's research, and everything will be good.

I find all the others waiting in the kitchen. D is in front of his laptop, which he closes and brings with him. I notice the temporary cameras and alarm systems and smirk. "Let's do this, team!" I call, clapping my hands. They all groan, but they are grinning. I head for the door and out so we can go explore.

We end up walking around the centre of Edinburgh, window shopping and taking pictures. We even climb to the castle where I ask a tourist to take a picture of us all. The guys pick me up and hold me sideways, making me laugh, and the picture has me smiling as we finally find a small pub and sit down for some beers and food.

For a moment, I just sit back with an unrestrained grin on my face as they all laugh at a story Isaac is telling. The food is good, the beers are cold, and the happiness in my chest is something I'm so unfamiliar with, I don't quite know what to do with it, but as I look around at their laughing faces, I know it's because of them.

Because of this team.

This family.

I don't think I could ever give it up now, and when D slings his arm around my shoulders and brings me back into the conversation, something close to love fills my chest.

After spending hours just enjoying our time together, we decide to wander back to the house. Along the way, Jonas spots a shop, and we all follow him in, only for him to buy a kilt. It makes me laugh, but I'm also ridiculously turned on as I imagine him wearing it.

Once we're back at the house, I grab a bottle of water and head outside, watching the sky while the others check the perimeter and D opens his laptop. Downing the bottle, I head back inside and bid them goodnight as I go up the stairs. Each step I take is slow and deliberate, as I know what is waiting for me up there—Louis and his promise to make me his tonight.

Shivering, I stop on a step and wonder if I'm really going to do this. Part of me knows it will change everything. I know he's giving me a choice to choose him—them.

It's an important moment, and it feels like something huge is on the horizon. My breath is shallow as I take the next step and the next, until I reach our bedroom to find him lying on the bed, his arms behind his head and a cocky, knowing smirk on his lips.

"Good girl, I knew you would come."

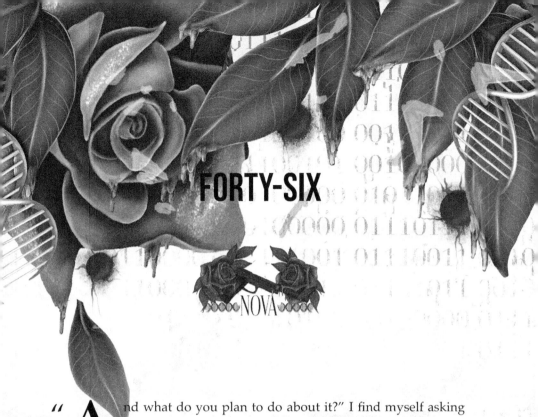

FORTY-SIX

NOVA

"And what do you plan to do about it?" I find myself asking as I lean there.

Smiling wider, he rolls from the bed in a smooth move and prowls towards me, hunting me before he cages me against the wall. His muscular arm comes up next to my head as he leans in. His chest is bare, and his muscles clench deliciously with his movements. His joggers are slung low on his hips, showcasing that incredible V, which has me licking my lips before I drag my eyes back up to meet his shining, knowing gaze.

"I plan to reward you," he murmurs, making my heart stutter and my breathing pick up. "All night."

He steps back, and I almost slump, as if I were released by him. Louis has this overwhelming magnetism. Before, I was always dominant, but he makes me submissive, and I find myself loving it, so when he barks a command, I jump to comply.

"Undress, love."

I don't just rip my clothes off though. I might like what he orders, but let's face it, I always have to rebel.

Even a little.

I drag my shirt over my head and kick my trousers off before strolling towards him in nothing but my lace thong and bra.

"All of it, Nova," he demands.

When I reach him, I slide my hand down his chest to cup his hard cock through his joggers, making him groan as I squeeze and lick his nipple. Suddenly, his fist is in my hair, yanking my head back.

"I said all of it," he grits out.

"Then make me," I challenge him.

Snarling, he turns me until my back hits his chest and then rips away my thong and bra, making me jerk before I moan. I rub my ass against his hard length, my nipples tightening in the cool air as his hand moves down to grip my throat.

"If you wanted to be punished, baby, then all you had to do was ask," he purrs in my ear as he wedges one leg between mine, pressing his thigh against my pussy. His free hand grips my hip and rocks me until my clit hits his solid muscle, sending sparks of pleasure spiralling through me.

My eyes close at the friction, and my lips part on a moan.

"Is this your idea of a punishment?" I mock.

"No, I'm just getting you nice and wet." He smirks, licking and sucking at my neck as his other hand strokes up my body, twisting my nipples meanly. He continues to work me up until I almost come just from this, and like he feels the pulsing of my pussy, he pulls away, leaving me cold and frustrated.

Before I can turn, I'm pushed down and my ass is dragged out.

A hard smack jiggles my ass, the pain heading straight to my clit. His hand soothes it away before gliding over the ink on my hip. "I love your tattoos. They look so fucking sexy." His tongue replaces his hand, stroking over the ink and then up over my stinging cheek. He trails his fingers over my parted ass to my pussy, where he plunges them inside of me before pulling back once more.

"You taste so fucking sweet, baby. Do you know that? All these hard, sharp edges, yet your pussy gives you away, sweet and soft and wet, begging for my big cock." There's a rustle, and then I gasp when his length drags down my pussy. "Do you want this big cock, Nova?"

Fisting the sheets, I push back, but he pulls away.

"Words, baby," he orders.

"Fuck! Yes, I want it!" I scream, throwing him a venomous look over my shoulder. I moan, watching as he grips his wet shaft and drags his fist up and down his length as he watches me. He's so fucking long, I actually shiver from the look of him. He's slimmer than the others, but fuck, he's so goddamn long, I know it's going to hurt in the best way.

"Good girl, and you'll take every hard inch . . . but not until I've had my fill." He steps back between my thighs and drops to his knees, slanting his mouth over my pussy as my eyes slam closed and my back bows in ecstasy.

His tongue flicks with expert movements, tasting my pussy before circling my hole and moving back up, teasing my clit until I'm humping his face. I push back rapidly, rocking and reaching for my release once more, but just as I'm about to come, he stills.

"Louis!" I groan.

"Beg me to make you come, Nova."

"Never," I hiss.

"Then you don't get to." He grins against my thigh as he licks and sucks at the skin there.

Panting, I squeeze my eyes closed before forcing the words out. "Please, Louis, please make me come."

"How?"

"With your tongue." I groan. "And then your cock. Please, just fuck me!"

"Good girl. If you behave, you get what you want." His mouth seals over my cunt once more, and within seconds, I'm screaming my release and coating his tongue as he laps me through it. Holding me against his greedy mouth with one hand, he keeps tonguing my over-sensitive flesh.

"No more."

His hand comes down in a smack on my ass as he nips my clit, making me jerk from the pain. "Not until I've said so. Now come again."

"I can't," I grind out.

"You can and you will. I want you squirting on my tongue, Nova," he orders, slipping his fingers inside of my still fluttering channel and stroking me before adding another, all the while he nips and sucks my oversensitive clit until I'm rocking into him.

He holds me there, between pleasure and pain, until he adds another finger, and then another. The pinch of pain as he stretches me is almost too much. "Good girl, take my whole fist."

I jerk, going to pull away, but he holds me in place as he adds his final fingers before pulling out and thrusting his fist back inside me.

His tongue drags over my pussy to my ass where he licks my asshole, all the while fucking me with his fist. The burn of pain and the stretch is too much, and with a scream, I come once more.

He pulls out as I fall forward, writhing in ecstasy from pleasure that's so great, I almost pass out.

When I can finally breathe again, I find him stroking his cock over my pussy, and without warning, he lifts me and impales me on it, like a rag doll.

The noise that leaves my lips isn't even human.

"So fucking beautiful, Nova. Such a good girl. Next time, you'll get my cock in your ass and my fist in your pussy," he growls, and it turns me on, making me grip his cock.

"Oh, you like that, don't you, you naughty girl?" He groans as I clench around him again. "You fucking love it."

"Asshole," I spit, even as I push back, finally recovering enough to move.

"You love it," he retorts. "Now be a good girl and take your man's cock. Let them all hear you fucking it like a good girl. No doubt they wish they were in here, and they are probably stroking their own cocks, fisting themselves in bed while imagining they're in this tight little cunt."

Shit, shit, shit.

Gripping my ass, he starts to speed up, fucking me harder. I grip onto the bed as I take it, his name a plea on my lips as he pounds into me from behind. Each brutal thrust rocks the bed into the wall in time with my moans. His huge length spears me to the point of pain, dragging across those nerves inside and making me wild.

One hand releases the globe of my ass and slips between my thighs to play with my clit, curling and flicking.

Over and over.

"Come for me, let me feel you gush on my cock, darling," he growls. "Let me feel you explode. That's it. You're so close, I can feel it. Fuck, you should see yourself. All hard muscles yet soft fucking cunt gripping my dick, begging for it. You're so fucking beautiful, my girl. That's it, good girl, come for me. Milk me."

Oh fuck.

He slams inside of me at the same time he flicks my clit, and it sends me over the edge once more.

I come all over his cock like he said. He strokes me through it as my legs quiver, my body locks up, and my pussy clamps around his cock.

"Good girl, such a good girl. Look at you, look at how prettily you came for me, wetting my cock like such a greedy girl." His words of praise fill my ears as he blankets my body, holding me until I slump, and then he slowly pulls out of my clenching cunt and flips me.

Breathlessly, I stare up at his possessive, lust-filled eyes.

Gripping my hips, he yanks me to the edge of the bed and lifts my ass from it, placing it against his stomach as he slides back inside of me like he belongs there. I press my feet to his shoulders and reach up, gripping the bedding as he starts to fuck me once more.

He moves with slow, purposeful thrusts until I throw my head back and my hands slide up to grip my swaying tits as he watches.

"Fuck, Nova, you're killing me," he growls.

I sit up and lick the sweat on his chest before falling back and lifting my hips to meet his thrusts. Snarling, he hammers into me now, watching me bounce with each thrust.

"Fuck, I've never needed someone as much as I need you. I've never been able to let go with anyone like this. You drive me mad."

"In the best way," I tease, sliding my hands down my body where I stroke through the wet mess of my pussy to grip his cock at the base as he hammers into me.

Grunting, he speeds up, his arms shaking and abs flexing with each brutal twist of his hips until he turns his head and bites my thigh, making me cry out as I come once more.

This time, though, I drag him with me, a roar leaving his lips as he pummels into me before stilling.

His release splashes inside me until he finally collapses on top of me. His sweaty body slides against mine as I wrap my legs and arms around him and kiss him, tasting the pleasure on his lips.

"That was only round one, baby," he murmurs, placing a soft kiss over my hammering heart.

I'm a wet mess, and I can't help but smile.

"Bring it on."

He does. I wake up later to his face buried between my thighs, and he orders me to come so many times, I actually pass out. The next time I wake up, it's with his fingers buried inside of me, which he quickly replaces with his cock, rocking into me from behind until I scream and he fills me with his cum.

I'm exhausted and fall straight back to sleep until the sunlight hits my face, slowly waking me up.

His hands explore my body, mapping every inch and stroking across the muscles in my stomach, over my slightly rounded hips, down and up my legs, over my toned back and shoulders, then down my breasts and back again.

I wake up wet and panting.

"Louis," I groan, burying my face in the pillow, even as I part my legs to give him better access to explore.

"I warned you, baby." He chuckles as he laps at my pussy before I feel his cock sliding into me.

He leans down to kiss me as he slowly rolls his hips, taking mercy on me and fucking me gently, each slow drag of his huge length making me gasp into his mouth. He swallows the sound, his own grunts making me feel giddy.

To have such an effect on such an incredible man?

Yeah, it's addictive.

My hands slide across his shoulders and down to his flexing ass, where I dig my nails in as I lick and suck at his lips, tasting his pleasure there.

"Shit, you're so fucking good like this. I don't want to blow just yet, baby, and if you keep kissing me like that, like I'm your fucking everything, then I will," he murmurs into my mouth before pulling from my body, leaving me blinking and unsatisfied, but I shouldn't have worried because he rolls down beside me and lifts me right onto his face.

My hands fall to his chest as I bow over him and he seals his mouth over my pussy, licking and sucking, using everything against me until I'm coming across his lips and tongue. I lean farther down and swipe my tongue across his hard cock, watching it jerk for me.

"Good girl," he purrs against me, the vibrations making me jerk away.

Chuckling, he drags me down, bringing his knees up to prop me up as his hard cock presses into me once more and he thrusts up from behind, spearing me on it.

He holds my hips as I face the stairs. "Ride me, Nova. Let me see that pretty pussy swallowing my cock."

Sighing in pleasure, I roll my hips before using my thighs to ride him with his help, while his fingers stroke my skin once more before grabbing my ass and parting it to see better.

"Fuck, I've never seen a more beautiful sight." He moans behind me, giving me all the control. "That's it, baby, take me, fuck me, use me for your pleasure."

I do, winding my hips and doing what feels good until a slow, rolling orgasm washes me away. I feel him sit up, changing the angle, and press his face to my neck, where he nuzzles and trails kisses as he bounces me on his cock, chasing his own release. The lazy thrust of his cock leaves me defenceless against this man, and he knows it.

He knows how to pull me apart and put me back together again, giving me no choice but to surrender his control.

It's so easy to see why the others follow him and trust him implicitly, and right now, so do I.

He fucks me right into another release, my name on his lips as he grunts and stills, pumping me full of his cum once more.

When the pleasure finally abates, he pulls free of my body, making me wince, and then tugs me into his arms, kissing my face and lips. "You did amazing, Nova, so fucking good. When I can walk, I'll bathe and feed you."

"Asshole," I murmur, even as I snuggle closer.

The chuckle makes his chest lift against me as he strokes my back. "No, that's for next time, baby."

Oh fuck.

FORTY-SEVEN

NOVA

I roll out of bed, finding the other side cold. Louis is gone, but there's a T-shirt folded on his pillow with a note on top.

Wear this. Let them all see whom you belonged to last night while I remember the way you came for me so prettily, baby. See you downstairs.

Flipping onto my back, I bite my lip to hold back my smile, feeling like a giggling schoolgirl. Hell, it's not a sweet, loving note, but damn, it's perfect for me and for them. Dragging myself up, I force myself to shower, wincing at the soreness between my thighs. It's that special kind of ache that reminds you that you've been good and fucked. I don't bother with knickers or a bra, and I leave my hair wet and my face bare as I pad back into the other room and slip on the shirt. I fold the note and shove it into my jeans pocket to keep. Not that I'll admit that to myself.

Walking downstairs, I hear them in the kitchen, their banter reaching my ears even on the second floor. It doesn't stop when I walk in, which makes me grin wider. Louis winks at me as he adds bacon to a pan, while Nico pushes him out of the way, eggs in his hand. Isaac is nursing a cup of tea and watching it all unfold with a paper folded before him, and he grins when he sees me. D is flipping sausages in a frying pan, and Jonas is doing push-ups on the deck outside.

"Morning, beautiful," D calls as I pass him, kissing his cheek as I head to the fridge. Nico beats me there, handing me a mug of coffee.

"Juice is on the table. Morning, baby." He kisses my cheek so close to my lips, I stumble for a moment, and then he whacks my ass with the spatula. "Go get Jonas and sit down. Breakfast is nearly ready."

When I pass Louis, he leans in and murmurs, "You look awfully good in my shirt, Nova." The promise in his tone almost has me skipping to the table. Putting my mug down, I pop my head outside.

"Hey, hot stuff, breakfast is ready!" I call.

Jonas stops mid jump clap push-up and grins up at me, his eyes bright. "I'll be right there—wait, get on my back. Let me use you as a weight."

Not needing to be told twice, I hurry over and sit on his back cross-legged. He doesn't even grunt at the added weight as he continues doing push-ups. The others look out and just shake their heads, and when Jonas is done, I climb down and offer him my hand. He takes it, and I hoist him up.

"Ew, you're sweaty," I tease, wiping my hand dramatically.

"Yeah, how about I make you all sweaty?" he flirts, and I point my finger at him.

"Don't you dare. I just showered," I warn, and his eyes narrow.

"Run, Nova," he teases.

I hurry back inside with him chasing me, laughing. I drop into Isaac's lap and wrap my arms around him. "I claim sanctuary!" I yell.

Isaac just wraps his arm around me and continues drinking his tea. "Leave her be, Jonas."

"Nah, now you'll both get sweaty." Laughing, he wraps us both in a sweaty, meaty hug, and when he pulls away, Isaac is sighing, but I see a smile twisting his lips. Kissing the top of my head, Jonas flops back into my chair and starts to pick up my coffee as Nico comes over to put a plate on the table and extracts it, handing it to me.

"Get your own," he tells Jonas.

"Rude, just because she has a vagina," he whines.

"Yup." I wink.

"Sexist," he tells me as he gets up.

Turning on Isaac's lap, I smile at him as he peers down at me with soft eyes. "Morning, how are you?"

"I'm fine," he replies as he holds me closer, pressing his face into my neck and inhaling. "Better now." His voice is husky, and it sends a shiver through me. It also doesn't escape my notice that something hard is pushing against my ass. I wiggle to be a brat, and he smacks my thigh.

"Unless you want me to bend you over this table and fuck you before breakfast, behave," he warns.

"No sex on the table, I just set it," D calls without even looking.

"Party pooper!" Jonas accuses as he sits back down with a mug. "There should always be time for sex before breakfast. It's like that fancy word for starter."

"Hors d'oeuvre? Appetizer?" I suggest, making him grin.

"That one. See? I knew you were a genius, Nova," he purrs, licking the rim of his mug while he watches me.

"Behave." Louis smacks his head as he passes to pop two plates down before Isaac and me. "And you need to eat. You burned a lot of calories last night." The satisfied smirk he wears tells everyone how I accomplished that, but they just laugh, not the least bit bothered that I'm fucking Louis now too.

No judgement, no hate, just pure acceptance, and I feel myself glowing as I tuck into the food, turning to share some with Isaac, who takes it gratefully, kissing my lips after every bite. When I look back, I find the others watching me with knowing, happy grins, and I just roll my eyes.

"So what's on the agenda for today?" I ask when the plates are clear. It's my turn to wash up, so I drag my feet, trying to distract them.

"I'm still waiting on any new information, so this morning we'll train and rest," Louis replies. "I want at least three hours of drills for everyone. We have been slacking while we've been on the road."

"Oh, does that mean I get to watch you all sweaty and half naked?" I bounce on Isaac's lap, making him groan again and grip me tighter.

"It means we get to watch you in skintight workout gear." Nico grins, making my mouth pop open.

I gasp. "You are supposed to be the well behaved one!"

"Oops," is all he says, sparking a surprised laugh from me.

"Wash up and then meet us outside," Louis orders, not letting me get away from my part in the group, even though I blew his mind last night.

"Can't I just suck one of your cocks and get you to wash up for me?" I grin.

Isaac laughs as he pushes me up, spanking me to get me moving.

"Oh, mine, mine!" Jonas calls.

"Deal—"

"No, wash up," Louis commands, shaking his head. "Lads, back outside."

They all grumble as they file outside, and I mutter as I clear the table and start to wash up, but I really shouldn't have complained because I get a free show as I do. I watch them strip their shirts off and warm up before working through Louis's drills. He does them with them as he calls them out, and I stop what I'm doing and just drool over all the tanned, exposed muscles.

I gawk, watching them do burpees, when Louis catches me and raises his eyebrows. Coughing to cover my awkwardness, I wash the pots as fast as possible and hurry upstairs. I change into some shorts, a sports bra, and a big T-shirt that I'll take off after warming up. Once I get back downstairs, I lace up my trainers and meet them outside. I stretch and focus on warming up my body while they work on their sets, and when I'm ready, I start with the drills they did—push-ups into burpees into jumping jacks. After I'm done, I pull my shirt off and put it on the table before stepping into the sled zone which they have fashioned out of the chairs with one of the guys lying on it. I pull it back and push it, barely breaking a sweat, and then Louis pulls off the kid gloves.

He doesn't go easy on me at all. Oh no, he pushes me to see how far I can really go, testing how strong, fast, and agile I am. Two hours later,

I collapse onto the grass, breathing heavily with that elated feeling I get after a great workout, the likes of which I haven't had in a long time.

"Need a hand . . . or some new lungs?" Nico grins down at me.

"Sadistic bastards. All of you," I retort, even as I groan and sit up, accepting the cold water he hands me. "But damn, that was good. I haven't worked that hard in too long."

"Oh, I don't know. I think you worked pretty hard last night," Jonas teases, wagging his eyebrows. I throw my water at him, making him laugh as he catches it and takes a big gulp.

Louis is about to respond when a buzz goes off, and all of us turn to the kitchen where D's laptop sits. Sharing a look, we scramble to our feet and race inside, hoping for the best, for more information to lead us to the next step.

FORTY-EIGHT

NOVA

We all gather around the laptop as D works through the information, but when he starts to get annoyed with us hanging over his shoulder, Louis barks at us to shower and hydrate. Realising it will be while, I kiss D's cheek to let him know it's okay and head back upstairs to shower once more.

I take my time and dress in a comfortable but moveable outfit in case we need to go out, sticking to my jeans, boots, and a jumper before grabbing my jacket and taking it downstairs with me. I hear bickering on the second floor.

"We do not share showers!"

"Then get out!"

"Get your dick away from me! Nova, help!"

Laughing, I shake my head as I head to the bottom floor. Louis is on the phone, shirtless with his workout shorts still on and coated in sweat, looking fucking delicious. His eyes heat and turn hungry as he looks me over, even as he carries on talking without even a hitch in his breath.

The possessive lust in his gaze makes me lick my lips before I turn to D and sit next to him. "Everything okay?"

He nods, typing away. I lean back, letting him work, but he blinks and looks over at me. "I'm sorry. I just get so into—"

"Never apologise." I lean over and drop a kiss onto his lips. "You want a drink while you work?"

He blinks at me slowly before a wide smile crawls over his face. "Coffee, please."

"You got it, babe." I wink as I stand, and when I pass him, he grabs my waist and hauls me back, tugging me down so he can kiss me properly. When I break away, breathing heavily, his eyes are molten. "I forgot to tell you that you look beautiful today," he purrs and then smacks my ass and goes back to work.

As I start making everyone coffee, Louis hangs up with a disgusted sneer on his lips. "Fucking soldiers and their sticks up their asses," he mutters as he leans back next to me. "Where are the others?"

"Last I heard, it sounded like Jonas was trying to scare Isaac out of the shower with his dick." I shrug, and we share a grin as we hear their thundering feet upstairs. "So, the usual."

"You are too good to us," he murmurs as I hand him a coffee.

"Don't forget it. Now go shower," I order.

His brow arches as he leans in. "Don't like me all sweaty, baby?"

"Oh, I do," I purr as I lick a long line up to his ear, tasting his musk. "But if you continue standing there shirtless, I'll end up fucking you and getting you all distracted."

"I wouldn't mind that," D calls out absentmindedly, making Louis and I chuckle as we break apart.

"Next time," Louis promises and drags himself away from me. I hear him heading upstairs as I turn back to the coffees, making them to each individual person's tastes.

"Fucking hell, Nico, get the knife out of his balls!" I hear him snap a moment later. "Behave, all of you. It's like living with animals. Jonas, stop chasing Isaac with your cock."

He sounds exasperated, and I giggle as D laughs.

Just as I'm laying out some biscuits and snacks, Nico comes in, wrapping his arms around me from behind and burying his face in my neck. "Save me from the madness."

"Nope, sorry." I pat his hands, leaning into him for a moment before dislodging him and handing him a coffee. "But here's a peace offering."

He takes it and sips it before his eyes close. When they flutter open, they are blazing as he backs me into the counter. "Fucking perfect."

"Yeah? Is it good? I've never tried that roast," I find myself asking.

With his eyes on me, he takes a big drink before grabbing my face and kissing me, letting me taste the coffee on his lips and tongue. When he pulls away, he's smirking. "Well, do you like it?"

"You're right. It's good," I rasp, my eyes wide.

"Either fuck or don't, but you're distracting!" D calls, making us both chuckle as we separate.

"Sorry, D!" we both call in unison.

We drink our coffee in peace until the others come down and wait with us. Ten minutes later, D leans back and blows out a breath before he chugs his coffee and wipes his mouth. He looks over at us and blinks before he blushes slightly, as if only just now realising we are here and watching him. "We have a location, but you might want to check with our bosses," he says mockingly.

Louis heads over and sighs before nodding, getting his phone out, and walking away. "It could be a while before we get permission, so today is an off day. Go have fun."

He doesn't have to tell us twice.

We spend the day wandering around Edinburgh before heading back to the house. D and Louis are busy with work, and Nico decides to go on a run with Isaac, leaving Jonas and me unoccupied, which is truly a bad idea.

We share a matching grin. "What bad things can we get up to?" he purrs as he prowls towards me, and I back into the garden. He thinks he's cornering me, but in reality, I'm leading him.

I glance away, scanning the garden before coming up with an idea.

I step into him and press my hand into his chest, sliding it down. "I can think of something," I purr and kiss him, nipping his lips before stepping back once more.

His eyes are closed, and when they blink open, they are dazed and euphoric. He watches me as I grab my jumper and strip it off along with my jeans, socks, and boots, leaving me in nothing but a lacy bra and thong. With a wink at him, I hurry to the hot tub, lift the lid, and climb in, sinking into the hot, bubbling water with a sigh.

My head tips back as the heat warms my chilled body, and then I move to the back row of seats and drape my arms across the edge as I lick my lips and meet his hungry gaze as he stands frozen, still watching me. "Well, what are you waiting for?"

He rips off his shirt and tosses his trousers away. He's naked under them, which I should have guessed. His huge, hard, pierced cock bobs as he walks towards me and climbs in. Pushing through the water, he doesn't stop until he's pressed against me, and I wrap my legs around him, grinding my cunt onto his cock.

I know D and Louis are just inside, and we are within view of them and the neighbours, but I don't care, especially when Jonas leans down and licks a trail of wetness between my breasts. Tugging my bra down, he uses it to push my breasts up before he nips and sucks my nipple. Keeping those dark eyes on me, he turns his head and sucks and nips the other. Pleasure arcs straight to my throbbing clit, even as the jets pound into my back, starting a lazy, hazy pleasure. My head tips back and my eyes close as his hands bracket my breasts, pushing them tight as he sucks and bites them. The stings of pain are followed by pleasure so great, I grind and moan against him without a care.

"Jonas." His name is a cry, and it drives him wild. He grinds his cock into my thong-covered pussy as he bites my nipple so hard, I jerk and scream. When he raises his head, I see he's drawn blood. Panting, I grip his hair and drag him up, kissing him.

Our tongues tangle as he reaches down into the water and rips my thong away, tossing it to the grass as his hands slide across my thighs to my hips and tilt me back so my clit hits his cock every time I wind my hips.

"I knew the moment I met you that I was yours," he murmurs into my lips, forcing me to swallow the words and sending them straight to my heart. "Knew I would worship you, that I'd be on my knees for the rest of my life if it keeps you at my side. I saw you, Nova. I fucking saw you and knew you were ours."

Fuck.

I moan into his lips, digging my teeth in and letting the pain flash through him until he grinds harder against my cunt, nearly making me come from that alone.

"But we are just as much yours." He groans. "So let them see that."

He grabs me and flips me around so I'm hanging over the edge of the hot tub, my tits pressed to the side and pushed up indecently. My nipples drag across the smooth plastic as his hand fists my hair and tugs. His other hand grips my hip and yanks me back onto the seat so I'm kneeling with my ass out for him, and then he lets go. I pant, feeling him moving in the water underneath me, and then he chuckles evilly.

Using my hips, he holds me tight and slams into me, taking my cunt the way I want him to. I close my eyes in agonised bliss as his hard cock fills me. The water churns around us as he pulls out and hammers back inside me.

"Let them hear you scream. Let them see the way I fuck you. You were made for all of us. We've been so lost, Nova, so fucking lost, and now that we have you, we'll never be again." The noise that leaves my lips is inhuman, his words ripping apart my heart. "Fuck, you feel so fucking good, too fucking good. It drives me crazy. It's all I think about, Nova: your pretty pussy. I'd be chained to your side and eating it every day all day if I could, begging for a taste, for the honour to be inside you. Look how well you're fucking taking me." His dirty words have me pushing back and impaling myself on his cock, and he bites my neck like an animal, making me cry out again.

His hand slides down to my throat and jerks my head up. "Eyes open, Nova. Look at what you do to us," he snarls, and my eyes pop open to see the others watching—all of them, their eyes hard and hungry.

Fuck!

I sway back harder, crying out, and then he repositions me, and I wonder why, but then I feel it.

A jet shoots right at my clit, making me writhe and scream. The intense feeling is too much, and I explode, coming around his cock, but he doesn't stop. He fucks me through it, keeping me pinned in place. The pressure on my clit is almost too much, and my eyes roll into the back of my head as he hammers into me.

"Ours, you're fucking ours, Nova." He grunts. "Look how you bring us together, how wild you make them. They never understood my madness until you." His voice is tight, harsh, as he bites and nips my skin, fucking me so hard, my hips slam into the side and I know I'll bruise.

The water splashes over the sides as my eyes open once more, meeting with those hungry ones of my other men as Jonas roars and hammers into me, forcing me tighter against the jet until I come alongside him. I cry out so loudly, everyone hears as I jerk and writhe on his cock and he pumps his cum inside of me. When I slump, he covers me, kissing my skin as his softening cock slips out of me, leaving me whimpering.

I almost slip into the water, but he holds me up as my legs twitch and my heart skips. "I love you, Nova."

I freeze and turn my head to meet his serious gaze. I was expecting it to be a joke, but there is nothing but sincerity in his eyes as he softly pushes the hair from my face.

"You don't have to say it back. I know you struggle with love, with trust, but this is enough for me, and even if I never get any more of you, that's okay. You hold my heart, though, all of it. I'm yours until the very end, and I'm not going anywhere. Where you go, I go. I will never betray you, never hurt you, and never leave you like everyone else, and with time, you'll believe that."

Tears fill my eyes as he voices all my fears. Leaning in, he kisses me softly.

"And one day, you will believe that I love you. I will wait for that day."

"What if it never comes?" I rasp.

"It will," he vows, his forehead pressed to mine. "Because we plan to show you every day just how worthy, important, and perfect you are so you'll finally see yourself as you are. Until then, I'll hold the shattered pieces of your heart and soul with mine."

FORTY-NINE

NOVA

After what I'm calling Hot Tub Fun, we spend the rest of the day checking our equipment and relaxing. It's strange, and we even watch a movie. We are waiting on confirmation from the military bros, as Jonas calls them, so in the meantime, we lie low.

When Dimitri suggests a BBQ, everyone seems excited. I don't help much with cooking, more moral support from the bean bag I'm reclining in with a beer. Louis and D are bent together over the grill, Jonas and Nico fight over setting the table, and Isaac sits next to me in the same double bean bag, sipping his beer and watching with a content smile.

I slip his arm over me and grin up at him as he directs that smile down at me, which only seems to grow and soften. That one look alone makes my heart skip and my voice hoarse when it comes out. "Are you okay?"

His grin turns smouldering as he starts to play with my hair and kisses my forehead so gently, so softly, my eyes close on a hard swallow. "Perfect now that you are here," he murmurs, his voice lowered to create our own little bubble.

"Good," I whisper, opening my eyes and meeting his.

Something passes between us, and breathing becomes hard. Our legs are intertwined, and our bodies are touching, and I realise I'm practically sprawled over him as lust pulses through me. Licking my lips, I watch his eyes blow with desire as he watches the movement, his teeth catching on his own.

"Nova." The way he breathes my name has me leaning up as Isaac leans down.

He meets me halfway, our lips coming together in a soft, loving kiss —one that burrows into my soul and takes root. His hand cups the back of my head as he tilts me backward so he's practically covering my body as he chases my lips. I part them for him, and he thrusts his tongue into my mouth, tangling it with mine.

What started as a soft, chaste kiss soon turns heated and wild.

I claw at his shoulders desperately, tugging him closer as he swallows my moan of pleasure. I nip his lip, and I feel him shiver against me, making me bolder. Pushing him back, I throw my leg over him and straddle his waist, all without breaking the kiss as I taste his hunger for me.

His hands grip my hips to help me before sliding down to my ass and hauling me closer, perching me on his huge, hard length. Grunting, he pulls back, his eyes blown wide with desire as he watches me.

Our hearts hammer in sync.

The others watch as they cook, and yes, we are having a nice family day, but I want to rip off my clothes and ride Isaac so I can feel him shatter below me as he keeps those loving eyes locked on me. Isaac makes me feel powerful, strong, sure, and in charge. He offers me comfort and happiness, and right now, I want that so badly, it almost hurts to stop.

So why should I?

It isn't anything they haven't seen before. Fuck the BBQ, I'm hungry for him, not the meat.

Biting his lower lip, I pull back and pop it free before sliding my hand down his chest and gripping his cock. "I'm hungry, and I can't wait," I murmur, and when he swallows, I grin, sliding down his body until my knees hit the grass. He slumps back into the bean bag, watching me with wide eyes as I tug down his joggers enough to free his cock.

I spit into my hand and slide my fist up and down his hard length, watching it jerk and leak for me as he groans.

He reaches down and tangles his hand in my hair. "Nova, you don't have to."

I blow over the tip of his cock, watching him writhe for me. "I want to," I murmur as I suck his tip into my mouth and moan. Desire hums through me, but I focus on his pleasure, knowing he never does.

"I guess she really wants his meat," Jonas jokes.

I flip him off as I roll my eyes up to Isaac's, watching him as I hollow my mouth and swallow his length. His head falls back, the veins popping in his neck as it strains. I watch his Adam's apple bob as he swallows hard, and then I feel his hand flex in my hair, tugging me closer.

God, I love this, love sucking cock and seeing the power I have over someone else. With Isaac, it's a heady feeling knowing I'm looking after the man who never lets anyone else look after him.

Only me.

Moaning, I grip his base and pull back, licking his length and tracing the veins there before sucking on the tip as his hips jerk. "Fuck, Nova!" he yells, making me grin as I pop his cock free from my mouth. The musky taste of him coats my tongue as he drips for me.

"Do you want me to stop?" I flutter my lashes innocently, but my smile is wicked.

"Oh, God, please, no!" he begs, tugging me back down.

Laughing, I go willingly and swallow his huge length all the way to the back of my throat, and then I linger there as he shakes beneath me. His thighs become taut as I pull up and then bob back down on his cock, speeding up and fucking him with my mouth. I keep my eyes on him the entire time, seeing the wild desire, love, passion, and friendship he feels for me as he watches me wordlessly.

Humming, I let him feel the vibration as I pull back and suck on his tip again.

"Oh fuck, I'm already close," he warns, his hips jerking. I swallow him all the way back, letting my throat close around him, and he cries out, thrusting his hips and widening his legs until he explodes with a yell.

Cum spurts down my throat. I swallow and pull back, letting it spill across my mouth, tongue, and lips as he watches.

"Nova." My name is a ragged cry as he reaches down and jerks his cock, spilling more cum across my tongue, and then I swallow as he slumps back, his cock wet and spent, and his face flushed and slack.

Sitting back with a smug expression, I use my finger to swipe up the mess on my lips and chin as he watches, moaning as I suck my fingers clean of his release.

"I'm full," I purr.

"Fuck, do you know how hard it is to cook with a stiff cock?" Dimitri calls, making me grin over my shoulder at him as I toss my hair back.

"I bet it's very *hard*." I pout over the word. "You should have let me help with that." His face heats as he watches me. "Or maybe you should help me." Turning, I press my back to Isaac's knees, and he reaches down and pets my hair as I watch the others. I spread my legs and drag a hand down my body.

Four sets of eyes track the movement, the food forgotten. A plate crashes from Jonas's hand as he lifts it into the air. "I volunteer."

"It's my turn to taste her cunt!" Nico snarls at him.

Louis watches it all with an arched eyebrow, but nobody notices D tossing his cooking utensils down, ripping off his shirt, and then prowling towards me. Grinning, I cup my pussy and grind into my hand through my shorts.

He drops to his knees several feet away from me and crawls forward, stopping to lick up my legs and across my shorts until his mouth covers my hand. "Fuck cooking, I'd rather eat," he whispers, rolling his eyes back up to mine, waiting for my decision.

Moving my hand, I cup his chin with it and sit up to kiss him softly. "Then lick my pussy until I come, baby," I order and sit back, letting Isaac pet my hair as I spread out between his legs. Dimitri instantly rips my shorts off, leaving me bare from the waist down.

Licking his lips, he grabs my thighs and tosses them over his shoulder.

"Fuck," Nico and Jonas say at the same time.

Louis turns off the grill, grabs a chair, and drags it to the side where he sits back with his legs spread as he watches us. Shit. My eyes close at the first touch of D's eager tongue. He laps at my cunt, tasting me as he slides his hands to my ass and lifts so he can access every inch of me.

"Fuck!" I scream as he sucks my clit before he drags his tongue down my pussy and spears it inside of me. I'm already dripping and on edge from blowing Isaac.

My head drops back to Isaac's thigh, and his thumb slides into my mouth, so I suck as Dimitri eats my cunt so good, I'm already close to coming.

His talented tongue fucks me before licking my clit in the way that drives me mad. My eyes open when he nips my clit, the wet sound of him going down on me ridiculously hot.

"Fuck, he's good at that. We should take lessons," Jonas comments, judging Nico.

"Speak for yourself." Nico grunts, smacking his back. My eyes dart to them before landing on Louis, who is smouldering, his hard cock outlined in his trousers.

Oh fuck, fuck, fuck.

My head falls back again as I grind and twist, chasing my orgasm, and when he pushes three fingers inside of me and curls them, I come all over his face with a scream. Holding him tight against my pussy, I ride out my release and then slump back, panting while Isaac pets my face and tells me how good I was, but I don't want to be a good girl.

I want to be bad.

Dimitri sits up, his face covered in my release, as he grabs his cock through his trousers and squeezes it, taking in my spread legs and my pussy that's on display.

"I want to fuck you all while you watch," I say, totally unashamed.

"You don't have to ask me twice," Jonas calls, hurrying forward.

Louis holds up his hand, and everyone freezes. "Are you sure, Nova?" His eyes hold a plethora of questions, but I simply nod. "Then we will do this my way. Nico, you have not had our Nova yet, have you?"

"No," he murmurs, watching me with unrestrained lust.

"Then you'll get her mouth. The first time you'll feel that incredible cunt will be alone. Jonas, you get her pussy, but don't make it hurt too badly because after you fill her with your cum, she'll get D's and mine."

Holy fucking shit.

Why is the thought of that so hot? Why is Louis taking charge and telling them how they are going to fuck me turning me on so much?

I don't know and I really don't care, because I get what I want—them for as long as I can have them—and so much pleasure I know nothing else will ever compare.

There are no secrets between us, and no lines we can't cross. We are all the same, a fucked-up little family, and I plan to fuck and keep every single one of them if they'll let me.

I'm flipped as Nico replaces Isaac. "Nico . . ." I swallow, knowing he doesn't need to.

"Open that pretty mouth and swallow my cock, baby," he orders, his head tilted to the side as he watches me, his eyes dark and hungry. "He's right. I get that sweet pussy when we are alone, not together, but for now, I want to fill that teasing mouth with my cum until you choke on it."

Well, fuck.

How could I resist?

Hands slide across my hips, yanking me up—Jonas.

Nico watches me as he pulls out his huge cock. My eyes widen. He's fucking massive. I knew he would be, but fuck. I don't think all of it will fit into my mouth. As if hearing my thoughts, he narrows his gaze. "You can and you will. You'll take me all the way down that pretty throat until all you can taste is me."

"Yeah, Nova, be good and suck his cock," Jonas taunts as his hand smacks my pussy, making me jerk and fall forward right onto Nico's waiting cock.

He fists my hair, and tears fill my eyes. Snarling, he presses the tip of his cock to my lips and then looks over my head, and just as I feel Jonas's tip at my pussy, I open my mouth, and both of them slam into me at the same time.

I jerk between them, the invasion too much, but they don't let me do anything except take it. Nico bottoms out in my throat, making me gag, but I dig my nails into his thighs to hold on as Jonas grips my hips painfully, pulls out, and pummels into me.

Moaning, I pant as Nico withdraws and thrusts into my mouth. Unlike Isaac, who let me take control, Nico takes what he wants, fucking my mouth as I choke and relent.

A loud slap rings out and I jerk, taking Nico deeper as Jonas's hand lands on my ass. Stinging pain comes after, and I whimper around Nico's cock as he rubs it in, my pussy clenching around him.

"Shit, Nova, I love how tight you get when I hurt you." He groans. "You should feel it, Nico. She clamps like a whore, watch." He smacks me again, the pain making me do just as he described as it explodes through my body.

"Is that right, baby?" Nico growls, his face feral as he thrusts up, taking my mouth hard and fast. "I wonder . . ." His eyes narrow further as he yanks me down, forcing me all the way to his base.

It hurts, yet I clamp around Jonas so hard, he groans. "Fuck, man, she really liked that."

I wasn't prepared for them both to work together against me, and it's so fucking hot that when Jonas spanks me again, I come so hard that Nico has to pull out of my mouth as I writhe and groan on Jonas's cock. He holds still, letting me come around him, and when I slump, he yanks my thighs back, pummelling into me as Nico thrusts into my slack mouth.

"You look so good taking their cocks," Louis comments, making my eyes widen as I simmer. "Doesn't she?"

"She does," Dimitri replies. "It would be even better if there was one in her ass too."

"Next time," Louis says.

"Look at her pretty tits practically spilling out," Isaac adds.

The fact that they are all here watching makes me push back, and I meet Jonas's feral thrusts. Hands slip across my body, one softer than the other as they slide over my skin, stroking me as I'm fucked by their brothers.

There are so many hands, the sensations are too much, and I practically squirm, but they hold me between them as they fuck me, each chasing their release. I can feel Nico's thighs quake below my fingers, and I know he's close. I want to feel it and taste him, so I lower my head all the way to his base and suck hard.

Fingers start to play with my nipples from both sides, tweaking and rolling, and I whimper, causing Nico to snarl before he comes with a roar, pumping his release down my throat. I swallow, but it spills over. Jonas growls, pummelling into my pussy before groaning, and then I feel his forehead hit my back as his hips jerk and he comes.

I slump down as Jonas pulls free, my body spent and wound up at the same time, but I don't have a moment to breathe because I'm turned.

"Sit that pretty pussy on his cock," Louis orders as I find Isaac lying back with one hand loosely stroking his cock. His length makes my mouth water as I crawl up his body, greedy for more.

Cum drips down my thighs and mouth, and yet I stop and lap at the tip of his cock, watching as his back bows.

Oh yes, this will be fun.

"Now, Nova," Louis snaps.

Giving him a pout, I slide up Isaac's body and place my hands on his chest, lining myself up with his hard cock, and then I sink down. Both of us groan as I wiggle, lift, and drop until I'm settled deep on his cock. His head lifts as he searches for my mouth, and I lean down and kiss him as I start to move.

I wind my hips, rocking and riding him as the others watch.

A hand slides up my back and to my hair, pushing down until I lie on top of Isaac, kissing him. I moan into his mouth as that same hand slides down my spine and wraps around Isaac's cock as it spears me.

Dimitri.

"You should see how good you look right now with him stretching you like this. It's almost as good as you will look with my cock in your ass." Biting Isaac's lip, I take out my desire on him as he groans and jerks below me.

A mouth slides across my ass, and a tongue slips down my crack to trace my hole, making me shiver. "I fucking love eating ass as much as I love fucking it, but that will be for later. For now, I'm going to get my cock all wet with cum so I can sink in deep and stretch you between us."

Oh shit.

I rip my mouth away, panting as I wiggle back. "Then do it," I demand breathlessly.

Louis chuckles. "You heard her, Dimitri."

"That I did." He grins against my ass and then he pulls back, taking his heat with him. I whimper, clenching around Isaac's cock. Suddenly, the thick head of Dimitri's cock is there, pushing in alongside him.

I fall forward, and arms wrap around me, holding me still. "Shh, it's going to feel so good," Isaac promises. "That's it, my good girl, take him as well. You know you can."

His praise has me wiggling, and Dimitri slips an inch deeper into my pussy. The burn is almost too much, and I let out a pathetic whimper as fingers slide down my dripping pussy and play with my clit. Desire roars back to life, quick and fast, and he sinks deeper.

Dimitri just sits there, letting me stretch around them as he circles my clit until I grind back, and then, in time with his fingers, he slides in deeper and deeper.

Finally, I feel every hard inch of him stretching my pussy to the point of pain, pressed to Isaac's cock.

Hurt and desire mingle together as he continues to flick my clit, and then they rock slowly, and, before I know it, I'm moving with them, chasing another release.

It builds inside me, and just as I'm about to topple over the edge once more, they stop. I cry out as Dimitri slides his cock free, leaving me sagging and unsatisfied.

"Good girl," Isaac praises, dotting kisses along my face as I shake frustratedly, until Dimitri's cock presses to my ass. Holding my cheeks in his hands, he pulls them open and slams into me.

The release that was fading away comes roaring back, and I shatter around them with a scream.

Dimitri turns my head and kisses me hard until I'm panting and barely able to breathe. "Fuck, your ass feels too good, Nova," he growls against my lips. "So fucking tight with him in your pussy too, and when you came, I nearly lost it."

"Fuck me," I beg.

"Oh, we are going to," Isaac promises with a wicked look, and he glances behind me before winking at me.

Dimitri keeps my head yanked up as he pulls out of my ass and slams back in. Isaac withdraws and thrusts in, and then they find a rhythm. They use me, both my ass and pussy stretched to the limits, as they hold me between them.

"You look so good right now, Nova," Jonas calls out. "Shit, I'm going to add this to my spank bank forever."

"I'm bloody hard again already," Nico grumbles.

"Good girl," Isaac praises, cupping my breasts, and Dimitri pushes me down, feeding them into his mouth. He sucks and licks my nipples until I'm gasping and writhing.

"Shit, she's close again," Dimitri growls in my ear. "I won't last if she keeps gripping me like this."

"Then don't," Louis replies. "Let her feel it, and fill her with your cum."

"You want that, Nova?" He groans long and loud in my ear. "Do you want us to make you come again as we fill every hole with our cum?"

"Fuck yes," I cry out, arching between them as Dimitri's fingers return to my oversensitive clit, the pleasure bordering on too much.

My heart hammers so fast, it scares me, and when D rubs my clit and Isaac bites my nipple, I come apart with a scream.

Dimitri hammers into my ass before stilling, his cum spilling inside of me and over my ass cheeks as he pulls out.

Moaning, Isaac fights his release, but as I keep clenching and riding the waves of pleasure, he finds his own, holding me tight as he grinds me down onto his length, and his cock jerks inside me.

I slump between them as Isaac moans my name and strokes my sweaty hair, and Dimitri rubs his cum into my ass before he moves away.

I'm limp.

Maybe even dead.

"My turn." Louis's voice startles me, and then hands are on me once more.

Louis lifts me with my back to his front, and then he slams me down on his cock. He tilts my head with his chin, nudging it to the side as he licks and nips my neck. "Look how badly they want you, Nova, and how crazy you make them." My eyes open and meet the others' gazes.

He's right; they look wild.

"Isaac, come lick this pretty pussy until she comes on me," Louis demands.

His hands shove my thighs wider as he thrusts up into me. Isaac readily drops to his knees and seals his lips over my cunt, uncaring about the fact Louis's cock is inside me.

"Good girl. Look at you, Nova. You are so goddamn beautiful and so powerful, you have us all on our knees for you," Louis croons in my ear, one hand on my throat and the other gripping my breasts as Isaac eats my pussy.

Louis leisurely fucks me like he has all the time in the world.

Nico is on his knees, watching me, and his huge cock is hard again as he licks his lips. Jonas strokes himself as he observes, and Dimitri is lying down with his gaze on me.

All of their attention is on me.

The power I feel makes me clench around Louis. "I can't come again."

"You can and you will," he retorts, biting my throat until I cry out. "You'll come all over Isaac's pretty face, and then you're going to come all over my cock."

"I can't." I shake my head as his hand tightens on my throat.

"You will," he warns dangerously, sliding his hand up until his thumb slips into my mouth. "Show me how you sucked him, baby. Show me how you sucked him so good, he couldn't help but come."

Groaning, I close my eyes as I suck his thumb, all while he keeps up his slow thrusts, driving me higher as Isaac's expert tongue circles my clit. Their touches are driving me wild, and even though I thought I couldn't, I come again, shouting around his thumb.

"Good girl," he croons as Isaac moves away with his hand on his cock.

Arching into me from behind, Louis speeds up, fighting through my clenching cunt as he growls dirty words in my ear that I can barely hear over my racing heart.

His heartbeat matches mine, echoing through my back as he takes me.

Claims me.

Fucks me.

With a snarl, he pushes me down onto all fours, grips my hips, and just hammers into me.

My head hangs down, and my body is limp in his grasp.

I am his—theirs.

He jerks, filling me with brutal thrusts before yelling out his release and dragging me along for another that makes me black out.

When I come to, I'm curled into him, my body covered in cum. My muscles are sore, but in the best way, and I have a smile on my lips.

"I think we burnt the food," I mutter as I flop back to the grass, making them all chuckle.

"Fuck the food," Louis mutters, and we laugh in shock.

Fuck the food indeed.

Even as I laugh, though, my heart skips a beat, and I know that when this mission is over, I might have to give them up. I don't know how I'll go back to life without them.

Without this.

This . . . unstoppable love.

FIFTY

NOVA

Eventually, we eat, since we were able to save some of the food, and then we all sleep in a big pile in the living room. I wake up early the next morning, grimacing at the sticky, nasty feel of my body, and I steal the first shower.

I am dressed and pouring coffee before they even start to stir, so when Louis's phone rings, I pick it up so he can rest. "Nova," I answer.

There's a moment of silence. "Put Louis on the line," a voice snaps.

Ah, the general.

"He's sleeping. What's up?" I purposely piss him off as I lean back, blowing on my coffee. Louis stumbles into the room, scrubbing at his adorable, dishevelled hair. His eyebrow rises, but he doesn't make me hand over the phone. Instead, he takes my coffee as he slips between my legs and holds me as he listens.

"Fine, tell him the location has been approved and to report his findings." He hangs up the phone.

Rude prick.

"Good morning to you too, asshole," I mutter as Louis yawns. "You hear that?" He nods, so I lean around him to see Jonas's naked ass on display as he bends and stretches, making Nico hit him with a pillow while D just watches with a chuckle.

"Get ready, boys. It's time to hit the next location," I call, and that causes them to switch to work mode.

We are ready and on the road in twenty minutes flat, heading out of Edinburgh as we make our way towards the old abandoned military base we found.

I lean back in my seat, watching the world go by as Louis drives. D and I are in his car, while Nico and Jonas are in the second vehicle with the equipment. The radio is on low as we drive farther into the middle of nowhere, but I trust them to know where they are going, so I close my eyes.

I jolt awake when we pull to a stop and sit up.

"Morning, Sleeping Beauty." Louis winks as he turns. "We are here."

Leaning forward between the seats, I frown as I survey the land below us. "Here?"

He nods. "Here."

The old base is surrounded by a new chain-link fence, so it would make sense, but the old grey buildings are mostly boarded up and falling down. The timeworn hangars and runway are empty and over-grown, and it looks deserted.

That's probably a good thing.

Sliding from the car, I stretch and twist, jumping on the spot to wake my tired muscles as the others get out and prepare. Rounding the back, I accept a bag from Nico and slip the backpack on. Next, I put in the earpiece and strap on the camera. D is going to set up in the first building we search so he can watch our backs since there are so many buildings to check, which also means that we all need to be prepared and on point.

Excitement races through my veins as I check the guns and strap them on before adding knives to my holsters. After putting my torch on my hip, I check everything once more before nodding. "Ready."

The others are equally strapped up, even D, who has his laptop in a case at his side, is holding a pistol. "Okay, so we know the plan. We take the gate after checking for alarms and tripwires. There is an inac-tive minefield to the left and right, so we need to ignore those. Once there, we take the security outpost. D, you set up and hack into any cameras if there are any left. If not, keep tabs. I will take Building L. Nico you take J, Jonas K, Isaac P, and Nova K. Keep in contact at all times. If you think you have something, call it out. We sweep and clean, boys . . . and, erm, girl. Let's do this."

"Fuck yeah." Jonas lifts his arm, and they all smash it, even me.

We don't speak after that as we carefully make our way down the hill, coming from the side so we avoid the main road and signs beyond. At the chain-link fence, D carefully cuts the padlock and slides it back. No alarms go off, and the cameras there don't move. We cut another one farther in, and then we are on the base.

We turn right, heading to the closed door of the security outpost. It's barely two rooms, and once we kick the door in, we can't all fit inside it, but the newer equipment here makes me frown. It has updated screens and monitors, and the desk is clean and tidy with a coffee cup growing mould in it. It's clearly been used recently.

"It couldn't have been too long ago," I murmur.

"No, so be careful. D, set up and let's see what we are working with. Until D lets us know, get into position." Nodding, we head out across the base. I move to the building in the back on the south side that has two floors. When I get there, it's labelled "Bunks."

I wait and scan the horizon as we let D work.

"I can't access the cameras. We are going in blind," D says.

"Got it. In three, two, one." I breach the door at the same time the others do.

The entrance is a simple hallway, with stairs on the right and doors all down the corridor. I sweep each corner, noting vending machines, a sofa, and a living area to the left. The doors all lead into bedrooms and bunks. I check every one meticulously before heading upstairs.

"Base level clear—nothing. Heading to second level," I call, keeping them updated.

"Copy, sweeping the third floor," Louis replies.

"Mine is empty, no sign of life for a long time," Nico responds.

"Same here," Jonas mutters, "apart from mouldy food and benches."

I don't reply, focusing on moving around the corner. I freeze at the top of the stairs. There are booted footprints in the dust. I follow them down the hall, stopping to check more bunks and showers. The trail leads to the very last closed door. "I might have something. Hold," I murmur, and the line goes quiet.

Grabbing the handle, I twist and shove it open, going in ready to fire.

There's a rumpled bed, a used shower, and discarded clothes and toiletries, but nobody is inside it, and it looks like it's been a while. "The room here has been used, but not recently. Maybe a week or two," I murmur. "My building is clear." I drop my weapon and head back downstairs and outside.

"Clear," Jonas calls.

"Clear," Louis says.

"Clear too," Nico and Isaac announce.

"That's the infirmary, bunks, armoury, cafeteria, and offices all clear. Maybe we were wrong?" D mutters.

"Maybe," I respond.

"There has to be something. Keep looking, D," Louis barks.

I step outside and eye the base, wondering why here.

Why? What makes this place special?

Wandering around the back of the building, I check out the view of the Highlands. The mountains are beautiful. My eyes drop to a dip in the terrain that is not easily visible until you are right on top of it. Heading towards it, I realise it's a depression covered in grit, but hidden away is a bunker with the door shut and clean.

"D, you seeing this?" I murmur into my comm.

"I am. It's not on the maps. Guys, we have a bunker. I think this is it. Meet southside. Nova, wait for us."

"Copy."

I wait even though I want to go in, but we don't know what's in there, so we need to do this together. It's the only place we have not cleared. This has to be it, but I know deep down what we will find.

More death.

It doesn't take them long to converge on me, and I move to one side of the door as Nico steps to the opposite side. The others spread out behind us, and when I nod at Nico, he rips the door open and I go in first.

"Clear," I murmur, feeling them moving behind me. I don't glance back, trusting them to protect my rear.

The bunker door leads into a small air lock with another door fifty feet in. I peer through the glass, but nothing except a darkened chamber waits on the other side. The emergency lighting is on, but it doesn't provide enough for me to see from here.

"I got it," D says as he moves to the panel and works his magic. Jonas and Isaac aim their guns out the bunker door, while Louis and Nico stand with me in case anyone is waiting on the other side of the second door.

There's a beep, and then D steps back, swinging his laptop around to pull out his gun. "Door opening in five, four, three, two, one."

It swings open, and we surge in as a line of three. I go forward, with Louis on my left and Nico on my right, as we sweep the entire room.

"Clear."

"Clear."

"Clear."

Relaxing slightly, I nod as Jonas hurries to the double door leading to a corridor beyond and takes up guard as we scan the room. It seems to be an entrance chamber, with computers, cameras, a locked metal weapons cabinet, and even labelled lockers. My eyebrows rise at that as D moves to the computers and starts to access them.

"This was on a different system, so I couldn't find it before . . . and I'm in. Okay, it seems we have power and lights. They are just all turned off for some reason. It's like it has all been powered down but the generator is fine. All the doors should work, and I can see there are some utilities still running. The cameras, however, are off. I'll stay here and try to get them back on."

"Good, do that, and turn any alarms off. I want no surprises. Who knows how big this place is? Isaac, you stay with D and guard the outer door. At the first sign of life, you lock it and call us in. I don't want to be trapped, but it's better to be safe than sorry. Nico, Jonas, and Nova, you are with me. If we come to any splits, Jonas, you are with Nova, and Nico is with me. We sweep this place. I want every

room, every fucking nook and cranny, searched. I want no surprises."
It's clear Louis doesn't like this situation, and I feel it.

An unknown bunker underground with a weapons system and separate locks in an abandoned military base? Yeah, not to mention the super creepy feeling I'm getting.

D turns the lights back on, flooding the place so brightly, I blink, and then I continue to look around warily.

This is our job, I refuse to back out, but something is telling me this place is important. They wouldn't have gone to such lengths to hide it if it wasn't, not to mention the systems are still running and someone was clearly here recently.

No, this is it.

I can feel it.

A change in our mission.

Lifting my gun once more, I stride to Louis's side. Jonas steps up behind me, and Nico takes his position at Jonas's back, ready to find out the truth.

Finally.

FIFTY-ONE

NOVA

The corridor is long, the floors under us are a spotless white, and the walls almost curve like the entryway. There are no windows, but bright lights flood the place, showing us the long, empty hallway leading to another set of closed double doors. When we reach them, I count down and open one, letting Louis and Nico sweep in before Jonas and I follow.

We communicate with looks and hand gestures, not wanting to alert anyone of our presence the farther we venture into the bunker.

The place seems to stretch, becoming wider and taller. The echoing chamber is almost the size of the base itself, and it makes me wonder if it runs under the entire structure. Probably. Maybe that's why they built the base here, to cover it.

Either way, it's too big to stay together, so we break apart. I move to the right, Jonas following me, while Nico and Louis take the left. In the middle are machines, generators maybe, and at the back, I spy a metal staircase leading up to another level above us. It's one giant room, where we can't even see the end. At first, the doors are opaque and labelled—toilets, kitchen, lounge, and bunks. It's clear they lived here or maybe even stayed here in shifts.

The doors to our right change, and I still. The wall turns into a glass, showing the labs beyond, and the farther I move, the more I see.

They are all fucking labs, which are empty, clean, and full of state-of-the-art equipment, waiting to be used.

"What the fuck?" Jonas hisses. "Do you think this is where they did all the experiments?"

"I don't know, but I don't like it," I murmur, and when I glance over, I see Louis and Nico finding the same labs on the other side.

It's like one big laboratory, and it is totally empty. There are no signs of life, not even any poor experiments like us.

Where is everyone? Were we wrong? Feeling dejected, I keep moving, speeding up with each empty lab I pass. Jonas doesn't protest, even though I know I'm being reckless. When I reach the stairs, I hurry up them, needing to see. A sharp command from Louis rings through the comm, but I ignore it.

There are more labs on this level, but they are bigger, with two on each side, taking up the entire place. The first two I pass are empty, with metal tables with bindings left forgotten and undone. I move across the metal walkway to the other side, finding the other labs unoccupied.

Dropping my gun, I lean over the edge to look down. "Clear. It's all fucking empty. Maybe they knew we were coming again?" I call.

"Maybe," Louis replies, looking around suspiciously. "Keep searching. Check everything. I want no surprises."

I nod, and after checking the labs up here, Jonas and I return to the ones downstairs, each going into one alone.

There aren't many places to hide, and even though I feel my ghosts rearing their heads at the stale air, the bright lights, and reminders of what I went through, I keep moving. Otherwise, I'll break down.

We need to find the research and destroy it, but how can we when this man seems to know our every move? When he is prepared and already gone?

Dad was right, he's dangerous, but we are fucking deadly, and we will end this. I have to believe that or we are fighting for nothing.

We search lab after lab, each one only making me more furious. It's clear they have been used. Was my father here? If so, then why couldn't he just give me a fucking list of places to destroy if he really wanted to make this right?

Is this all one big game?

I'm tired of fucking playing.

I want to win.

Past the labs, I check the kitchen, finding half-eaten food and water on the table and counters. A door clicks behind me, and I swing around with inhuman speed, my gun raised.

There, with one hand on the door and the other gripping a bloody knife, is a man.

He's dressed in army fatigues and coated in blood and sweat. His short blond hair is sweaty and stuck to his head, and his face is pale. His eyes are wide, but with pain, not fear, and something else.

Shock, I realise.

He's tall, taller than even me, and built like a Mack truck.

It's clear he's military from the way he moves and the clipped bark that comes. "Who are you?" he demands, his voice thick with a Scottish accent.

"I should be asking you that," I respond calmly, still looking at him down my gun.

I could call out, but he could attack faster. I can take him, and he's obviously injured and weak. Who knows how long he's been here? He could be half crazy, but I'm faster and stronger, so I drop the gun and arch an eyebrow.

"I'm here to find out what the fuck they were doing here," I say, telling him the truth.

Laughing, he drops the knife with a groan and slides down the wall with an audible thump. His legs are oddly bent, like he can't move them anymore. It's then I spot the first-aid kid to the side, used and covered in blood.

"Then you found it . . ." He gestures at himself and then promptly passes out.

Shit!

"Guys!" I yell as I rush to his side. I press my fingers to his clammy skin, focusing on the steady thump of his pulse. Pushing up his shirt, I search his chest, finding multiple wounds and even a surgery site. It's clear he tried to close them and fix himself.

I sit back and eye him.

Is he an experiment?

Are the fatigues even his?

The door bursts open, and Jonas instantly aims his gun at the man. "Don't," I command sharply as Louis storms in. I look up at him. "Get Isaac, he's dying."

"Shit," Louis calls out and then comes closer. "Are you okay?" he asks me as he regards the man carefully.

I nod, looking back at him. "I think he's like us. I think he's an experiment, and they left him to die."

We wait nervously while Isaac works on the man. Louis helped carry him to the closest lab, and once there, they stripped him and quickly started working on putting the soldier back together again. He has so many incisions, and he had sewn himself so badly, Isaac actually swears. He spends hours putting in drips, fluids, and sedatives before cutting and sewing him. Isaac cleans his wounds and dresses them before checking him over.

We wait the whole time, and when Isaac comes out, exhausted and coated in blood, I straighten. "Well?"

"He'll live, but barely. I have no idea how he survived what he did. He has been tortured and experimented on, and the bastards must have left him cut open. He tried to close the wound. He's dehydrated, in shock, and his body is shutting down. If we didn't find him when we did, he would have been dead."

"Did he say anything to you?" Louis asks me.

"Only that we found what we were looking for," I murmur, my gaze on the deathly still man. He looks massive on the table, and I turn to Isaac. "You find anything?"

"Dog tags and a tattoo. He's military alright. Since when do they experiment on active soldiers?" he snarls.

"I don't know, but we need to find out. I want someone on him at all times in case he wakes and attacks. I also want Isaac here too. The rest of us will gather everything and start to figure out what the fuck happened here," Louis orders.

"I'll stay." I nod when Louis arches an eyebrow. "I'll be fine."

He pulls me in and kisses me quickly before barking orders, and the others hurry to their tasks. Isaac sighs, and I melt into his side for a moment.

"What did they do to him?" I ask softly.

"What didn't they do? I don't even know how he's alive. He's one tough son of a bitch, that's for sure. I hope he survives. I really do."

"Me too," I murmur, squeezing his hand as he goes back in to keep an eye on his patient while I take up guard in the corner of the room, but I don't think he's a threat.

Not from the anger I saw in his eyes when he fell.

He's just as much of a victim as us, and he hates it.

FIFTY-TWO

NOVA

"Do you think he'll wake up?" Annie asks through the phone, worrying her lip and even in the tiny screen I can sense her anxiety.

I'm sitting on an uncomfortable chair with my legs thrown over the side, the unconscious soldier still sleeping soundly despite Isaac stopping the sedative hours ago. We decided to stay until he wakes, and then we will be able to move him without hurting him. It means we are all on high alert, sleeping and patrolling in shifts. I refuse to leave the soldier's side, though, knowing he'll need a familiar face when he wakes up.

I glance back at his sleeping form and sigh. "I'm not sure. He is clearly strong if he survived what they have done to him."

"Poor man." Annie frowns with tears in her eyes. "What are you going to do with him if he wakes?"

"I don't know," I admit honestly. "He will need to be debriefed, but he's not good to us like this. He needs to heal somewhere safe, where they can't get to him."

She nods, her eyes hardening as she straightens in bed. I see her laptop and work spread out around her, and there are circles under her eyes. I'm worried, but she ignored my question about her resting. "You should bring him here. I can look after him. After all, it's my specialty. I can help him heal and work through his PTSD."

"Annie." I sigh. "It's dangerous. They will look for him—"

"Then they will have to go through me," she snaps before scrubbing at her face. "I need to help."

"You are," I murmur.

"More than this. I can do this, Nova. It's who I am. I heal. Let me heal him. Our father did this to that poor man, so his daughter should save him. You can't, since you need to be out there stopping this, but I can, and this will be the last place they'll look."

I follow her logic and sigh. "I'll propose it to the others, but no promises. The military will probably want him back."

She scoffs then, her eyes flashing with fire. "And you know what they will do. He will go missing." Her blonde hair flips as she glares at me. "Over my dead body."

"When you're mad, we are awfully similar." I grin, and she barks out a laugh.

"God, I hope so." We share a grin as I look her over.

"How are you really, Annie?"

"I should be asking you that." She arches an eyebrow at me. "Though in all honesty, despite the anger you are clearly feeling, you look . . . good, healthy, and happy." There's clearly a question in her words, and I look out of the glass door but see none of the others.

"I am," I hedge.

"Tell me!" she gushes, flipping onto her stomach, and I can't help but grin.

Is this girl talk? Sharing stories about boys with my sister?

I can't help the twinge of happiness that goes through me despite the situation.

"Come on, spill the dirt, which guy is it? They are all very attractive, if not terrifying." That makes me laugh, and I lower my voice.

"All."

"All?" Her eyes widen before she laughs, smacking the bedding. "Fuck yes." She pops her hand over her mouth at the curse before grinning. "You never did anything by halves."

"I guess not." I grin.

Her cheeks redden as she looks at me. "All of them . . . together?"

"Sometimes." I wink as she blushes. "But it's more than that, Annie. They fill something inside me I didn't know I needed. I was so lonely and so scared all the time, always on the move, and they . . ."

"Fill that," she murmurs knowingly.

I nod. "They make me happy. They make me laugh. They make me forget about my past, even for a moment, and they happily use my skills and support me. They hold me through my nightmares and fight at my side. I've never felt something like this before, never mind for more than one person. It can't work, surely."

"Who said so?" she snaps. "People have multiple wives or partners. Do whatever the fuck makes you happy, Nova. God knows you deserve it."

"I—" I look away, and she calls my name. When I look back, she wears a determined expression.

"Do they make you happy?" she demands.

"Yes," I reply without hesitation.

"Do you love them?" she asks.

"Yes." I shock myself with that answer, and she grins.

"Then that's all that matters. Fuck what anyone else thinks. You all need each other. I saw that when I met them. They need you, and you need them. Together, you're just . . . stronger. Stop fighting that and accept it. Some love is just meant to be unconventional, and you might have been brought together by a common cause and traumas, but it will be love that keeps you together. You'll have to fight for it, but you've always been good at that."

"When did you get so wise?" I croak.

"I always was." She winks.

I lick my lips. "What if they don't love me back? What if they leave?"

"You cannot control how others feel or what might happen in the future, only what happens now. Are you going to let your fears and doubts stop you from finding happiness, even if it will possibly end in the future?" I shake my head, and she nods. "Good, then stop doubting yourself and getting in your own way. You're brave, Nova, so be so now. Plus, I saw those men. They are head over heels in love with you. You're never getting away, so stop worrying and just enjoy it, and let your little sister live vicariously through you."

I laugh at that. "I have missed you so much."

Her eyes soften once more. "I missed you too. Now get back to your hunks and keep my patient alive. I'll speak to you soon, sis."

"Bye." I hang up, my eyes going back to the patient. She's right. She's the best place for him.

And my best place is here, with my men.

It's time I stop running so hard and embrace this. It might be forever, but even if it's not, it's going to be one hell of a good time while it lasts.

FIFTY-THREE

NICO

I don't let her know I listened to her conversation with her sister.

I stop in the kitchen with a frown marring my face. Louis is there, making food for everyone, and Jonas is sprawled out, snoring, or pretending to. Isaac is asleep, and D is working.

Louis freezes when he sees my expression. "What?" Jonas is instantly up, but I wave away his concern as I debate if I should keep it to myself or not.

She loves us.

How could she ever doubt that we would feel any different?

Have we not shown her? We need to every day.

From the moment I laid eyes on Nova, I knew she was ours. I knew she would be my everything, but I never could have imagined the depths of my feelings. I can barely breathe without her in my sight, and every smile and look she shoots my way steals another piece of my soul.

"Nothing. I overheard Nova talking to her sister."

"Good, they should heal their relationship." He stares at me though. "What is it?"

"I . . . Do you love her?" I ask, needing to know. I will protect her, even from my family.

"Nico," he snaps. "What is it?"

"Do you love her?" I question more forcefully, staring him down. He searches my face with a perplexed expression before sighing.

"Well, I was hoping the first time I said it, it would be to her, but yes, I love her, as do you."

"Me too!" Jonas adds helpfully.

"You are in this forever and not just for now?" I press.

He carefully puts his spoon down and meets me head-on. "When do I ever do anything halfway? I am all in with her. We all are. I tried to resist to keep us safe, but we both know that didn't work. She's mine, and I'm hers. Now tell me."

"She loves us," I croak, and I hear the disbelief in my voice.

"Of course she does. We are amazing and have great dicks," Jonas says.

"How can she love us?" I whisper, and Louis sighs as he squeezes my arm.

"Because we are worthy of it—*you* are worthy of it, and if you let her, Nico, she will prove that to you. But how do you feel about it?" There's our leader, always trying to protect us.

"Like I've won every fucking lottery in the world," I growl. "Like I don't deserve it, but I'm going to take it anyway and hoard it, never letting her go."

He grins then, a wicked one. "Then I guess we better keep our girl happy." Turning, he bowls her some soup and hands it over with a spoon and a water. "Let's start with this. She gets grumpy when she is hungry." I nod and take it, still humbled as I head back to her.

How could I do anything else? I need to be at her side at all times.

"Oh, and Nico? Don't let her know you listened in. Respect her privacy. She will tell us when she's ready. I do believe our Nova is more stubborn than us," Louis calls.

Jonas waves me on, and when I head back to her, I quicken my steps.

I need to tell her or, better yet, show her, so she never doubts us again and she stays with us forever.

I know she's not used to a family, but she needs to get accustomed to it quickly because we won't let her go, even if she wants us to. We won't chain her like her father, but we will follow her anywhere.

"Hey," she says softly as I enter, her eyes sparkling. Her hair is tied up in a bun, and she's looking way too fucking beautiful. For a moment, I freeze and just stare, feeling unworthy and far too scarred for her, but then she pulls a chair over for me and pats it. I sit beside her and hand over the food.

She arches a brow but takes it. "Thanks." She starts to eat as I nod. Nova watches me, probably realising something is wrong.

Think, Nico. Speak before she finds it weird.

I have nothing.

All I need to do is prove I love her.

The way to do that is to lay myself bare so she knows every part of me, even the parts the others don't.

"I hate tight spaces," I blurt, and her spoon pauses before she swallows.

"I know," Nova says, and I stiffen. "I notice things."

I look away for a moment, but her soft hand lands on my thigh encouragingly. Her touch is so soft and warm, it thaws my bitter, cold soul. "He used to lock me in them, and they were so small, I could barely breathe, couldn't move, in the dark."

"Nico." She puts her food down and before I know it, she's on my lap, cupping my face. I press my forehead to hers. "You don't have to tell me. We all have our issues from what they did, but all that matters is the future."

"I know, but I want you to know all of me," I admit softly. "Not just who I am now."

She kisses me, and when she pulls back, I grip her hips, tugging her close to give me strength as she straddles me.

"I hate the dark."

She shrugs. "I hate labs."

"I'm terrified of tight spaces and being locked away and forgotten."

"I'm terrified of needles," she admits.

Her confessions give me strength. "My favourite colour is black." I grin, and she laughs.

"Mine is red. How boring are we?"

Smiling, I stroke her back. "I'm still scared of your father, even though I'm an adult now."

"So am I, and he's dead," she replies, as if daring for me to keep going and try to tell her something that will change her feelings.

After all, isn't that what I'm doing? I'm admitting shit because I'm scared that once she finds out about it, she will stop loving me.

"I love cupcakes even though they are usually cute and frilly. I hate scary movies and I listen to Taylor Swift more often than I should admit to," I blurt.

"I love Taylor Swift; only psychopaths don't." She giggles, running her lips over mine. "Cupcakes are incredible, we can get them together, and I love scary movies so you can hide behind me."

"I'm scared I will never be enough for you."

She gasps, her nails digging into my cheeks as she brings my gaze back to hers. "Do not ever fucking say that again."

"I am," I whisper brokenly. "I'm scared I'm too fucked up for you to ever truly love me. That one day you'll realise it and leave."

"I will never leave," she snarls. Her eyes flash with that fire that gets me hard. "They would have to drag my dead body from you. I am here forever, Nico, and nothing you could ever tell me would change that. Fuck, you could tell me you dress up as a unicorn for fun or that you like plain vanilla ice cream and it wouldn't change how I feel. We are all fucked up, Nico, but that's why we work so well together."

"But what if you change your mind?" I ask, laying my fears bare. My fingers tighten at the idea of her trying to run. "I don't think I could let you go, even if you wanted me to."

"Good, don't, not ever," she purrs, licking my lips until I part them for her, and then she bites down on my lip until I shiver in pleasure. "Stop doubting yourself, Nico. I don't, and neither do the others. We will figure this out together, but I'm all in. We are in this together, and I'll remind you whenever you need me to."

Swallowing, I search her gaze before my hand grips the back of her head, spanning most of it since my hands are so big, and I slam my lips onto hers. I swallow her moan as she presses her hot chest against mine. My other hand kneads her ass and rocks her against my hard cock as I tangle my tongue with hers, showing her everything I wish I could say.

Telling her I love her too.

There is a groan behind us, and we pull apart, both leaping to our feet as we hurry to the soldier's bedside. His eyelids are fluttering, and I quickly move to the door and call for the others.

"Where am I?" he rasps.

"You're safe, hold on."

"Not safe, coming. They are coming." He gasps and begins to struggle.

"Who's coming?" Nova snaps as Isaac slides into the room.

"The ones . . . The ones who did this to us," the soldier grits out before passing out.

"He's out cold," Isaac observes. "Should have been for hours—"

We look at Louis then. "We have to trust his word, even if it's wrong. Doc, get him ready. We are moving out and moving out now."

FIFTY-FOUR

ISAAC

I keep him stable as we load him into the plane, and after a few hours, we land near the mansion again and transport him there. When we arrive, Ana is ready, and the lab has been changed into a medical room. She helps me hook him up as I explain what he needs.

She's clearly smart and capable, and I finally trudge upstairs, trusting her to care for him. Stripping, I jump into the shower.

The plane is going back for Louis and Nico, who stayed to pack our stuff, but we had to move fast just in case what he said was true. D did set up some cameras so we could keep watch, but so far nothing has happened, so I take the time to wash.

I watch blood swirl down the drain as exhaustion tugs at me. This week started out so well. I was happy and in love, surrounded by my family and my girl, and now I wash off the blood of an almost dead soldier who has been experimented on.

I know that the feeling of being lost and so far behind the man who is responsible for all of this is weighing on all of us.

I feel like a failure for not figuring it out and keeping the man downstairs safe.

For not being able to protect my family.

Like my misery calls to her, Nova wraps her arms around me from behind, her wet, naked, hot body pressing against me. I shiver and tears fall from my closed eyes.

"Are you okay?"

"No," I admit, my voice choked. "Not at all."

Turning me, she pulls my head to her chest, but I drop to my knees and press my forehead to her stomach. She strokes my hair and back as she whispers comforting words before falling to her knees and wiping my tears away. "You did everything you could."

"Did I?" I whisper, searching her gaze.

I feel raw and weak.

"I feel like I failed everyone. We keep fighting, but is it enough? People are suffering, and I can't save them."

"You cannot save everyone," she retorts, making me still. "We save who we can, but I will not let you lose or destroy yourself to selflessly save the world."

"But—"

"No, you are used to looking after everyone else, but I will look after you, Isaac. I will take care of you when you won't. You did everything you could, and that's what we will continue to do, but not at the expense of your happiness and soul. So tell me now, and we will stop and turn our backs."

"We can't—"

"We can if that's what saves you and what keeps you with us," she argues, her eyes gleaming like she would fight the fires of hell for me.

I think she would, this damaged, scarred warrior. I think she would fight everything to protect us.

"I love you," I admit without shame.

"I know." She grins. "I love you too, and that is exactly why I won't let you self-destruct."

Pulling me close, she holds me as I break, and then she washes me before drying my body and helping me into some clean clothes. Nova sits me on the closed lid of the toilet as she brushes my hair, and the entire time, I keep my head pressed to her stomach, listening to her thumping heart.

I rebuild myself while she takes care of me, and I have to admit, it's nice to have someone looking after me. When she tilts my head up and kisses me, looking me over and nodding, my heart swells.

"Perfect," she declares.

I lose that last little part of me to her, to my Nova, my protector.

My love.

"You decide your future, Isaac, and wherever it is, your family will follow. We can't do this without you."

I know she's right and the others look to me. I might not be the strongest or even the fastest, but I'm the healer, their confidant, and friend.

"I-I need to see this through. We do. I just had a moment of weakness."

"We all do," she murmurs softly as she strokes my face lovingly. "But you will never have to go through them alone."

I smile then, pulling her close and kissing her until there is a knock at the door. "Plane's here." That is all that's said, the voice knowing, and I wonder if he heard it all. D is good at that.

"The plane is here," she whispers. "We have to keep going so we can end this. That's how we save him and all the others. Are you with me?" She holds out her hand and without hesitation, I lay my hand in hers.

"Always."

FIFTY-FIVE

JONAS

"So where to?" I ask as I kick my feet up onto Nico's lap and press my head to Nova's. She grins down at me, stroking my hair as her eyes refocus on Louis as the plane door shuts.

"We have one more location, somewhere Ana was able to decrypt from the doctor's message—Greenland. We are going to Greenland."

"Never been." I look up at my girl then, watching her eyes flitter over all of us before landing back on me. They seem to soften, and a grin tugs at her lips that mirrors my own and makes my cock hard. "Have you, baby?"

"Nope. I guess there's a first time for everything."

"I guess." I snuggle closer when Nico groans and pushes my feet off.

"Dude, your boner is near me!"

Nova giggles as I wink at Nico.

"Wouldn't be the first time. You remember when—" Nova covers my lips with a laugh, and Nico's lips twitch. Louis shakes his head with a roguish smile, D laughs, even Isaac grins as he kisses Nova's cheek as he passes.

Her eyes track him for a moment before she looks at Louis. "Then let's hope we find something. I think we all could do with that."

"Yep. Get your rest because we'll hit the ground running."

After a few hours of annoying the others, I flop onto the bed in the back, huffing. I've always hated being bored, so when Nova sneaks in with a wicked grin, I sit up. My cock is already hard as I reach for her.

"I'm bored," she whispers, since the others are sleeping.

"Me too. Want to play?" I tease, making her laugh as she bounces on the bed. I quickly grab her and pin her beneath me. Her eyes sparkle as she grips my hair and pulls me down for a hard kiss, stealing everything, including my soul.

"Jonas," she murmurs as I slide down her body.

Sitting up slightly, she tugs off her top and bra, making my mouth water as I stare at her breasts before wagging my finger at her. "Behave," I warn as I slip off her jeans and thong, sliding them down her thick thighs. My cock twitches at the sight of her laid out below me, naked and beautiful.

She is a work of art, all tatted skin, long lush hair, and sexy muscles, and she watches me hungrily. She parts her legs for me, knowing exactly what she wants and not shy to ask for it.

"Well, are you going to make me come or just stare?" she taunts, her lush lips curved up in a mocking smile that makes me want to go to war for her.

I'm utterly obsessed with everything that is Nova, but when she gives me that look, I feel like I could take on a million armies just to crawl between her thighs and toss them over my shoulders.

With my eyes on her, I seal my mouth to her cunt and suck. The force makes her back bow, and her hands tangle in my hair and tug. Her moans bounce off the walls as I finally release her and lap at her clit as she pants.

Her flavour makes me snarl in hunger, so I slide lower and thrust my tongue into her, searching for more of her addictive taste. Her legs tighten as I attack her pussy, switching between thrusting my tongue inside and lapping at her clit. It leaves her unbalanced and before long, she cries out, coming so prettily on my tongue.

I lick her clean, wanting another taste, but she drags me up. Grumbling, I stop to lick, bite, and suck her nipples before kissing her, letting her taste her cum as she whimpers below me.

I pull back. "I fucking adore you."

"Back at you." She grins, rolling her body against me until my cock can't be ignored anymore. I need her.

It's almost loving, something I'm not used to. It feels right when I flip her. She arches, wiggling her sexy body against mine as she pushes her round ass into me, urging me on. Gripping her hair, I push her head down with a snarl and drag my cock along her dripping pussy.

"Jonas," she begs.

"That's it, baby, call my name for them all to hear," I demand, leaning down to bite her perky ass. She groans, and I grin as I lean back, seeing my teeth imprint there. I press my thumb to the bite mark and she jerks. "I might get this tattooed. Now scream, Nova."

"Make me," she demands, pushing back.

"Oh, I plan to." I fist her hair with one hand and grip her hip with the other, then I slam my cock inside that taunting wet heat. Both of us moan at the sensation. The feel of her tight, wet cunt gripping me makes me wild. I hammer into her, taking her roughly now. I need to hear her screams, and I love the sight of her clenching the bedding as her beautiful body pushes back to take me.

It's always so perfect between us, the mix of pain and pleasure making us crazed. "That's it, beautiful," I purr. "Fuck, look at how sexy you are, split open around my cock."

Grabbing my phone, I live stream it to the others, hearing them beyond the door as they get the video. Moaning indecently, she swallows my cock with her tight pussy, arching back as I fuck her.

I slide my cock out to the very tip and then drive in so hard, she finally screams. Her body contorts around me as her cunt milks me with her orgasm, and I still fuck her, watching as she squirts around my cock and stains the bedding.

"Fuck, just like that. Again. Squirt," I demand, driving in harder and dropping the phone to rub her clit. I release her hair and slide my hand down her back to press my thumb into her asshole. I fight off my release, feeling it building. Lightening sparks down my spine, and my balls tighten.

Fuck, she feels too good.

Fighting to get her to come again, I make the mistake of giving her everything, and when she screams once more, squirting around my cock, I yell my own release as it takes me by surprise. She groans, and when the pleasure releases me, I slump into her.

"Made you scream," I croak.

"So did I." She smirks as she rolls onto her back, her delicious tits swaying with the movement.

Leaning down, I lick her juices from the bed. She laughs and tugs me up and into her arms.

Our sweaty bodies press together, and we hold each other with lazy satisfaction and love. I don't let her go back to the others, even though I feel time passing, and I keep her with me until I can't anymore.

"Come on, assholes, we are landing soon. Time to get to work."

"Oh, asshole? Next time, I get yours." I wink, making her laugh.

NOVA

We land on an airfield in the middle of nowhere and disembark. We have to rent some off-road vehicles to get to the location, and it's over a day's drive. We continue into the night, switching drivers until Louis calls it and we hunker down.

The next morning, I'm stretching my legs when my phone buzzes in my pocket. I move away from the cabin we rented for the night and sit in the grass, and then I answer the FaceTime. Ana is in the lab, and she smiles softly at me when she sees me. She still looks tired though.

"I'm glad you got there safely," she greets.

"How's our patient?" I ask.

"See for yourself?" Grinning, she tilts the camera, and I see the soldier sitting up. He waves at me with a wink.

"I wanted to thank you for saving me," he begins. He glances at Ana. "Both of you." His eyes seem to soften and almost heat when he looks at my sister, and my eyebrows rise. "I never told you my name before I passed out. It's Sam, Sam Danes. I was a soldier before I was recruited to be part of a clinical trial. We were never told what it was for, and by the time we were in, it was too late. Most of my unit died from what they did to us. Only I survived, and just barely." Ana moves closer, and he offers me a stern look. "I know you are going after them. Make them stop. Make them pay."

"That's the plan." I nod. "Ana, look after our patient. Sam, look after Ana and make sure she sleeps."

"I will." He grins, and Annie ducks her head with a blush.

"Let us know when you find anything. We will be here," Annie says.

"Of course. I'll let you get back to it." I snigger. "Bye, love you."

Her eyes widen as they fill with tears. The words had been an instantaneous reaction, but I don't regret them. "I love you too, Nova. Be careful."

Dropping the phone, I see the others loading up the trucks, so I head over to help them.

I am ready to get back on the road and to this next location, hoping it holds something since they never went to the location in Scotland like Sam thought. It seems we have to hunt them ourselves, and that's just what we will do.

It's time to end this once and for all.

FIFTY-SIX

DMITRI

"You have got to be kidding me?" I groan as I sit at the side of the road, scanning the maps on my laptop. "It seems we have gone past it. The bloody roads all look the same here."

Louis sighs when he peers over my shoulder. "They want it hidden. It's a good sign at least." I nod as I stretch and accept the water Isaac hands over. Nova is stretched out on the truck's roof, sunbathing, with Jonas next to her, and for a moment, my eyes linger on her.

Like she feels my gaze, she lifts her head and gives me a wink. "You find it yet, babe?"

"I think so." I know I'm blushing, especially when she does an incredible roll and flips off the truck to land on her feet before she heads my way and kisses me softly.

"That's my boy," she purrs and looks at Louis. "Well, let's go then. What are we waiting for?"

Once we're back in the trucks, I keep a careful watch on the satellite phone and navigate us through winding hills and topography. Louis is right; they want this hidden and hidden well.

Is that a good sign or a bad one?

LOUIS

"There's life," I murmur, watching through the sniper rifle's scope.

Our earpieces are in, and D is back at the trucks, trying to access their systems. Nova is with Nico on the other side of the hills, hidden behind foliage, Isaac is protecting D, and Jonas is with me.

The location is right in the middle of mountains, completely hiding it from view. We had to hike to get here, and I wanted as many angles as possible. Passing the scope to Jonas, I grab my camera and shoot as many pictures as I can, needing them to come up with a plan. I know Nova will be doing the same.

But there's life.

I see planes on a runway, bunkers with doors open, and buildings with soldiers and scientists streaming in and out.

We've finally done it. We've finally found their main location.

This is our chance.

"Okay, let's regroup at the trucks to make a plan. We'll observe tonight, and then tomorrow, we'll attack."

I leave Jonas to keep watch as I climb back down and meet at the trucks. An hour later, Nova appears, leaving Nico in position as well, just in case.

We all look through the pictures. It's a fortress, that's for sure, with electrified fences and gates. Soldiers guard the perimeter in shifts, and cameras are placed strategically around the area . . . and that's only the stuff we can see.

It doesn't matter, though, because we need to get in there and find the truth, destroy the research, and end this.

"Okay, we switch at five. Get some rest. I want to know everything about that place before we go in."

"We go in tomorrow, right? I think under darkness would be better. They would be less likely to see us," Nova murmurs.

"Maybe. Give me a few hours, and I'll have a plan."

"Yes, boss." She winks. "Then I guess I'll get some sleep."

My eyes wander to her ass as she climbs into the back of the truck before I turn away. I need to concentrate despite the fact that I want to curl up behind her and hold her close, because I know one thing—we aren't coming out of there unscathed.

FIFTY-SEVEN

NOVA

I switch out with Jonas and watch the base for most of the night. The moon is shining down on it, and no matter how much I try, I see no weakness.

It's impregnable, but if anyone can do it, it's us.

We just have to get in. I'm almost frothing at the mouth to.

When Isaac comes to relieve me, I head back down to hear the plan, eating the canned food we pass around as Louis stares down at a map D made from the pictures. His eyebrows are deep slashes, and there are bags under his eyes. He clearly hasn't slept, and I have no doubt that the same thing we are all thinking is keeping him up.

How are we going to get out of there after?

And if we do, will we all be in one piece?

It's Louis's job to keep us safe, or so he thinks, but it's time I showed him he doesn't have to.

"Talk through it out loud," I call.

Louis's head jerks up, and he looks around at us and then back at the map. Scrunching his face, he sits back heavily, his shoulders rounded with his responsibilities. I need him to smile, so I head over and sit on the ground between his thighs, feeling him soften. When his voice comes, though, it's hard.

"We could disarm the alarms, if possible, and cut a hole in the fence, but it might be too noisy. We could try to talk our way in, or we could bust our way in. They all have cons and are too risky. I don't like the odds."

"You never do," D says softly.

Looking up at him, I mull over his words. "There's one more option."

"What's that?" he asks, looking down at me hopefully, almost begging for another way to do this.

"I think we can draw the soldiers out, set a fire or something and trigger the alarm system that lines the mountain side. When they come, we can knock them out, steal their uniforms and vehicles, and drive ourselves back in, Trojan horse style."

For a moment, he just stares at me, calculating the odds, and then his mouth drops open. "Fucking hell, that just might work." He yanks me up and slams his lips onto mine. Blinking, I meet his smouldering gaze. "You are too fucking clever, baby. When we finish this, I'll remind you of that with my tongue in your cunt."

"Erm, can I join?" D asks, making us laugh and break apart breathlessly.

"So that's what we'll do," he murmurs. "It just might work. Okay, D—"

And so the plan forms.

There are still downsides and things that could go wrong, but we have to try.

None of us can live without succeeding.

We wait for nightfall to make our move.

Everything is set, and everyone knows their positions. I wave up at D, who's watching our backs with a sniper rifle. Nico and Jonas are on branches above the position we chose, waiting to pounce, and I'm crouched behind a rock. Isaac is farther down to alert us of their approach, and Louis is ready to light it up.

We all know what's at stake. Nothing can go wrong, and when Louis's call comes, I tense, ready for this. I'm dressed casually, so it will be easy to strip off and get into their uniforms. My gun lies across my lap, and I have a knife at my hip. I don't need much more since I am a weapon.

The fire is small and contained, but it will draw their gazes since this area is abandoned, and ten minutes later, Isaac's signal comes. Two minutes after that, I feel the thrum of their engines, and the next minute, I hear the rumbling of a truck. They have to stop at the edge of the trees just beyond like we planned. We didn't want them running or ramming us, after all.

A few minutes of silence pass, and I remain motionless. I am like a statue, and unless you were looking for us with our exact location, you would never see any of us. I see them creeping through the trees in formation—ten of them, and they aren't messing around at all. Their guns are up, the torches on top sweeping the area.

We wait.

And wait.

Five of them step towards the fire to investigate, while the others break off and head into the trees just like we wanted. I turn away, letting Nico and Jonas handle those near the fire, and then I pick through the bush and sneak up on a male. Pressing my back to a tree, I barely breathe, and when he passes, I step out behind him and break his neck before he can turn. Catching his body, I lower it gently to the ground, switch off the light, and move back into the darkness as another approaches.

"Simons," the person hisses, straining to see right until they stumble over the body and fall. I pull my knife, and I'm on them in an instant, slashing his throat then covering his mouth. I watch his eyes drain of life before clicking off his light too.

I don't see any others, but I do look over in time to see Jonas and Nico drop down from the trees, right on their prey. Jonas simply rips through his two, blood going everywhere. Nico knocks one out, and he snaps the other's neck.

I let out a whistle to let them know I'm clear, and the others respond, so I stand and drag the bodies into the clearing. Louis comes out with two more, and D strolls in with his sniper rifle slung over his shoulder and puts out the fire as Isaac emerges from the dark.

We silently strip the men and finish off the ones that are still alive, tossing them into a ditch we found and covering them so they aren't discovered right away. We check their weapons and then we change, having to pick the uniforms without any blood. The trousers are too big for me, so I have to roll them up, but the shirt is loose enough not to show my breasts, and with the jacket I slip on, I look like a slim man. I tie my hair up and stuff it under a cap, then I pull the cap down, shielding my face. I stand to see the others are also ready in their fatigues. Louis has a radio, and he checks the scene before grinning at us.

"Good job, team. Now let's waltz into the enemy's lair."

The truck is easy to find, with the doors open and lights on. There's one man still in there, shifting nervously, and D slips in behind him and slides a rope around his neck. Within moments, he's dead, his body tossed aside as we climb in. I huddle in the middle seat, concealing myself, while Nico drives, grumbling at how tight the pants are. Louis sits in the front seat next to him.

Jonas leans into me. "You look hot in cargo."

"So do you." I grin, gripping his hard cock. "But lose the hard-on. They might find that odd."

"Then don't look at me, touch me, breathe . . . or even exist." He chuckles, and the others laugh as I huff.

D snickers at my side. "I second that."

"Third," Isaac adds.

"Fourth." Nico winks back at me.

"Fifth," Louis says.

I cross my arms and slump down. "I'm dressed like a dude, and it's doing it for you?"

"You could be in a bin sack covered in shit, and I would still want to fuck you," Nico replies, making my mouth drop open.

"True." Jonas chuckles.

"You are all insane. Madmen, I tell you."

"I guess that makes you our madwoman," D purrs in my ear, sliding his hand up my inner thigh as we drive through the trees.

"Behave, all of you." I smack his hand away, but he just puts it back, and a smacking contest begins when Jonas joins in.

"Children." Louis laughs. "The gate is coming up, behave."

"Yeah, behave." I stick out my tongue, and D leans forward and bites it, making me moan.

When he releases it, he licks my lips. "I will when you do."

They settle as we approach the gate, the lights shining into the forest. "Showtime, boys."

"If it all goes wrong, we'll just shoot them," Jonas adds helpfully. "God, I hope it goes wrong."

Yep, insane, the lot of them, and I might just be the worst because I agree as I tug my gun out.

FIFTY-EIGHT

NOVA

W hen we pull up to the gate, we slow down and try to look as relaxed as possible, even though we are all stiff with tension. A bored-looking guard heads over, shining his torch in the truck, but he doesn't seem to recognise us or care. "What was it?"

"Some brush caught fire, but we put it out. Nothing to worry about," Louis murmurs.

"Okay, head back. It's time to switch shifts anyway." The guard barely contains his yawn as he waves us in and the gate buzzes. He either didn't care or was dumb or both, but it works in our favour.

Having studied the layout of the base, Louis drives slowly towards the hangar that's farthest from the rest of the compound. We all step out of the truck and into the darkness to gather our thoughts. Jonas grabs some explosives and places a few around the truck, and then we head to the building that we've seen the most activity at.

We slowly march through the darkened base, placing explosives in a few places so we can set them off when we need to.

The car charges will go first, causing a distraction to get us into the buildings, and the others are in case everything goes wrong.

We'll blow this place sky high—an agreement we all made.

We manoeuvre into place down the side of the huge, two-story brick building with two guards posted outside. D works his magic, and when he nods, I know he has control of the power and cameras, which is just what we need.

Jonas lifts the handheld detonator, and with a mouthed, "Boom," he flips it. The car we were in explodes into a fiery ball, lighting up the sky. Alarms immediately blare as soldiers rush to the car from every corner—except for the two at the door. Nico nods and moves around the building to the other side, and when I peek out, we slip out in sync. I drive my knife into a man's chest, pushing him to the wall and covering his mouth as D kills the lights and cameras. Nico does the same, and with a matching grunt, we tug the bodies behind the building and into the darkness.

They will eventually be found, but it gives us time to get in first, especially since the alarm still shrieks, drawing everyone on the base to the burning truck.

"Let's move; the clock is ticking. We go in low and use the element of surprise. D, I want those cameras off inside as quickly as possible, and you are in charge. Nico and Jonas, you are the battering ram. Isaac, stay in the back with D. Nova, you're with me." We all nod, and when we step in front of the doors, Jonas pulls the pin on something and tosses it inside before slamming the doors.

There's a flash and some groaning, and then he opens the doors and we peer through the smoke to see disoriented soldiers as Nico and Jonas rush in, knocking them out as they go.

I follow them in, wincing at the smoke, but we push through into an entryway where soldiers are scrambling about. I don't hesitate to kill them because if they are here, then they know what's being done.

They know, and they helped hurt their own.

And children.

It's what keeps me going as we move as a unit, never faltering.

The element of surprise works for us. D blocks the door after us so no one can get in or escape, we find a security office where we quickly dispatch the guards, and Dimitri sets up shop. Isaac stays with him as we keep moving.

The building is a maze, but D quickly barks instructions in our ears after locating us through the cameras and taking them over so no one else can see us. "There are four giant labs on the second level. First level is living and relaxation. Third level does not have as many cameras but seems to be an office of some sort, and there's motion inside."

"We take the labs and keep as many subjects alive as we can, and whoever is here? Let's hope he's in charge," Louis murmurs, and we all agree.

We form a square as we move through the first floor, which includes reception areas, kitchens, lounges, and even some bedrooms.

We engage with more guards, but they are either unprepared or just not fast enough. Others are highly trained soldiers, and I can appreciate their sharp eyes and quick movements, but they are not quick enough for us.

I watch the moment of shock on their faces when they realise what we are before we end their lives.

It's almost too easy.

We sweep room after room, leaving bodies in our wake, but they hear us coming now and they are prepared. At the back of the first floor, they have created a barricade of tables and chairs, the tops of their heads just peeking above them when they start to spray fire across the hallway. I roll to the side and into the open doorway of a room, yanking Isaac with me as he groans. Pushing him against the wall, I scan him for injury. He's focused on the others who are all ducked into side rooms, but my focus is on him when I see he's bleeding just above his pants. Ripping up his shirt, I find a single bullet wound.

Glancing down, he blinks in surprise. "Oh, I didn't even feel it. I'll be okay. It will heal." He peers over his back. "It looks to be a through and through, so just leave the shirt to tighten on it and collect the blood. Nova?" He peers down at me worriedly as I stare at the blood dripping from the wound on my love.

On my healer.

On the man who has been tortured his whole life when he just wanted to help.

Something snaps in me, and before Louis or the others can call for me to stop, I'm moving out into the corridor with a snarl on my lips. Power surges through my body, making me faster, stronger, and smarter, just like Father wanted.

He wanted to see what I'm made of?

He wanted to see what perfect soldiers we could be?

Well, that's what he gets.

I shoot as I move, sliding across the hallway to avoid their fire. I shoot twice.

One shot into the man spraying the hallway, his head exploding as he falls back.

One into the man peeking up over the edge, firing straight through his eye.

I run towards the wall and flip off it, firing as I go. I spray the whole other side of the barrier before I land and roll, pulling two blades as I drop the now empty gun. I rush the barrier as more guards and soldiers try to pull the dead away, flinging my body over it with a snarled yell.

"They. Are. Mine!" I tear into their masses with my blades, spinning faster than they can track as I cut throats and disembowel others.

I sense the moment a gun is aimed towards me, and I turn, throwing the blade with such strength, it impales the man in the throat and throws him back into the wall, pinning him there like a trapped butterfly as he dies.

Yet I still feel more strength in my body, more anger, so I let it loose.

I release all those years of bottled rage, pain, and fear for the first time ever, my tight grip on it easing, and those would who blindly protect the person willing to kill, torture, and maim children and men pay the price.

I let them see just exactly what they are protecting.

I show them I am unstoppable.

I spot some trying to retreat, but I don't allow it. Picking up a weapon, I cut them down, and when it clicks empty, I swing it like a bat, smashing their faces in. Bodies fly through the air, but I don't hear anything over my thundering heart and breathing. When I swing around, searching for a target, holding a blade I picked up midair, a hand catches my own.

Snarling, I try to rip my hand back, but I'm suddenly backed into a wall, even as I fight, until lips descend onto mine.

I gasp and still, and then they slowly pull back. I blink away the haze I seemed to be under to meet Louis's hard, hot eyes. "Finished, baby?" he purrs.

Swallowing, I search his gaze as his eyes crinkle with a smile.

"While I think watching you hack up bodies with a blade is hot, I have no intentions of it being mine. You like it too much, so behave, and let's keep moving."

"Sorry," I pant, peering over his shoulder. I'm mortified when I see at least twenty dead bodies splayed around, looking like they have been torn apart by a wild animal. I close my eyes and hide, barely able to meet the others' watchful gazes.

I don't want to see the horror and reproach.

"What did he do to me?" I whisper.

"Nothing, baby, you are perfect," Louis promises.

A hand cups my cheek, and I turn into it, dropping the knife as I let Louis pin me there so I don't hurt anyone else.

"Look at me," comes a sharp command. I squeeze my eyes shut, and the fingers clench my jaw until it hurts. "Now, Nova."

I open my eyes to find Isaac before me. I worriedly search his gaze for disgust, but I simply see love. "You would never hurt one of us," he murmurs knowingly. "You did that, all of that, because they hurt me—because they hurt your family."

"I—" I shake my head, feeling lost and raw despite where we are. "I don't trust myself," I finally admit.

"Well, we do," Nico snaps, crowding behind Louis as Jonas moves to my other side.

"You were fantastic." He sighs lovingly, making me smile slightly.

"When we found another dead kid and we first came together, I lost it," Isaac tells me.

"And when Nico was hurt while we were hunting your father years ago, I tortured four men to get answers," Louis says.

"I just like to kill everything . . . everything but you guys." Jonas grins.

"You might be dangerous, deadly, fucking wild, and messed up, but we all are, Nova," Louis tells me, "and you would do anything to keep our family safe, just like we would. This just proves it, so trust us. We will always be right behind you, watching your back."

"And feel free to use your blade on me anytime." Jonas chuckles.

Sighing, I close my eyes and bang my head back against the wall. "Are they all dead?"

"Oh yeah, baby." Nico chuckles. "They are very fucking dead, but we are going to be too if we don't start moving," he reminds us.

D's voice sounds in my ear. "Nova, listen to them. What we do to protect our family is nothing to be ashamed of, nor is what you are and what you're capable of. If you are a monster, then so are we, and I love that you fight every day just to survive. After all, not everyone could." I feel the name on his lips.

Bass.

"But Nico is right; we need to keep moving. Soldiers are trying to bash through the doors right now, and we need to get to the labs before they end any of their experiments or anyone makes a getaway."

"I'm here. I'm okay." I shake it off and straighten, and Louis searches my gaze before nodding, trusting me.

"Then let's do this." Louis plucks the blade from the ground and hands it over, while Isaac offers me my guns which are now reloaded. I take them carefully, blood coating my hands and arms.

Isaac leans in and kisses me deeply. "I love you too," he murmurs, "and when this is over, I'll show how much that meant to me."

Smiling, I push from the wall and step over the bodies, not sparing them another look.

Maybe it should haunt me and killing should be harder, but it's not.

It's almost too easy when it's for my men and to stop what my father started.

Shaking my head, I refocus as we head upstairs and into a whole different level. This one is filled with labs and hiding scientists. I see some running, but I pay them no mind. They won't get far, and they can't hurt us.

Not now.

I keep to the middle to allow my heart to slow as we break into pairs without orders. The first lab is empty, bar a partially cut open body of a soldier on the bed, which makes me snarl. I grab a sheet and cover him gently, which is the least I can do for him for now. The next room has a scientist, and he throws us a panicked look as he plunges a needle into the neck of an unconscious soldier who's tied down.

"No!" I yell as I rush him, shoving him away. I grab the needle and lift it. It's half full. "What's in this?"

He tilts his head back, even as his eyes dart around for an escape.

"Tell me," I roar in his face.

"It is to kill him. It's painless. The research is to be destroyed rather than taken," he stammers.

"Research? Research? He is a person!" I scream before lowering my voice. "Let's see how truly painless it is," I sneer and stab it down into his neck, depressing the plunger. He falls back with a yell and yanks it out, covering the wound with his hand as I watch with a cruel twist of my lips.

It doesn't take long. He drops to his knees, his mouth opening and closing as he wheezes like he can't breathe. His entire body shakes before turning into full-blown seizures, causing him to froth at the mouth before he stills.

"I guess not very," I spit before turning. Nico is standing with his fingers pressed against the soldier's neck, and when I ask silently, he shakes his head.

Grinding my teeth, I hurry to the final lab, meeting Louis and Jonas there.

I need to save just one person from this hellhole.

Only, there is just a scientist standing there in his white coat, and his eyes are hard as he watches us.

Louis moves over and picks up his badge. "Lead Scientist Tyrion. Are you in charge?"

"Only of the labs," he murmurs, shooting us worried looks. "You are them, aren't you?"

"Them who?" Louis asks.

"The children. The first experiments. His legacy. We heard you had been sweeping labs, and we were on lockdown. You are magnificent," he whispers, "just like he said."

"Oh, looks like we're famous." Louis turns to us with an arched brow as we all laugh humourlessly. "Then I guess you know what comes next," he tells the man.

"Please." The first sign of fear breaks through his facade, his voice warbling. "It's just a job."

"Not to us," I spit, stepping to Louis's side. "Not to those dead soldiers out there or the countless dead children."

"I had nothing to do with you or the other kids!" he yells. "I swear, I was only brought on a few months ago before your father died. I didn't even know what it entailed until I took the position, and it was too late."

"Lies," I sneer.

"Please," he begs, holding his hands up as tears well in his eyes. "I was only following orders."

"You all were," I scoff. "History is filled with men and women simply following orders and committing horrendous crimes. You made your choice. You did this, and now you should suffer the consequences."

"Please, I have a family," he babbles. "I did it for them. I never wanted to, please. You'll never hear from me again."

Dropping the gun, I jerk my chin at him. "Get out of here, and if I see your face again, you're dead."

I show him the mercy that was never shown to us, and I hope I am right in doing so.

"Nova?" Louis asks.

"Leave him. He's not worth it." I whirl and leave the labs, heading to the stairs at the very end of the hall.

Hopefully, we'll find the man in charge because I have some things I'd like to discuss with him.

FIFTY-NINE

NOVA

The stairs have a closed, locked door that D opens for us.

"I've got you," he murmurs. It feels wrong to be doing this without him, but then again, he's right there, in our ears, watching us.

We surge up the stairs, knowing that with each second that passes, they could escape.

This might have started with my father, but it will end here with this man—the one tugging at a door as we rush into an ornate office. There are bookshelves to the left filled with pictures of him and military commanders, and even a fucking president. There is a sofa to the left, and a huge desk taking up the back placed in front of some windows. Beyond is a plane gearing up to depart.

The man tries to escape through the locked fire door as he glances back at us with purpose and hatred.

He's not what I was expecting, but then again, I guess the bad guys never are. After all, he's just a man. Just a fucking man. Nothing more.

He's middle-aged and moderately attractive, with salt and pepper hair. His face is angular, with bright blue eyes, and his body is encased in an expensive three-piece suit. He's neither tall nor short, fat nor slim.

He would be forgettable if it weren't for the shark-like smile he aims at us when he swings the door open. "He's making a run for it!" I yell and sprint across the office to see him leaping into the plane.

We have to roll when he looks back and pulls out a pistol, aiming badly, but it keeps us down as the plane starts to lift.

"Shit! He can't get away!" Louis roars.

Putting my gun away, I throw him a narrow-eyed look. "Then let's stop him." Without waiting for his approval, I push into a sprint, aiming for the plane.

We can't let him get away.

I pump my arms faster.

This has to end.

I duck my head.

He dies today, giving us freedom.

With a roar, I leap into the air.

I manage to hit the closing back door and turn to see the others running. Louis makes it, Nico too, then Jonas and Isaac. D breaks out of the door and sprints across the deck. With my hand stretched out towards him, I let the others anchor me as I reach for him, unwilling to leave him behind.

We end this together.

"Hurry!" I yell at him.

Eyes glittering, he moves like lightning just as we take off into the air. Our hands slap together, and I grip him tightly as he swings. Staring into his determined eyes, I haul him up, and we fall into a heap in the plane's belly.

Panting, he rolls off me, and Louis helps me up as I pull my gun. He nods at me. "D, you're with me. We'll get them to land safely. Everyone else, check for soldiers and secure the leader."

He sneers the word, echoing our feelings as we climb up the ramp and into the small plane. He's there, banging on the cockpit, and when he sees us, his nostrils flare as he takes aim once more.

"Not a good idea," I call. "Sure way to crash the plane." I shrug.

"Maybe, but it might be worth it," he replies. "Unless you want to find out, weapons down."

Playing nice for now, I slowly lower my gun to the floor and leave it there as I straighten, smiling at him. "I don't need a weapon to kill you."

"No, you wouldn't, would you, Nova?" He arches a brow.

I look him over as he steps closer, still aiming his gun at me. Nico and Jonas slide down each side to circle him.

"I don't know you."

"Oh, but I know you. I watched you be born. I watched every moment of his research on you. He always told me you were the future, you kids, his pet project. I believe differently, but here you are. He was right. You are incredible." He shakes his head. "We could have done such amazing things together if you hadn't grown a conscience."

"Who are you? He never told me your name."

"He wouldn't. After all, your father plays the long game. Name's William Moss. I was your father's silent partner from the beginning. The money, the operations, nothing would have happened without me."

"And that's something to be proud of?" I distract him as the guys move closer.

"I would say so. Just think of everything we can achieve and how much money we will make. I will obviously have to kill the men who are with you, since they were all failed experiments and we don't need that pollution, but you?" He shakes his head. "Perfect. You are the perfect blend, and we can work on your obedience."

"Never," I spit.

"Ah, stop or she dies. We might all go down, but you'll watch her choke on her own blood first," he sneers at Nico and Jonas. "Yes, Nova, this isn't the end like you want it to be. This is just the beginning."

"When I kill you, it will be the end. It will finally be over, and your precious research? I'll destroy it all and let it burn with your body."

"And then what?" he asks. "You'll live happily ever after? A normal life isn't for you. You are a weapon. All of you. You couldn't exist any other way. You need the adrenaline and the fight to stay alive. Tell me that you haven't felt the best you ever have while following his breadcrumbs."

"Shut up," I spit, moving closer.

He just smiles "And you followed it so willingly, so happy to do exactly what he wanted while showing just what you are capable of—the final and best experiment. The final test."

I still, searching his eyes. "You mean your test."

"His." He smiles slowly.

"He's dead," I state bluntly.

"Is he?" He grins. "Then yes, my final test, and you passed with flying colours, though we never anticipated you would form such a close bond with the others. That will be severed though, not to worry, since we need you clear-headed."

"Shut up!" I roar as I press against his gun. "Kill me and be done with it."

"Oh, Nova, you still don't get it, do you? All of this was to bring you home. No, you won't die, but they will." He swings the gun, ready to fire, before I slam my arm down, breaking his.

He falls back with a roar and the shot goes wide, hitting a window.

The air is instantly sucked out, and the plane rattles and nosedives for a moment before it straightens. I'm about to end this, to end him, when the hole gets bigger and the chairs rip from the walls and slam through the windows. I grab the wall and hold on.

"D! Cockpit!" Louis roars as he tries to get to me.

D crawls past me, ripping open the door and slamming it shut. Looking out of the window, I watch a chair hit the engine, and we start to nosedive again. I feel D struggling to try and right the plane. He yells that the side of the mountain is rapidly approaching, and I know we are going to crash.

Whipping my head back around, I leap for William to end this just as we hit.

We are all thrown about as we hit. D manages to straighten us as much as possible, and that's the only thing that saves us. Even so, I feel my shoulder pop out of place and my ribs crack. My head smacks into the side until Nico catches me as I fly about and pulls me into his arms, wrapping himself around me as we hit once more, and everything goes dark.

I open my eyes with a groan as I feel his arms slipping from around me. Rolling, I see Nico's out cold. Panic instantly takes hold, but his chest is rising and falling. Isaac is groaning and clutching his bullet wound on his side. Louis is on his knees, coughing. Jonas holds onto a rope that was once on the side and not the ceiling, and he lets go and falls to his back with a thump.

Staggering to my feet, I rush to the cockpit, ripping open the door to see D in his chair, wiping at a head wound but alive.

My eyes then swing to William.

He's groaning and holding his stomach, where a metal bar is speared through his gut, pinning him in place. Dropping to my knees before him, I watch the blood pool around his hands as he tries to staunch the flow. He blinks repeatedly, his mouth moving.

Shock.

Gripping my shoulder, I pop it back into position with a grunt. There's not much I can do about the other aches and pains, but we are all alive, and that's what matters.

William, however, is dying, and I let it happen, surrounded by his creations, his experiments, and his enemies as he does.

Forgotten and unimportant.

"Is that all the research back there?" I demand, needing answers.

"Yes, in the vault, the other . . . The others are at your father's house and lab." He coughs, splattering blood on his lips and chin.

His head falls back, but he holds my gaze. "I guess we all think we are so invincible, so immortal, until the end," he jokes bitterly. "But you? You truly are unstoppable, like he promised."

I don't speak, and he smiles, his teeth and lips covered in his blood as he chokes on it, just like he threatened to do to me.

"He's alive." He coughs, the force racking his body.

Snarling, I grab his shoulders and slap him until he focuses on me again.

"Who is?" I demand as he groans. "Who is?" I yell.

His head lolls back as his eyes start to close, and his whisper comes out half broken and dead. "Your father. Your father is alive."

"No," I whisper.

"This . . . This was all his plan." He coughs again, the sound wet and rattling. "To get you back. One last experiment."

Then I watch as he takes his last breath.

"Nova, it could be a lie from a dying man, one last way to hurt you," Louis murmurs. I didn't even know they were close.

I can't speak over my panic because deep down, I believe him.

There's one way to . . . Reaching forward, I search through his pockets until I find his phone. Using his thumb, I unlock it and scroll through his call list and hit the last number.

The only number he has rung.

The ringing is loud, even over the groan of the plane and the flames licking at it.

"We need to move," Louis says. "It's over, Nova. Let's go!"

I don't move, don't speak, as it rings in my ear.

There's a click.

"Hello?"

My world falls apart as I hear my father's sharp and commanding voice.

One I would know anywhere.

One that sends shivers of fear through me.

"Hello?" There's silence then. "Novaleen, is that you?" He sounds way too overjoyed about it.

"You're alive," I croak.

"And you found him for me. Thank you for that. I wish I could have seen it. Is he dead?" he asks curiously.

"You're alive," I repeat.

"Do not state the obvious, girl," he admonishes, his usual cold tone snapping me from my shock as I tighten my blood-soaked hold on the phone.

He's alive.

The bastard is alive and has been playing us this entire time.

"I'm coming for you. Nowhere is safe," I snarl, and before he can answer, I crush the phone in my grip then turn to see five shocked faces.

"This isn't over. Not yet." I stand and storm from the plane, ready to hunt my father down.

The man who started all this.

The one who's supposed to be in the ground.

I thought I was unstoppable, but what if it was all a lie?

What if it was all a pretty lie . . .

CONTINUE THE ADVENTURE...

Want to find out if Nova gets her revenge? Unbreakable is coming soon and is the conclusion to the Pretty Liars duet!

ABOUT K.A. KNIGHT

K.A Knight is an USA Today bestselling indie author trying to get all of the stories and characters out of her head, writing the monsters that you love to hate. She loves reading and devours every book she can get her hands on, and she also has a worrying caffeine addiction.

She leads her double life in a sleepy English town, where she spends her days writing like a crazy person.

Read more at K.A Knight's website or join her Facebook Reader Group.
Sign up for exclusive content and my newsletter here
http://eepurl.com/drLLoj

ALSO BY K.A. KNIGHT

Pretty Stormy

Pretty Wild

Pretty Hot

Pretty Faces

Pretty Spelled

Fallen Gods - the omnibus 1

Fallen Gods - the omnibus 2

FORBIDDEN READS (STANDALONES) *CONTEMPORARY*

Daddy's Angel

Stepbrothers' Darling

PRETTY LIARS *CONTEMPORARY RH*

Unstoppable

Unbreakable (Coming soon!)

FORGOTTEN CITY

Monstrous Lies

Monstrous Truths

Monstrous Ends

STANDALONES

IN DEN OF VIPERS' UNIVERSE - CONTEMPORARY

Scarlett Limerence

Nadia's Salvation

Alena's Revenge

Den of Vipers

Gangsters and Guns (Co-Write with Loxley Savage)

CONTEMPORARY

The Standby

Diver's Heart

SCI FI RH

Crown of Stars

AUDIOBOOKS

The Wasteland

The Summit

Rage

Hate

Den of Vipers *(From Podium Audio)*

Gangsters and Guns *(From Podium Audio)*

Daddy's Angel *(From Podium Audio)*

Stepbrothers' Darling *(From Podium Audio)*

Blade of Iris *(From Podium Audio)*

Deadly Affair *(From Podium Audio)*

Stolen Trophy *(From Podium Audio)*

Crown of Stars *(From Podium Audio)*

SHARED WORLD PROJECTS

Blade of Iris - Mafia Wars *CONTEMPORARY*

CO-AUTHOR PROJECTS - *Erin O'Kane*

HER FREAKS SERIES *PNR Dystopian RH*

Circus Save Me

Taming The Ringmaster

Walking the Tightrope

Her Freaks Series - the omnibus

STANDALONES

PNR RH

The Hero Complex

Collection of Short Stories

Dark Temptations (contains One Night Only and Circus Saves Christmas)

THE WILD BOYS SERIES *CONTEMPORARY*

The Wild Interview

The Wild Tour

The Wild Finale

The Wild Boys - the omnibus

CO-AUTHOR PROJECTS - *Ivy Fox*

Deadly Love Series *CONTEMPORARY*

Deadly Affair

Deadly Match

Deadly Encounter

CO-AUTHOR PROJECTS - *Kendra Moreno*

STANDALONES

CONTEMPORARY

Stolen Trophy

PNR RH

Fractured Shadows

Burn Me

CO-AUTHOR PROJECTS - *Loxley Savage*

THE FORSAKEN SERIES *SCI FI RH*

Capturing Carmen

Stealing Shiloh

Harboring Harlow

STANDALONES

Gangsters and Guns - IN DEN OF VIPERS' UNIVERSE

OTHER CO-WRITES

Shipwreck Souls *(with Kendra Moreno & Poppy Woods)*

The Horror Emporium *(with Kendra Moreno & Poppy Woods)*